THEN SHE VANISHES

ALSO BY CLAIRE DOUGLAS

THEN SHE
VANISHES

A Novel

CLAIRE DOUGLAS

HARPER

NEW YORK • LONDON • TORONTO • SYDNEY

HARPER

Originally published as *Then She Vanishes* in Great Britain in 2019 by Penguin Random House UK.

FIRST U.S. EDITION

Library of Congress Cataloging-in-Publication Data has been applied for.

ISBN 978-0-06-300155-8 (pbk.)
ISBN 978-0-06-309273-0 (library edition)

21 22 23 24 25   LSC   10 9 8 7 6 5 4 3 2 1

THEN SHE VANISHES

PROLOGUE

March 2012

I FEEL CALM AS I WATCH THE SUN RISE BEHIND THE ROW OF ICE-cream-colored houses. Not as I imagined a person would feel who's about to commit murder. I'm not nervous, or sweaty palmed. My heart isn't even racing. There's no adrenaline pumping through my veins. Not yet, anyway. Maybe that will come later. But now, in this moment, I'm overcome with a kind of peace. As though everything that has happened in my life so far has led up to this point. There's no going back.

Now, which house?

They are all Georgian, beautiful, tall, and elegant, with their perfectly proportioned windows and arched front doors. They remind me of an illustration in a children's book, some long and thin, others stocky and square. They face toward the choppy, wind-beaten sea and the small port, with its handful of fishing boats, marooned on the sloping sands now that the tide is out.

Perfect holiday homes, even out of season. Even on a cold, gusty March day such as this.

Powder blue, soft peach, pale pink, clotted cream. Which one?

And then I see it. A brilliant white with cobalt-painted window frames, dwarfed by the taller, more graceful houses either side of it. It's the West Ham sticker nestled into the corner of the top right-hand window that sways me.

That's the house.

I pick up the shotgun from the footwell, enjoying the weight of it in my hands, the power of it, and for the first time I feel a frisson of . . . what? Fear? No, not fear. Because I've never felt less afraid. What, then? Control? Yes, that's exactly it. At last I feel totally and utterly in control.

I step out of the car. The wind has picked up and I almost trap the end of my scarf in the door. It's as if the elements are out to get me. To stop me.

It's just gone 6:30 a.m. The road is quiet, the front gardens tidy, with a row of black wheelie bins left out for the refuse collectors. One has been pushed over by the wind, its contents spilling onto the pavement and coating the tarmac with potato peelings, empty baked-beans tins, and wet kitchen roll. To my left I can see a solitary dog walker on the beach, just a black silhouette in the distance. They are too far out to see me. And what I'm about to do.

I move the shotgun to eye height and stride toward the white house, confidence brimming with every step I take. Everything has taken on a surreal quality, as if I'm in a video game. I stop when I get to the front door. I pull back the trigger, firing a single shot, and the lock splinters. The noise is bound to alert the neighbors and the occupants. I'd better be quick.

I kick the door open and stride into a narrow hallway. The staircase is straight ahead and I dart up it, every one of my senses alert. At the top is a door. I push it open and see a man getting out of bed. On his bottom half he's wearing a pair of striped pajama trousers, his large stomach hanging over the waistband. He has a gold rope necklace at his throat and wiry gray hairs covering his chest. The gunshot must have woken him. He's older, late fifties, with thinning hair and broad shoulders. I'm repulsed by the sight of him. He tries to stand up when he sees me in the doorframe, his mouth slack, his brow furrowed. "What the . . . ?" Before he has time to finish his sentence I aim the gun at his head and watch in fascination as his blood splatters the Regency-striped wallpaper behind him. He flops back against the duvet, staining it red, his eyes still open.

I turn to leave. A woman is blocking my way. She's even older than the man, and has white candyfloss curls. She's wearing a flowery nightie. She's stunned at first, her eyes widening in recognition at the sight of me. And then she starts screaming. I silence her with a bullet to her chest, which propels her down the stairs as though she's a rag doll. She lies in a crumpled heap at the bottom and, calmly, I step over her to leave. I can hear a dog barking somewhere in the house, maybe the kitchen, and I falter for just a few seconds. Then I stride out of the front door.

A young guy wearing Lycra is in the neighboring front garden, wheeling his bin down the path. When he notices me all the color drains from his face, his jaw slack. I must look mad with my unwashed hair and crumpled clothes. It's almost funny. I ignore him and get into the car, throwing the gun onto the back seat.

I can see Lycra Guy through my rearview mirror as I pull away. A mobile phone is pressed to his ear and he's gesticulating. I think I hear another scream although it could be the seagulls lined up on the wall, their beady eyes watching me, judging me.

It's only then that I begin to shake uncontrollably. I can't be sure whether it's the adrenaline, or the realization that there is definitely no going back for me. For us.

This is just the beginning.

1

Jess

BRISTOL AND SOMERSET HERALD

Tuesday, March 13, 2012

DOUBLE MURDER SHOCKS
SLEEPY SEASIDE TOWN

by Jessica Fox

A MURDER investigation is underway after two people were found dead at a house in the seaside Somerset town of Tilby on Friday.

Detectives were called to the beachside property in Shackleton Road just after 7 a.m. When the police entered the cottage they found two bodies, thought to be local businessman Clive Wilson, 58, and his mother, Deirdre Wilson, 76. They had been shot. The property was cordoned off and police and forensics officers were at the scene throughout the day.

A third person, 32-year-old Heather Underwood, was found unconscious at a caravan park less than half a mile away. She had sustained a self-inflicted gunshot wound to the chest and is currently in a critical condition in hospital.

Detective Chief Inspector Gary Ruthgow of Avon and Somerset Police said officers were called to the Georgian property by paramedics. He confirmed that detectives are not looking for anyone else in relation to the deaths. He said: "This is a small town and I would urge anyone with any information that could assist with our investigation to please get in touch."

Neighbors on the well-heeled street, which consists of a boutique hotel as well as permanent residences and second homes, are shocked and saddened by the horrific murders.

I sit back in my chair and reread the article. The deadline is in twenty minutes. It's taken me nearly an hour to write just five paragraphs. If I don't send it soon it won't make the front page tomorrow, and my news editor, Ted, will have my guts for garters (one of his favorite phrases and always said in a droll tone).

I glance out of the window at the rooftops of Bristol. I can see the cathedral's spire from up here and the buildings that cluster around College Green. I can tell it's raining by the sea of colorful umbrellas obscuring the pavements, moving almost as one.

A line of traffic chugs up Park Street and a double-decker bus belches smoke as it heaves itself up the hill, like an unfit runner.

Ever since I spoke to DCI Ruthgow this morning I've not been able to get the interview out of my head. His words are eating away at me. I'm dying for a cigarette but I daren't leave my desk until I've filed this story. I glance across at Jack, my smoking companion. He's hunched over his computer, tapping at his keyboard, a phone cradled between shoulder and chin. Sensing me watching, he lifts his head and pulls a silly face. And then, in a placatory voice, he says into the receiver, "Yes, yes, I quite understand, madam. No, I didn't realize they would use that photo of your cat . . . I agree, quite inappropriate given his untimely demise . . . Uh-huh, yes, not Fluffy's best side admittedly but, no, I didn't think he looked fat."

I can't help but smile and turn back to my computer, studying the words on the screen again, trying to push away the thought I've had since speaking to DCI Ruthgow earlier. But it won't budge.

Is it *my* Heather?

Tilby is a small town. I should know: I grew up there. And this Heather Underwood would be the same age as the Heather I went to school with. The Heather I was *best friends* with. We lost touch when we left school, but for a while—for a good couple of years, in fact—we were inseparable. As far as I remember, there was only one caravan park in Tilby, and it was owned by Heather's family. The surname is different—she was a Powell back then—but it's too much of a coincidence, although not beyond impossible. Heather isn't that unusual a name. I flick back through my notebook, trying to decipher my shorthand. Yes, in our interview Ruthgow confirmed that, after killing two people, Heather Underwood went back to the caravan park where she lives with her husband and young son and tried to take her own life.

Heather always wanted to leave Tilby. Would she really still be living at the same address after all this time?

"Haven't you finished that yet, Jess?"

I turn to see Ted standing over me, his breath smelling of coffee and cigarettes overlaid with a faint hint of mint. He runs a hand over his beard. It's the color of a tobacco stain, the same as his hair.

"Yep. I'm just about to file it."

"Good." He peers at my screen. "Didn't you go to school in Tilby?"

"I did." I don't remember telling him that, although it's on my CV. But the man's like a bloodhound.

"You're about the same age, aren't you? Did you know this girl?"

I take a breath. "I'm . . . Actually, I'm not sure. I was friends with a Heather. But . . ." But the Heather I knew would never have been capable of something like this, I want to say. The Heather I knew was sweet, quiet, kind. She always had so much time for people. The old woman with the beginnings of dementia whom we'd bump into in the corner shop: Heather would help her home when it was obvious she couldn't remember the way. Or she'd pilfer blankets from her house to give to the homeless man who slept beneath the underpass when it was cold. She was always polite and well mannered, remembering to say thank you to bus drivers and shopkeepers when I always forgot, desperate to eat my sweets or get to my destination.

Yet there was another side to her too. I remember the last time I saw her: her green eyes had blazed, her fists clenched at her sides. That was the only time I'd ever seen her in a rage. I had been scared of her sudden unpredictability, like a horse I'd always thought placid that was now about to rear and buck. But it was toward the end of our friendship, when everything went wrong and she was angry with the world. With me. It was understandable.

I've tried not to think about Heather in recent years, but now a picture of her forms in my head, like a reflection in water, slowly sharpening and gaining focus. Dressed in a long, floaty skirt and DM boots, twirling around on the lawn, singing along to "Charlotte Sometimes" by The Cure; the tinkling sound of the many bangles jangling on her arm; cantering on her little black pony, Lucky, her long dark hair cascading down her back.

I take a deep breath. I really need a fag.

Ted makes a smacking sound as he chews gum in my ear, reminding me he's still standing beside me. "You better get your butt down to Tilby," he says, in his Essex accent. He's lived in Bristol for years but has never managed to pick up the West Country twang. Although, when he's had a few, he likes to rib me about mine. "And take Jack with you. See if it's the Heather you knew at school. She's unconscious so the police can't charge her yet."

The subtext being that we can print what we want until they do.

Ted doesn't often show excitement or happiness or any other emotion apart from grumpiness. Unless he's had a few beers, when his humor shows through like a slice of sunlight beneath a gray cloud. Most of the time he wears a harassed expression and, when he's not smoking or drinking coffee, he frantically chews gum, his jaw going nineteen to the dozen. But now his small blue eyes shine with rare delight, as though he's a pitbull about to be given a slab of raw meat.

"I was about to look on the electoral roll—see if she still lives with Leo or Margot."

"Don't worry about that now. Even if it isn't the Heather you knew, you still need to be there. Interview whoever she was living with. Describe where she shot herself for color. You know the drill."

I do indeed. I could do it in my sleep. Yet before, when I worked in London, I never knew the people involved. Now, if it's my old friend Heather . . . I shake my head, not allowing my thoughts to go there. I have to treat it as any other job.

I stand up and pull my sheepskin coat from the back of the chair. It's heavy and warm (it's always so cold in here—the heating rarely works properly) and I wrap it around myself gratefully. I got it in the charity shop on Park Street, where I buy most of my clothes, and it's the color of toffee with a shaggy cream collar and cuffs. Jack's still on the phone so I scrawl a quick note, saying I'll meet him outside.

"Nice coat, Jess," calls our receptionist, Sue, as I scurry past, shoving my notebook into my bag. She's in her late fifties with a crop of silver hair and twinkly eyes that crinkle when she laughs. She's like a lovely cuddly aunt who always refers to me as "a girl," asking me about my life and my boyfriend, as though living vicariously through "my youth" even though, at thirty-one, I'm not particularly young. Some days I feel very, very old. And very, very jaded. Like today.

"Thanks," I call back, taking the cigarettes from my pocket as I head out of the reception area. "Got it for a bargain in BS8."

"And I'm liking the new fringe," she adds. I touch it self-consciously, although I know it frames my face, softens my blunt bob, and the platinum blond contrasts with my chocolate-brown eyes. "Very Debbie Harry."

I laugh off her compliment—although I'm secretly delighted—promising to bring her back a coffee (the machine stuff in the office tastes of plastic), then shoulder my way through the door, down the stairs, and onto Park Street.

Our offices are in a red brick building directly above a newsagent's. There are only six of us who work out of here—two snappers; two reporters, including myself and a trainee called Ellie; Ted; and Sue. Our headquarters are in an office park a few miles out of town. We type up our copy, then send it down the line to the subeditors at HQ. Jack and I often joke that our office is where the dregs are sent. The staff they don't want to get rid of, but don't want hanging about the main newsroom. I can't understand what Jack's done to warrant such a situation. How could anyone dislike him? I tell him that he's only here because he was the last in. As soon as a snapper leaves HQ (and it's amazing how high the turnover of staff is there, how quickly they jump ship to a daily like the *Bristol Daily News*), Jack will have left before he can say "digital camera." I doubt the other photographer, Seth, will ever go anywhere else. He's long past retirement.

I can't allow myself to wonder how I'd cope without Jack if he left. I know it will happen eventually. Jack pretends otherwise, but underneath his easygoing persona he's ambitious. It's only a matter of time before he moves on. I, on the other hand, am happier here in our little office, away from prying eyes and ears. And Ted is a good boss. Despite his grumpiness, he trusts us and leaves us to make our own decisions (and most afternoons he leaves early to slope off to the local pub). I don't want to be stuck out in some soulless office park. I like being able to walk out onto Park Street. I love the hustle and bustle, the shops, the cafés, the buskers. It reminds me of London. Not to mention that I can walk to work from where I live.

I've been given a second chance and I'll always be grateful to Ted for that. He took me on when nobody else would.

We have our own entrance: a single blue door set into the brick wall. There's no sign, nothing to suggest that a newspaper operates behind it. Sometimes a homeless man huddles under a dirty blanket in the doorway. He's called Stan. I often bring him a coffee when I'm getting one for Sue. Today he's not here, just an empty can of Foster's scrunched up in the corner and the faint whiff of urine. I shelter in the doorway and light a cigarette, inhaling it deeply.

The rain is still coming down. It's fine and drizzly. I like the rain. I always have, the heavier the better; the way it smells, the sound it makes as it clatters into drains, the whoosh of it as tires part puddles. Even nicer if it's accompanied by thunder and lightning. Most people think it odd, but Heather felt the same as me. I remember the sound of it drumming on the aluminium roof of the barn at her family's caravan park. We loved that barn, with its mezzanine level where they kept the hay for the horses. They had so much land, acres of it. It had been her uncle Leo's idea to set up one of the fields as a caravan park. We used to escape to that barn with our art pads, tartan blankets embedded with yellow hairs from the family's ancient Labrador, Goldie, pulled over our knees as we tried to sketch the pond or the fountain in her garden, or the caravans in the field beyond, a ribbon of sea glistening enticingly in the distance. Her house was amazing: five bedrooms and a room they called the Den. So much grander than the cramped cottage with the low ceilings that Mum and I shared. Although Heather's house wasn't posh: it was lived in, with old-fashioned furniture, sanded original floorboards, and checked blankets thrown over the back of well-worn sofas, very different from the pristine yet sparsely furnished two-up-two-down we had.

Heather tried to teach me to ride. She had such patience, leading me endlessly around the paddock on Lucky, while I tried to get the hang of it. She would tell me funny stories of her mishaps, like the time she thought she'd lost the use of her legs after one of the horses bucked her off. "I was such a drama queen about it," she'd said, giggling, "lying in the middle of the field insisting I was paralyzed. My instructor just told me to stop being silly and get back on the horse." Despite Heather's best efforts I never took to riding. I preferred spending time grooming the pony and French plaiting its tail.

Heather had a menagerie of animals in that barn—a goat she'd rescued, chickens, a pet rat. She spent time with each one, tending them with such love I could only watch with a mixture of awe and envy. My own mother never allowed me to have any pets, saying they were a tie, but Heather's mum, Margot, was happy for her to have all sorts of animals parading about the place. They even had a peacock that strutted across the field, showing off its feathers. Sometimes, guiltily, I wished my mum was more like Heather's.

I keep trying to imagine that same sensible girl as a grown woman walking into a house and shooting dead two people.

Tilby's only fifteen miles away. It won't take me and Jack long to get there to find out for certain. If he ever turns up. I keep the car parked at my flat on the Welsh Back. It's only a ten-minute walk from here.

I take another deep drag of the cigarette, instantly feeling calmer. I've given up everything else that was bad for me: London, the *Daily Tribune*, binge drinking, the odd recreational drugs, the constant moving around, living with different house-mates. But I can't give up this. I need some vices.

I blow out smoke slowly. An old lady wearing a clear plastic hairnet shoots me a disapproving look as she shuffles past. Undeterred, I carry on puffing until only the butt is left. Why is Jack taking so long?

Tilby Manor Caravan Park. The name pops into my head. That was what the Powells had called it. I'd forgotten. I can still remember how much I loved spending time there. We spent our days sketching, or playing house in one of the empty caravans, or spying on Heather's big sister and her boyfriend. It was idyllic, really. I spent more time at her home than I did my own.

Until our childhood was cut brutally short in 1994.

I went back to her house only a few times after that, and our friendship, which had once been so strong, began to weaken and break, like a strand of my now overprocessed hair. By the time we were doing our GCSEs we were acquaintances, mumbling a hello to each other as we passed in the corridors.

If this woman, *this killer,* is the Heather I knew at school, the story could help my career and put me back on the map, which I desperately need after what happened at the *Tribune.* I know so much about her and her family. Too much.

But is that what I really want? And at what cost?

2

Jess

WE SPEED DOWN THE M5 IN MY MINT-GREEN NISSAN FIGARO, JACK looking uncomfortable in the passenger seat. He's been forced to lean to the side slightly so that he can get his legs in, even though he's pushed the seat as far back as it will go. His camera bag sits on his lap and he cradles it like a beloved puppy.

I quickly fill him in on the story, casually throwing in that I once knew a Heather from Tilby. He's not fooled. He knows me too well. I try to concentrate on the road to avoid the concern in his eyes. "It's got to be her, hasn't it? Do you want me to look it up on my phone? I can get the electoral roll. See who's registered there?"

I shake my head emphatically, pushing away any doubts. "It's not necessarily her. It would be extremely out of character." I'm not sure if I'm trying to convince him or myself. "And no point looking it up. We'll be there soon." I'm trying to put off the inevitable.

"But you said you haven't seen her since you were teenagers. People change. Something might have happened to turn her into a killer."

I shrug, trying to look like I couldn't care less either way as I concentrate on ignoring the little voice inside my head that says, *Do you remember what she told you? It was a secret you promised never to tell. And if you had told, it might not have happened.* I mentally shake myself. I was fourteen. It was nearly twenty years ago. How can I be sure I'm recollecting it all correctly?

Jack shuffles against the seat. "I'm glad to be getting out the office. Honestly, if Mrs. Hodge rings up one more time complaining about the photos I took of Fluffy . . ."

I giggle. "Fluffy? Seriously?"

"It had been a quiet news day." He grins, then shifts his weight and winces. "I'm in pain here. Just saying."

"How tall *are* you?" I laugh as I move into the left-hand lane. The turning for Tilby is coming up.

"Nearly six five and most of that is leg." He raises an eyebrow as if daring me to contradict him. Not that I would. It's true, he's all limbs.

"You're practically a giant compared to me." I'm at least a foot shorter.

"Yes, well, my height is a slight disadvantage when I'm forced to travel in Noddy's car," he says, his eyes twinkling.

I smack him hard on his bony thigh. "And what do you suggest I drive? Some corporate BMW or Mercedes? You can always take the bus next time." But I'm smiling as I say it. Jack is one of my favorite people. Nothing ever seems to get him down. Five years younger than me, he's full of spark, of life, always ready with a quip or a joke. When he started at the paper last summer we soon bonded over our shared love of cigarettes and Kraftwerk. At that time I'd been working at the *Herald* just a few months. Now he's one of my closest friends in Bristol. Actually, he's my only friend in Bristol, apart from my boyfriend, Rory.

Jack cranes his neck, like an elegant giraffe, to get a better look out of the windscreen. "Where is this place?" he says, as I swing right at the roundabout. "I thought we were going to the beach." Jack is from Brighton but moved to a flat in Fishponds with his police-officer boyfriend, Finn, nine months ago. I know he misses living by the sea.

"The caravan park where Heather Underwood was found is about half a mile inland," I explain. "To get to the beach you have to take a left at the roundabout." I haven't been to Tilby for more than a decade, not since my mum remarried and emigrated to Spain, but I remember the way.

The address Ted gave me was number 36 Cowship Lane. I never took much notice of road names back then—I'd been fourteen the last time I was at Heather's house. And, anyway, I always took shortcuts. I had to trudge through fields of cowpats and long grass to get from my house to hers, but even so, I know that was the name of her road because I remember us laughing at it, nicknaming it Cowshit Lane.

The road narrows and I see the familiar landmarks: the

church on the corner where Heather and I used to sketch the gravestones, the Horseshoe pub with its mock-Tudor exterior—we'd stood outside one summer, spying on her uncle Leo and his hot new girlfriend—the row of identical cottages with the playground opposite. I point to number 7. "Me and my mum lived there," I say, my heart unexpectedly heavy. I haven't seen Mum in too long.

"Oh, aren't they sweet? They're like little toy houses," says Jack, pressing his nose to the glass. Jack is what my mum would call posh. He grew up in a big, rambling house with sea views and speaks the Queen's English, not a dropped *h* in sight. He went to boarding school and skis at his family's lodge in the winter. His mother's a barrister and his dad is a partner in some big corporation. But there's no side to Jack. He's not being snobby in his assessment of the cottage I grew up in. He just says things as he sees them. "They're full of character, aren't they?"

"Yes. But you'd be permanently stooped living in one," I acknowledge.

I slow down as we drive along the high street. There's a Costa now and a WHSmith. Greggs is still there—Heather and I used to club together to buy one of their sausage rolls on the way home from school. It's been updated with an awning and a few rain-spattered bistro tables outside—one of the chairs has toppled onto its side in the wind. The Gateway supermarket has been replaced by a Co-op. And then I come to the clock tower. It's smaller than I remember and sits in a triangle between a fork in the road. It's where I—along with most of Tilby's youth back in the day—used to hang out when we couldn't be bothered to walk the ten minutes to the seafront. But that was after Heather, when I'd tried to fill the chasm she'd left in my heart by turning my attention to Woodpecker cider and boys. "Shit," I say, as a lorry beeps at me and I'm forced to move lanes. "It's all one-way now." I take a sharp left onto a narrow track. "This is Cowship Lane. Look out for number thirty-six."

Most of the properties are detached with land. Some are bungalows, others barn conversions and then, toward the end of the lane with a huge corner plot and the sea in the distance, I spot it and my stomach convulses.

It's the house from my memories.

There's a huge sign now with *Tilby Manor Caravan Park* emblazoned on it at the entrance to the driveway. I'm sure they didn't have that back then.

Even though, deep down, I'd known it would be her, I still feel a sudden crushing sadness as I turn into the sweeping graveled driveway with the familiar stone house in front of me. Everything comes flooding back: the long summer evenings, the smell of hay that would tickle my nose and make me sneeze, the tinkle of the pond, the dust motes floating in the fading sunshine of the barn. I know that, from the main bedroom at the back of the house, you can see the sea; her sister's bedroom overlooked the front lawn, and Heather's the caravan park in the distance. For a short time in my life this was like a second home.

I swallow the lump in my throat and pull in beside a battered

Land Rover. Behind the house is the caravan site—a two-acre field that used to accommodate about eight static caravans, with space for ten tourers—although it's not visible from here. To the right-hand side of the house is the barn where we used to hang out. It has police tape surrounding it now, a piece of which has come loose and is fluttering in the wind. Is that where it happened? Where Heather shot herself? I'm struck by the horror of it.

It's nothing new, I tell myself. I've seen it all: a family carried out in body bags after the father killed them all and then himself because he was in debt; the bloodied pavement where a terrorist attack took place outside Madame Tussauds; a tent erected in the woods after a missing teenager was found dead. With each story I had to remain detached for my sanity. But this. This is different. This is Heather.

I turn off the engine and stare straight ahead, my hands gripping the steering wheel. The front door is around the side. But from here I can see into the bay window of the living room. I remember that room. Heather and I used to snuggle under blankets during the winter, the smell of burning wood and ash from the open fire making our nostrils itch. I take a deep breath. I can almost remember the smell, the feeling of contentment. There's a woman at the window, partly obscured by the gossamer net curtains. Her face is in shadow, but by the set of her hair in its familiar chignon and the shape of her long, elegant neck and sharp nose, I know she's Heather's mum, Margot.

"So?" Jack asks, turning to face me. When I don't say anything, he adds gently, "The shooter. It's your onetime friend, isn't it?"

I nod and blink away tears before he notices. He'll tease me mercilessly. Tears don't go with my persona as a hard-nosed journalist. Jack often says I'm as hard as nails. I think he admires it.

"Shit," he mutters, under his breath, but I notice a light in his eyes. Of course he's going to be excited by this—I would be, too, if I were him, if it was someone else. Anyone else. But not her. Not Heather. Jack's hoping this will be our way in, and I've had the same thought. Yet it could be a hindrance. I might be the last person Margot wants to see. I wouldn't blame her. I can still recall her final words to me on the phone all those years ago, her acidic, accusing tone, her once friendly voice brittle and strained. I grip the steering wheel, unable to move, uncertain of the reaction I'll get.

Jack opens the passenger door and turns to me before getting out. "Well, come on. What are you waiting for?" He assesses me, his eyes softening. "Don't tell me the nerves are kicking in? That you really are human, Jessica Fox." I know he's teasing me but he's closer to the truth than he knows. Usually, when faced with a task like this—a death knock or doorstepping a celebrity, a disgraced official—I hide behind my journalist facade. But Margot knew me before I was a journalist. She knows the real me. It will be like I'm standing before her naked. I'll have nothing to hide behind.

I take a deep breath and follow Jack. He's got his camera case slung across his body but he still looks conspicuous. Paparazzo. I turn to him. "Perhaps you should stay here a minute. I don't want to spook Margot." I remember her as a straight-backed horsey woman, kind and caring, like Heather, but on first impressions she could be brusque and no-nonsense. A little intimidating.

Jack shrugs good-naturedly. "Sure, whatever you think. I'll wait in the car."

I hand him the keys and smile at him gratefully, hoping Margot hasn't spotted us already.

I walk slowly around the side of the house to the front door. Nothing much has changed—even the door is painted the same olive green—and I see the fountain in the distance, the hedges that hide the fields beyond and the caravan park. And in that moment I imagine I'm fourteen again, calling for Heather. I almost expect to hear the soft bark of Goldie and I feel a lurch in my heart. Don't be soft, I tell myself. That was a long time ago.

I rap on the door and wait, my heart hammering despite the bollocking I'm inwardly giving myself for being a wuss. I need another fag but I know that would be unprofessional. *Oh, come on, Margot. Open the door. I know you're in.*

And eventually, after what feels like years, the door opens and she's standing there in a waxed jacket and cream jodhpurs, a furious look on her face, her arms folded. Her once raven hair is streaked with white, and her eyes are lined, her neck jowly. She would only be in her late fifties but looks older, more weathered, although she's still striking. Tall and slim, she's wearing a slash of red lipstick that is darker around the edges. Her green eyes assess me but I can tell she doesn't recognize me. "I don't want to talk to you," she snaps. "Leave us alone. I've told the other one and I'm telling you the same. If you come here again I'll call the police."

I lift my eyes to hers. "Margot," I say softly. "It's me. Jessica Fox. Heather's old friend."

And then, with a jolt of recognition, her face pales. And in that moment I can see that she's unsure whether or not to slam the door in my face.

3

Margot

THE CRUNCH OF TIRES ON GRAVEL MAKES MARGOT GO TO THE window. Her heart leaps at first, thinking it's Adam and little Ethan coming home. But no. Instead of their black saloon, there's a small vehicle that looks like a replica of one of her grandson's toy cars parked next to hers. She sees two people get out: a slight blond girl and a lanky lad carrying a camera case. They look like they're having a discussion and then the lad gets back inside the car.

Margot experiences a burst of rage that's become more frequent since it happened. Bloody journalists. She's sick of them. She's already sent one lot packing with a flea in their ear. She can't stand them. They're like crows, the way they peck over the remains of other people's misery. What sort of person would choose to do a job like that? Thank goodness Adam and Ethan aren't home yet. They don't need this, not when they're facing the prospect of losing a wife, a mother. She reprimands herself. No. She mustn't think negatively. Heather will *not* die. She'll be fine. Margot's already lost one daughter and she's sure as hell not going to lose another. God can't be that cruel.

If it is a journalist, she'll give them a piece of her mind. Her anger propels her out of the room and down the hallway. She wrenches the front door open. This one is younger than the last and swamped in a coat that looks like it's been shaved from a llama.

Oh, Margot enjoys the ticking-off she gives her. It feels good to vent some of her anger. But then the young woman looks up at her and her big doe eyes soften and she says, "Margot. It's me. Jessica Fox. Heather's old friend." And Margot's stomach falls. Jessica. *The* Jessica. She remembers her daughter sobbing in her bed after Jessica's betrayal. Margot had held Heather in her arms while her daughter tried to make sense of it all. Especially after everything she'd been through, the grief over her dad and losing Flora. It was cold and unfeeling. Margot had never forgiven her.

"So, you're a journalist now?" she asks instead, folding her arms across her chest in a way she hopes displays her disapproval. It's not surprising, she thinks, as she surveys the woman standing in front of her. Jessica had been fourteen the last time she saw her, hanging around the clock tower with a new group of friends, drinking and generally behaving like a little tart, draped over some boy. Margot had felt so angry that she'd called Jessica at home and reprimanded her about how she'd treated Heather. She wasn't proud of her behavior, looking back. Jessica was only a teenager.

Jessica hesitates. "Yes, I am . . . but that's not the only reason I'm here."

Margot rolls her eyes. Of course it is! Why else would she come?

Jessica obviously notices because she adds, "I also wanted to say how sorry I am. For the way . . ." She swallows and, for a brief moment, Margot thinks she notices tears film Jessica's eyes. But, no, she must be mistaken, for Jessica Fox has no heart. ". . . For the way I treated Heather, back then."

"For abandoning her," Margot states. *After all, let's call a spade a spade*, she thinks. "After she lost her father. Her sister."

Jessica nods, her shaggy fringe falling in her face. The gesture gives her vulnerability and unexpectedly reminds Margot of Heather. "Yes," Jessica says, in a small voice. "I treated her badly, I know that. I was a kid, and I was stupid and selfish. I didn't think about Heather's feelings. I just . . ."

Jessica doesn't have to finish her sentence. Margot knows exactly what she must have been thinking all those years ago. She'd wanted to get away from Heather and all her bad luck. Maybe she'd thought it was contagious.

"Why now?" demands Margot. "Because Heather's in hospital, accused of killing two people? It's a juicy story, I'll give you that."

Jessica shuffles, clearly uncomfortable. "I moved away. I've only been living back in the West Country for a year."

"And you didn't think to look us up before? You didn't feel like apologizing then?"

Jessica opens her mouth but no words come out. *What can she say?* thinks Margot. *Where's her defense?* Then, eventually, she says, "It's been years, Margot."

Margot's suddenly had enough of this conversation. She doesn't want to look into Jessica's big brown eyes, doesn't want to feel anything for the girl standing before her.

She pulls herself up to her full height and can almost feel her heart hardening. "I have nothing more to say to you." Before Jessica can utter another word Margot closes the door firmly in her face. Then she leans against it, her heart pounding. She places a hand on her chest and takes a deep breath.

"Margot." She hears Jessica's voice through the door. "The press, they're going to keep hounding you until you give your side of the story. And wouldn't you rather speak to me? Someone you know? If you give me an exclusive, they'll go away. Margot? Margot, please, just think about it." She hears the letter box clatter behind her as Jessica pushes something through it. Margot counts to ten before turning and picking it up. It's a business card. Margot rips it in half and throws it into the wastepaper basket.

MARGOT WATCHES FROM THE SAFETY OF HER LIVING-ROOM WINDOW until Jessica has driven away, then goes upstairs and changes out of her riding gear. Downstairs again, she locks the house and almost runs to her Land Rover, as though she's expecting the press to be hiding in the surrounding bushes ready to pounce on her with their microphones and cameras. But nobody else is around. There's only one static caravan in use at the moment, by their long-term tenant Colin. He turned up five months ago, on the weekend the clocks went back, and hasn't left. Not that she's complaining. He doesn't say much, but he pays on time and it's an income, even if it's only small. She thinks he's probably lonely. For once, she's thankful they're out of season. Adam usually manages the camping site but, understandably, he's not been able to cope with that at the moment. The poor man is out of his mind with worry. And so is she. Because all she can think about is what awaits Heather when she finally wakes up. She refuses to think *if* she wakes up. She knows Heather's made of strong stuff.

At this time of day it takes Margot just over half an hour to drive to the hospital in Bristol. She tries to avoid the rush hour if she can and the ICU is open from 10 a.m. until 8 p.m. She parks, then walks the ten-minute journey from the multistory to the hospital reception. It's been only four days since Heather was admitted but already Margot feels she's too used to the atrium that reminds her of an airport terminal, with its many shops and cafés, and the weird smell—a mixture of chemicals, coffee, and vegetable soup.

When she first arrived on Friday, not long after Adam had rung to tell her about that life-changing phone call he'd received from the police, Margot had wondered if she'd ever get used to finding her way along the maze of corridors. Then, she'd been almost blinded by shock and fear. Her mind had screamed that it couldn't be true, that her daughter wasn't capable of such a horrendous crime. Why? Why would she do it? It made no sense, not when she had everything to live for. A lovely home, a supportive husband, and a beautiful baby boy. No, there had to be some mistake. She'd arranged to meet Adam in the atrium and the two of them had stumbled toward Heather's room, as if they were disaster survivors. And then she had seen that there was no mistake. The woman lying alone in the bed, attached to so much machinery she wondered how anybody could get near her, really *was* her daughter.

Sheila, her friend and stable hand, had been the one to find Heather in the barn. She'd come in at 8:15 a.m. to feed and groom the horses. By then Heather had been lying unconscious for at least an hour. It's a wonder she hadn't died there and then. Margot had been away at a yoga retreat with her friend Pam— something she'd never done before—and had been due home later that day.

Adam had cried when they'd met at the hospital that day and she'd been mesmerized by how his tears trickled into his thick brown beard. She'd seen Adam cry before—when he'd married Heather, when Ethan was born—but happy tears. Never this. He told her he'd not been at home when Heather shot herself, because he'd been taking Ethan to nursery, then gone to see a friend. Margot had thought this was strange. Adam and Heather never took Ethan to nursery earlier than 8 a.m. She could tell he was hiding something, but didn't want to probe. It wasn't the right time. She was aware that things hadn't been great between them for a while but didn't want to interfere by asking too many questions. After all, she knows what marriage is like. She'd had enough of her own problems with Keith, God rest his soul.

Margot slows down as she approaches the door to Heather's room. As always, her stomach turns over when she sees the police officer standing guard outside. It's a different one today. A woman this time. And, inappropriately, she thinks how masculine the female constable looks in the unflattering navy slacks and black workmen's shoes. The officer looks up at Margot and smiles. It's brief and professional. She's young, younger than Heather, with auburn hair tied in a low ponytail and clear, pale skin. She stands aside to let Margot pass. Margot has to concentrate on suppressing her desire to give the officer a telling-off. *Why are you here?* she wants to scream. *How can Heather pose a risk when she's bloody unconscious?* But she doesn't, of course, because this woman is an official and Margot was brought up by her strict councillor father to respect officials. Instead, she pulls the strap of her handbag further up her shoulder and pushes through the door into the room.

The quietness strikes her, as it always does at first. The only sound to be heard is the bleeping of the monitors. Heather's long dark hair has been brushed and, apart from her pale face, which has lost its usual healthy glow, there is nothing to indicate that she's fighting for her life. She looks peaceful, as though she's sleeping. There are no obvious signs of trauma, no bruising or surgical dressings on show. However, Margot knows that underneath the regulation hospital gown, Heather's chest and shoulder are tightly bandaged and, obscured by that fine head of hair, there's a shaved patch on the back of her head, with a five-inch gash now stitched and covered with gauze.

Margot dumps her bag on the floor and sits beside her daughter, taking her hand. The left one. The one she used to kill two innocent people. The one she used to point the gun toward her chest. The pellets had grazed her left breast and shoulder, thankfully, but she'd banged her head when she fell. Ironically it was the injury to her head, not the gunshot, that had put her daughter into the coma. This information, imparted by a serious-faced specialist when Heather was first brought in, gives Margot hope. It means Heather's suicide attempt wasn't serious. She could have shot herself in the head if she'd really wanted to die, or under her chin. The girl's been around guns since she was a kid. They used to own a farm in Kent before they moved here. Heather knows how to use them properly, and she knows what to do to kill, she tells herself.

The shotgun had been Margot's, used mostly for bird shooting, kept in a special cabinet in a shed under lock and key, although Adam sometimes borrowed it. They were both members of a shooting club about two miles away, although Heather was never interested in joining. The license was up for renewal. Maybe she should have got rid of it. Guns, it seemed, brought nothing but bad luck to their family.

Four days. It's now been four days that her darling Heather has been in this state. The doctors warned her that the longer she spends in the coma the less likelihood there is of a full recovery. She brings Heather's hand to her cheek—her daughter's skin is still so soft. *Oh, please wake up, please . . . please*, she silently begs.

Margot glances toward the All About Me board on the wall. The hospital issues them to all ICU patients so that their families have a place to display photographs or other information that might be useful. Adam's written down Heather's favorite radio station—Absolute 90s—and he's pinned up some photos. Margot's heart breaks every time she looks at them. There's one of Heather, her face wide and smiling, holding a newborn Ethan just after she'd given birth. In this very hospital, in fact, only eighteen months ago. There's another of Adam and Heather's wedding day ten years before. Heather looks so beautiful, young and innocent in a simple yet elegant gown, her hair piled on top of her head, tendrils framing her face. Adam, tall, dark, and brooding, is next to her in a suit that looks a fraction too small. They married young. Too young, Margot had thought at the time, but they'd been so much in love—they'd shone with it. Then Ethan came along, a much-loved and wanted baby, after years of trying. Heather suffered—*suffers, she's still alive, she's still here*—from polycystic ovaries, which made falling pregnant difficult. Things hadn't been plain sailing since Ethan was born. Heather had had postnatal depression in the immediate weeks following a traumatic birth, and found it hard to cope. But things had been getting better. At least, she'd thought they were.

What were you thinking, sweetheart? she wonders, for the umpteenth time, her daughter's hand still in hers. *Why did you kill those two people?*

4

I CAN HEAR VOICES. ARE THEY REAL OR IMAGINED? *I* CAN'T MAKE THEM OUT. *Every time I think I've understood a word or phrase, they disappear so that I can't catch them, like bubbles bursting in front of me. I can remember the weight of the gun, the sound of it going off. The drugs are too strong. They're dragging me back under, stopping me remembering, preventing me from hurting. And I don't want to remember. Because I think I've killed someone.*

5

It's late and already dark by the time I leave work.

After returning from Margot's earlier, I'd parked my Nissan in the underground car park beneath my flat and walked back to the newsroom, Jack chewing my ear all the way about how we should be staking out the Powells' farm and that Ted was bound to be disappointed in us. Loitering is something I would have done in the past. It just doesn't feel right under these circumstances. Now that I know it *is* my Heather who is the killer, I wonder if I'm too close to do this story justice. I instantly bat that idea away. It could also work to my advantage. I can't let the opportunity pass. After everything that happened at the *Tribune*, I need this story.

It's still raining as I cut across the city center and head toward the river, the wind tugging at my umbrella. Streetlights reflect in puddles. A few regulars are heading into the Llandoger Trow pub as I pass, but as I take a right along the river it becomes quieter and darker, people falling away, not wanting to risk the journey to pubs or restaurants in the area on a Monday night in this weather. Before long I'm alone.

It's bleaker along here at this time of year. The trees are still bare, beaten by the wind and rain, and the one boat that serves as a café in the late spring and summer is now depressingly empty. But walking alone in the dark never bothers me. And it's built up along the Welsh Back, the riverside soon hidden behind the buildings on either side of me, although there is a lack of street-light here and the cobbles are slick with rain.

And then I hear it.

Someone calling my name.

Jess-i-ca.

I turn around but nobody's there. I must be imagining it. It's the wind buffeting between the buildings, that's all.

I quicken my pace, my grip tightening around the handle of my umbrella. I'm not far from my apartment. The other build-ings along here—mostly offices, with the odd residential block thrown in—seem deserted. There aren't even any cars driving down here. It's only 7 p.m. Not even late.

Jess-i-ca.

I stop when I hear it again, spinning around, fury mixed with fear, but there's no sign of anyone. I refuse to run, to show I'm unnerved. I'm tired; it's been a long day. That's all this is. I take the umbrella down anyway, not caring that the rain soaks my hair. I can use it as a weapon if need be. I continue walking as fast as I can without actually running.

And then there are footsteps behind me. Loud and thudding. I almost trip on the cobbled road as I break into a run, no longer caring about showing any fear. I don't stop until I reach my apartment block. My hand is shaking as I delve into my bag for the keys and I let the umbrella fall from my hand in my eagerness to get inside. Is it him? I imagine his bulldog-type face, his sneer, his anger, the last words he said to me ringing in my ears: *I'll kill you, you fucking bitch.*

I grab the umbrella from the ground and hold it out in front of me, like a truncheon, as I push my shoulder into the door. And then I fall into the lobby, my heart hammering. As I close the door I take the opportunity to glance out into the street, but it's empty.

I take the stairs two at a time to the second floor. The smell of cooking hits me as I walk through the door of our flat: beef and onions. I feel foolish now. I completely overreacted. I can't let that thug scare me. I've been living here for nearly a year now and there's been no sign of him. It was just an empty threat he made, I remind myself. I can't live in fear.

I kick off my boots and hang up my coat before wandering into the open-plan kitchen–living room. The football is on the too-large widescreen TV. It's not even Rory's team but that doesn't bother him; he'll watch any match going. He has his back to me as he stands at the hob, stirring mince in a frying pan, watching the football out of the corner of his eye. He's wearing an apron over his jeans and T-shirt, with a naked man's torso on the front in frilly pink underwear that one of his brothers bought him for Christmas.

Without speaking, I go to the doors that lead to the balcony and throw them open, even though it's raining. The extractor fan is so ineffectual that we need another way of letting out the steam and cooking smells. I step onto the balcony and take a few deep breaths, the fresh air hitting my lungs and causing them to hurt a little. I really should give up smoking. Rory will be able to smell it on me. But after my fright earlier I'm desperate for a fag. I lean over the railings a little, enjoying the wind against my face. If I close my eyes I can pretend I'm on a boat. The flat can feel a bit claustrophobic at times. It's on the second floor so has no garden. If it wasn't for the views of the waterside I wouldn't want to live here. I glance down along the river, which looks dark and unwelcoming in this light. I'm half-expecting to see a figure lurking, but there's nobody. I can see Victoria Bridge from here, all lit up, the lights refracting in the water.

We hadn't planned on moving to Bristol, so close to where I grew up. But when Rory's sister, Aoife, was offered a promotion at a pharmaceutical company in Amsterdam, she said we could live here and pay enough rent to cover her mortgage, which is next to nothing as she bought the flat twelve years ago. Her idea was a godsend and benefited both of us. A place to run away to. Away from London, the *Tribune,* and all that went wrong there. We've lived here for nearly a year now but the flat still doesn't feel like home. Everywhere you look there are signs of Aoife and her life: photos of her and her friends on the white walls, the French-style bed that she bought from an expensive boutique, the charcoal linen L-shaped sofa that I'm terrified of messing up. Home is Rory's flat in Streatham where I spent most nights toward the end, desperate to get away from my annoying housemates. Despite my reservations I'm grateful to Aoife. I had to take a pay cut going from national to local news so the cheap rent has helped us financially, especially as Rory is supply teaching while looking for a full-time job. Rory gave up a lot for me, and when we decided to leave London for good he'd shyly asked if I'd like to move in with him, properly.

As soon as he spots me, he leaves the kitchen area to grab the remote control and turn off the TV. He knows I hate football.

"Don't do that because of me," I say, going over to him and planting a quick kiss on his lips.

He laughs. "You know I only watch it so my brothers don't beat me to a pulp."

"Well, you do need to sound like you know what they're talking about," I reply, mock-serious.

"You're right there. It's research."

It's our in-joke. Rory pretends he needs to learn how to be an alpha male, like his brothers, when really we both know he loves football.

He chuckles to himself as he returns to his cooking and I dart into the bedroom on the pretense of drying my wet hair. But really I want to look out of our bedroom window. From here I have views of the street I've just walked down and I pull back the roller blind to get a better look. A young couple are weaving across the cobbles, laughing too loudly, arm in arm and obviously holding each other up. Across the road from us, a derelict building is going through the planning process; it'll be converted into apartments. Is that a figure I see loitering in the doorway? I press my face to the glass but, no, it's just a trick of the light. There's nothing to be afraid of.

I comb through my damp hair, then go and find Rory in the kitchen, happy now I know there's no threat, just my imagination running away with me. "Thanks for making dinner," I say to him. I don't need to add *again*. He's always the one cooking. He says he enjoys it and finds it relaxing, even though it looks like a bomb has hit the kitchen after he's finished with it. I survey it now: a dirty spoon left on the black granite worktop, dishes and cups filling the sink. He usually leaves all the clearing up to me. I don't mind—I'd rather stack the dishwasher than cook any day. Jack jokes that if I married Rory the cooking would soon stop, that it's his way of lulling me into a false sense of security. But I don't believe him. Rory's too honest.

He brushes back my hair so that he's looking at me. Really looking. He has these brilliant blue eyes and when he stares into mine I almost squirm because it's as though he can read my mind, as though he knows every evil thought I've ever had, or the horrible dark things I've done, like the real reason we had to leave London last year. Or the guilt I carry about what I did that summer of 1994.

"What's going on, Jessie?" he says now. He's the only one who's allowed to call me that. The way he pronounces it in his sexy Irish accent gives me a little thrill. "Something's bothering you, isn't it?"

I move away from him to pick up a spatula and dump it in the sink. He's still studying me when I turn around. "It's just work."

"I thought it would be better now. Local news. Twice-weekly deadlines instead of daily, you know?"

"It *is* better. Or, rather, it was . . ."

He frowns. "But?"

Something sizzles and hisses. "Shit, it's the food," says Rory, darting to the hob and turning the heat down. His dark hair flops in front of his face as he picks up the wooden spoon and stirs the mince. I hop up onto the counter to watch him. He turned thirty-five last month but there is no sign of aging, no softening of his chiseled jaw, or extra fat on his lean frame. He still looks boyish.

He pours in his legendary homemade sauce that his mother taught him how to make. He once told me that growing up as a geeky, skinny kid in the countryside of County Cork he preferred learning to cook with his mum to climbing trees like his brothers. Aoife, the only girl, preferred the tree climbing, so it was only Rory, out of all of Rowena's children, who learned any culinary skills.

"So," says Rory, once the mince is back under control. "What happened today? I thought you liked working for Ted." He gently moves my legs aside so he can get to the cupboard for a pan.

I jump off the counter and switch on the kettle. "I had to go to Tilby. To doorstep the mother of a woman who killed two people."

"Oh, yeah, I heard about that on the news. Pretty shocking. Especially for Tilby." He pours spaghetti into a saucepan of cold water.

"Well, it turns out that I went to school with the killer."

"What?" He stares at me in shock.

"For two or three years she was my best friend." Best friend. It seems so trivial to call her that when she'd been so much more. Our friendship had burned with an intensity I've never experienced with anyone since. Not even Rory. I didn't realize how rare it was at the time. I'd taken it for granted. And thrown it away as though it was nothing, not knowing I'd never have another friendship like it. I've spoken about her to Rory a few times in the two and a half years we've been together, in passing, and only in reference to something that happened at school. Like the time we got a detention for accidentally flooding the girls' toilets or were sent out of chemistry for laughing at the back of the class. Heather was the quiet one of the two of us, softer than me, but she had a wicked sense of humor and would often have me in fits of giggles at the most inappropriate times. Yet none of the anecdotes I shared conveyed the true depth of feeling I had for her back then. For a moment in time she meant everything.

I'm hit with a sense of melancholy for that schoolgirl. So innocent. What changed? What went wrong for her?

Although I know some of it. We both changed after what happened in 1994.

"Blimey!" exclaims Rory, when I've finished filling him in on today's events. "Are you allowed to report any of this, considering she's in a coma?"

I drop tea bags into two mugs and nod. "The case is only active if she's charged. And she can't be charged because she's unconscious."

Rory runs a hand through his hair. "What was she like at school? Did she have violent tendencies? Was she the kind of kid to pull the legs off a daddy longlegs?"

"Of course not!" I cry, a little too quickly. Heather would never hurt an animal, or insect. "She was just a normal schoolgirl."

Except she wasn't.

WE WERE ALMOST TWELVE WHEN WE FIRST MET. MUM AND DAD had only recently divorced so we'd moved from a four-bedroom detached house in Bristol to the little cottage in Tilby in time for me to start the one and only senior school there at the beginning of the Easter term. At first I didn't have much to do with Heather. A girl called Gina, big and butch with spiky hair and too many piercings, took me under her wing. She was popular and I was easily accepted into her group. I always did have the gift of the gab, as my mum would say, and I found it easy to make friends. Heather, on the other hand, was a bit of a loner. Apparently, according to Gina, she'd only recently moved to the area from Kent and was finding it hard to fit in.

I first noticed her in our art lesson. We were put together by our art teacher, Miss Simpson. Heather didn't really speak to me much, just sat beside me drawing the bowl of apples we had been asked to sketch, her long dark hair falling over her shoulder and pooling onto the desk, deep in concentration. I was mesmerized by the way her hand sped across the page, shading in the apples with expert precision and flair. I could tell, even then, that she had a talent. I enjoyed art but she was so much better than me.

"Wow, that's amazing!" I'd exclaimed, when she'd finished. Mine looked like two blobs on a plate while hers were so lifelike.

"Oh, thanks," she said, smiling and blushing slightly. When she turned to look at me I was struck by how pretty she was. Her eyes were hazel with flecks of green and her pale skin flawless—unlike mine with a few stubborn pimples on my chin—with a sprinkling of freckles over the bridge of her nose. She was wearing the ugly green school uniform, just like I was, but she managed to make it look exotic. There was something about her, and I couldn't put my finger on what it was, but she seemed different from the other girls. She was quiet but she appeared self-assured rather than painfully shy; she didn't need to flock around in little cliquey groups like I did.

After that I made sure I always sat next to her in art. And even though she still didn't speak much she would often pass me one of her earphones, the other in her ear, so I could listen, too, to her Walkman (art was the only lesson in which we were allowed to do this). She loved The Cure, and even though I didn't know much about their music, I soon started to look forward to those art lessons.

One day, toward the end of year seven, we were asked to make something for Father's Day. She'd turned to me and said, "My dad's dead."

I'd stared at her, appalled by her forthrightness and not knowing how to answer. She didn't look embarrassed or worried by my reaction. I paused, then said, "And my dad's done a runner so . . ."

"Does that mean we get this lesson off? I'll ask Miss Simpson."

She went to put her hand up and we both collapsed, laughing.

After that I asked Gina about Heather but she'd scoffed, professing her "weird." At home time I often saw Heather leave school with an older girl. "That's her sister, Flora," said Gina one day, standing beside me and crunching mint Polos in my ear. "She's in year nine. They live up on Tilby Manor. Own the caravan park there. Moved here last year. Think they're snobs."

They didn't seem snobby to me. They were like two pretty cats. Aloof. Mysterious.

After that I began to seek Heather out. She usually disappeared to the library at lunchtime to read or to draw. One day I followed her and saw that she was writing what looked like a story. I loved writing, and would spend hours in my bedroom making books out of A4 paper that my mum would bring home from her office job especially for me to use. I knew Gina and the others would take the piss out of me if I told them about my hobby. It wasn't cool to be clever at Tilby High in the early 1990s. But I was getting bored of Gina and her cronies, their incessant talk of boys, and who fancied whom. I wasn't ready for all that. I didn't want a boyfriend; I wanted a friend. A best friend. Someone I admired, who had similar interests. And I quickly realized that the person I was looking for was Heather.

6

Jess

BRISTOL AND SOMERSET HERALD

Friday, March 16, 2012

FAMILY DEVASTED BY SEASIDE SHOOTINGS

by Jessica Fox

THE FAMILY of a mother and son who were shot dead in the sleepy seaside town of Tilby are shocked and saddened by their "senseless" deaths.

Deirdre and Clive Wilson were killed in their own home just a week ago today.

Lisa Wilson, 29, Deirdre's granddaughter, described her grandmother as a fun-loving, bubbly lady, who was fit and active and loved to ballroom dance.

Deirdre, who had been a widow for over twenty years, had only moved to the cottage where she died a month previously.

"My gran loved the sea so decided to save up so that she could buy the cottage. She was so happy to finally put down roots in Tilby," Lisa said. "Gran had admired the area for a long time and, in the short time she was there, she threw herself into the local community, joining the Women's Institute and volunteering at the church café. My uncle Clive had his own place in Bristol, but they were close so he often stayed with her. I don't think Gran liked living alone. They were just two normal, kind people. Gran loved dogs. She used to breed those beautiful chow chows that look like teddy bears. It's tragic to think all her planning and saving came to nothing. She only got to live in that house for a month. Why would someone want to kill an old lady who never hurt a fly?"

Police are waiting to question local woman Heather Underwood, 32, in connection with their deaths. She is currently in a coma in hospital after trying to take her own life.

Lisa's father, Norman, 56, added, "My brother Clive was a gentle soul. He lived a quiet life with my mum. He'd had a few financial difficulties over the years, a few businesses that went bust. I regret to say I didn't see them that much over the years after me and my family moved to Reading, although we kept in touch by phone. But I can't understand why somebody would want to shoot him or my mother.

I've never heard of this Heather Underwood. And, as far as I'm aware, my mum and brother had never met her. For her to break into their home and shoot them . . . well, it beggars belief. The family want answers."

Lisa and Norman Wilson aren't the only ones who seem baffled by this senseless killing. The police are also perplexed and can find no motive . . .

I STOP TYPING AND READ WHAT I'VE WRITTEN SO FAR. IT'S NOT TYING together in the way I want it to. I need to convey who these people were and ask why anyone would want to hurt them. Maybe I should take out the bit about the police being perplexed. It might make them look ineffectual, even though when I spoke to DCI Ruthgow on the phone earlier that was exactly how he'd sounded. He more or less admitted they have no motive, no reason why Heather would shoot those two people. Just evidence: the shotgun she used to try to kill herself was the same one used to kill Deirdre and Clive, then the fingerprints, the type and size of the cartridges used, and other forensic results they must have at their disposal, which I can't report at this time. If Heather wakes up, will she plead temporary insanity? Did she do it because she was depressed? Had she, momentarily, lost a sense of reality? They are all things I'd love to ask Margot, but since she practically shut the door in my face on Monday I haven't tried to speak to her again, though it's only a matter of time before Ted sends me back.

And I refuse to give up on Margot until I get her story.

I reread the article. I need to think of how to end it before filing it ready for the deadline tomorrow. It will be in the newspaper on Friday and I can't write anything that Margot might read and disapprove of. Not if I want to get her onside.

I flip through my notes. I'd spoken to Lisa and Norman Wilson this morning and they were very forthcoming on the phone. Lisa had cried, her voice sounding thick beneath her tears, as she described her grandmother. I look again at the photos she emailed. There's a lovely one of Deirdre sitting in a garden at the end of last summer, a puppy on her lap. Its fluffy teddy-bear face makes me think it must be one of the chow chows Lisa described. Deirdre is wearing a straw hat and is smiling, surrounded by peach roses. She looks younger than her age, her eyes clear and blue, her white hair bobbed to her shoulders, her face plump and rose cheeked. She appears happy, contented. She looks like a lovely, kind, devoted grandmother. I wonder how she'd felt when Heather had burst into her home carrying a gun. Had Clive been shot first? Or her? The police didn't say. I try to imagine her fear and shudder, feeling nauseous.

I scroll down to the next photo. Clive. It looks like it was taken in a pub. He's sitting with a pint in front of him, grinning. His blurry eyes give away that he's had a few. He looks his age: the whites of his eyes are bloodshot and, even though the photo is only of his top half, I can see that he's stocky. He's wearing a football shirt in gray and maroon—West Ham? Rory would know—and a gold chain around his neck. The hand holding the glass has a fat sovereign ring on the middle finger.

Who were Clive and Deirdre Wilson?

I sense Ted watching me. I look up and meet his eyes through the glass of his office—I say office, it's more of a cubicle. He's on the phone and is leaning back in his chair. Who is he talking to? Is it about me?

Stop being paranoid, Jess. I turn back to my computer. He's probably talking to Jared, our slimy editor at the *Herald*, who thankfully works at HQ. When he comes here—luckily for us, only very occasionally—he stands too close to me and Ellie, our trainee reporter, and addresses us by our names too many times for it to be natural. Apart from Ted, the office is quiet today. Seth is at his computer slowly going through images. Ellie is out on a story with Jack. Sue sits around the corner so I never see her unless I go to the loo or am heading out, although I can hear her on the phone—her voice is unusually loud—more often than not chatting to her sister about her "good-for-nothing" husband.

I log onto Facebook. A few times over the years I've tried to search for Heather under her maiden name, Powell. I was intrigued, I suppose, to find out what had happened to her. To see what she looked like now. To know if she ever married or had children. For those two years of my childhood the Powells had felt like family, and even though I could never go back, a part of me missed them. Although numerous Heather Powells came up, they were never her. But now I know her married name I search for Heather Underwood.

Her page is the first to appear and I click on it eagerly, wanting to know more about her life. I'm disappointed to find that her settings are restricted so that I can see only a profile photograph of her. I click on it anyway, intrigued to know what the adult Heather looks like. It's a close-up and obviously taken on holiday, judging by the palm trees in the background. She's squinting slightly but my stomach flips at the familiar sight of her: the long dark hair, the almond-shaped eyes, with new lines fanning out at the edges, the clear skin. Oh, Heather.

"Attractive woman."

I jump at the sound of Ted's voice by my shoulder. He's as stealthy as a bloody cat. I place my hand on my chest theatrically. "I was just seeing what information I could get but her privacy settings are too tight." I don't want him thinking I'm skiving by being on Facebook.

"Fuck." He draws breath through his teeth. "We need something. Come on, Jess. Where's that killer instinct you're famous for?" I cringe, remembering how it could have landed me in prison. "You know the family. You have an in. The *Daily News* and the fucking nationals are all over this story and it's already Wednesday. It'll be just a matter of time before this photo hits the red tops. We need something more. We need an exclusive."

He's right. I can't let what happened at the *Tribune* put me off. It's shaken my confidence, but I need this. I push back my chair and gather up my coat and bag. "I'll try Margot again."

"Good." His eyes glint. "And remember, do whatever it takes. But stay the right side of the law."

Despite myself, my stomach drops as I pull into Cowship Lane, oppressed by the narrow road with the hedges rearing up on ei-

Claire Douglas

ther side. Dark clouds gather in the distance, heavy with rain. I take a deep breath. This isn't just some random woman I'm trying to interview. It's Margot Powell. But before last year would that have bothered me? I don't think so.

Up ahead I can see cars blocking the exit to Tilby Manor Caravan Park as well as a local TV news station's van. I slow down. There is just enough room for me to pass but I can't get into the driveway. Has Margot decided to speak to the press after all? I can just imagine Ted's wrath if that's the case. He hired me despite my previous history because he thought, no doubt, there would be something to gain from my *tenacity*. I can't let him down.

I park in a lay-by further along the lane and walk up, trying to look confident. I pull my bag further onto my shoulder as I approach the small gathering of journalists. "There's no point," I say, in a loud, clear voice. "She won't talk to you. She's signed an exclusive with me."

A woman a little younger than me, with a pointed face and hair in a swishy blond ponytail, steps forward. I recognize her from the *Bristol Daily News*. Harriet Hill. She folds her arms across her bust. She looks smart in a long camel coat and black trousers. She assesses me through narrowed eyes, a hint of disgust on her face, no doubt taking in my retro patterned tights and shaggy coat. "She's signed an exclusive?" she asks, in a haughty voice. "With which paper?" She gives a fake laugh. "Don't tell me— the *Herald*." She spits out the name of our paper as though it tastes horrible. She swivels on her heels to one of the journalists standing beside her—a man I recognize from the *Daily Mail*—shaking her ponytail in disbelief. "The *Herald* is a *biweekly*." She smirks and he looks at the ground.

I ignore her, and push past them. "She won't answer," calls Harriet, but I continue striding down the long driveway with a confidence I don't feel. I can see a Range Rover parked in front of the barn as I walk around the side to the front door. I know Margot won't answer so I call through the letter box, hoping I'm too far away for the other journalists to hear me. "Margot, it's me, Jess. If you open the door I guarantee the rest of them will go away."

I stand back and wait, my heart thudding. I count. One, two, three. *Come on. Come on.*

Then, eventually, I hear movement behind the door. I call again through the letter box just to be sure. "Please, Margot. If you let me in the others will go. I promise."

I stand tall, waiting with bated breath as the front door slowly swings open.

7

Margot

IT'S BEEN RELENTLESS. FOR DAYS ON END MARGOT'S HAD TO PUT UP with the swarm of insects—because that's what they are, *pests*, feeding off her misery—outside her house. She's had to drive past them every time she visited Heather. She rang Adam and told him to stay at his mother's with Ethan for a few days. She can't let them be subjected to this.

And now here's another. Knocking on her door. She'd thrown a glass of water into the face of the last; a cocky young man who tried to charm her with his fake compliments. Oh, no. She's no fool. She won't be hoodwinked into talking to anyone.

It's beginning to wear thin. There's only so much front she can put up. They're getting in the way of her business, spooking the horses when she takes them for a ride or preventing would-be campers from inquiring about a caravan or a pitch. She knows it's a quiet time of year but they still get business some weekends leading up to the Easter holidays.

She's necking a Valium that her doctor kindly prescribed when she hears someone calling through the letter box. Of all the nerve! She strides to the front door, ready to give them a ticking-off, when she recognizes Jessica's voice.

". . . if you let me in the others will go. I promise."

Her hand falters on the doorknob. Surely she's just saying that. Another ploy to get her to speak. Oh, she's heard them all: "A chance to tell your side of the story, Mrs. Powell"; "You can defend your daughter by putting your side across"; "Don't you want the public to see that your daughter is a person? Not just a killer?"

Despite her reservations she pulls back the door to see Jessica standing there with an apprehensive look on her face. If she didn't know better she'd think the girl was nervous. But that lasts only a millisecond as Jessica's expression changes to its usual assertive response. Margot notices the girl is still wearing the hideous llama coat.

"Margot," she says, in an urgent tone. "I've told the other reporters you've agreed to talk exclusively to me." She holds up a hand when Margot opens her mouth to object. "I know it's a lie but if they think it's true they won't bother to stay. There'll be no point. So please. Just let me in."

Margot glares at Jessica, then over her shoulder at the other journalists all waiting at the end of the driveway. There's something about the way they're standing—the six or seven of them who have congregated—that puts her in mind of a pack of beagles about to go on a hunt.

Silently Margot steps aside to allow Jessica over the threshold. "It had better work," she mutters, as Jessica walks past.

"It will," says Jessica, confidently.

"Go through."

Jessica does as she's told, then stands awkwardly in the farmhouse kitchen, which hasn't changed since she was last there eighteen years ago. She notices Jessica's eyes sweeping the room and landing on a photograph of Flora and Heather as teenagers. "Sit down," instructs Margot, turning away to fill the kettle. She hears the scraping of chair legs on tiles.

Margot replaces the kettle on the Aga. It hasn't long since boiled. She has no clue as to whether Jessica's plan has worked because the kitchen is at the back of the house, overlooking the garden and the fields beyond. In the distance she can see the tree they planted in Flora's memory—a stunning beech that has now grown tall in the intervening years—and beyond that her own black stallion, Orion, with Heather's pony, Lucky, grazing. Oh, how Heather loves that little black, even though she outgrew him years ago. She swallows a lump in her throat when she thinks of her daughter lying so still in that hospital bed.

"I'm sorry," says Jessica, in a small voice from the table behind her. "I can't stop thinking about Heather."

Margot's shoulders tighten. How can she tell if Jessica is genuine? She wants to reply with a caustic retort but she doesn't have the energy. Instead her shoulders sag under the weight of her worry. "Tea?" she says instead, as the kettle starts to whistle.

Jessica nods. "Thank you. That would be lovely." She looks wistful as she stares out of the window. "I regret how our friendship ended," she says. "Me and Heather, I mean."

"You dumped her when she needed you most." Margot's jaw hurts with all the vitriol she's tried hard to suppress. She places a cup in front of Jessica too roughly, so that the tea spills over the top and gathers in the saucer. She doesn't apologize.

Jessica fiddles with her saucer, her eyes downcast. "I know. And I regret it. It was a tough lesson. I don't have many"—she sighs, still not looking at Margot—"female friends."

This doesn't surprise Margot in the least.

Margot takes her teacup and sits opposite Jessica. The girl looks worn out. There are dark circles under her eyes and her face is drawn. Margot takes a sip of her tea, then asks after Jessica's mother. She's surprised to see Jessica's face fall at the mention of Simone. Has she put her foot in it? Did Simone die?

But then Jessica says quietly, "Mum remarried and moved to Spain about ten years ago. I see her once or twice a year."

Only once or twice a year. Margot can't imagine that. Since losing Flora she's made sure to see Heather as often as she can, which is easy as they all live in such close proximity, although she tries to give them their space. When Heather and Adam married they moved into the stone cottage on the edge of the caravan site and did it up, decorating the walls with pale pastel colors, Heather sanding down furniture in the shabby-chic style she loves so much. She can still remember Heather's excitement when she painted the nursery while heavily pregnant with Ethan. She'd been too scared to do it before she got to thirty-five weeks, worried about jinxing it.

"I can't imagine that," Margot mumbles. To her shame she feels her eyes well with tears, thinking of life without Heather. If she gains consciousness she'll be incarcerated for murder. Margot will lose her either way. No. That's not true. Because at least in prison they'd see each other weekly, sitting across a table from each other in a sterile visitors' room. They'd still be able to talk and confide, maybe even laugh. She'd still have her funny, sensitive, beautiful daughter.

Jessica must sense her weakness because she reaches out a hand across the pine kitchen table and touches Margot's fingers gently. "I know Heather wouldn't have shot those people unless there was a reason," she begins. "She's not a cold-blooded killer."

Margot stiffens. Keith's angry red face pops into her head, and a ten-year-old Heather, cradling the lamb in her lap knowing she wasn't allowed to.

Margot blinks and tries to focus on Jessica. She has to clear her mind. "Of course she's not a cold-blooded killer," she says instead. "I don't understand what drove her to commit this . . . *this mad act*. It's so out of character. You knew Heather. She's a gentle soul, kind, loving . . ."

Jessica bites her lip and nods. But something passes across her face that makes Margot wonder whether she suspects the truth.

8

Jess

I CAN SENSE MARGOT WAVERING. SHE'S CONTEMPLATING CONFIDING in me, I can tell. I don't want to do or say anything to distract her. I need to lead her carefully now, no wrong moves. I take my hand away and sip my tea. Waiting.

Behind Margot there is a photo on the wall of Heather and Flora, taken around the time I knew them. Their heads are pressed together, their silky dark hair falling over their shoulders and merging so you can't tell where Heather's begins and Flora's ends. They are giving wide, toothy grins. Eyes shining. Young. They are in sharp focus, the background muted greens and browns, but from their short sleeves and tanned arms I can tell it was taken in the summer. My heart contracts and I swallow a lump in my throat as I realize it was taken that *last* summer. There are others on the mantelpiece behind me that I spotted when I walked in. I long to go over to them, pick them up and examine them. But I can't.

When I think of Flora, the familiar guilt tugs away at my insides.

I place my cup back on the kitchen table, yellowing and over varnished but it's the same table I sat at with Heather. I can tell by the knots and the whorls. There's one near the edge that looks like a witch's face. Once, Heather painted eyes on it as a joke. Nothing has changed. Even the roman blinds at the kitchen window are the same, with their green-and-white tree-print design, faded now in parts. The only difference is there is no longer any dog at our feet. Goldie used to follow us everywhere until she got too old to do much more than sleep. When I first stayed the night I wore a pair of oversize slippers shaped like pigs and Goldie chased me around the kitchen, trying to nip them. She thought they were toys, I suppose. I smile at the memory.

Margot notices. "What?"

"I'm just remembering being here. Before. With Heather. Remember how Goldie used to be obsessed with my slippers. Those pig ones?"

Margot chuckles. The sound lifts me. "I'd forgotten that. I miss the dog."

"Did you ever get another after she passed away?"

Margot shakes her head. "No. Too much had happened by then."

"Margot, I—"

I'm interrupted by a man striding into the kitchen from the back door, bringing with him fresh air and the faint smell of rain. He's tall and outdoorsy, with a padded vest and heavy boots, handsome in a rugged Bear Grylls type of way. In his arms, he has a small boy, who can't be more than eighteen months old. He has on soft biscuit-colored corduroy dungarees and is chewing a plastic toy giraffe. By his red cheeks and gnawing I can tell he's teething. I've learned a lot about babies from Rory's brothers' kids. He has a mass of dark curls and eyes like Heather's. I smile at him and he ducks his head behind the man's shoulder.

Heather's husband and son.

My heart contracts. They must be going through hell.

Margot stands up. "Adam. What are you doing here? I thought you were staying at Gloria's."

He scowls. "I refuse to let those parasites drive me out of my own home." He turns to me, his brow furrowed. "Are you one of them?"

I avert my eyes. "I . . . Well, I'm—"

"She's a friend of the family," interjects Margot, much to my surprise. "She was Heather's best friend at school. This is Jessica Fox. And this is Heather's husband, Adam."

"Heather's never mentioned you," he says, fixing me with his cold, hard stare. It's like he's punched me in the stomach. Heather and I were friends for such a short time in the grand scheme of things but our friendship meant something. It was important. Did she not feel the same? Did I hurt her so badly she refused ever to think of me again? She never knew what I did back then. It's a secret I've carried with me all these years. I shake my head to stop my thoughts. What's happening to me? Being here again, in Margot's home, in her kitchen with all the memories, is harder than I thought it would be.

Adam turns back to Margot. "Ethan wanted his own bed. He's been crying for his mother."

Margot looks stricken. She holds out her arms and Ethan wriggles into them. She hugs the little boy to her and he snuggles against her knitted jumper. The change in Margot is immediate. The hard exterior she's worn with me dissolves into something soft and maternal as she kisses the top of Ethan's dark head. It reminds me again of when we were kids. Margot always made time for us, sitting with us around this very table, helping us with our homework, or letting us bake a cake—which usually ended up tasting rank. Once, during a heat wave, she showed us how to make lemonade.

"The kettle's just boiled," says Margot to Adam, her cheek resting on Ethan's hair.

Adam goes to the kettle to make himself a coffee. I don't know what to say so I pick up my cup again, sip my tea, and wait. The tension feels too thick and I know it's down to my presence. What I can't understand is why. He doesn't know I'm a journalist yet. Is this what he's always like? Or is grief making him act this way?

"Have they all gone?" Margot asks Adam, as he pulls out a chair next to me. His hands are red and raw as he cups the mug. It's unusually cold for March, even with all the rain we've been having.

"The vultures?"

Margot nods, not looking at me.

"Yep. Thank God. I don't know what you said to make them bugger off. Maybe they've gone home for their tea."

"Jessica got rid of them for us."

Adam turns to me, expression quizzical. "And how did you manage that?"

I push down my unease. "I'm a journalist too," I say, in a voice that belies my apprehension.

"Of course you fucking are!" he says quietly, menacingly, into his mug.

"Adam," Margot warns, "little ears." She covers Ethan's with her hands to make her point. I can't believe Heather has chosen to spend her life with this bullish man. She'd had a huge crush on River Phoenix when we were teenagers; she'd imagined him to be sensitive and artistic. The fact he died young only romanticized him in her eyes. Adam couldn't be more different.

His eyes flash at Margot. "Why have you let her in, Marg, when she's one of them?"

"I'm not here to do any harm," I insist. "Heather was my friend."

He glares at me. "You lot never print the truth. You twist everything and you'll twist this." He turns back to Margot. "Don't trust her. You can't trust any of them."

"Listen," I say, trying to keep my voice steady and firm. "If you don't tell your side of the story then someone *somewhere* will print what they want. They'll dig and they'll find stuff. They always do. But if you talk to me"—I ignore the grunts—"*if* you talk to me then it will be your side of the story. I'll print exactly what you want me to print. An exclusive."

He laughs cruelly. "You've got to be kidding me. Are you listening to this, Marg? Don't tell me you're taken in by her."

"I won't print anything about Heather or the family without you reading it first," I promise, desperate to say, *to do* anything to make him trust me, even though it goes against my normal practice.

"You don't understand," he says carefully. "I don't want *anything* in the papers about us. Full stop."

I slap my hand against the wooden surface of the table. "And *you* don't understand. It *will* get in the papers whether you want it to or not. For crying out loud, it's already *in* them!"

We stare at each other. My heart feels like it's going to leap out of my chest. He breaks eye contact first, slumping back in his chair. Margot assesses us silently, rocking Ethan backward and forward in her arms. I wonder what she's thinking. But I've already noticed a thaw in her since I sent the rest of the reporters packing.

Adam places his head in his hands and groans. "I just can't believe we're in this situation," he says, his deep voice muffled between his fingers.

"I'm so sorry," I say gently, relieved that he's calmer. "I haven't seen Heather for years, but this seems unbelievable to me. Completely out of character. Have you . . ." I dart a look at Margot. "Have you wondered if there could be some mistake? Was it definitely Heather who did this?"

Margot's face hardens again. "That's what the police believe. There were eyewitnesses . . . and they're more or less sure that her own gunshot wound was self-inflicted."

"More or less sure?" I ask. "Is there any doubt?"

Adam interrupts. "There is no doubt," he snaps. Why do I get the impression he's hiding something?

Ethan starts to whimper, fidgeting and trying to get down from Margot's lap. Adam stands up. "He needs to go to bed," he says, taking him from Margot. "But we can carry on this conversation later, Marg. Alone." He shoots me a look before turning back to Margot. "Don't make any decisions yet."

He stalks off, Ethan in his arms, without saying goodbye to me, the back door banging behind him.

The sky has darkened and Margot glances anxiously out the window. "I'd better get the horses in. It looks like it's going to be another bad night." Then she sighs heavily. "I'm sorry about Adam. Underneath all that . . . brusqueness, he's a nice guy. He's a good husband and father."

I'm not sure I believe that. He seems threatening and aggressive to me but I don't say so. Instead I try to look understanding. "It's a stressful time for you all."

To my horror, Margot's face crumples and she pulls out a tissue from the sleeve of her jumper. "I can't lose Heather as well," she says, tears spilling down her cheeks. "I don't know how I'd bear it."

"Oh, Margot." I get up and, without even thinking about it, I put my arms around her. She still smells exactly as she used to all those years ago. Yardley perfume mixed with saddle leather. I breathe her in, remembering a time when I was still only twelve and on my first sleepover with Heather. I'd woken up, sweating and agitated, after a dream about my dad. I'd been upset, the divorce still too fresh, and I missed Dad, who had disappeared back to his job on the oil rigs, never bothering to keep in touch. Margot must have heard my crying because she'd come into the bedroom wearing a purple dressing gown and she'd hugged me, my face nuzzled against the soft velour. I'd felt safe in her warm arms and reassured. I'd instantly calmed down and fallen back to sleep. "I'm so sorry," I say to her now, the irony not lost on me that I'm the one comforting her. "I'm so, so sorry."

As I drive along Tilby's high street a deep sadness descends upon me. The pavements are sleek with rain but I can almost see Heather and Flora hunched together, laughing. Once on our walk home—when I was finally allowed into their inner sanctum—we could hardly put one foot in front of the other as we doubled up with laughter after a car drove past, dousing us with rainwater so that our skirts were drenched. I remember running through the fields to their house, the mud splashing up our legs and over our white socks, then drying off with old towels in our favorite barn—the one where Heather was found at death's door.

I should be feeling ecstatic. I have no doubt that Adam and Margot will agree to talk to me now, which could be a turning point for my career, and Ted will be overjoyed—but I can't stop thinking about them, most of all Margot. Seeing her again, meeting Adam and little Ethan has stirred everything up. As a teenager I was more than a little obsessed with the family. I never got to meet Heather's dad as he'd died a few years previously, before they moved to Tilby, but her uncle—Margot's younger brother, Leo—was always there. A handsome, jovial guy with the same thick, dark hair as Margot used to have and twinkly green eyes.

I'd been more than a little envious of them, really, Heather and Flora. Being an only child, I'd always wanted an older sister. And they seemed so close.

They had everything—or so I thought then. Even, later, when I got to know them better, when Heather became my best friend, Flora still remained that glamorous enigma.

And then, in August 1994, sixteen-year-old Flora Powell disappeared.

9

August 1994

FLORA GRABBED HER SISTER'S HAND IN A SUDDEN RUSH OF EXCITEMENT. The fair had come to Tilby and it was the most thrilling thing that had happened in their boring little town all year. More amazingly still, their mother had allowed them to go. In the evening. Without her or Uncle Leo tagging along.

Different tunes clashed together so all that was discernible was the heavy beat of the drums. Lights flashed from the rides and laughter rang out in the normally empty field. The sweet scent of candyfloss was heavy in the air, mixed with something else, roasted meat, perhaps. Heather glanced at her sister, seeming unsure. Heather was only fourteen and this was the first time she'd been allowed to go to the fair at night without her mother. Unknown to her, Flora had snuck out last year when everyone was asleep. She'd been brave enough then to go to the edge of the caravan park and watch from that safe distance as the lights of the Big Wheel dazzled and the thump of music floated through the night.

But this year was different. This year Flora had turned sixteen. She was practically an adult. Plus she wanted to meet *him*.

She didn't know his name. But she'd bumped into him on the high street yesterday when she was in Gateway getting some shopping for her mum. She'd spotted the flyers attached to lampposts and nailed to fences. The Smithwick traveling fair was back for its second year. It meant the town was flooded with new blood and she, for one, couldn't be more ecstatic. She was fed up with the boys in her year at school and it wouldn't be any different in September, even though she'd be in the sixth form. They either followed her around trying to twang her bra strap or they hurled offensive remarks at her, words like "dyke" and "frigid," just because she didn't fancy any of them. She hated walking past them where they all seemed to congregate at the clock tower, drinking Diamond White and smoking, trying to look hard. She didn't find any of them attractive or cool.

Flora had been leaving the supermarket, the handle of the plastic carrier bag digging into the flesh of her forearm, when they almost collided. She could tell straightaway that he wasn't a local by the dark hair that touched the collar of his patterned psychedelic shirt and his tanned face. No boys in Tilby would dare to dress to stand out, scared they might get beaten up. He was older than her by a couple of years at least, and when his sea-blue eyes met hers, she actually felt butterflies flutter in her stomach.

"Oops, sorry," he said, in an accent she couldn't quite place. London, perhaps. Definitely not West Country. "Nearly sent you flying." His eyes swept over her long black skirt with the tasseled hem, her lacy cream blouse, the many chains around her neck, and her DM boots. And then he gave an audacious whistle. "Actually, I take that back. I'm not sorry at all. You look like a beautiful gypsy girl."

Flora had blushed, not knowing what to say or how to react. Instead she muttered something about having to go and scurried past him down the street, but he called after her: "Come to the fair tomorrow night. I'm working on the Waltzers ride there. I'll look out for you, Gypsy Girl." She'd grinned to herself as she hotfooted home, her cheeks still burning in the breeze.

And now here she was. But where was he?

She felt Heather stiffen beside her and snatch her hand away. "I'm not sure about this," she said. Her voice sounded very small and Flora could hardly hear her above the cacophony.

Flora felt a flash of annoyance toward her sister. She didn't want to walk around the fair by herself. Why was Heather being such a baby? It wasn't as though their mother had forbidden them to come.

But she took a deep breath, making an effort to swallow her irritation. This was what Heather was like. Quiet and unsure about trying new things. She knew she should have asked Jess along too. Jess was good at bringing Heather out of herself. Her sister was too introverted at times, closeted in her bedroom listening to too much goth music. Flora liked The Cure as much as Heather did—although she preferred All About Eve now. The trouble with Heather was that she didn't want to open her mind to new experiences. Flora had never been properly kissed, just a peck from Andy Waters back in junior school when they pretended to get married. It was her time.

"Come on," Flora pleaded, trying to keep her voice light and not too desperate. "We'll have fun!" And the only bloke I've ever truly fancied has said he's going to be here, she silently added.

"I don't really want to be here . . . It's all a bit loud." She looked bewildered, like one of the neighbor's sheep after it had strayed into the wrong field and got caught up in barbed wire.

It took a while but Flora eventually managed to coax her sister toward the Waltzers. The sun was going down and the sky was streaked with pink, orange, and purple. It gave the evening an unreal quality and Flora's heart quickened even more. The dance beats seemed to pulsate inside her. She just knew something exciting was going to happen for her tonight. If only Heather would stop being such a wuss. This was their father's fault. He'd shouted and nagged and bullied them for most of their childhood. But he'd been dead for more than four years now. Yet Heather still seemed cowed by him. Flora knew her sister needed to let her hair down a bit, to stop her incessant worrying.

"I'm not going on that," said Heather, her eyes wide with terror as she watched the Waltzers spin and dip as though they were dancing. "I'll be sick."

Flora wasn't planning to go on them either. She was just there for the sexy boy she'd bumped into yesterday. Where was he? And then she spotted him jumping from one car to another, whirling them around to the squawking delights of the passengers: three teenage girls with too much lipstick and hair spray, she was irked to note. He was even better-looking than she remembered. Her insides actually fizzed, like a Refresher on her tongue, at the sight of him.

Then he noticed her and his face brightened. He jumped down to where they were standing on the steps, much to the obvious annoyance of his groupies in the car. "Well, hello, Gypsy Girl. I was hoping you'd make it."

Flora's cheeks flamed and she just about managed to mumble hi. She sensed Heather staring at her in disbelief. She didn't dare look at her sister because she knew she'd see judgment and disappointment in her expression. "Fancy a go?"

Heather stepped back in horror. "Not for me, thanks. I've just spotted Jess," she said, her voice full of relief. "Come on, Flora. Mum said we had to stick together, remember?"

Instantly Flora felt irritated. She wasn't going anywhere. She turned up her face to the boy, whose name she still didn't know, and said, "I'd love a go, as long as you spin me."

HEATHER STOOD FOR A WHILE, WATCHING HER SISTER GIGGLING AND flirting with the fair hand. She'd never seen Flora act like that before. It made her feel uneasy and she turned away in disgust. She could see Jess standing at the Big Wheel, holding a giant candyfloss on a stick and waving her over. She was alone. That was what Heather admired about Jess. She was brave. She didn't worry about turning up at something like this by herself. Heather hated crowds and loud noises.

Flora was off the Waltzers now, looking a bit green and giddy. The fair hand was holding her up, his arm snaked around her waist. He looked smarmy to Heather but she could see how much her sister fancied him. He was too old for Flora, not like the boys at school, and he walked as though he had something in his pants. Then they sashayed past her, Flora not even glancing in her direction. No, this wasn't right. Heather stepped forward, arms folded, calling after them, "Where are you going?"

Flora tossed her long dark hair over her shoulder. "Just for a walk around the fair. Dylan is on his break."

Dylan. Of course, that would be his name, something cool and a bit different, not Peter or Mike or Paul, like the boys at school. Oh, no, bloody *Dylan*. "Mum said we had to stick to-gether . . ." But her words were already lost in the hubbub and the music. Flora was too busy giggling at something Dylan was saying. She watched as they wandered off, his arm slung around her shoulders and hers around his waist.

"Who was that?" Jess was suddenly by her side, her lips glistening with pink sugar. The fluffy candyfloss was as big as her head.

"Some bloke Flora met off the Waltzers."

Jess linked her arm through hers. "Don't worry. She's a big girl, she'll be fine. Come on. Why don't we go and see if Zac and his mates are here?" Jess brushed her mousy blond fringe from her face. Was that blue eyeliner she was wearing? Heather felt the all-too-familiar anxiety tug at her insides—first Flora going off with some strange lad and now her best friend wearing makeup and talking about finding that moron Zac and his mates.

She turned away, trying desperately to spot Flora. But her sister had been swallowed by the crowds.

"Hey, she'll be okay," said Jess, watching Heather intently. "You worry too much. Come on."

Heather tried to smile, but she suddenly felt a sense of foreboding so strong she had to pause to catch her breath. She pushed down her unease and followed Jess further into the fair.

10

I MUST BE DREAMING BUT I'M REMEMBERING YOU AND THE FAIR, THE MUSIC, THE crowds. I start to feel scared, just like I did the first time I went there, and I begin to thrash around, my legs jerking, but it must be my imagination because I know I can't move. I feel like I'm underwater and that the surface is up ahead, glinting enticingly, the sun beaming down, like the light at the end of a tunnel, but I can't reach it. I can't pull myself out of the cold darkness. I can't reach you.

I don't know if I let out a moan. Is that voices I hear? A hand stroking my brow? Is it my mother? I'm desperate to talk to her, to explain. I need to tell her what happened, and why, before it's too late. But I can't move, I can't speak. Is this what it feels like to be dying?

My mind slips back to the fair. It's all I can think about. And even in my muddy, confused state I know that the fair is very important. That it all started there. I mustn't forget. It's the link to everything.

11

Jess

BRISTOL AND SOMERSET HERALD

Friday, March 16, 2012

WOMAN BRANDISHING A GUN
SPOTTED BY NEXT-DOOR NEIGHBOR

by Jessica Fox

AN EYEWITNESS to last week's shootings saw a woman leaving the property with a gun on the morning of the double murder in Tilby.

Peter Bright, 37, who lives next door to where mother and son Deirdre and Clive Wilson were shot dead, described seeing a "dark-haired woman" leaving their cottage with a gun used for "hunting."

He said: "I had just come back from a run and thought

I heard a shot, then a thump and a bang coming from next door. I didn't think too much about it until I was putting the bins out. And then I saw this dark-haired woman stride down their garden path with what looked like a shotgun slung over her shoulder as though about to go and shoot birds. She had a deranged look on her face. I watched her get into her car and then I heard screams from my wife. When I turned back I saw what Holly was screaming about. The Wilsons' front door was wide open and Deirdre's body was slumped at the foot of the stairs. That's when I put two and two together and realized the woman I saw had just shot Deirdre Wilson."

Mr. Bright continued, "I couldn't believe what I was seeing. The woman was totally calm when she left the house. She got into a sky-blue estate car. I remember thinking it was weird because I'd passed that car over an hour earlier while on my run, which must have been about 6 a.m. And that same car had been heading into Tilby Manor Caravan Park and had been driving very erratically."

Avon and Somerset Police are appealing for more witnesses to come forward.

I FILE THE STORY IN TIME FOR THE LUNCHTIME DEADLINE SO IT WILL appear in tomorrow's paper, then take a long slug of coffee.

Peter had been twitchy when Jack and I visited him first thing this morning. We'd just turned up on the off chance he would be in. He worked from home, he said. Something in software. He was obviously a keen runner as he was still in his Lycra when we got there, although he didn't look as though he'd just been exercising; he was surprisingly fresh faced with no hint of sweat. His wife, Holly, made us a cup of tea served in floral bone-china cups, then sat next to Peter on the sofa in their small, immaculate living room, too close so that her right side was pressed up against his left. There was an overpowering smell of plug-in air freshener in the room, but despite the bright furnishings the cottage was dark and a bit gloomy. It was the views of the beach and the sea beyond that were the selling point. Holly had seemed nervous, too, and didn't want to go on record or give any quotes, even though she described to us the full horror of finding Deirdre Wilson slumped on the hallway floor.

"There was so much blood," she said, shredding a tissue into her lap. "More than I thought there would be, not that I knew what to expect. Her eyes were wide and staring . . ." She gulped. "I'll never forget it."

Peter placed his arm protectively around his wife's shoulders. Then he explained to us that their house was the mirror opposite of Deirdre and Clive's. "And as it's a terrace I could hear every bang. I didn't know they were shots. Obviously you don't expect to hear gunshots, do you? That's why it was such a shock to see that woman carrying a gun leaving their house. She acted like she didn't care who saw her. I mean, she could have come in the middle of the night. Under darkness. You know?"

I'd sat and nodded as I took notes. I still found it hard to believe we were sitting there talking about Heather. And where had she been coming back from at six in the morning? Why had she not been at home, tucked up in bed with Adam? Or downstairs feeding her little boy? Had she spent the night somewhere else? With someone else?

The shootings had taken place around 6:45 a.m. So what had she been doing before that?

"I don't understand why anybody would want to kill them," said Holly, into a tissue. "I know they hadn't lived there very long but they seemed normal. Deirdre spent most of the time either pottering in the garden or walking her dog along the beach. A few older ladies would drop in from time to time, with a cake. I think she held the odd coffee morning. She was in the Women's Institute, you know . . ." She sniffed and dabbed delicately at her nose. "Clive kept himself to himself. He would also walk Hulk . . ." I raised an eyebrow and she laughed. "I know. Odd name for a dog that looks like a teddy bear. I think they wanted something masculine. It was plain to see he loved that dog. I'd sometimes bump into him on the way to the newsagent's where he'd always go to collect the *Radio Times* on a Saturday morning, or coming back from the pub as I was putting out the bins. He always said hello. They weren't loud people. They didn't play music or bang around the house. They just seemed"—she stared up at me with woeful eyes—"decent."

After I'd finished interviewing them, Jack took Peter outside so he could photograph him standing in the front garden, with the Wilsons' cottage in full view behind him. I stood watching, hoping the rain would hold off long enough for Jack to get a decent shot. The house was no longer cordoned, but seven or eight bunches of flowers had been left to wilt in the Wilsons' neat front garden. While Jack was busy repositioning Peter and snapping away, I wandered over to take a closer look at the Wilsons' house. The curtains were closed but the place was tidy, with garden gnomes and stone animals dotted around the front garden and between the well-tended plants. There was a Neighborhood Watch sticker in the living-room window and a wrought-iron umbrella stand in the corner of the front porch. I wondered if anybody had been in there to clean away the blood in the hallway.

Then I drifted over to the flowers. Most of the messages attached had faded in the rain but there was one from Deirdre's granddaughter, Lisa, with *To a wonderful Gran* scrawled on a card attached to a drooping bouquet of lilies and another from "the ladies at the Women's Institute" on some wilting peach roses.

I was about to walk away when I saw a bunch of carnations that looked fresher than the rest. The card wasn't signed, but I could tell there was writing on it. I crouched to get a closer look. Written in large block capitals were the words *THIS WAS ONE BULLET YOU COULDN'T DODGE.*

Intrigued, I ripped it from the cellophane wrapping and, before anyone noticed, I pocketed it.

12

Jess

Have you shown that card to Ted yet?" asks Jack, wheeling his chair over to me with a glint in his eye. "This could be a story in itself."

"Not yet," I reply, tapping at my keyboard, my eyes glued to the screen. I've filed the eyewitness story, so I'm working on a Clive and Deirdre background piece. But now I'm worried I've done the wrong thing. I shouldn't have pocketed the card. It would be interfering with a crime scene. If Clive or Deirdre had enemies, the police will want to know. I can't afford to take one step out of line. Ted had told me that when he offered me the job.

Jack had been so excited when I showed him the card in the car. He'd turned it over in his fingers and kept asking me what I thought it meant.

"It means that one or both of them had enemies," I'd said. Other than that I didn't fully understand why I'd decided to take it. Maybe to prove Clive Wilson wasn't the squeaky-clean uncle, brother, and son that his family had tried to portray. Unless the message had been meant for Deirdre. I doubted that. She looked like a lovely, doting grandmother. Maybe the killer had shot her because she'd got in the way or had come home unexpectedly. But, then again, perhaps Deirdre wasn't who she'd appeared to be.

I still can't bring myself to think of Heather as the killer.

There has to have been some mistake.

I recall my conversation with Margot yesterday. She'd insinuated there might be some doubt, although I found it interesting that Adam had quickly shut her down. Something doesn't seem right there.

"You don't think Heather was in it with someone, do you?" asks Jack now. "Or someone paid her to do it?"

I can't help but laugh at Jack's wild imagination. "She's not a professional assassin. And this is Tilby we're talking about, not some big city. It's the biggest crime that's been committed there for as long as I can remember."

Since Flora, I think, although I don't say that to Jack.

"But how do you know?"

I swivel in my chair so that I'm facing him. "I'm sure the police would have noticed if she'd received a large payment recently."

"Could have been made in cash."

"I'm sure the police are in the process of going through everything."

Jack shrugs. "They have a caravan park. Money must go in and out all the time. It might not be noticeable. Maybe they were in debt. Maybe her husband was in on it too."

I think of Adam. What is his background? His story? I know nothing about him, other than that he's a brooding, abrupt man to whom I've taken an immediate dislike, even though I can't put my finger on why. I'm sure he's hiding something. How could Heather have ended up with someone like him?

But still. Jack's theory does sound a bit far-fetched. I can't imagine Margot would let her caravan park be used as a front for criminal activity. But I don't want to burst Jack's bubble.

"This could be a good story, Jess. It's only Thursday," continues Jack, eagerly. "We've got until Monday lunchtime to find out more before the deadline for Tuesday's paper."

I suppress a sigh. Jack looks like an eager puppy, but then I remind myself this is probably the biggest story he's ever worked on. He's hungry for it. I can't blame him for that. "Like what?"

He flops back in his chair. "I don't know. You're the reporter. I'm just saying it looks dodgy. Clive had enemies. This card implies that someone isn't surprised he's dead."

I hold up my hands in mock-surrender. "Okay, okay, I get your point. I'll talk to Ted and see what he suggests." I glance across the desk at my mobile. It's disappointingly quiet. I'd been hoping Margot would call. I'd thought I was getting somewhere yesterday. I bet Adam talked her out of speaking to me.

I get up from my seat while Jack scoots his chair back to his own desk, a self-satisfied smile on his face at the thought we might get to play detective. I sometimes wonder why he didn't go into the police force, like his boyfriend.

I stand at the threshold to Ted's "office" and, when he doesn't look up from his computer, I clear my throat.

"Yep," he says, still not looking at me.

I push the card across his desk, explaining where I found it. He glances at it, then at me, interest registering on his usually cynical features. "You know you'll have to give this to the police."

I nod.

"We can't withhold any evidence, Jess. You know that, right?"

I blink, my cheeks hot. Does he think I've learned nothing from what happened at the *Tribune*? "Of course," I mutter. "I don't know why I took it, really."

"You could have just snapped it with your phone," he says, watching me carefully.

"Yes."

"Can you drop it over to Bridewell? But take a photo of it first. All right?" He pushes the card toward me, then turns his attention back to his computer screen. I slink out of the room as though I'm a naughty schoolgirl who's been sent to the headmaster's office.

I glare at Jack as I return to my desk. I set the card near my keyboard and quickly snap it with my phone.

"What?" he says, coming over as I shrug on my coat and grab my bag, opening it for my purse.

"I shouldn't have nicked the bloody card." I slip it into my purse. "Now I have to take it to the police station."

Jack bites his lip, his eyes worried. "Shit, I'm sorry. I never thought."

I lower my voice. "I need Ted to trust me."

"He does trust you."

"You don't understand . . ."

Jack sighs. "Of course I bloody do. I'm not an idiot, Jess. I know what went on in London. I remember the scandal. It was all over the news. I wondered if you might have been caught up in it."

How long has he known this about me? I've not told anyone about it since leaving London. The thought that Jack, the only friend I've felt a connection with since Heather, has insight into this dark, ugly part of me makes me feel sick with shame. No wonder he jokes that I'm as hard as nails. He couldn't be more wrong.

I stare at him for a few seconds, thrown, my cheeks burning. How could he know this about me and still want to be my friend? He opens his mouth to say something but I hold up a hand, signaling for him to stop. There's nobody else in the newsroom apart from Sue but I don't want her to hear. I pull the strap firmly over my shoulder and gesture for him to follow. Sue's on the phone as we stride past, but I sense her looking up at us. "I've told you," I can hear her saying, "to give him the bloody elbow. He doesn't deserve you, Sal."

It's raining when we get outside so we huddle in the doorway. There's no sign of Stan. "I can't be long," says Jack, wrapping his arms about his thin frame. He's wearing a trendy suit and his legs are like pipe cleaners. "Ted wants me to finish uploading some photos before I leave tonight." He clears his throat and shuffles, seeming embarrassed. "Look, we've been friends for nearly a year. You can tell me anything—you do know that, don't you? I'm never going to think any less of you."

To my shame, my eyes fill with tears. I touch his arm. "Thank you. Do you want to meet for a quick drink after work?"

He peers at his feet. His trousers are a tad too short, but they look cool on him, like a fashion statement. He's wearing funky socks, yellow with little blue birds all over them. "I promised Finn we'd go out tonight. He wants to take me for a meal. He's been working so hard lately. He's meeting me at the Watershed at seven."

I've met Finn a few times, and once the four of us went on a double date. Although he seems a lovely guy, he's much quieter and more introverted than Jack. When we were out, Jack did the talking for both of them. He never left Jack's side, and if Rory or I tried to engage him in conversation his eyes would search out Jack, as though willing him to intervene.

Since then Rory and I have tried to arrange another foursome but Finn always seems to have an excuse: he's on shifts, he's too tired, he's ill. I worry that he doesn't really like or approve of us. Or, rather, of me.

I pull my coat around myself. The rain is getting harder, running along the pavements and dribbling into the drains. "Please, Jack, just a quick one. I need someone to talk to. What about I meet you there first, straight after work? Don't worry, I'll make myself scarce as soon as Finn arrives."

Jack looks up, his face softening. "Oh, go on then, just a quick one." He winks at me. "You always get me into trouble."

13

Jess

MY HEART FALLS WHEN I WALK INTO THE POLICE STATION AND SEE DCI Ruthgow standing behind the counter. He's talking in a low voice to the duty officer: a middle-aged woman with a severe dark brown fringe.

I've only met Ruthgow once, at a police conference at the end of last year, although I've spoken to him numerous times on the phone, but he's as I remember him—he always looks like he's spent the night sleeping on his face. His craggy brows are threaded with gray, and he's smartly dressed in a crisp dark suit. I imagine he's the type of guy who wears aftershave and changes his shirt every day—unlike Ted, who can wear the same clothes for three days on the trot. When I reach the desk, recognition flickers across his face. "Jessica Fox?"' he says, in his deep, croaky voice.

I smile confidently while my mind races for excuses as to why I've taken a potential piece of evidence from a crime scene.

I reach into my purse and hand him the card. "I was at the Wilsons' house earlier." I notice the duty officer moves away to talk to someone who has come in behind me. "And I saw this attached to a bunch of flowers. It sounded threatening. Thought it might be important." Let him believe I've done him a favor.

He pushes his black-framed glasses further onto his nose and frowns down at the card. "Right," he says, glancing up at me, his eyebrow raised questioningly. "And you took it because . . . ?"

"Like I said, I thought it might be important. And I didn't want it to blow away or get lost."

He doesn't say anything else but rests his finger lightly on the card, as though worried I might snatch it back. "Right. Anything else I can help you with?"

I stand up straighter. This could work to my advantage. "While I'm here, I was wondering . . . Do you have any more information on the victims? Like, what kind of people were they?" I nod toward the card. "It sounds like they could have had enemies. Were they—Clive particularly—into anything . . . I don't know"—I lift my shoulders—"dodgy?"

"Dodgy?" Ruthgow rubs the skin between his eyebrows as if he's never heard the word before. "I'm afraid I can't reveal anything at this point in the investigation."

"But you think it's an open-and-closed case? That Heather Underwood committed the murders?"

He sighs. "We're not taking anything for granted."

"So someone else could be involved?"

"I'm not necessarily saying that."

"Does Clive have a criminal record?" I persist. It comes out of nowhere but is a last-ditch attempt at finding out something.

Ruthgow falters. "I . . . Not exactly. No. There was a complaint made about him."

I mentally rub my hands together. "What sort of complaint?"

Ruthgow shoots me a warning look. "This is off the record. But someone complained about him and the police were called. He was issued a warning but no further action was taken." He holds up his hands as though to ward off any further words. "That's all I can say at this point." He turns his attention back to the card. "You know, you shouldn't tamper with a crime scene."

"I thought I was doing the right thing." I smile sweetly.

"You shouldn't have taken this card." His voice is stern but fatherly.

I glance at my watch and roll my eyes theatrically. "Jeez!" Jeez? I've never said that in my life before. "Better be off. On another job. Busy day."

He opens his mouth, the puzzled expression not leaving his face.

But I hurry away before he can reprimand me further.

By the time I've walked to the police station and back, I'm a bit late to meet Jack. But he's waiting at the table nearest the door, his expression serious as he taps out a text on his phone, a pint of beer untouched in front of him. His dark blond hair flops in his face and he keeps pushing it back with one hand, distracted, his brows knotted together. I'm struck again by how handsome he is. Not as striking as Rory, I think loyally, but still a very attractive man. Once, during a drunken chat when we were first getting to know each other, Jack let slip that he'd broken a few hearts before falling in love with Finn three years ago. As a result Finn could be a little possessive at times.

"I'm sorry I'm late," I say, as I slide into the seat opposite him.

He looks up, his face brightening when he sees it's me. "About time. Thought you'd been arrested for taking that card from the Wilsons' garden."

"Ruthgow wasn't happy. You know what he's like."

He rolls his eyes. "He's so intense. Isn't he up for retirement yet? He looks like he's going to croak any minute." He clutches his throat and puts on a raspy thirty-fags-a-day voice: "*You know this is the only information I can give you on the record.*"

"He's not yet sixty. You make him sound like he's about to get a telegram from the Queen any minute." I get up. "I'm just going to the bar. Do you want anything?"

He jumps up. "I'll get it. You sit down. You could do with a rest." He grins. "After all, you're getting on a bit yourself now."

"Oh, fuck off." I laugh, but I sit down anyway. My feet are hurting in my new boots. I'd bought them for a steal at a vintage shop after falling in love with them, but they're half a size too small.

"What do you want?"

I contemplate asking for a glass of wine but settle on a Coke. When I left London I promised myself I wouldn't drink during the week. My glass of wine a night was turning into two, and then three. It's hard to keep to my no-drinking rule sometimes, though.

Jack strides to the bar, attracting stares from a blond woman at a nearby table in his well-cut suit. He gets paid a pittance at the paper, but he always seems able to afford nice clothes. I don't know where he gets the money from.

He returns with my drink and two packets of spicy crisps that he knows are my favorite.

"Thanks, mate," I say, taking a long glug of Coke. Out of the corner of my eye I can see the blond woman looking toward Jack and giggling to her friend.

Jack's oblivious and regards me seriously. When I return my glass to the table he asks, "Are you okay? You know you can tell me anything."

He's right. I can tell him things I've not even told Rory. That's the problem.

Rory is so *good*, with a very strong moral code. That's what I'd fallen in love with. Somehow being with him just made me *better*. Nicer. His softness sanded down my edges. We complement each other—I help him when he needs to be tougher, and he makes me see reason when I'm being too hard. And I've never doubted his love for me. But sometimes I worry that he sees me as he wants me to be rather than as I really am. And I've let him because I prefer myself through his eyes. When I'm with him I can believe I really am a good person.

My moralistic radar is so off kilter sometimes that I don't always know if I'm doing a good or a bad thing. But since the mess I left behind in London, I've really been trying. Yet today, with that card, I feel as if I've failed some test.

I try to explain this to Jack, but he stares at me with confusion. "I don't think what you did with the card was wrong, though. You've got a good nose for a story. That's what being a journalist is all about. There's a story behind that card. Clive—or Deirdre—had enemies. That's worth exploring."

I fidget in my seat, feeling uncomfortable. "It's not just that." I fiddle with my beer mat. Behind me a few lads whoop and cheer at something and Jack flinches. I turn around but they're busy thumping one of their group on the back and congratulating him about something. "I need to tell you what happened in London."

Jack frowns, his eyes flickering to the lads, then back to me. "Like I said earlier, I think I know. The scandal. It was all over the news. Were you involved?" He rips open both packets of crisps and places them between us with a help-yourself gesture.

Behind him, through the window, I can see that it's already getting dark. It's still a few weeks until the clocks go forward. People are scurrying past on their way home from work, huddled under umbrellas. I think of the walk to the Welsh Back and shudder, remembering the footsteps the other night, the sense that I was being followed. I could really do with a glass of wine.

Jack shovels a handful of crisps into his mouth and I take a deep breath. I need to get this off my chest. "Yes. It was immoral.

I know that now. A teenage girl was found dead after overdosing on drugs. She was missing for a few months before that, and during that time we—we hacked her phone, as well as her stepdad's."

He takes a sharp breath, nearly choking on the crisps. "I had an inkling that's what you were going to say. But were you arrested?"

"No. My news editor was. The buck stopped with him. But"—I blink back tears—"I was involved. So was my colleague Mark. We shouldn't have done it. We knew it was wrong, but we were running on adrenaline. It was a big case. A missing teenage girl. We all assumed her stepdad might have had something to do with it. Things had become *shady*. The boundaries were unclear. I was sacked, along with Mark and a few others, including my editor. We were so desperate for the story. We thought if we hacked their phones we'd find out something incriminating about the stepdad . . . It was stupid. Reckless."

Jack swallows. "Shit, Jess. Does Ted know?"

I nod and shuffle in my seat. I pick up a crisp but don't eat it, just hold it uselessly. "Yes. I had to be honest with him. He would have found out anyway. But he took me on, providing I kept on the right side of the law, of course. He gave me a second chance and I'm so grateful for that. Oh, God, Jack, it was just horrible. The worst. The embarrassment. The fear I'd be arrested. Charged. Prison, even. The trial is still hanging over my editor and others . . . Well, you'll have read about it, no doubt. I felt so guilty—I still feel guilty, especially toward the girl's family."

Jack exhales through his nose. Then, "What does Rory think?"

This is the bit I'm most ashamed of. "I never told him. Not about me. He knows my editor was arrested and charged but that's it."

Jack's eyes are round with shock. "What? How could he not know?"

I put down the crisp, feeling sick. "He wouldn't have a clue what goes on. He's not a part of this murky world, thank God. And I wasn't charged. I told him they had to get rid of me because of cutbacks."

He groans. "You lied? Oh, Jess."

I close my eyes. I have a headache coming on. "I know," I mumble, massaging my temples. "Rory thinks the best of me. I suppose I didn't want to disappoint him by admitting I was also involved."

I open my eyes. Jack reaches across the table and takes my hand. He doesn't say anything—he doesn't have to—just squeezes my fingers gently.

I feel close to tears but I won't cry. "He would look at me differently. He wants marriage, kids, the whole fairy tale. And I want it too. After my upbringing"—I swallow a lump in my throat—"I want a good man. A family man. I just . . ." I lower my voice so that it's barely audible. "I just don't know if I deserve it."

Jack leans forward, still holding my hand. "Of course you do. You realize you made a mistake. Nobody's perfect, Jess. Blimey. Certainly not me and I bet certainly not Rory, whatever you think. But you should tell him."

"I know." I take my hand from his and push the crisps packet away from me. I've completely lost my appetite. "There's more," I say.

Jack stays silent, waiting, as he regards me over his pint glass.

"The case I'm talking about. It was Marianne Walker-Smith."

He snorts. "Shit."

I don't need to tell him what happened. The whole country knows. Marianne, a fourteen-year-old schoolgirl, went missing on Christmas Eve fifteen months ago from Reading. Everyone, including the press, suspected her stepfather, a rough-looking local hard nut made good. Wayne Walker was a builder who made a lot of money but couldn't shed his thuggish image despite his flash cars and fancy suits. He was arrested but released with no charge after lack of evidence. A few months later, and just before I was sacked, Marianne's body was found on Clapham Common. A heroin overdose. She'd got in with the wrong crowd, the police said, and run away from home. There had been sightings of her with an older man, but nothing to suggest she'd been murdered.

But Wayne was angry and wanted someone to blame. One evening, when I still lived in London, I was on my way home from a night out with friends when he accosted me as I was walking alone to the tube station, slamming me into a wall and breathing into my ear that he would fuck me up, among other things.

"You weren't the only journalist who slagged him off in the press," says Jack, when I finish telling him. "Why did he come after you?"

I run my finger around the rim of my glass. "I don't know. Someone saw, yelled out, and he ran off. But I knew who he was. I recognized his bulldog face."

"It was just an empty threat. He wouldn't do anything. He can't know where you live now."

I remember how scared I'd felt the other night when I'd thought I was being followed. "No. You're right. It just freaked me out."

"Not surprising. He sounds like a nasty piece of work."

"I think he knew something about the phone hacking. Maybe someone in the police tipped him off. It was before my editor was charged—"

I'm interrupted by Finn walking through the door. He looks smart, dressed in drainpipe jeans, a white shirt, and a pin-striped blazer. He's shorter than Jack, although still tall at about six foot, with white-blond hair and blue eyes. He reminds me of Matt and Luke Goss from Bros. He's a year younger than me, and I know that I, of all people, shouldn't judge but it's hard to believe he's a cop.

He shakes out an umbrella and looks around until he spots us. Irritation briefly passes over his face when he sees me sitting with Jack. "Oh," he says, coming over to us, looking flustered. "I didn't realize you were meeting Jess first."

I stand up so quickly I feel light-headed. "I'm just going."

"You haven't finished your drink," says Jack. "Don't go yet. You don't mind, do you, Finn?"

Finn looks like he does mind. Very much. But he's too polite to say so. Instead he hastily scouts around for another chair while I squirm with embarrassment, wanting nothing more than to make a swift exit. I don't want to play gooseberry.

He pulls up a seat between me and Jack. "So, how's things?" he says to me. "You okay? How's Rory?"

"Fine. We're both fine. You?"

"Busy with work. You know. Hoping to be made a sergeant so have to put the hours in."

I nod politely but the conversation feels formal and stilted. I love Jack so much. I just wish I felt as comfortable with Finn.

"So, what are you working on at the moment? Still the Wilson case?" he asks.

"Yep. Can you give us anything? Tip-offs, et cetera?" I try to sound playful but his expression darkens.

"You know I can't. It's unprofessional," he replies stiffly.

Jack rolls his eyes. "Always the professional, eh, Finn." He winks but Finn doesn't look amused.

I down the rest of my Coke so fast it gives me indigestion and I suppress the urge to burp. "Anyway," I say, in a voice that sounds like I've inhaled helium, "I'd better be off. Rory will be wondering where I am."

I rummage in my bag for my umbrella and, telling Jack I'll see him in the morning, I rush outside, the cold air instantly cooling my cheeks. I take a few deep breaths and stand under my umbrella for a minute, looking through the window at Jack and Finn. Finn's back is to me but I can see Jack glancing at his boyfriend tenderly, his hand over Finn's.

I walk briskly along the Watershed and cross the footbridge over the river. I wouldn't normally go home this way—it can feel a bit lonely in the dark walking through Queen Square at this time of night—but it's the most direct route to our flat from the pub. Queen Square is deserted, as most of the Georgian buildings that line the pavements are now offices, and I quicken my steps, trying to stop my imagination running away with me. But I'm sure I hear footsteps again. They sound heavy, like men's boots. The rain is harder now and the wind tugs at my umbrella. I focus on my destination, walking as quickly as I can without running, and soon I exit the square and am passing the Llandoger Trow pub. I can see a few people huddled together outside it, smoking under an umbrella, the light from within casting an amber glow onto the cobbled pavement. A woman carrying a briefcase emerges from the building opposite and walks briskly in the other direction and I instantly feel safer, until I turn right onto the river and I'm alone again.

I'm sure I can still hear the footsteps. Heavy and determined. I stop and turn around, ready to confront whoever is behind me, but there is nobody. Someone laughs, piercing the silence. I walk on, but as the river falls away and I'm enveloped by the tall buildings either side of me I can see shadows lurking in every doorway. It's my imagination, I tell myself. There's nothing here. I'm just feeling unnerved after reliving past events this evening, that's all. But I deliberately walk in the middle of the cobbled road anyway, praying no cars turn down this way, until I reach my block.

I fumble for my key, but don't allow myself to panic. I turn the lock and let myself into the lobby, closing the heavy glass door behind me with relief. But as I do so I notice a light flash in the lower window of the derelict building opposite. A torch, perhaps. But it's gone.

Before I have time to think any more about it, my phone vibrates in my coat pocket. I retrieve it to see Margot's name flashing up on the screen.

14

August 1994

FLORA WAS FALLING IN LOVE. SHE WAS CERTAIN OF IT. SHE'D NEVER felt like this before. And Dylan was so different from anyone she'd ever met. They'd only been seeing each other for seven days, but it had been the best week of her life. Dylan made her feel so special. And he was nineteen. *Nineteen*. Three whole years older. She still couldn't believe her luck that he was interested in her when he could have had anyone. She saw the way other girls flicked their hair and fluttered their eyelashes whenever he was around.

The country was in the middle of a heat wave, and every day seemed hotter and more humid than the last. When they weren't at the fair, they were at the beach, sunbathing or splashing about in the extremely cold Channel.

"I don't know why you keep mooning over that boy," Heather had said that afternoon, after Flora had begged her to go with her to the fair yet again. Heather was on her bed, an A4 sketch pad on her knee, getting away from the incessant heat. "You know the fair will move on in a couple of weeks and him with it. A girl in every town, I bet."

Flora had scowled in response. It wasn't like Heather to be mean, yet here she was acting like a jealous ex. "You're my sister," she'd replied. "You're supposed to be supportive."

It had had the desired effect, as Flora had known it would. Nothing like laying a guilt trip on Heather to get her to do what Flora wanted. It worked both ways, though—they'd been doing it to each other for as long as they could remember. So Heather reluctantly agreed to accompany her to the fair for the fifth time that week. On the days that Heather had refused, Flora had gone anyway. Her mother hadn't noticed, too busy with customers. The caravan park was only in its second summer and the business was starting to take off. But Flora didn't like to disobey Margot's rules too often, if she could help it. She knew her mother's strictness came from a good place, and that she cared more than anything for her and Heather. Which was more than could be said about Heather's friend, Jess: her mother didn't seem to give a toss where Jess was half the time, or for how long. Jess might as well have lived with them, the amount of times she stayed over.

Jess was here now, standing by the coconut stall wearing a crop top and too much makeup. She was jigging along to "Saturday Night" by Whigfield, which was blaring out of a nearby boom box. God, Flora hated that song. Someone had brought a tape back from their holidays in Benidorm and unfortunately it seemed to have caught on. There was even a bloody dance. She'd caught Heather and Jess doing it the other night in Heather's bedroom. They'd looked mortified, midpose, when she came bounding in, Jess in particular. Flora knew Jess wanted her to think she was cool.

Jess blushed now at the sight of them. "Hi, Heather, Flora."

Flora smiled kindly, then cast her eyes about for Dylan. Where was he? She couldn't see him in his usual spot on the Waltzers.

"Right, I'm off to find Dylan," she said to Heather, undoing the top button of her lacy blouse and repositioning her yin-and-yang velvet choker. She gathered her hair away from her neck. It was nearly seven thirty but it was still stifling hot and the air smelled sickly sweet. "I'll meet you back here about nine fifteen. Okay?"

Heather folded her arms across her chest. "Fine. But don't be late. I don't want to piss Mum off."

Flora sighed. Heather was such a party pooper. "I won't be late." Over her sister's shoulder she spotted Dylan in the distance. He was with another bloke. Someone she didn't recognize, not that she'd met many of Dylan's friends yet. This bloke looked a lot older than Dylan, with a hard face and lots of piercings. Flora didn't want to sound all middle class about it, but she thought he looked a bit . . . unsavory.

Jess took Heather's arm and led her away, chattering in her ear, although it didn't look as though Heather was listening.

Flora wanted to reassure her sister, tell her not to worry. But she knew it would fall on deaf ears. Even though Flora was the elder, it was Heather who was more sensible and reliable, Heather who had looked out for them both when their dad died.

Flora waved at Dylan, who raised a hand in return, but he didn't smile. He was in deep conversation with Mr. Piercings. She stood where she was, waiting for them to reach her, not wanting to interrupt.

There was something different about Dylan tonight, thought Flora, as he approached. He was attempting a smile, despite a tension around his mouth. "This is my gypsy girl, Flora," he said, putting an arm around her shoulders. "And this," he indicated Mr. Piercings, "is Speedy. My mum's boyfriend."

"Hi," said Flora, wondering why he had that nickname.

He held out a hand. She noticed his fingernails were yellow and bitten down. Flora took it dutifully, not wanting to appear impolite. *Manners. Manners. Manners.* Her mother had drilled it into them since they were little. But really Flora wanted to recoil. He was even odder-looking up close, although younger than she'd initially thought. He had a distinctive tattoo on his neck of a green parrot. How could Dylan's mum fancy this guy? She'd not met her, of course, considering she'd only known Dylan a week and he was living on-site with the other workers at the fair. But he'd shown her a photo of a delicate pretty blond, with the same dazzling blue eyes as his own. His mum had had him young, he said. She'd only been seventeen, and he'd never known his dad.

"Nice to meet ya," said Speedy. He had a similar accent to Dylan—London, with a hint of West Country. His eyes lingered a little too long on the open neck of her blouse.

Dylan, as if noticing, pulled her closer to him. "Anyway, Speedy just popped in to say hi. He's off home now. Say hi to Mum for me."

Speedy grinned in response. "Yep, that's right. I'm going. But I'll bring your mum next week. It's been a while since she's seen you. Think about what I said, though, yeah?"

"Yeah," said Dylan, his jaw set.

"Great." Speedy smirked at Flora, then at Dylan, before turning around and walking off.

Dylan didn't say anything for a few moments, watching Speedy weave his way through the crowds. It wasn't until he'd disappeared that Dylan turned to her. "Sorry about that. He's a bit of a prat."

"He's your stepdad?" Flora said, unable to believe it.

"Not stepdad. My mum's boyfriend. It won't last five minutes. He's all right, really."

"You just said he was a prat."

Dylan grinned. "He's all right . . . for a prat. But he's harmless. And he's good to Mum."

Something didn't feel right but Flora couldn't put her finger on it. She wasn't used to boys, but she felt he was hiding something from her.

"Is he local? I thought you said your mum lived in Swindon."

He shrugged. "She does. And he lives with her. For now. He

came to give me this." His eyes lit up as he disentangled himself from her and retrieved something from his jeans pocket. Then he held it flat against his palm as though it were diamonds. It looked like a bag of herbs to her.

"What is it?"

"Pot."

She frowned. "Pot? As in . . ."

"As in weed. Grass. Skunk. Whatever you want to call it." He folded his fingers around it and slipped it back into his pocket.

Flora gasped. "Shit, Dylan. Drugs."

"Sssh," he hissed, looking wildly around him as though expecting the police to be lurking at the coconut stall. "I was hoping you'd smoke some with me."

Flora stared at her feet. Drugs. She didn't even smoke cigarettes. She realized how provincial and out of her depth she really was. Despite the heat, she suddenly felt cold. "I don't know . . ."

"I thought you were cool." He sounded disappointed. "But maybe you're too young for me, after all."

Her head shot up. She couldn't let him think that. She'd let him touch her in places she'd never been touched. She hadn't known her body could respond to someone like that, hadn't known she could desire someone so much. She wanted him to be her first. If he dumped her now she wouldn't be able to live, to breathe, without him. He occupied her every thought. It was like she was possessed.

She jutted out her chin defiantly. "I'm not too young."

His eyes lit up. "So you'll smoke it with me."

She nodded. Of course she would.

HEATHER WAITED BY THE CANDYFLOSS STALL, AS THEY'D AGREED. Jess said she'd stay with her until Flora arrived. Jess didn't have a curfew and thought nothing of walking back through the fields to her cottage alone in the dark. Heather admired her friend's guts, but couldn't understand why she was allowed so much freedom—she herself would hate it. Sometimes she wondered if, deep down, Jess hated it too. She seemed lonely at home, and was spending more and more time with them.

They'd had a fun evening and, before long, Jess had made Heather forget about Flora and Dylan. She brought Heather out of herself, made her remember she was just a fourteen-year-old girl and that she wasn't responsible for everyone and everything.

That's what Heather had first liked about Jess when they'd met in the art class. She'd been honored that this popular, funny girl had wanted to be friends with her. She knew everyone else in their year thought her weird, with her goth tendencies, but Jess didn't. Jess made her feel normal. Jess made the darkness in her mind disappear, at least for a while. And they'd had fun tonight, gossiping and singing along to "Baby, I Love Your Way" by Big Mountain while attempting to win a teddy at the shooting stall. Heather had won a prize, of course. She was an expert with a gun. It was a big fluffy chick and she'd given it to a delighted Jess. Her friend held it under her arm now and Heather felt a stab of fondness for her and her love of anything cuddly.

But then she started to feel anxious. Where was Flora? It was gone nine fifteen and if they weren't home by half past Mum would go nuts.

And then she saw her and Dylan striding toward them. Well, Dylan was. Flora was stumbling more than striding, and she looked ill, as though she couldn't put one foot in front of the other, but she was giggling, her head lolling on Dylan's shoulder.

"What's wrong with her?" Heather hissed, turning to Jess with concern.

Jess frowned. "I dunno."

"Take a chill pill. She's fine," said Dylan, stopping in front of them. Heather wanted to wipe the stupid smirk off his face. "Your sister's just a bit tired, that's all."

"Has she been drinking? Is she drunk?" demanded Heather.

"She's definitely not drunk."

Flora's eyes looked huge and dark, the green irises almost obscured by her enlarged pupils. "I'm fine," she insisted, as she attempted to stand up straight. "We'd better get home."

"I'll walk with you," said Dylan. "Make sure she gets home okay."

His suggestion instantly grated on Heather. She was more than capable of looking after her sister. She grabbed Flora's arm and pulled her away from Dylan. "She'll be fine," she said firmly. "Come on, Jess."

Heather was almost the same height as Flora, despite being two years younger, and Flora kept trying to rest her head on

Heather's shoulder. Jess took the other arm and they whisked Flora away, leaving Dylan standing in the middle of the busy fair with a vacant expression on his face.

"What has he done to you?" demanded Heather, trying to keep the panic out of her voice. "Has he spiked your drink?" She'd heard something about this in a newspaper report recently.

Flora giggled in response.

Heather and Jess half dragged, half carried Flora away from the fair and across the field. It was almost dark now, with only a sliver of a bright orange sun left on the horizon. When they got to the turnstile where they usually parted ways with Jess, they stopped. From here they could see the edge of the Powells' caravan park and the main house beyond that. Heather noticed her mother's bedroom light was on. Would she be worried yet? They were ten minutes late.

Jess hesitated. "Are you going to be all right?"

Heather nodded. "It's not far now. Thanks for helping, Jess." She flashed her friend a watery smile but inside she felt like crying.

Jess returned the smile, then untangled Flora's arm from around her neck. "Good luck with your mum."

"Thanks."

Heather watched as Jess almost vaulted onto the stile, scuffing the toes of her bloodred DM boots, jumping down the other side, and running over the neighboring field toward her cottage.

Flora groaned. "Just leave me here. I'm too tired to go any further."

"Don't be ridiculous. We're already late."

"You're such a goody-goody."

Heather sighed. "Yep. So you keep saying." The things she did for her sister, she thought, as she helped her across the field. Flora kept stumbling. It hadn't rained for weeks and the grass was hard, with patches of dusty, dried mud. Didn't Flora care about being grounded? Heather certainly didn't give a toss. It would be Flora who suffered, not her, Flora who wouldn't be able to meet up with her precious Dylan anymore.

They entered through the side gate, bypassing the caravan park, but it led to the path that ran parallel with the paddock. Uncle Leo was bringing in Margot's horse, Saba, for the night. He turned when he heard them, a frown on his face. "What are you doing?" he whispered. "Your mum's going insane in there." He waved toward the house.

"We're only ten minutes late," said Heather, thinking on her feet. "Flora fell over and twisted her ankle so it took longer getting back."

He took in Flora's unsteadiness and her glassy-eyed look. "Has she been on the wacky baccy?" he hissed.

Heather was certain that Flora had taken something. She wasn't that naïve. She'd read about drugs and they'd had to watch a video at school last term. But she wasn't about to tell Uncle Leo that.

Leo sighed, pushing his dark curls away from his face. Margot was now striding out of the front door and marching toward them.

"Say nothing," he said. "I'll cover for you. But get Flora into the house."

"Sorry, sis," called Leo, as Margot approached. "The girls were just helping me with the horses."

"They're late," she snapped, glaring at her daughters and folding her arms over her chest. "I told you to be back at nine thirty."

Before Heather could open her mouth to defend herself, Leo interjected, "They were here. Flora had sprained her ankle so was just sitting on the grass. That's why I didn't see them."

Flora groaned, and Heather wasn't sure if she was playing along or it was the effect of whatever she'd taken.

Margot uncrossed her arms, instantly thawing. "Oh, right. Was it the left one?" When Heather nodded, Margot turned to Flora. "Are you okay, honey? You have to be careful with that ankle." Flora had broken it when she was six in a skipping accident, which had weakened the bone. Heather felt a sudden stab of guilt that they were playing on Margot's worries.

"And while Flora was recovering," Leo continued, winking at the girls when Margot wasn't looking, "Heather helped me with Saba."

Heather was terrified their mother would be able to see the real reason for her elder daughter's state, even if it was now dark.

"She's fine," Heather said hurriedly, moving her sister away and heading toward the house. "I'll help her to bed," she called over her shoulder. "Don't worry."

"Make sure to put on that supportive sock," Margot called after them.

Heather was gratified to see that her sister was limping. So she was playing along. She couldn't be that drunk or drugged. It was okay, Heather thought, breathing a sigh of relief. It was all going to be okay. She just needed to keep her sister away from Dylan. Just for a few weeks, until the fair moved on. That was all. And to do that she'd need Jess's help.

15

GUNS. THEY WERE SUCH A BIG PART OF OUR LIVES, WEREN'T THEY? FIRST at the farm in Kent, and then later, when we moved to Tilby. We were never scared of them, even as kids. We'd learned to handle them when we were young. Our father had made sure of that.

Guns. We've caused so much destruction with them. And as I lie here, questioning whether I'll die, I wonder if Mum and Dad ever regretted showing us how to use them.

16

Margot

I<small>T'S BEEN NEARLY EIGHTEEN YEARS SINCE</small> M<small>ARGOT SAW</small> DCI G<small>ARY</small> Ruthgow but as soon as she spots him from across the field she recognizes him straightaway. Her stomach drops. Why would someone as important as him come all this way? She doesn't think she could bear more bad news.

As he strides toward her she can tell he's put on weight, and now walks with a slight limp, but he still has a good head of hair, although it's peppered with white now. He's always held himself well, upright and commanding, as though about to address the room. He's wearing a thick wool coat that reaches his knees, with a navy suit underneath. He'll get his shoes mucky walking across the grass, she thinks, as she steps down from the caravan. Her green Hunter wellies are thick with mud. She brushes imaginary horsehair from her vest as she swallows her panic. She knows everything's okay with Heather. She was only with her a few hours ago and there was no change: she's still in a coma but stable. So what horrible life-changing news is he here to impart this time? She thinks of everyone she loves, mentally ticking them off on her fingers: Ethan is at nursery, Adam is catching up with some bookkeeping, and her brother, Leo, is at his partner's house in Bristol, although she hasn't seen him for a while. She thinks it's yet another girlfriend. One she hasn't met. She'll probably be the same as the others, though: tall, pretty, and young. Too young for him, most likely. Yet she doubts Gary Ruthgow has come all this way to talk about her brother.

Margot will never forget the dreadful day when she first met Ruthgow. Before that, before he came on the scene, there were other officers. The first was a woman who took notes while Margot cried on Leo's shoulder, pleading with them to do something, *anything* to find Flora and that, no, she wasn't the sort of girl to run away from home and, no, she'd never done anything like this before. And then a detective—a man this time—had questioned everybody, those staying on the campsite as well as Leo, Heather, Jessica, Flora's friends—not that there were many—and the boy she'd been "seeing," Dylan Bird. This had shocked Margot. She'd told the male officer, DC Lovelace (she'd never forgotten the name, mainly because it didn't fit with the square-jawed, gruff young officer), that she hadn't known Flora had a boyfriend. That was a mistake, of course, because then it was assumed that Flora was the type of girl to keep secrets from her mother, her family, that she was precocious, up to no good, and had probably run away. But her savings account hadn't been touched, her passport hadn't been taken from where Margot kept it, along with hers and Heather's, in an old suitcase on top of the wardrobe in the spare room. Her clothes and possessions were untouched. There were no signs that Flora had run away. And Margot knew, in the sixth-sense way only a parent can, that something bad had happened to her daughter.

And then, after Flora had been missing for three agonizing days, when Margot had thought she'd go out of her mind with worry, Gary Ruthgow had turned up.

He was a detective sergeant then and had sat in her living room, next to a female detective, who looked like Anita Dobson, on her shabby old sofa with the dog hairs and the threadbare arms and told her they'd made "a significant discovery." Flora's bloodstained blouse had been found in the undergrowth at the end of the lane, which turns onto the high street, sniffed out by a dog. It was the blouse she had been wearing the day she disappeared.

Margot had had to stuff her whole fist into her mouth to stop herself screaming and the woman officer had placed a hand on her arm, her blue eyes full of warmth and sympathy. Leo had come in then, and he'd held her as she sobbed, telling her it didn't mean anything. That Flora could still be alive. It was only a blouse, he'd said. *Only a blouse.*

But she knew. She just *knew*. Flora was dead.

Flora, her firstborn, her beautiful, dutiful, intelligent daughter, who'd never put a foot wrong in her life, wasn't the sort of girl to go off without telling her family. The three of them were tight-knit, even more so after Keith died. And, okay, maybe Flora hadn't mentioned this boy, this *Dylan Bird*, but that was probably because it hadn't been serious. It had only been a few weeks or so, according to Heather, who'd eventually had to spill the beans, even though Margot could tell she felt disloyal by doing so.

And that had been that. No more discovered clothing, no body, no leads. The last known sighting of her had been on Thursday, August 25, 1994. A witness came forward to say he'd been driving along Tilby's high street and had seen Flora walking alone in the rain at around 9 p.m. Her curfew had been nine thirty. Margot had made only two stipulations that summer: that Flora and Heather stick together, and that they were home before it got dark.

Yet Flora had broken both those rules. She hadn't stayed with her sister. And she'd never come home.

"Margot Powell." Ruthgow extends a gloved hand rather formally and Margot takes it.

"How are you, Gary? Long time."

He smiles tightly. "Indeed."

Was she being too familiar with him? They'd begun to grow closer at one point, all those years ago, the grieving mother and the grieving widower. They'd even gone for a drink at the local pub, the Horseshoe, where she'd cried into her glass of wine and he'd promised he'd do everything he could to find Flora. But he'd not kept his promise. After the TV stations and the newspapers, and even the town, began to view Flora's disappearance as old news, Gary Ruthgow had put in for a transfer, left their little local police station (since closed down), and fled to Bristol. A new start. A new life. Hers had crumbled around her ears so that even getting up each day and putting one foot in front of the other was a mammoth challenge. She kept going only for Heather. And then, later, for Ethan.

If Heather died too, her life was all but over.

"What brings you all this way?" she asks, when it's obvious he's not about to make clear the reason for his visit. He shuffles his feet and blows on his hands as though biding his time.

"It's rather delicate, I'm afraid. It concerns Heather. And Flora to an extent."

Margot's heart drops. What does he mean? Does he have new information about Flora?

She can see Colin moving about in the caravan next door so she suggests to Ruthgow they go into the house. She doesn't want Colin to hear anything that the detective might have to say. She's not fussy to whom she lets her caravans, or who pitches a tent in her field, as long as they look after the place, are clean and tidy, and pay their way. But there's something about Colin that she can't put her finger on. Something that makes her feel uneasy. She often wonders if he's running away, hiding out in the back of beyond. Either that or he's just a loner. He's got to be in his late fifties at least, with a paunch and a haggard face, wearing the same cable-knit sweater and brown cords day after day. Yet he's been renting the caravan for nearly six months now and seems to have no intention of moving on any time soon.

She can't complain, though. It's an income. She's never had much time for small talk with the customers, but she's seen Heather talking to him. Heather seemed quite fond of him, bringing him cups of tea and cooking extra casserole for him. Her daughter always was softhearted. The irony isn't lost on her that that same woman is now the only suspect in a double shooting.

Margot locks the caravan behind her and picks up the basket of cleaning paraphernalia at her feet. "Come on, then. I'll put the kettle on. It's cold out here." As they trudge across the field she gabbles at him, asking how he's been and if he enjoys living in Bristol. What she'd really like to ask is whether he ever thinks about her. Or Flora, the girl he couldn't save.

Ruthgow follows her through to the kitchen and she tells him to take a seat. Does it feel weird for him, she wonders, being here again after all these years? Another Powell daughter, another case. She sees him glance at the framed photograph of Flora and Heather on the wall. Everybody notices that photo when they come into the kitchen, even if they've been here many times before, and they all get the same look on their face: a mixture of sadness and relief that it's not their loved one who's gone.

He asks for coffee. Black, no sugar. Different from how he'd had it eighteen years ago. She's always had a good memory for silly, irrelevant details. Like she remembers that the last time she saw him he was wearing a pale blue shirt with creases crisscrossed along the front, as though it had come straight out of its packet, and his hands had trembled slightly as he held his coffee cup. He'd been too thin then, and he'd smoked too much, and even though he'd told her later that his wife had died a few years before, he still wore a single gold band on his left hand. She notices now that he no longer wears it. He's clean-shaven and his shirt is ironed and, if it's possible, he's grown even more attractive. She dismisses this thought straightaway. That part of her life is over.

He was always a man of few words but he's hardly said anything since he arrived, just short answers to her many questions about his life in Bristol. It doesn't sound like he ever remarried. Another thing they have in common.

She hands him his coffee and sits down opposite him. She didn't make any for herself. She couldn't stomach it. "So?" she says. "What have you come all this way to tell me?"

He looks serious, professional, and sits up a little straighter. His body fills the chair and she can smell an expensive after-shave on him. "First, Margot, I need to apologize. For never finding out what happened to Flora." He runs a hand across his chin and she jolts at the memory of the familiar gesture. "It haunts me. I've never given up. I want you to know that."

"You don't think she ran away?" It was always her fear that the police wouldn't take Flora's case seriously, believing she was just a teenage runaway, even after the blouse was found.

"You know I don't," he says shortly. "And I haven't changed my mind about that. We took the case very seriously. You have my word on it."

"How can somebody just vanish?" She can hear the desperation in her voice. It was the same question she'd asked herself every day for eighteen years.

"You'd be surprised by how many people go missing in the UK each year."

She shakes her head. "Sometimes I don't think I can bear it . . ." Then she, too, sits up straighter, her jaw jutting out. She can't fall apart now. She's been strong all these years. And she has to remain so, for Heather. For Ethan.

He assesses her with his calm expression. "I'm sorry, Margot." His pale eyes are sad, his mouth set.

She assesses him with a cold, hard stare. "I'm assuming there's no development with Flora and that you're here about Heather."

He has the good grace to look regretful. "I know you've been asked this before, when you were first interviewed after Heather was taken into hospital, but have you thought more about the victims, Deirdre and Clive Wilson? Are you sure you don't know them?"

"No. I've never heard of them. Neither has Adam—Heather's husband. We can't think of any link between Heather and those people."

"Have they ever stayed at the caravan park?"

"Not that I know of, but I haven't checked the register. And I don't recognize them from the photos that have been in the paper. We've not been very busy, really, since about October. It's too cold for camping."

He reaches inside his coat and takes out a little notepad. He flicks through it and Margot's unease intensifies. Eventually he says, "Your husband, Keith Powell."

"Yes."

He consults his notes. "He was killed on the twenty-first of April 1990 on the farm you used to own in Kent. Is that correct?"

Margot suddenly understands why Ruthgow has come all this way. "That's right." Her mouth is so dry she has to get up to pour herself a glass of water. They'd once bonded over the death of their spouses. He hadn't known then, of course, exactly how Keith had died. It was a secret she'd hoped she would take to the grave.

Ruthgow waits until she's returned to her seat before continuing. "He was killed with a shotgun. Similar model used by Heather to shoot Deirdre and Clive Wilson."

Margot blinks back tears. "It was an unfortunate accident, that's all. No charges were brought."

Ruthgow doesn't say anything, he just surveys her with those calm, unreadable eyes, and she realizes it's not just his appearance that has changed in the intervening years: back then he was more emotional, warmer. She'd felt she could tell him anything after Flora had gone missing. He was on her side, more than any other officer working on the case at the time. She'd sensed some of them saw Flora Powell as a typical teenage girl who'd lied and kept secrets from her family, including a boyfriend. Not Gary Ruthgow.

And now here he is with his thinly veiled accusations.

"I'm sorry, Margot, I really am, but this doesn't look good. A dead father, a missing sister. And now two more dead."

Margot stands up, pushing her chair back. She knows exactly what he's insinuating. Hasn't she thought the same thing herself in her darker moments? "I want you to leave. Please, just go!"

Ruthgow stands up, too, looking pained. "I don't want to up-set you. We have to look into every possibility. You know Flora's case isn't closed. It's cold, that's all. Margot, please . . ." He holds out a hand and in his expression she sees the man he used to be, the man she cried and got drunk with, opened up to—about Keith and how much she missed him even though he hadn't al-ways been the perfect husband or father. And, in turn, he'd con-fided in her about coping with his wife's sudden death in a car crash. But now she was on the other side: no longer the innocent victim whose precious daughter had been snatched away so cru-elly. Now she was the mother of a killer.

"She was just a kid," she says hotly, as she walks him to the front door. But Ruthgow leaves without saying anything further.

Heather was only ten years old when Keith died. She was only ten years old when she pulled the trigger on the gun that killed her father.

17

Margot

Margot watches from the living-room window as Ruthgow gets into his unmarked police car and drives away. How did he find out about Keith's accident? When Flora went missing it never came out—the police force in Kent had handled it, and back then Margot hadn't thought of the implications. Heather had been fourteen when Flora had disappeared. And it had never once occurred to her that Heather was responsible. Why would it? But now . . . No. She refuses to believe it. Heather loved Flora more than anyone in the world; she would never have hurt her. If anything, what had happened to Keith, then to Flora, has obviously destabilized Heather to such an extent that she'd flipped. Maybe Deirdre and Clive Wilson were targeted completely at random. Heather probably didn't even know what she was doing. Surely it was temporary insanity.

Yesterday she'd contacted a defense lawyer in the likelihood that Heather will go to court—because her daughter *will* wake up, and when she does they need to fight her case. Together. Damn Ruthgow. He must be near to retiring. Does he want to solve Flora's case before he leaves the force? Is that what this is all about? And if he and the rest of his team pin it on Heather, it's a closed case, ends neatly tied up. Ruthgow can walk off into his future with a clear conscience and a pat on the back.

She closes her eyes and remembers the day Keith died. It had been a beautiful April afternoon, the girls' favorite time of year because that was when the lambs were born. They'd loved the farm in Maidstone, Kent. She had foolishly thought it was an idyllic place to bring up children. She'd always told the girls to respect the guns, never to handle or hold them without permission and supervision. Both she and Keith had been so strict about that. The girls could shoot, of course. Keith had trained them well. But he'd drummed it into them that they were never to pick up a gun unsupervised. So why had Heather picked up the gun that day? Keith had been using it himself only five minutes before. She knew he was always strict about locking the guns into the cabinet after use. He'd had to kill a cow that was ill and in pain. She remembers seeing him striding toward the barn with the shotgun over his shoulder and a look of determination on his face. Little did she know it would be the last time she'd see him alive. Less than ten minutes later, while she'd been putting out the washing, she'd heard a gunshot ring out. It hadn't frightened her. She'd thought Keith was killing another animal. But then there was a scream. A child's. And a deathly silence that had made her flesh turn cold. She knew the girls were playing in the barn with the lambs so she'd run as fast as she could around the side of the house just in time to see Keith staggering backward and clutching his chest, her daughters looking on in horror, and then the gun slipping from Heather's grasp onto the grass, fear and shock etched over both girls' pale little faces.

By the time Margot had reached her husband he was already dead, his eyes rolled back in his head and blood blooming at the front of his shirt. She'd furiously checked for a pulse, even though she knew he was gone. And then she thought of her daughters, and how they must be feeling to see their father dead like that on the ground. She had no choice but to leave him lying there while she ushered the girls back into the house. Heather said it was an accident. That Keith had left the gun on the ground by the barn after shooting the cow and she'd picked it up. Keith, realizing his mistake at leaving the gun unattended, had shouted at her to put it down. "She swung the gun toward Daddy without thinking and it just went off. It was an accident," Flora had explained, backing up Heather's version of events.

And Margot had had no reason to doubt any of it. Until now.

MARGOT STANDS IN THE FRONT PORCH AND PUSHES HER FEET BACK into her recently vacated wellies. The sky is brooding but there's no rain yet so she takes this chance to make her way across the field to the caravan park. The wooden shed that they've converted into an office for the site is empty but she can see through the window of the coach house that Adam is in. His face is illuminated by the computer screen. Has he picked Ethan up yet from nursery? It's nearly six. She raps on the door and he lifts his head, annoyance crossing his features at being disturbed. When he sees it's her he waves, although he still doesn't smile. He gets up and she imagines his lumbering gait as he goes to answer the door.

"You okay?" he says, as he pulls the door open.

"Do you want me to pick Ethan up from nursery?"

"Nah, you're all right, Marg. Mum's gone to get him. He's staying the night at hers. I think being here makes him miss Heather more, y'know?"

She nods, trying to quash the jealous feelings in the pit of her stomach at the thought of Gloria spending all this time with her precious grandson. She knows it's for the best, but she wants him.

Adam stands aside to let her in and the two of them take up most of the space in the small, square hallway. The ceilings are low, and there are parts of the house where Adam has to stoop. Margot had been thinking lately that as Heather and Adam extend their family they could move into the main house and she'd come here. The house is too big for her now. All those empty rooms, Flora's still as it was when she last used it. She wonders what will happen if Heather doesn't wake up. Or if she goes to prison. Will Adam still want to be here, running the caravan park? Leo's already left. She bought him out five years ago. After Flora went missing, all his spark and humor slowly seeped out of him, and he spent longer and longer away from Tilby. Then, one night a year or so later, when he was out of his head on whiskey, he admitted that he couldn't stand being here any longer, that he was fed up with the stares and silent accusations of the locals that he, the only young man living at Tilby Manor at the time, must be responsible for Flora's disappearance.

"Do you want a cuppa?" asks Adam now. He looks haggard, thinks Margot. She wonders if he's eating properly. In the week that Heather's been in hospital Adam has sometimes joined Margot for dinner, and a few nights he's stayed in one of her spare rooms for company, but most of the time he's sequestered in here.

"I'm fine, thanks. Just wanted a quick look at the register. The police were here earlier . . ."

His eyes narrow. "The police? Why?"

She holds up a hand to prevent him going off on one. It's always been Adam's way. Talk first and think later. It had taken Margot a long time to like him, if she was being honest with herself. Heather had been so young and innocent in that department. She'd never had a boyfriend before—not one Margot knew about anyway. But when Heather was just eighteen she'd met Adam at the annual barn dance to raise funds for the church hall. He was from a little village in south Gloucestershire, but had been staying with his uncle Saul on his farm a mile or so from Tilby, learning the trade. Adam's cousin, Ezra, had had a crush on Heather, but it had been strong, silent, gruff Adam who had stolen her heart. She'd seemed besotted with him from the outset, which had worried Margot. She couldn't help but think he was a crutch, after Keith and Flora. They were inseparable. Heather was never one for lots of friends, especially after Jess, but she'd kept in touch with a few girls from college. Soon, they had fallen by the wayside as Heather spent all her time with Adam.

She often wondered if Adam had convinced Heather to stop seeing her friends. Heather had let slip once that he was a little possessive. But as time went on and Adam and Heather took over running the caravan park, Margot began to see another side to Adam. He was fiercely loyal to Heather and, under the gruff exterior, he was warm, especially to animals. He seemed more comfortable with the horses than he did with people. Despite her reservations, he's been a good husband and father. It's only in the last few months that she's noticed a change in him—snappy with Heather, less patient when things went wrong. Just before Heather's "accident," she saw him fling files across the office in a fit of rage. He hadn't noticed she was outside. When she asked him about it later he'd been red faced and apologetic, saying he was looking for some paperwork and had got frustrated. He had reminded Margot of Keith, toward the end.

"It's nothing," she lies now. She's definitely not going to tell him they suspect Heather might have had something to do with Flora's death. "They just wanted to ask if I could have a look through the register and see if Deirdre or Clive Wilson had ever stayed here. They're trying to find a link."

The lines in his forehead deepen. "We've already told them we don't know the bloody Wilsons. Why won't they listen? Why can't they see that Heather's been struggling? The postnatal depression . . ."

"They're just trying to do their job," she says levelly.

He exhales and runs a hand over his beard. "Let's go to the office, then," he says, moving toward the front door. Margot follows. It's raining now and they have to make a mad dash across the yard.

It smells damp as Adam opens the door, despite its insulation, as though nobody has inhabited it for a while. But the desk, as usual, is messy, papers, books, and pens strewn haphazardly across it, with a half-drunk mug of week-old coffee standing by the monitor, spores of green mold floating on the top. Even the keyboard is covered with papers so that only the ends are visible. Adam looks mildly embarrassed as he rummages—no wonder he can never find anything, she thinks—until he comes to two A4-sized leatherbound diaries. He pushes them toward Margot. "These are 2011 and 2012, although there's only a few pages marked in that one," he says.

Margot takes a seat at the desk and moves the debris aside, flicking through the pages of the 2012 diary. She takes out her reading glasses from the inner pocket of her vest, slipping them on to peer through the list of names.

"Right, well, I'll get going," says Adam.

"I'll lock up," she says, without glancing up. "Come over for dinner later, if you like. You need to keep your strength up and I've got a casserole in the slow cooker."

"Thanks, Marg." He's the only person who has ever shortened her name. It would annoy her coming from anyone else. But in Adam's West Country burr it seems natural. She hears the door bang shut behind him as he leaves.

She licks her index finger before turning over the page. There aren't many recent names on the list, out of season, so she doesn't bother to read the first few pages of 2012. Instead she concentrates on the 2011 diary, flicking back to the summer when they were at their busiest. All the names of the customers who stayed on the campsite are there, in either Heather's loopy writing or Adam's more stilted hand. *Sean and Sally Peeves, Caravan One, August 6, 2011, one week. Lawrence and Felicity Dawes, Caravan Two, August 6, two weeks. Petra Anderson, pitch for one tent, four nights.* It's tedious work. And how far should she go back? They've been running this caravan park for nearly twenty years. Does she even have the old records? She recalls dumping a load of notebooks in the attic a year or so ago. Maybe she'd give them to the police and they could go through it all. And even if the Wilsons did stay here, what does it prove? That Heather knew them? But it doesn't explain why she'd want to shoot them.

She turns to the beginning of the book, January 2011. She flicks to the next page, then to March. A year ago. But nothing. She sighs, pushing the diary aside and picking up the 2012 diary. And, to her surprise, there it is, on the second page, written in familiar looping handwriting.

Deirdre Wilson, Caravan Three, February 3, 2012, two nights.

She takes her glasses off and rubs at the corners of her eyes. She was here. Deirdre was here just over a month ago. And, judging by the handwriting, Heather had met her.

18

Margot

MARGOT STARES AT HEATHER'S HANDWRITING, STUNNED AT HER discovery. There it is, in blue biro, the proof of a link between her daughter and the Wilsons.

Sliding the diary under her vest to protect it from the rain, Margot locks the office and darts back through the caravan park. There is a light on in Colin's caravan and it seeps around the edges of the closed gingham curtains that Heather had run up on the sewing machine. Her heart lurches at the sight of them. From the windows on the other side of the caravan, Colin will have a view of the cliffs and the sea in the distance. She wonders how he feels about what's happened with Heather. He seemed very fond of her, although he has only once asked how she is, and Margot felt he took pains to avoid the subject of the shootings, shuffling his feet and keeping his eyes on the ground. When she cleaned his caravan yesterday she found a Get Well card with a cartoon dog holding a bunch of flowers on the front. But he'd only got as far as writing Heather's name inside. Margot hadn't meant to pry; it had fluttered to the floor in the breeze she had created when she opened the caravan door. She imagines him now, sitting alone in front of the tiny inbuilt TV with his meal for one, and feels real empathy with him for the first time.

Margot jogs across the field that separates the caravan park from the house, past the paddock, and through the garden. One of the horses neighs from the stables. Winnie, she thinks, and the sound comforts her. When she reaches the porch she kicks off her wellies and enters the house.

Only last month Deirdre Wilson stayed here on their caravan site. There was no sign of Clive's name, but what does it mean? Is it just a coincidence?

She turns on the light in the living room, shuddering as she spots a figure standing at the edge of the driveway. Another journalist? It's a bit late. She flops onto the sofa, with the diary on her lap. She knows she'll have to tell Ruthgow about Deirdre.

Margot's head is reeling as she tries to process all this new information. Now the police know about Heather's involvement in Keith's accident she's sure it won't be long before the papers sniff out the story, and she knows they'll go to town. But can she bring herself to call Jessica? She'd given Margot her business card again yesterday, after Margot was forced to admit she'd ripped up the last one. If she doesn't talk to a journalist soon, one of them will go ahead and print something without her consent.

She sits up, leaning forward to get a better view from the window. There's definitely someone out there. She's sure it's the same pest who was here this morning. Honestly, they're like horseflies: you get rid of one and another pops up in their place. This morning's had been a solitary man, who looked a bit worse for wear, with a three-day-old beard and his hair flattened by the rain. He'd stood at the gate, staring up at the house. When she'd driven past on the way to see Heather she'd wound her window down and told him there was no point in him waiting there: she'd agreed to do an exclusive with another newspaper. He'd opened his mouth, to convince her or to swear at her, she couldn't be sure which, but she'd driven sharply away before he could speak, gratified to see that her wheels had sprayed mud over the bottom of his trousers.

Adam will be in soon, she tells herself, and she'll send him out to get rid of the journalist. She stands up so he can see her. He's illuminated by a lamppost, a fine rain falling on the hood of his parka. "Bugger off!" she shouts, gesticulating, although she knows he can't hear her. He bows his head, almost as if he's apologizing, then turns around and gets into a car parked further down the lane.

Before Margot can change her mind she picks up her phone from the coffee table and taps out Jessica's number. She knows Adam won't approve of what she's about to do; he'd tried to talk her out of it last night. But Jessica's words have eaten away at her, like maggots on meat, and she can't ignore them any longer. She can't have faceless journalists digging away at her past.

Who knows what else they'll unearth?

Adam flashes into her mind.

He's definitely been acting oddly since it happened. She can't push away the thought. He's never been the most communicative of men. At least, not to her. He's probably different with Heather, although Margot remembers Heather complaining about her husband's brusque ways over the years. Like the time they'd attended that village fete and Adam really didn't want to go so was abrupt and short with everyone. If he was in a bad mood he wouldn't hide it. It had embarrassed Heather, who's always had impeccable manners, thanks to Margot. She was very firm about that when her daughters were growing up. Adam still dutifully visits Heather every day, but for only half an hour or so. Margot usually waits outside the room if she arrives at the same time. She can see through the glass in the door that Adam holds Heather's hand, although she can't hear what he says to her. But his lips move, so he's obviously saying something. Yet by his rigid posture she knows he's angry and confused.

Now she'll have to tell Adam about Heather killing Keith before it all comes out. She knows Heather's never uttered a word about it to anyone. That was what they'd all agreed when they left Kent to make a new start in Tilby back in 1991.

The phone rings a few times before it's picked up and Margot recognizes Jessica's voice as she says hello. She sounds a little out of breath and, dare she say it, scared.

"Jessica?" She knows it's her. She just needs to be sure someone else—maybe another journalist—hasn't got hold of the phone. She still can't quite believe she's doing this.

"Margot! Hi. Thank you so much for ringing," says Jessica. She sounds like she's somewhere echoey.

"I'm"—Margot hesitates—"I've been thinking about what you said. Yesterday. If I gave you an exclusive, would everybody else leave us alone?"

"I promise you they will," Jessica says. "And if they don't, call me. I'll come over and tell them where to go."

She laughs, sounding so like the girl who used to stay with them all those years ago that Margot can't help but smile. But just as quickly she remembers that Jessica is a journalist now. And that she hurt her precious Heather. She puts up the barriers again. "Adam doesn't want me to do it."

Jessica pauses. "Okay. But I promise you and Adam will get copy approval before anything is printed."

Margot shuffles in her seat. Her back aches. She spent too long out with the horses after visiting Heather earlier, then that jaunt across the field. She turns sixty next year, and keeps forgetting she's not thirty anymore. She'd cleaned one of the static caravans too, as a family wants to rent it this weekend. It smelled strongly of dog and there was a wee stain on the lino so Margot had had to get down on her hands and knees and bleach and scrub until it was spotless. During the summer months she has a cleaner, but in the off season she wants to save the money. And then the whole thing with Ruthgow. It's too much. It's all just *too much*.

She sighs. "Okay. Fine. Can you come over tomorrow? I'd rather do it face-to-face, if you don't mind."

Jessica sounds thrilled and Margot feels the familiar lurch in her stomach. Can she trust her?

They arrange a time for the next day and Margot hangs up. She sits for a while longer, staring at the phone in her hand, wondering if she's made a huge mistake by allowing Jessica Fox back into her life.

19

I'M FEELING COLD NOW. TOO COLD. IT DOESN'T MATTER HOW MANY BLANKETS *I'm swathed in, I can't stop shivering. Your face flashes through my mind, as well as Dylan's, Uncle Leo's, Jess's.*

Jess.

In my mind she's still the same fourteen-year-old. More or less neglected by her own mother and so desperate for attention from ours. I could never blame her for that. She thinks nobody knows about the secret she's kept to herself all these years.

But she's wrong.

20

Jess

I HARDLY SLEPT LAST NIGHT FOR WORRYING ABOUT WHAT I'D TOLD Jack. Could Wayne Walker really have found me here? I wasn't imagining it last night when I noticed that light in the derelict building opposite. Was someone in there, watching my movements?

I have to be honest with Rory. Jack's right about that. He's been so good to me. He deserves better. Tonight. I'll tell him tonight. I'll cook dinner for a change. I'll make an effort.

And in the meantime I need to see Margot.

Ted was ecstatic when I told him this morning that Margot had agreed to an exclusive interview. He didn't show it, of course. That's not his way. But I could tell by the shine in his eyes and the way his chewing slowed down, the gum moving around his mouth less frantically than normal. He told me to take Jack and get as many photos as possible. "And if you can get some of

Margot's personal ones of Heather growing up that would be even better."

I told Margot on the phone last night that I'd be there at noon. She wanted to go to the hospital to see Heather first thing, she'd said. But at eleven Jack still hasn't turned up for work. I text him, mentioning that Margot has agreed to talk, but when there's no response I ring his mobile. In desperation I leave my desk to find Ellie, the trainee.

She's on a computer in the corner uploading press releases onto the *Herald*'s decrepit website. It's supposed to be updated daily, but Ted hates anything too technical and because it's so out-of-date hardly anybody reads it. Ellie has sprayed the ends of her brown hair blue today. Usually it's pink. The odd occasion it's been green. I ask her if she's seen or heard from Jack yet today, but she shakes her head, without looking up from the keyboard.

Seth is painstakingly sorting through photos in his side room. I go up to him and stand in front of his desk. He looks up and smiles kindly, pushing his black-framed glasses further onto his face. "You all right, girl?" He calls everyone "girl." Even Sue. But nobody is ever offended. If Ted said it, or Jack, it would come across as condescending. But Seth is old school. A Cockney who worked in Fleet Street back in the day. Getting on for seventy now, he should have retired long ago but he loves his job. And it's not as if he goes around brushing up against us or slapping our arses. Even Ellie, twenty-three and a staunch feminist, doesn't seem to mind. In fact she calls him "Pops" in retaliation, and he loves it.

"Just wondering if you've heard from Jack. I've tried to call his mobile but it goes straight to voicemail."

Seth glances at the clock on the wall, his brow furrowed. "No. Now you mention it I haven't. He's never late."

A sense of unease settles in my stomach. Has something happened? It can't have. I left him with Finn last night. Maybe they'd had a late one and he's overslept. But even as I think it I know that's wrong. Jack is always on time. Diligent. Professional to a T.

"We're supposed to be going on a job." Although he wouldn't have known that last night.

Seth sits back in his chair. "I'll give him a call. Find out where he is. I'm sure it's nothing to worry about."

I thank him and go back to my desk. I need to leave soon if I'm going to get to Margot's for midday. I pick up my phone to check again, and as I do so it buzzes in my hand. I breathe a sigh of relief when I see Jack's name flashing up.

"Where are you?" I hiss into the phone. "Are you okay?"

"I'm fine." His voice sounds muffled and I can hear traffic in the background. A car horn beeps and I hear Jack telling them to fuck off. It's unlike him to be aggressive and I flinch. "Sorry about that," he says. "Some twat almost knocked me over."

"Where are you? We need to go over to Margot's."

"I'm sorry. Can you meet me downstairs?"

I glance at my watch. "Sure. What shall I tell Ted? Can you come with me to Margot's or shall I say you've rung in sick?"

"No. It's fine. I'm fine. Just . . ." He sighs impatiently. "Please, I'd rather meet you outside. Okay?"

I put the phone down, puzzled. Why's Jack being so evasive? And grumpy. He's usually so good-natured.

I gather up my things and call to Ted that I'm off to see Margot and meeting Jack outside. Then I hurry off before he can reply.

Outside Jack is smoking and talking to Stan, who's huddled up in the doorway beneath a blanket. He's drinking a takeaway coffee that I suspect Jack has bought him. Stan takes his filthy cap off to me, like he does every time I see him, and grins toothlessly. He smells of stale lager. I smile back and I'm about to indulge in a bit of banter, which Stan always enjoys, when I notice Jack properly and freeze. He's sporting the ugliest black eye I've ever seen. It's so puffy and swollen that he can hardly open it. He also has a cut lip. Instantly tears spring to my eyes at the thought of anyone doing this to him.

I rush toward him. "What happened? Oh, Jack . . ." I put my hand to his lip. "Who did this to you?"

He covers my hand with his. "I was mugged. Last night. Some fucker tried to take my camera but I fought them off—not before they gave me this, though." He takes his hand away to point to his face.

I frown. "But you were with Finn last night."

Jack steers me away from Stan. "Let's walk and talk or we'll be late. Where's your car?"

"At my place."

"Come on, then. We'd better be quick."

He gives the rest of his cigarette to Stan, saying it hurts his cut lip to smoke it, and we walk down Park Street, trying not to notice the occasional stare directed at Jack.

"Where was Finn when this happened?" I ask, as we cross the center and head toward the Welsh Back.

He hangs his head. "We had a row."

I clench my fists in anger. Bloody Finn. "What about?"

"Oh, nothing, really. It just escalated and he walked off in a huff. Got the bus home and left me to sit in the pub by myself. So I had another drink and left. But then I encountered this chancer. Thought he could take me on. But he underestimated me."

"Jack!" I cry, exasperated. "You've been beaten up."

He tries to smile but with his swollen lip it's more of a grimace. "You should see the other guy."

MARGOT IS FUSSING AROUND JACK WHEN WE ARRIVE, ASKING IF HE'D like some ice for his eye. It reminds me of what she used to be like, when Heather and I were friends, always so motherly. Caring. Making sure everybody was okay. I always thought Heather and Flora were so lucky to have her. Even then I could tell she was different from my mum. And it's not as if my mum didn't care. She loved me—*loves me*—I know that. It's just that she was preoccupied and busy a lot of the time, working as a secretary at the one and only legal firm in the high street. At weekends and in the evenings she was either fitting in the chores she hadn't managed to do during the week or sorting out my grandmother, who was in a care home in Clevedon, or going on dates. She was happy that I was out of her hair for a few hours. *Anything for a quiet life.*

That was her motto. Margot was just more *present*, I suppose. But she had her brother Leo around to help. And she worked from home.

I wonder who's around for Margot now that Heather is in a coma. It doesn't look like Adam is much company, from the little I've seen of him. The words "gruff" and "unsympathetic" spring to mind. And I heard Leo moved away not long after Flora disappeared. Even then I couldn't help overhearing the rumor that he must have had something to do with it, and the gossip surrounding his "penchant for young girls" because one of his old girlfriends had been much younger than him. I remember her, Hayley, tall and slim with long, wheat-colored hair.

Margot ushers us into the living room. It hasn't changed much: still the same old sofas (although with different throws covering them), the old-fashioned heavy walnut furniture, and the cozy open fireplace. In the corner, by the French windows, there is a box of toys that must belong to Heather's little boy. I still find it hard to believe that she's a wife and mother. I can't imagine ever being either.

Jack and I sit side by side on the sofa while Margot bustles out of the room again. Five minutes later she's back with a bag of frozen peas that she hands to Jack. "For the eye," she says. "Hold it there for a good five to ten minutes to reduce the swelling. That's it. Now, I'll go and fetch some tea."

She leaves the room again and Jack turns to me. He's moved the bag of peas from his left eye to his swollen lip. "She seems really nice," he says, his voice muffled by the bag.

"She is. She's thawed a bit since I first called round. You don't want to get on the wrong side of her, though. She's . . ."

I fall silent as Margot returns, carrying a tray and setting it down on the coffee table. She pours us both tea and leaves us to add milk as she settles herself in one of the armchairs. She seems chirpier today and I wonder if she's had news about Heather.

"How is Heather?" I ask, stirring my tea. "Is there any change?"

"No. But she's stable. The doctors say there's no reason why she should still be in a coma. Apparently it's her body's way of resting. There is no longer any swelling or bleeding on the brain. So it's good news." She smiles, tucking her slippered feet underneath her. For once she's not wearing jodhpurs but a pair of jeggings and a long jumper with a horse on the front. "I'm hopeful."

"I'm so pleased. I'd . . ." I hesitate, trying not to look at Jack. "I'd love to see her again. When she wakes up. That is, if she'd like to see me."

There's so much I wish I could say to her. To apologize for.

Margot's expression is steadfast and I'm worried I've gone too far, asked for too much. But, to my surprise, she nods. "I think she might like that. Yes."

I'm so relieved and grateful that I can feel myself smiling back gormlessly. Then I remember why we're here. I reach down to the bag at my feet and retrieve my notebook and pen.

Margot's eyes go to the notebook and I see her stiffen. I try to ease her in gently, just asking some anodyne questions, about the business and Heather's setup with Adam and Ethan. Margot's answers are guarded and my heart falls. If she's like this now, how will she react when I start probing further?

"So, the day of the shooting. Last Friday . . ."

"I can't believe it's only a week ago today," she mumbles. "So much has changed."

Only a week. It feels much longer. "So that day," I try again, "where were you when you heard?"

She fidgets. "I was away. I hardly ever go away, and the one time I do . . . the one time . . ."

"Who found Heather?"

She sniffs. "Sheila. Do you remember her? She still helps out with the horses once or twice a week."

I nod. I do remember Sheila, a buxom, gossipy woman, who used to chat to everyone and anything incessantly, animals included. Heather and I used to giggle when we heard her talking to the plants.

"She came in that day because I was on a yoga retreat with my friend Pam."

I scribble it down in shorthand. "Where was that?"

"In Devon. But we were due back that day."

"And what time was this?" I ask.

"Sheila found her at about eight thirty a.m. in the barn. Heather had been unconscious for quite some time."

I swallow, trying not to think of Heather lying in our favorite barn, bleeding and unconscious. "And Sheila called the ambulance?"

"Yes. And then she called Adam. I was traveling home with

Pam when Adam phoned me. He was distraught. He said they'd argued the night before and he'd walked out, staying at his mum's with Ethan."

This is news to me. I sit up straighter. "What did they row about?"

"He didn't say. Just that she'd been a little delusional and obsessed."

"Delusional and obsessed? About what?"

Margot stares at her lap. "I don't know."

I glance at her, wondering if she's telling the truth. "You never asked him?"

"I—I didn't want to pry."

"But," I begin tentatively, "it might explain her state of mind."

She suddenly looks unsure. "Yes. That's true."

There's something not quite right here. Is she scared of Adam? If not, why wouldn't she ask him?

For now I change tack. "So when Adam called you, did he know that Heather had shot the Wilsons?"

She shakes her head. "Not at that stage. All he knew was that it looked as though Heather had tried to take her own life and was in hospital. In a coma. So Pam drove me straight to hospital. On the way Adam called me again to say he'd heard from the police. That's when he told me what she had done. He was waiting for me in the atrium when I arrived, and he was devastated. As you can imagine . . ." She leans forward and places her teacup on the side table with a trembling hand.

The room falls silent as we take in her words. Out of the corner of my eye I can see Jack moving the frozen peas back to his eye with a grimace.

"Did they have proof?" I ask.

"Yes. The gun. It was the same one that was used to kill the Wilsons."

"And you've never heard her mention Clive or Deirdre Wilson? She's never had any dealings with them that you know of?"

She swallows, playing with the rings on her hands. She has two on her wedding finger and a signet ring that I recognize on the little finger of her right hand. Heather and Flora used to wear them too. Family rings, Heather called them. "I didn't think she knew them. And it might be a coincidence. But Deirdre stayed here in one of the caravans. About five weeks ago. I saw it written in the register"—she glances up at me, pain etched on her face—"in Heather's handwriting."

So Heather had met Deirdre Wilson. What happened between them? Did she do or say something to make Heather kill her?

"But she'd never mentioned her to you?"

"Never," she says firmly. Margot uncrosses her legs and reaches for her tea.

I wait for her to settle back into her chair before asking, "Can you explain what Heather was like as a child? I know I became friends with her when we were twelve, but before that, when you lived in Kent."

Margot looks wistful, her gaze going to the French windows as though a child version of Heather is out there, playing on the lawn. "She was sensitive. A born worrier. My mother, when she was alive, said that Heather lived close to the well. She cried easily."

I don't remember ever seeing Heather cry. Even after Flora went missing. But I keep quiet.

Margot chews her lip thoughtfully. "Flora was more fanciful, I suppose. Heather . . . well, Heather was practical. She looked after Flora, even though she was the youngest. And she was always so self-contained, even as a child, content in her own company, sketching or writing or playing alone with her stuffed animals. But she loved being with Flora too. They didn't seem to need anyone else." She sighs. "I shouldn't be talking about her in the past tense. Heather's still here, still with us."

I remember how honored I'd felt when I was finally accepted into their little group. How Heather had cared for me when I was ill once with a tummy bug, holding my hair back as I was sick and looking after me until my mum got home from work.

"The waters run deep with Heather," she says. "You never really knew what she was thinking. She never wanted to be any trouble. After Ethan was born she suffered postnatal depression but she didn't tell anyone for ages that she was feeling so awful. It was only when she couldn't hide it any more that she admitted it. She didn't want to make a fuss." She closes her eyes as if the memory is too painful, and my heart hurts for her.

When she looks up there is a different expression on her face, as though she's contemplating telling me something she isn't sure she should.

"What is it?" I ask gently. This is one of my strengths as a journalist: knowing when to speak and when to keep quiet. I'm good at reading people and I know, right now, there's something important she wants to say.

Jack, who has been silent until now, suddenly sits forward in his seat. He can sense it too. I will him to remain quiet. I don't want to interrupt Margot's flow.

Margot sighs. "Detective Ruthgow was here yesterday. About what happened to Heather's dad. My husband, Keith."

I'm holding my breath.

"I don't know if Heather ever told you, Jessica, what happened to her father but I doubt it. She never spoke of it. She was so closed about it all and I think it was her way of coping. We probably didn't handle it right, in hindsight."

Heather hardly ever mentioned her dad, apart from that time in our art lesson when she blurted out that he was dead. She'd also once said he'd been a bit of a tyrant. I wait. I can sense Jack crossing his legs and out of the corner of my eye I notice he rests the bag of peas in his lap.

I shake my head, my pen poised, adrenaline pumping through my veins.

"She killed him. With a gun. By accident."

I stare at her in shock. Of all the things I'd thought she might say I'd never expected this.

"Oh, God. Poor Heather. And your husband. I'm so sorry," I manage.

The image I've always held of my onetime best friend is warping and distorting in my mind, like a perfect photograph that has been damaged by water.

She blinks. "Yes," she adds curtly. "Well, Heather was only ten. She couldn't have known what she was doing. It was an accident."

"Of course."

"I'm only telling you because it's bound to come out. And I'd rather you—well, the public—heard it from me first. I don't want there to be rumors flying, people filling in the blanks. Do you know what I mean?"

I nod vigorously, my heart racing. "I do." I pause. "Can you explain what happened?"

My shorthand can hardly keep up—and I'm fast at 120 words per minute—as Margot explains what happened on that April day back in 1990 at their farm in Kent. When she's finished there's a stunned silence.

Oh, Heather. I can't believe she never told me. We were so close. I'd thought we told each other everything but there was this huge secret between us. I can't believe Heather shot and killed her father. Something as traumatic as that must have changed her. Who *is* Heather?

I'm still trying to process all this when I hear a door slam. I glance at Margot, who's looking toward the hallway. I follow her gaze. Adam is leaning against the doorjamb, even surlier than before, and I'm glad that Jack has accompanied me. But he barely acknowledges us. His face, under all that facial hair, is deathly white.

Margot stands up. A woman who's accustomed to hearing bad news, she senses straightaway that something's wrong. "What? What is it?" she says, her eyes darting about frantically, searching his face for clues, I imagine. "Is it Heather?"

He shakes his head. "No. No. I've had a call. From the police. They've found . . ." He turns to us. "This is off the bloody record, all right?"

I nod, although Jack's face is impassive.

"They've found *what?*" asks Margot, her voice rising.

"Another set of fingerprints on the gun."

21

Margot

THE AIR SMELLS STALE IN THE POLICE STATION AND MARGOT'S SURE somebody has recently been eating egg sandwiches. She sits in the waiting room, her bag on her lap, trying not to make eye contact with some of the undesirables, her gaze trained on the posters with local helplines stuck to the wall opposite. A youth in the corner with a nose ring has already bared his teeth at her. He's waiting with an extremely skinny young woman, who, she's sure, must be a drug addict, judging by her greasy hair and marked arms. It's mid-March but the woman is in a vest top and sweatpants, although it's unbearably hot in there. Margot can feel sweat breaking out on her back. She shouldn't have put on her padded coat but she doesn't want to take it off and draw attention to herself.

She shuffles in the uncomfortable plastic chair. How long is Adam going to take? The horrible blue walls are beginning to close in on her.

Adam was quiet in the car on the drive over while Margot had found it hard to suppress her excitement. Another set of fingerprints found. Which means it might not have been Heather who killed those people after all. She's always known, deep down, that Heather wouldn't do this. Not in cold blood. Keith was different. Keith was an unfortunate, tragic accident.

Jess had been understanding when their interview had had to be cut short. She'd asked if she could go over to the caravan park and talk to Colin. Margot had agreed. She can't imagine Colin would know anything, and she wanted to appease Jess after running out on her like that. Adam hadn't looked particularly thrilled by the prospect of Jess and that nice boy, Jack, entering the caravan park, but he rarely looked thrilled about anything so Margot told herself not to dwell on it.

She checks her watch. It's almost two. She wanted to go back and see Heather. What if she wakes up and nobody's there? She's agitated by the thought.

The drug-addict woman approaches the duty officer behind the desk and starts arguing with him. Margot shrinks in her seat, wanting to make herself even smaller. Just when she thinks she can stand it no longer and will have to get some fresh air, Adam emerges, grim faced.

She leaps to her feet. "All done?"

He nods.

"Can we go?"

"Yep. Let's get out of here."

As soon as Margot steps outside she gasps for air. Oh, how she hates being cooped up inside. It makes her feel like she can't breathe. Heather's always been the same. They share the love of the countryside, the open spaces, the lush greenery, the hills. Some mornings, before breakfast, they'd saddle their horses and ride across a stretch of land they called the Gallops. It was when Heather said she'd felt the most free—free of the constraints of being a wife and a mother. How would she cope in prison?

She wouldn't. That's the truth of it. For the first time Margot wonders if it would be better for her daughter if she never woke up.

"So, what did they say? The police."

Adam shrugs. "Not much. But it's nothing to get excited about, Marg. I've used the gun in the past and so have you. Our fingerprints are bound to be on it."

Her heart falls. Of course. That's all this is. Nothing to get her hopes up about. It *was* Heather who killed those people. She was *seen*, for crying out loud. There are witnesses.

She feels despondent as she gets back into the car. Adam turns the radio on. It's still tuned to Absolute 90s and Margot has to swallow the lump in her throat when Sinéad O'Connor's "Nothing Compares 2 U" comes on. An image pops into her head of her daughters belting out this song into hairbrushes in Flora's bedroom. It had been a few months after Keith had died and she remembers being thankful that they'd seemed like their old selves. She'd been terrified their lives would be defined— ruined even—by the one idiotic moment that had cost Keith his life. But there they'd been, singing into their hairbrushes like any other normal ten- and twelve-year-old.

But they weren't normal, were they? A thing like that was bound to have left its grubby mark on their once clean souls.

"Are you okay, Marg?"

Adam's voice brings her out of the past and she realizes she has tears on her cheeks.

IT'S NOT UNTIL MUCH LATER, FOLLOWING AN AFTERNOON SPENT SIT-ting beside Heather, brushing her lovely long hair and talking to her about the horses, her husband and son, that Margot gets the phone call. Adam's gone to his mum's, promising to bring Ethan back to spend the night. He'd popped in to see Heather too, but he didn't stay long. She's noticed his visits are getting shorter. Margot had to get the bus back. She wasn't a fan of public trans-port. Too enclosed with not enough air, and she always seemed to end up squashed against the window with the person next to her invading her space with their pointy elbows.

She'd walked into a dark, empty house—it's at times like these that she misses a dog to greet her—to the phone ringing.

It's Ruthgow, who informs Margot that Adam's fingerprints are on the gun. As well as her own. But there is another set that doesn't match those of anybody they have on record. Someone else, other than Heather, held the gun that day.

22

Jess

Jack and I stand in the porch and watch as Adam speeds out of the driveway in his blue estate. Jack is still clutching the bag of peas Margot gave him. He holds them up to me; the bag is melting and water drips at our feet. "Forgot to give them back. I'll just leave them here." He bends over and dumps them by a pair of dirty wellies.

In the distance a dog barks but there are no other sounds. The sun is struggling to come out from behind a gray cloud. "I forgot how quiet it is in the country," I say. "Come on, it's this way."

We trudge through the long grass, the dew darkening the hem of Jack's trouser legs. "I'm not decked out for this," he observes, as he almost slips on the grass and clutches my arm, panic written all over his face. "Isn't there a main path?"

I stifle a giggle. "I'm afraid not. Sorry, Jack, you're going to have to get your posh designer shoes a little bit dirty."

He grins, which gives him a sinister look with his swollen lip and black eye.

We pass the fountain where Heather and I would spend hours sprawled on the lawn, sketching, and walk until we get to a thick hedge with a large arch in the middle.

"It's through here?" Jack asks, as though he expects to be walking into a pit full of tigers.

"Yes. It's clever, isn't it? It means the main house has privacy away from the caravan park." It's neater than it was in 1994, now pruned and shaped. I imagine, in the summer, the arch is filled with flowers.

I walk through the gap first and stop in surprise. It's much smarter than I remember, with a row of static caravans in one area of the field and in the other a smattering of pod tents. Behind that is the old coach house where Heather and Adam now live. In 1994 it was more or less a shell and was used for storage. Once we saw her uncle Leo and his girlfriend Hayley sneaking out of it with sheepish expressions, Leo adjusting the belt of his jeans and Hayley pulling at the hem of her micro miniskirt. We had been in one of the caravans and we'd fallen about laughing so much that Heather nearly wet herself.

"It's quite nice," says Jack, nodding in approval.

"Not that you've ever camped in your life," I acknowledge, remembering that Jack had turned down a lads' weekend "glamping" because he didn't want to "rough it."

"I'm camp in other ways," he says, winking at me.

I roll my eyes. "Right. I wonder which caravan Colin's staying in."

"Maybe the one with the light on."

I shove him playfully but he winces and holds his arm. At first I think he's mucking about, but from the pain that flashes across his face I realize he's serious. "Oh, Jack! Are you okay?"

"Bruises. From the mugging."

"Shit, I forgot." I rub his upper arm tenderly. "I'm really sorry."

"Don't worry. Come on." He moves away from me and strides toward the caravan with the light on. There are little gingham curtains at the window and I imagine it's cozy inside. Jack's already rapping on the door before I've even reached him. "Eager beaver," I tease, when I catch up with him.

Before he can reply the door opens and a short, balding man with a large stomach stands blinking at us. He has glasses perched on his pointed nose and he reminds me of a mole. He frowns. "Yes?"

Jack opens his mouth to speak but I interrupt him by introducing myself. "Margot said it was okay for us to talk to you."

He hesitates. "I don't have anything to say."

"It's just about Heather."

His eyes widen and he leans closer to me. He smells of beef stew. "What about Heather? Is she okay?"

"There's no change, I'm afraid. But the morning she shot herself, were you here?"

His face closes up. "I don't know anything. I've told the police this already. I was in bed. Asleep. I heard nothing. I saw nothing." He retreats back into his caravan.

"Please, Colin. It could help Heather."

"No. It won't." And he shuts the door in our faces before I can ask what he means.

THE REST OF THE AFTERNOON GOES SLOWLY. JACK IS SENT OUT ON another job with Ellie and I'm left in the newsroom to type up my unfinished interview with Margot. Ted slopes off to the pub early and, as soon as he's gone, I escape too, so that I don't have to walk home in the dark, with the now ever-present fear that I'm being followed. Plus, I'd promised Rory I'd cook dinner tonight.

It's twilight as I make my way through Queen Square after a detour to Tesco to pick up ingredients. Even so, as I head across the square I sense I'm being followed again and the back of my neck prickles, as though someone's eyes are boring into me. I turn quickly, while still walking, hoping to catch whoever it is off guard. A man is walking several paces behind me with a baseball cap pulled over his eyes. In the fading light it's hard to make out who it is, but my stomach drops. Is it Wayne Walker? Has he been following me all this time? I squint, trying to get a better look, but the peak of the cap has cast shadows over his face so I can't make out his features. He's tall. Too tall for Wayne, I think. There's something about his gait that reminds me of Adam. I know he went to the police station with Margot earlier, but it's possible she went back to Tilby on her own and he stayed behind to spy on me. What does he want? How can—Oomph! I walk straight into a bin, banging my leg in the process. I swear under my breath, rubbing my leg, hoping I haven't bruised myself. When I turn around, the man is walking in the opposite direction.

I'M SURROUNDED BY MESS: CHOPPED VEGETABLES ON THE COUNTER, noodles spilling out of an opened bag, the carcass of a waxy pepper and its core. The wok is too hot and some bean sprouts and chicken strips are sticking to the base, already burned, but I dump the noodles in regardless. A stir-fry. How hard can that be? Bloody hard as it turns out.

"You're supposed to keep stirring," says a voice, over my shoulder. I jump. Rory's home too early. I didn't hear him come in. This was supposed to be a surprise.

"I hate cooking," I mumble, picking up a spatula and prodding the noodles, feeling sweat prickle under my armpits.

He laughs in my ear, wrapping his arms around my waist. "I've noticed." He spins me around so that I'm facing him. He's still wearing his coat and his nose is red with the cold. I can smell rain on him. "But it's the thought that counts. And you know stir-fries are my favorite." He kisses me.

I bat him away good-naturedly, turning back to the cooking. "You're distracting me."

"Okay, okay. I'm going to take my coat off. I'll leave you in peace." He retreats with his coat folded over his arms.

He's in a good mood. The job must be going well. I'm going

to tell him. Once I've finished making his favorite food and opened a bottle of wine, I'm going to be honest about everything. I know I wasn't being paranoid earlier in Queen Square. That man had been following me, and when he saw I'd noticed he turned and went back in the opposite direction. If it is Adam, then why? What does he want from me?

We sit at Aoife's little round table in the dining-room end of the open-plan kitchen–sitting room, with a view of the river. Rory makes a good stab at the food despite its charcoal aftertaste. He knows I've done this for him. He holds my hand across the table and tells me about his day in one of the tougher Bristol schools and uses words like "rewarding" and "challenges." All the while the food churns in my stomach and I hardly touch my wine.

Rory's always been honest with me about what he wants. Marriage, and babies, a big, happy, bustling family like the one he came from. He wants loyalty and honesty; he doesn't believe in lying. Even little white lies. Once, I didn't want to go out with his university friends. It wasn't that I don't like them; they're good fun and I love hearing stories about what they got up to when they all shared a house together. They called Rory Mrs. Mopp because he was the one who cooked and cleaned. But on that particular night I was tired and just wanted to stay in and watch TV. I asked him to make an excuse for me, but he didn't. He told them the truth when they came by to pick us up. "Sorry, mate, Jessie would rather stay in and watch *Mad Men* tonight," he said while I squirmed. Rory didn't mind. He was good-natured about it and went out anyway. "I don't see the point of lying," he'd said, when I'd questioned him about it afterward. And I love that. Really, I do. But sometimes it's a lot to live up to.

I take a deep breath. "I need to be honest with you. I've done something," I begin.

His face falls, the fork to his lips. "Oh, God. What have you done? Have you poisoned the food?" He laughs.

"Rory. Be serious. This is important."

"Okay, okay." He takes a forkful of noodles, his eyes shining.

"I lied to you," I blurt out, "about why we left London." And then I tell him everything, about the phone hacking and Wayne Walker and his threats and how I think he—or someone—may be following me now.

His eyes widen and he swallows. "You got *sacked*?"

"I was lucky I didn't get arrested," I say, putting my fork down.

"So we left London and my job—which I loved—so that you could run away?" He puts his fork down too.

"More of a fresh start," I mutter. "Not running away. As such."

"And this Wayne guy? You think he's followed you here?"

"I don't know," I admit. "I feel like I'm being followed."

He leans back in his chair. "Jesus. Phone hacking. What were you thinking?" And there it is. That look. The look I've been dreading. He's seeing me for who I really am. He's not going to want to marry me, or have babies with me, or any of the other things he's planned and I feel . . . *relieved*.

"It's better that you know now . . . who I really am."

His frown deepens. "What are you talking about? You're not a bloody murderer. You made a mistake. Wayne Walker should never have threatened you like that anyway, regardless."

"But I lied."

"I know. And it makes me feel sad that you weren't honest with me at the time. But, Jess, why are you telling me this now?" And then it dawns on him. He's not stupid, my Rory. "You've found the ring, haven't you?"

That sodding ring. The antique ruby ring I'd stupidly admired in that boutique in Clifton during the summer. Ever since I found it nestled in his underwear drawer a few weeks ago, I've been waiting for the proposal. And I'm just not ready. I'm not ready to settle down and become somebody's wife. Why can't things stay as they are?

"I wasn't snooping. I was looking for some socks." He knows I'm always stealing his socks, even if they are too big, as one of mine always seems to go missing.

He pushes his plate away. He's lost the color in his face. He doesn't say anything, just stares at me as though wondering who I am. I look away, unable to witness the pain I see in his eyes. Eventually he asks, "Don't you want to be with me anymore?"

My stomach twists. "Of course I do. I love you. I just . . ."

"You don't want to get married to me?"

Tears spring to my eyes. "Just not yet."

He sighs. "Jess. We've been together for nearly three years. We've been living together for a year."

"I know."

"I'm thirty-five. I want kids. Lots of kids. I want to move back to Ireland eventually. I thought you wanted all that too."

I hang my head.

"What are you so afraid of?"

My head shoots up. "Nothing." I clench my fists in my lap. "I'm not afraid of anything. It's just moving too fast. Okay. We live together, don't we? We haven't even bought our own place yet. We're not in a position to get married. Financially."

He doesn't say anything for a few minutes, but then, "We could afford to buy our own place in Ireland. That's why we're living here practically rent-free. So we can save."

Ireland again. This is his dream. Not mine. And then what? He'll saddle me with a couple of kids and do a runner, like my dad, leaving me to bring them up on my own. In a country I'm not familiar with. Away from my friends and family. Not that I've got much family . . . or that many friends left. I gulp.

He reaches across the table, as though reading my mind. "I'm not your dad, Jess."

"I know," I say. "I know that."

"I don't think you do," he mumbles, getting up from the table and taking our plates to the sink.

I sit there for a while, staring at the half-drunk bottle of wine on the table. The lights twinkle in the distance, reflecting in the dark, undulating river. I feel as if I'm at a crossroads in my life—I was at the same point a year ago when we moved from London. But I didn't want to face it then. I wanted Rory. I still want him, but I don't know if I'll ever be ready for marriage and kids. I look across at him in the kitchen. He's standing staring at the kettle as if wondering what it does and my heart sinks. I should go to him, reassure him, tell him how much I want to make our relationship work. He bought me a ring because I said I loved it. This funny, sexy, kind man wants to spend the rest of his life with me. *Me*. And I'm scared. Rory was right about that.

Rory turns to me, the hurt still in his eyes. He looks like someone's kicked him in the stomach. "I'm going for a drink," he says, moving toward the hall for his coat.

I get up from the table and follow him. "On your own?" Rory never drinks alone.

"One of the other supply teachers I'm working with asked if I'd meet him for a drink tonight. I said I couldn't. Obviously. But now . . ." He shoves his arms into his navy duffle coat, his dark hair falling over his forehead as he fiddles with the toggles. I call it his Paddington Bear coat. It suits him. It makes him look bookish, but sexy. I long to go to him, to reassure him, but I'm rooted to the spot, unable to do anything but stare as he slips his shoes on without undoing the laces—the same ones he wore for work. He still hasn't had the chance to get changed.

"When will you be back?" I try not to sound whiny. That was how my mum sounded when my dad went out all hours, before he left for good.

He looks at me then, our eyes meeting properly for the first time, and his face softens. "I just need some space to take in what you've said." He attempts a smile. "I'm disappointed but I'll get over it. You know I'll wait until you're ready." He reaches for my hand, squeezing it. "I don't want anyone else."

And then he's gone, leaving me standing alone in the hallway, wondering what I've done.

I WISH THERE WAS SOMEONE I COULD ASK FOR ADVICE. I HAVE TRAN-sient relationships with the friends I do have, colleagues I've worked with, friends from university, and I still keep in touch with Gina from school—although she's moved to Denmark now—yet nothing deep, no dark confessions over a glass of wine, no insights into what I really think or feel. I've never really let anyone in, apart from Heather, and look what happened there. Even with Rory and Jack I still keep a part of myself hidden, preserved.

I slump onto the sofa, my mobile in my lap. We don't have a landline. It's easier that way. I think of my mum in Spain, not really knowing anything about my life, too busy with her husband, her friends, and her expat community. We've drifted further apart over the years. But I call her anyway, suddenly desperate to hear her voice. It rings for a while and just when I contemplate hanging up, she answers.

"Hello, Jessiebobs," she says, her voice tinkling and light, but behind it I can hear the drone of indistinct chatter, the clink of cutlery, the faint laughter that tells me she's out. Jessiebobs. She used to call me that all the time when I was a kid. "This is a surprise."

I'll say. We haven't spoken in months. There are no weekly calls from Spain, no texts to check that I'm okay, not like Rory and his mum.

"Just thought I'd ring to catch up," I say.

"It's a Friday night." She sounds puzzled. Of course. I should have realized. My mum has a better social life than I do. "I'd have thought you'd be out."

"You obviously are." I can't help the note of bitterness creeping into my voice.

She sighs. "Yes. Yes, I am . . ." Her voice is suddenly drowned by a burst of laughter. "Listen, Jess, I can't talk now. Can I ring you back tomorrow?"

"I . . . Yes, that's great."

"Speak soon. Love you." And the phone goes dead.

I stare at the screen for a few moments before tossing it onto the sofa. It's only seven thirty but now the evening looms ahead and I feel lonely and trapped in this apartment that doesn't feel like mine. I wander into the bedroom with photographs of Aoife and her friends taken on various nights out over the bed, and open the top drawer in Rory's side cabinet, retrieving the little square box. I sit on the edge of the bed and admire the ring again. It really is beautiful. I try it on to find it's only a little bit big. Why can't I be normal? Heather got married. Heather had a baby.

My mind goes back to when Margot let us spend the night in one of the static caravans. It must have been only a few months before that fateful summer and the caravan park was quiet, the season not yet kicking in. We took a four-berth right on the edge of the park, with views of the cliffs and the bay of Tilby. We could have had a bedroom each but we'd slept in the living-room part with the sofa folded down into a bed. It was early April and cold, and we'd huddled together in our individual sleeping bags, talking of all the things we would do when we left school.

"I never want to get married," I'd said, pulling the edge of the sleeping bag up to my chin. It smelled mildewy. "I want to travel. See the world. Not be tied down by some man."

"Same," agreed Heather, wriggling like a maggot in her luminous yellow sleeping bag. "I want to go to Paris and write and wander along the Left Bank and maybe take a lover."

We'd laughed at this. Take a lover. It was something we'd heard in a film and now it was a running joke. We weren't going to be tied down. We'd just take a lover.

Yet Heather never left Tilby or, as far as I can work out, took a lover. She met Adam at eighteen and married him at twenty-two. Margot had said he was her first and only boyfriend.

I'd been twenty-nine when I'd met Rory, and he definitely hadn't been my first. Far from it.

I push the ring back into its padded box and hide it under Rory's socks, so that I can no longer see it, as though the sight of it would burn my retinas. I turn off the light and I'm about to leave the room when my eyes catch something across the road through the bedroom window. I step forward, half-hidden by Aoife's retro-print curtains. In one of the upstairs windows on the third floor of the derelict building I can see the faint silhouette of a person. I can't make out whether it's male or female but they're holding a torch and directing it right at me. Can they see me? They probably could earlier when I was sitting on the bed with the curtains open and the lights on. I shudder at the thought.

The building used to be an old granary and flour warehouse. Are squatters living there? Or is someone hanging out there to spy on me? I step forward and draw the curtains tightly.

As I head back into the living room I hear my mobile ringing. I grab it from where I'd slung it on the sofa, hoping it's Rory, but I'm surprised when Margot's name flashes up.

"Jess?"

I've noticed she calls me Jess now, like she did when I was a kid.

"Speaking. Are you okay?" She sounds upset.

"I—I know I'm interrupting your evening and you're probably busy . . ."

"I'm not busy." I give a fake laugh. "I'm actually home alone."

There's a pause. "Oh. Right. I thought you'd be out. You always were such a social butterfly."

Was I? I suppose I was once. Now the only thing I seem to do is work or come home and slump in front of the TV with Rory, watching box sets, broken up by the occasional drink at the pub with Jack. "I don't go out much." When did that happen? Since we left London? Or before?

"Anyway," she continues, "I had a call from the police. About the fingerprints on the gun. They've identified mine and Adam's but also, another set."

I stand up straighter. Now this is interesting. "Really? Whose?"

She sighs. "They don't know."

"But," I begin pacing the room, "this is good, right? It means Heather might not have pulled the trigger. Someone else was there." I realize, with a jolt, that I'm desperate for Heather to be innocent. How can I be objective in my reporting now?

"I—I'm not sure . . ." She sounds lost and my heart aches for her.

"Margot? Is Adam with you? Have you told him about the other set of fingerprints on the gun?"

The line crackles a little and I go to stand near the balcony doors. "He went to see Heather. And the . . ." Her voice cuts out, then comes back in again, like a radio being tuned. "I think he's at his mum's with Ethan." She sounds very far away.

"Margot," I shout, so that she can hear me. "Can I come over?" It will only take twenty minutes to get there at this time of night.

"Now?" More static. "Are you sure?"

I've never been more sure of anything. My own mother might not have time for me, but Margot always has. "I'll see you soon." I abort the call, then scribble a note for Rory telling him where I am, grab my keys, and rush out of the door.

I take the lift down to the basement and dart to my Nissan. The car park is small and well lit and there are other vehicles, although no people. I can't help but feel a little unnerved as I unlock the door and slide behind the wheel. I immediately click on the central locking and start the engine. It's not until I drive out of the exit that I notice it in my rearview mirror, and I know that this time it's not my imagination. There's definitely someone standing by my building, watching as I pull away.

23

IT'S FUNNY WHAT YOU DREAM ABOUT IN THIS STATE OF NOT-QUITE-HERE. I'M *not dead but at this moment I'm not living. I'm in limbo. Waiting to wake up, in and out of consciousness, with images from my past drifting through the fog, like a surreal version of* This Is Your Life. *I don't like to think of my long-ago dead father, but I hope that if I end up joining him, if there is an afterlife, then he'll forgive us.*

He wasn't always a nice man. He bullied the two of us for years, didn't he? Even Mum. We were better off without him in so many ways. But if he'd lived, if we hadn't had to leave him behind in Kent, then what followed might never have taken place.

I would never have ended up hurting you.

Mum. She needs to know the truth. If I die now, my story will disappear with me.

I can't allow that to happen.

24

Margot

THE POLICE HAD REVEALED SOMETHING ELSE TO MARGOT ON THE phone. Something she's desperate to tell someone about. That was one of the reasons she'd called Jessica. In that moment she felt Jess would understand, knowing Heather as she had.

After she'd put the phone down to Ruthgow, she immediately rang Adam, who had sounded his usual cynical self, warning her not to take it too seriously, that it didn't mean anything, it could be a fingerprint from ages ago, and she found she couldn't tell him the rest. He'd only find a way to downplay it and she needed something. She needed hope.

She'd been distracted momentarily by the arrival of a couple wanting to rent a caravan. It was unusual at this time of year: it gets very cold and windy up here as the field with the camping site has views of the sea, although the occasional punter did turn up, usually a rambler who was braving the cliff walks. But it wasn't until Easter that business began to pick up and that was still three weeks away.

The couple who turned up were young, around Heather's age. They looked mismatched: him tall and gangly with glasses and not much to say, and her pretty, petite, and bubbly, talking for both of them. She'd asked a few probing questions about Heather, saying she'd read about it in the newspaper. It made Margot wonder, as she showed them to a caravan, if they were journalists. Even so, she wasn't about to turn away their business. If the newspaper they worked for was foolish enough to pay for them to stay, she'd take their money, thank you very much. But they wouldn't get a word out of her. And she knows Adam would never talk. Sheila has been a friend for years—yes, she can be a bit of a gossip, but she's loyal. Margot made sure she was polite to the couple, but she evaded their questions expertly—she's had enough practice this last week—telling them where she was if they needed anything, not that they should: the caravans are well stocked, with a running shower and hot water.

But when she got back to the dark, empty house she realized there was nobody to call. She's definitely found out who her friends are since this happened. Women from her shooting club, whom she's known since she moved here, have shunned her. Even the postman, whom she's been chatting to for twenty years and who is always so cheery, avoided eye contact when she saw him scuttling up the path yesterday. And then there are the others, friends who have lost touch over the years now ringing up to get the lowdown. Pam had popped in briefly two days ago, but had seemed edgy and uncomfortable, going out of her way to make sure she didn't utter Heather's name.

When Flora went missing everyone rallied around. For weeks her friends would sit with her, or bring homemade lasagnas, letting her talk or cry, comforting her, helping her with the business and the horses. But those same people are now acting as though she has a contagious disease. She's no longer somebody to be pitied. She's the mother of a killer.

Margot's never felt more alone.

So, when Jessica suggested coming over Margot found herself agreeing, desperate for company.

It's just gone eight when the doorbell rings but Margot's ready for it, like a dog that's been left in the house for days by its owner. She opens the door onto the starless night, a moth buzzing around the outside light that's illuminating Jessica. Beyond her is darkness, thick and encompassing, as though they're under a giant tent. The campsite isn't visible from here, or the stables, but she can hear the horses whinnying to each other.

Jess isn't in her llama coat today. Instead she's huddled in an oversize parka that swamps her frame and makes her look young and vulnerable. She also seems tired and a little sad. Gone is the hard-faced journalist expression she usually wears, making Margot wonder if it's all just an act. She doesn't blame her. By the sound of it, the poor girl has had to stand on her own two feet for so long that it's not surprising she had to toughen up. She remembers Simone as a crisp, efficient woman, who made sure Jess was clean and fed and clothed in the latest fashions, but she wasn't particularly warm toward her, and would think nothing of leaving her alone all day and late into the evening. When Heather had mentioned it, worrying about her friend in her usual way, Margot's heart had ached at the thought of small, scrappy Jess sitting alone in the house with nobody for company, having to help herself to her own microwave dinner while she waited for her mother to get back from work or her latest date. So, Margot had welcomed her into their family.

It feels like she's doing the same again, if under different circumstances this time.

Her breath fogs out in front of her and Margot thinks again of the young couple in the caravan, trying to get warm. At least Colin is now hardened to it.

"Thank you for coming over," Margot says, opening the door wider to allow Jess over the threshold. She starts to take off her trainers, but Margot tells her not to. "The boards need resanding. This place is going to the dogs." It's too much upkeep, now that it's just her.

She ushers Jess into the kitchen. The Aga is on, and Jess stands next to it, warming her hands.

"I don't know if you've eaten already, but I've got some chicken soup," she offers, going to the pan simmering on the hob. "Do you want some?"

Jess grins. "I hardly ate my dinner. I'd love some. Thank you."

She sits at the kitchen table while Margot dishes out soup for them both, and rummages in the bread bin. There's a loaf Adam brought home a few days ago from the farm shop. A bit stale but it will be okay with soup. Margot hasn't had the chance to go shopping since Heather's been in hospital.

She sits opposite Jess, placing a plate of the stale bread between them. "Is everything okay?"

"I should be asking you that," says Jess, her brown eyes full of concern. "How's Heather?"

Margot swallows some soup. It's too hot and scalds her mouth. "The same. I worry, sometimes, that she'll be in a coma for years. The doctors assure me that's rare. But they also say with head injuries everybody is different."

Jess nods, then eats a few spoonfuls before adding, "And how's Adam coping?"

Margot tears off a piece of bread and sinks it into the soup. She hasn't got much appetite. She's eating, sleeping, washing, feeding the horses, cleaning mechanically, like a robot. "Adam is . . . struggling, I think. He's never been the most communicative of men, but now it's like he's gone into himself." He'd be furious if he knew she had Jess here.

"I can understand that," she says. "And the fingerprints. The police think someone else held the gun that morning? Not just Heather?"

Margot hesitates, suddenly unsure if this was a good idea. She knows she's agreed to an exclusive but this information is so new, so precious, that she feels she wants to nourish and protect it, like a seedling, giving it time to grow. But, on the other hand, if those fingerprints put doubt on the fact that Heather carried out the horrific shootings, well, she'd want everyone to know it.

Jess must notice her conflicting emotions because she sits back in her chair, putting the spoon down. "I'm here tonight as a friend. Not as a journalist," she says.

Can Margot believe her? She studies her face. She's hardly changed, not really. Aged, of course, but underneath the new fine lines and the makeup and the heavy fringe she sees the same Jess who practically lived with them for two years. She was like a member of the family for a time.

"In that case let me open a bottle of wine. I could do with a drink," says Margot, getting up and going over to the wine rack. She picks a Chablis and pours them both a glass. "I just wish I knew exactly what happened that morning," she says, passing a glass to Jess. "If only Heather had an alibi."

Jess hesitates. "I'm not supposed to drink in the week and I'm driving."

Margot wonders why Jess can't drink in the week. Has she been forbidden to? Keith used to try to boss her about, telling her what she could and couldn't do. Is that what's happening with Jess? She can't imagine it. It's obviously a self-imposed rule. "Just one won't hurt," she says, and Jess takes it, setting it down next to her bowl.

"Was it normal for Heather and Adam to argue to such an extent that he'd walk out?" she asks, surprising Margot.

'I don't know. I didn't think so. But they live in the coach house, near the caravan site, so I wouldn't always know."

Jess frowns. "And you still don't know what they argued about?"

"I've never asked." She probably should, but Adam is so private and she's worried about upsetting him. He has so much to deal with right now. He must feel guilty about leaving Heather alone like that, especially if she was feeling depressed and suicidal. "I don't want to believe Heather would be capable of such a thing. She's not trigger happy. She's not particularly into guns. She's never been interested in coming clay-pigeon shooting with me. But that neighbor of the Wilsons—he saw her. He saw her leaving the house with a gun. If it wasn't Heather, how do you explain that?"

Jess pushes her fringe out of her face, her expression troubled.

"And I know," Margot continues, desperate to get it all off her chest, now that someone is here to listen, "that Heather shot my husband. And I keep telling myself that it was an accident. But what if it wasn't?" It must be the wine talking. She's drinking it too quickly and it's going to her head. All her dark fears are spewing out of her mouth and she can't control them. "He wasn't always a good husband. Or father. He could be cruel."

Jess raises her eyebrows. "Heather never said."

"It wasn't anything abusive. He didn't hit us. I would have left him if he had. He was ex-army and hard. A bully, I suppose, looking back, although I didn't think so at the time. He instilled fear in the girls. If they put a foot wrong, he'd scream at them. They were nervous wrecks around him. It's no wonder Heather shot him by accident—I can just imagine his rage when he found her fiddling with that gun. She would have been nervous and her finger would have slipped." She sighs heavily. "He wasn't like that when I first met him, or when the girls were really little. But he changed. I think he suffered from mental-health problems. Depression, maybe PTSD, but twenty years ago we weren't so aware of these things." She doesn't know why she's telling Jess all of this.

She's surprised when Jess reaches across the table and takes her hand. "I think you're amazing."

Margot's cheeks flame. "Amazing? I'm anything but."

"I always thought you were an excellent mum. And the way you coped with what happened to Flora. Now this . . . and I didn't even know about what you went through with Keith."

Margot chews her lip. She's not used to someone being so kind to her and she's annoyed with herself when tears sting her eyes. "Oh, shush," she says. "There's nothing I can do but carry on, is there? I need to be there for Heather when she wakes."

Jess nods and removes her hand.

"Are you okay here with me on a Friday night? Shouldn't you be with your fella?" says Margot.

Jess toys with the stem of her glass. "He wants to get married and have kids," she blurts out, "and I'm not ready. I feel like the worst person ever because I love him. He's so good, you know. I'm realizing how hard that is to find . . ."

"There's no rush. You're still young."

Jess smiles stiffly. "Yes."

Margot studies her. "Are you worried about your career?"

Jess shakes her head. "No. Not really. To be honest, since I've moved away from London I've been a bit disenchanted with the whole journalism thing."

Margot doesn't understand what drove Jess to become a journalist in the first place, but she doesn't want to say that. It's obvious the poor girl is suffering some inner turmoil and she doubts there's much she can say to help without knowing the facts. She does wonder, though, if it's to do with Jess's upbringing. She was practically neglected by Simone, and there was never any sign of the father, but it seemed to be socially acceptable because the Foxes were considered middle class and Simone had a good job as a legal secretary. She wonders now if it would have been different if Jess had been from the only council estate in Tilby. She would probably have been hauled into the care system.

"DCI Ruthgow turned up yesterday," she says, watching Jess carefully. "He worked on Flora's disappearance."

Jess looks interested. "What did he say?"

Margot sighs. "I'm worried he thinks Heather had something to do with it."

She's relieved to see that Jess looks suitably shocked. "With Flora's disappearance?"

She nods.

"Bloody hell. Surely not. What does he think Heather's done? Shot her, too, and then buried the body?"

Margot winces. She would never have believed Heather capable of something like that. But, then again, she'd never have believed Heather could shoot dead two people.

"She was only fourteen at the time," says Jess. "Jesus."

Heather was only ten when she shot her father. But Margot pushes the thought away. Ruthgow is wrong. She knows that, deep down, no matter what else Heather has done she'd never hurt Flora.

She remembers the white blouse she'd had to identify. The bloom of blood at the front. Could that have come from a gunshot wound?

Margot feels sick at the thought. With trembling hands she pours herself another glass of wine and offers more to Jess.

Jess declines. "I'd better not."

Before Margot has the chance to think about it she says, "You can stay here tonight. If you like?" She doesn't know why she makes the offer, really. Maybe it's because she's so fed up with spending the night alone in this big old house. It would be lovely to have some company again.

Sometimes, when Adam was away or she wanted some space, Heather would stay over in her old room. And when Ethan came along he would stay with her. Those were Margot's favorite times, when it was just the three of them.

Jess opens her mouth, looking surprised. "I . . . Well, that's really kind of you, but I'd better not. Rory—my boyfriend—he'll be expecting me home."

Margot tries to look understanding despite the hard stone of disappointment lodged in her chest.

"I've been thinking about Deirdre a lot," Margot says, trying to move the conversation on. She hasn't seen Jess in nearly twenty years and now here she is, asking her to stay over. Jess must think she's lonely and desperate. "And wondering what transpired between her and Heather when she stayed here earlier this year. I haven't told the police yet."

"Oh, Margot! You should," says Jess. "I think Clive was into some dodgy dealings. I found a card outside his mother's house, the kind that comes with flowers. It said, 'This was one bullet you couldn't dodge.' He obviously had enemies."

Margot pushes her bowl of soup away from her. She's hardly eaten any and it's cold. Since Heather was taken to hospital the weight has been falling off her. Now her collarbones jut out and her once tight-fitting jodhpurs are loose. "But his mother, Deirdre. Surely not her." *This was one bullet you couldn't dodge.* Where has she read that before?

Jess shrugs and Margot notices she hasn't eaten much either. "I don't know. I'm in the process of gathering more information about them from the neighbors. But as they haven't lived there that long . . ." Jess sighs.

Margot stretches, her back hurting on the hard chair. She suggests they move into the living room and Jess nods encouragingly. She can see, by the clock on the wall, that it's gone nine. She doesn't want Jess to leave yet.

It's not until they've settled at either end of the sofa, Margot with another drink in her hand, Jess with water, that she reveals the nugget of information she's been keeping to herself.

"When the police called about the fingerprints, they said something else," she admits. "About Heather."

Jess sits forward, her eyes brimming with expectation.

"Her car was caught on CCTV earlier that morning. The morning of the shootings. At around five a.m. Fifteen miles away. In Bristol."

Jessica's eyes widen. "In Bristol?"

"Yes. Southville."

"What would she be doing there?"

"I don't know. The police asked if we know anyone who lives in that area but we don't. I just don't understand what she would have been doing in Bristol at that time in the morning. I keep thinking about it. Was she looking for her victim, with a shotgun in the car? I just . . ." Margot covers her face with her hands.

"Oh, Margot . . ."

They're interrupted by the shrill buzzing of Margot's phone. They both turn toward where it sits on the coffee table. Margot reaches for it. "It's Adam. I'd better answer," she says.

Margot's never heard her son-in-law sound so animated. "I've had a call from the hospital, Marg. It's Heather. She's come around. She's awake."

25

Margot

MARGOT DOESN'T THINK OF THE MILLIONS OF QUESTIONS SWIRL-
ing around in her brain, or that she's just left Jess sitting outside
the ICU as though she's no more than a chauffeur. All she can
concentrate on, as she runs down the corridor, only half-aware
that Adam is following, and brushes past the policewoman still
standing guard and into Heather's room, is that she's awake. Her
daughter is awake.

The doctors warned Margot when it first happened that
Heather might not be herself if she came around. That the longer she spent in a coma the higher the chance that she could be
in a permanent vegetative state. No, all Margot cares about is
having her baby back in her arms. Her warm-blooded, breathing, conscious daughter.

Heather is propped up by pillows when she comes in, although her face is pale and she's still attached to a drip. Margot

rushes over to her and tentatively gathers her into her arms, careful of the wires. "Oh, my darling," she says, into Heather's hair. And then she sits beside her on the chair and takes her hand.

Heather stares at her, and just as Margot begins to wonder if her daughter recognizes her, her face breaks into a watery smile. "Hi, Mum," she says, and it's like music to Margot's ears. The sweetest, most wonderful sound she's ever heard. She wants to bury her head in her daughter's lap and sob, with relief and fear. But she doesn't. She needs to be stoic. She knows there's still a long way to go.

Instead she blinks away the tears. "Oh, sweetheart." She brings Heather's hand to her lips. "We've been so worried about you."

"My mouth is dry." Her lips are sore and cracked. Margot takes the cup of water from Heather's side table and places it to her lips. Heather leans forward to take a few sips, then leans back against the pillows. Margot can see through the glass panel in the door that Adam is outside talking to the doctor. Why hasn't he rushed in here to see his wife?

"How are you feeling, sweetheart?" she asks, aware of what a silly question it is.

"I feel like I've had a fight with a bus. Was I in some kind of accident?"

Margot's stomach tightens. *She doesn't know.* "Um. What exactly has the doctor said?"

Heather looks around the room, bewilderment in her eyes. "That I've had an accident."

Margot brings the cup back to Heather's lips. "Well, let's wait to speak to them, shall we? Can you remember anything?" *What were you doing in Bristol? Why did you kill Clive and Deirdre Wilson?* She has to bite her lip to stop her questions spilling out of her mouth.

"They said I was in a coma."

Margot puts the cup down. "Yes. That's right. For seven whole days."

Heather touches the bandage on her head gingerly.

"Is it sore?" Margot asks.

Heather shakes her head, then winces. "A little." She's struggling to keep her eyes open. "Ethan?"

"Ethan's fine. He's with Gloria."

"I feel so tired," she says. Margot's heart hammers. Heather closes her eyes again. Is she back in the coma? Margot leaps up. "Heather." She shakes her gently. "Heather. Sweetheart."

Heather groans a little and her eyes flutter open. "I'm just tired," she says, and closes them again.

Dr. Khan comes into the room, Adam following close behind. She's the same female doctor that Margot has seen sporadically during the week. "She was talking to me," says Margot, trying to quell her panic, as though she'd been given this wonderful miracle only to have it snatched away again.

Dr. Khan, who looks to be in her late thirties, with gold-rimmed glasses and a glossy dark bun, bustles over to Heather, checking her vital signs. Then she turns to Margot and Adam. "Don't worry. She's just sleeping. Coma patients are often tired when they come around. And it can take a few days—longer in some cases—for the disorientation to wear off. Heather only woke up a few hours ago."

A few hours. Why didn't someone ring before? Why hadn't Margot been with her? Or Adam? Heather had woken up and been alone. She must have felt scared, wondering where she was and what had happened.

"I've just been explaining to Mr. Underwood," Dr. Khan smiles reassuringly at Adam, "that we've done all the necessary checks and the signs are very encouraging. Heather has regained full consciousness."

"What about brain damage?" Margot asks.

"As far as we're aware, there is no sign of damage or trauma to the brain. However, it does seem that Heather has trouble remembering the"—she swallows and pushes her glasses further up her nose, glancing briefly at the sleeping Heather—"incident that brought her here. But, again, this is sometimes the case."

"She knew who I was," Margot says.

Adam strides past her and perches on the chair Margot only recently vacated. He takes Heather's hand in his large one and, with the other, smooths her silky dark hair from her forehead. "Hello, love," he says to her. "It's Adam. I'm here."

Her eyes flicker open and lock with his, and Margot sees such intimacy between them that she feels as though she's intruding.

Even though Margot wants never to leave Heather's side again, she knows they need time alone and steps out of the room, along with the doctor.

They glance at the policewoman, who's still standing outside Heather's door, like a security guard or a bouncer. Margot would love to tell her to bugger off and that she's encroaching on a private family moment. Instead she moves away and Dr. Khan follows. "It's really encouraging," Dr. Khan says again, when they're out of earshot of the officer. "This is the best possible outcome we could have expected for Heather."

"I know visiting hours are over, but can I stay?"

She flashes Margot a regretful smile. "I think Heather needs rest right now. She's in the best hands, Mrs. Powell, I can assure you of that."

MARGOT GOES TO FIND JESS IN THE MAIN WAITING ROOM. IT'S NOW eleven o'clock, and the room is dimly lit and nearly empty, apart from Jess flicking through a magazine in the corner, and a bloke staring into space, sipping from a coffee cup.

Jess jumps up when she notices Margot. "How is she?"

Jess looks tired, Margot thinks, and some of her mascara has smudged around her eyes. "She's surprisingly well. No sign of brain damage. Although she's very tired. Adam's still with her but the doctor said it would be best for me to come back first thing."

Jess rushes into Margot's arms. "I'm so pleased," she says, giving her a hug. "That's great news. It must be such a relief."

Margot steps away, suddenly feeling like a traitor. What would Heather think if she knew that Margot had been fraternizing with her onetime best friend? Would she mind? "Do you need a lift home?" says Jess, pulling her parka around her and stifling a yawn.

"That's really kind but I'll wait for Adam. Thank you, Jess. For tonight."

Jess smiles shyly. "I'm glad I could help. And I'm so happy that Heather's going to be okay."

She gives Margot a wave and leaves the room. Margot watches her go, unable to stop the smile spreading across her face. Heather's awake. And now, at last, they might finally get some answers.

26

Jess

BRISTOL DAILY NEWS
Monday, March 19, 2012

THE SEASIDE SHOOTER'S FRIEND REVEALS ALL

by Harriet Hill

A FAMILY friend of the alleged Seaside Shooter who killed a Tilby couple revealed the moment she found her.

Mother and son Deirdre and Clive Wilson were shot dead in their home last Friday, the 9th. The suspect, Heather Underwood, 32, is currently in a coma in hospital after turning the gun on herself.

Sheila Bannerman, 58, who has worked with the family for years, had arrived at Tilby Manor Caravan Park at around 8 a.m. on the 9th to put out the horses to graze. She explained: "I'd gone into the main barn, as that's where the tack room is, to get a head collar for one of the horses when I found Heather. She was on the floor with the gun beside her and a wound to her chest. There was also a pool of blood surrounding her head. I thought she was dead, that she'd been murdered. I called the ambulance and they arrived within minutes. When I later found out that she was the one who had killed those two people and tried to take her own life—well, I couldn't believe it."

The Powell family, who have owned the caravan park since 1991, have had their share of tragedy. Margot Powell's elder daughter, Heather's sister Flora, disappeared in 1994 when she was only sixteen. The police never solved the case, although many locals, including Sheila herself, believe that Flora was murdered. "I knew the family back then," she said. "Flora's bloodstained blouse was found but never her body. Her uncle Leo was arrested at the time but released without charge. Leo always has had a liking for younger women and I think a lot of the locals believe that there's no smoke without fire, especially now he's left. We all wonder what he's running away from. Tilby's a safe, sleepy seaside town. For two awful tragedies to befall one family is particularly heart wrenching."

Sheila described Heather as a "happy, smiley woman," who is a brilliant mum to her son, Ethan, eighteen months. She said: "Heather was always quiet and thoughtful, but unfailingly polite. I've never heard a cross word from her, even as a teenager. She was exceptionally close to her sister, Flora, and I think her disappearance messed her up more than anyone would have thought. She suffered postnatal depression after her son was born and, as far as I'm aware, she was still on antidepressants. I think she must have just flipped. It's Margot I feel sorry for. She lived for those girls, you know."

Police are remaining tight lipped about what occurred on the 9th, but Heather Underwood is currently in hospital under police guard.

Avon and Somerset Police are urging anyone with any information to come forward.

I STARE IN DISBELIEF AT THE FRONT PAGE OF THE NEWSPAPER THAT Ted has slammed down in front of me.

"Why has the *Daily News* got this fucking story in today's paper, not us?" he bellows in my car.

I flinch. My heart is racing but I try to remain calm. I can feel Ellie's and Jack's eyes on me and my face burns. "Because I've been working on the exclusive with Margot Powell. It's nearly finished. Plus, I'm the only journalist who knows, at the moment, that Heather has actually woken up from her coma." It's not fair of Ted to compare. The *News* is a daily whereas we come out on Tuesday and Friday.

"Well, write it up as quick as you can and it can be our front-page headline tomorrow. Ellie can put it on the website too."

He pauses, as if considering something. Then, "And can you get hold of this Leo? Sounds like he was a suspect when Flora Powell went missing. He might know more about the current shootings or give us some insight into Heather's past."

What will Margot think if I go after her brother? I'm once again torn between wanting the story and my loyalty to the family.

"I thought the exclusive was going to be the front page." I'd spent all weekend working on it, mainly to avoid Rory, who still isn't really talking to me. I could hear him moving about the flat while I hid in the bedroom. He'd slept with his back to me on both nights, and I'd lain beside him craving a hug, but too stubborn to make the first move.

"That can go on page two."

Will Margot be cross if I reveal that Heather is awake? Ted won't care because, as far as he's concerned, we've got the exclusive now: she's signed the contract and can't go back on it. But, I realize with a jolt, I care. Margot and I are becoming friends. I enjoy her company and would love to see Heather again—despite what she's supposed to have done. I still want to believe she's innocent, that there is another explanation. And I don't want to turn my back on them, like everyone else has. Like this so-called friend of theirs, Sheila Bannerman. Am I turning soft? Ted would think so.

The newsroom is deathly silent as we all await Ted's next tirade. I brace myself.

"And have you followed up on Clive Wilson? Talked to neighbors? Found out why someone would leave him such a threatening note when he was already dead?" he barks.

"Jack and I had planned to do that today."

He looks mildly mollified, his shoulders relaxing a fraction. He chews his gum in silence for a couple of moments. Then, "Right. Good. But first you can write five hundred words on the fact Heather has come out of her coma and send it over to HQ. You've got an hour."

He stalks off before I've had a chance to reply and everyone lets out a collective breath when Ted is safely back in his "office." Jack widens his eyes over Seth's head with a "What's his problem?" gesture.

I bash out the five hundred words that Ted wants, keeping it as simple as I can, so that Margot doesn't find it offensive. I hesitate over revealing what Margot said about Heather not being able to remember. I was at the hospital as a friend on Friday night, not as a journalist, and it doesn't sit right with me that I'm somehow betraying the family by writing this.

But what choice do I have? I need this job.

I BREATHE IN THE SALTY SEA AIR, THE STRESS OF THE PAST FEW DAYS slowly ebbing away from me. Shackleton Road and the house where Clive and Deirdre were murdered are directly behind me. I'm standing where eyewitnesses say Heather parked, next to the wall overlooking the beach. The beach where we'd sometimes hang out, when we could be bothered to make the fifteen-minute walk. Tilby is hilly, and the town center a good hike from the beach. You have to walk up some very steep cobbled streets to get to the shops. It was always fun to walk down, but walking back up the steep hill was a different matter. If we had the money we'd get the bus.

The tide is out today and the sand spreads before me, new and unmarked, like freshly rolled pastry. The boats in the harbor are marooned and it's funny to see them beached. When the tide is in, though, the water reaches right up to this wall.

I've managed to get hold of Leo. He was surprised to hear from me. He lives in Bristol now, and has agreed to meet me after work at a café in Park Street. I feel apprehensive at the thought of seeing him again, especially as I kept it from him that I'm now a reporter. He thinks I'm only interested in catching up.

Jack is standing beside me, looking thoughtfully out to sea, a hint of a smile on his face.

"It's not exactly Brighton, is it?" I laugh. Jack has been in a strange mood today. He's quieter than normal and a lot of my banter has gone straight over his head.

He shrugs. "I'd like to live here."

"Really?" It's not a particularly sophisticated or happening place. The town is mostly full of chains or pound shops, the only arcade further up the hill. And, driving along the high street to get to the beach, it doesn't look like it's changed much. "I lived on the other side of town. No sea views for me."

He laughs. "Still. A beach on your doorstep is a good thing."

"It was hardly on my doorstep. I was surrounded by coun-tryside mostly. There were a lot of cowpats."

He turns so that he's facing the row of terraced houses on Shackleton Road and starts taking more snaps. I follow him as he enters the Wilsons' front garden. There are no new flowers or cards, and the bouquets that were left there after it happened are all dead, the leaves paper thin and brown. I wonder who will remove them. A family member, perhaps. I think of the message, *This was one bullet you couldn't dodge.* Who could have written it? And why?

I still can't believe this happened. That Heather did something so . . . *brutal.*

"I want to try the other next-door neighbors again," I say to Jack, as he stands back, checking his viewfinder. They were away on the day of the shootings, but they might know something about Clive or Deirdre.

I walk to the house on the right of the Wilsons'. It's painted a pale ice-cream pink, with shutters at the windows. It has an extra floor, dwarfing Deirdre and Clive's house. I knock, Jack at my shoulder, and wait, hoping they're in. It's eleven so they're most likely at work. Jack and I really need to try in the evening. Just when we're about to retreat down the front path, the door opens revealing a woman in a dressing gown. She's around forty, with a tissue pressed to her nose. She looks like she's just got out of bed.

"I'm so sorry to disturb you," I begin, then introduce myself and Jack. "Do you mind if I ask you some questions about your neighbors, Clive and Deirdre Wilson?"

She blinks at us, as though the light is too bright for her eyes. "Which paper are you from again?"

"The *Bristol and Somerset Herald.*"

She shrugs and, to my surprise and excitement, she lets us into the house. "Excuse the state of me," she says. "Terrible cold.

Taking a sickie. But don't put that in the paper." She laughs, then coughs dramatically while Jack and I look on helplessly.

When she's recovered she indicates that we follow her into the living room. It's spacious, decorated in various shades of gray, with a huge bay window and high ceilings. "Lovely place you've got here," I say. The view is even better from here than it is at the Brights' house, on the other side of the Wilsons', which is slightly obscured by the lifeboat station.

"Thanks. Please, sit."

Jack and I perch on the sofa, as far away from her as possible, not wanting to catch her germs. I reach into my bag for my notebook. "So, your name . . . ?"

She perches on the window seat. "I'm Netta Black."

"And how well did you know Deirdre and Clive?" I ask.

She pulls her dressing gown further around herself. It's nearly floor length and a deep sable velour. She glances at Jack self-consciously. "I've been here four years, and they moved in not that long ago, so I didn't know them very well, mostly just to say hello to, although my husband, George, went down the local pub—you know the Funky Raven?" I shake my head. "—with Clive a couple of times. Until he was barred."

"Your husband was barred?"

She laughs, then splutters into a handkerchief. "No. Clive was barred. I'm not sure why. Some disagreement with the owner. George didn't really know much about it. And Clive didn't always live here anyway. He stayed with his mum a couple of times a week but I think he'd got a place Bristol way."

This is news to me. His brother, Norman, had said Clive had had to move in with their mum because he was having financial troubles. I think of Heather and the fact she was spotted on CCTV in Bristol on the morning of the killings. "Do you know where in Bristol?"

She chews her lip. "Hmm. I think George mentioned it was in Southville."

Southville. That was where Heather had been. She must have gone looking for Clive earlier that morning. But why? And if she had, the murders weren't down to a spur-of-the-moment temporary insanity. They were premeditated. Planned. Jack's words about Heather being some secret assassin come back to me. No. That's not real life. Heather is a normal suburban wife and mother. Not some kind of hit woman. Then why?

I glance across at Jack, but he looks bored, his eyes unfocused, as though he's thinking about something else. I turn my attention back to Netta.

"And what did you make of Clive and Deirdre when you saw them?" I ask.

She chews her lip again, thinking. Then, "They seemed nice. Particularly Deirdre. I'd see her walking her cute dog on the beach. She was just an old lady. Honestly, it's dreadful what happened. This woman who the police say killed them—who was she?"

"I don't know," I lie. "And Clive?" I'm trying to get the conversation back on track. "What was he like?"

"Gruff. Typical bloke. He chatted to my husband but he seemed a bit awkward around me. Wouldn't look me in the eye, that kind of thing. George said he was just shy. But he wasn't young. He was a bit . . . what's the word? . . . rough at the edges. He wore sovereign rings and a gold chain around his neck. He had tattoos. You know the type?" She pulls a face and I'm shocked at her snobbery. I wonder what her assessment would be of me, sitting on her plush velvet couch with my bleached blond hair and my secondhand clothes.

I rearrange my legs, which are starting to go numb. "So, you weren't aware of any enemies he might have had?"

"Hmm. Well, the landlord of the Funky Raven for starters. And there might have been others."

"What's the landlord's name?"

"Stuart Patterson. He's a nice guy. Friendly. I don't know what Clive did to get on his wrong side because, as far as I'm aware, it's quite hard to piss off Stu."

I decide that's our next destination. I stand up. Jack does too, looking relieved to be going.

Netta follows suit, glancing at Jack's camera fearfully. "You don't want to take my photo, do you?"

Jack grins. "No, don't worry."

"Phew. I look a mess." She pats her expensively highlighted waves. Even though she's ill, it's still obvious she's an attractive woman.

"Thank you for your time," I say, as she shows us out. "And you're happy for us to name you in the newspaper?"

"Of course. My fifteen minutes of fame." Her gaze goes over my shoulder to Jack. "And if you want a photo, do come back another time when I'm in a better state." I'm sure she winks at him. Then she closes the door on us.

"Think you've got a fan there."

He laughs. "Well, you've either got it or you haven't. Maybe she likes the vulnerable look." He indicates his black eye that's now turning purple. I'm just about to retaliate when I freeze. There's a man in Clive and Deirdre's front garden. He's bent over a dying bouquet of daffodils, anger on his face, a fluffy dog that looks like a bear at his feet. I prod Jack in the shoulder blades and incline my head toward him. Jack widens his eyes and clears his throat.

There's only a small wired fence between the two front gardens and the man looks up. He's tall and lean, with receding gray hair. He's wearing a scarf wrapped tightly around his neck and a padded black coat. His face is long, thin, and weathered.

"Hi," he says, looking a little shifty and leaning back on his heels. "I'm not trespassing. My brother and my mum used to live here." He indicates the dog. "This is Hulk."

I recognize his voice instantly from the phone conversation we had. He looks older than I imagined, though, and more scraggy. "Norman? I'm Jess from the *Herald*. We spoke last week."

His eyes light up in recognition and he shakes my hand heartily over the fence. "What are you doing here?"

I quickly explain about the card I found with the flowers. "So I've just been asking the neighbors if they know if anybody had a grudge against him."

Something dark passes across Norman's face. "And what have they been saying?"

"Oh, nothing really. That Clive kept himself to himself."

He seems satisfied with this response. I daren't tell him I'm on the way to the Funky Raven to ask the landlord why Clive had been barred.

He thrusts his hands into his pockets and toes the lawn with his boot. "Yes, well, I think Clive made a few enemies along the way, if truth be told. He got into something dodgy back in Bristol. He didn't say what—but I got the impression he was running away, hence the move out here."

"Do you think the woman who killed Clive and your mum was hired?" Jack pipes up from behind me. I turn to glare at him. I'm the one who's supposed to be asking the questions. Why is Jack so obsessed by that ridiculous, far-fetched theory?

Norman looks shocked. "But why kill my mum? She's done nothing wrong. She was just an old lady." He runs his hand along his bald patch, and mumbles, as if to himself, "To be shot like that by a *woman*. I've heard the suspect is a wife and mother. Clive's no angel, don't get me wrong, but I can't help but think they were in the wrong place at the wrong time, y'know. This woman obviously has a screw loose and just snapped." He bends down to pat Hulk's head.

I haven't even mentioned to Jack yet what Margot told me the other night. That Deirdre had once stayed at the caravan park and Heather had met her. Was that just a coincidence?

And if Heather had just "snapped," why had she got into

the car and driven here? Why had she been in Bristol—near Clive's house—earlier that morning? Had she been looking for him?

Norman turns away, his face set, and begins picking up the dead flowers strewn on the lawn, throwing them into a black bin liner, Hulk at his heels. But I can tell from his body language there's something he's not saying.

27

August 1994

FLORA PEERED OUT OF HER BEDROOM WINDOW. ON THE LAWN BE-
low, shaded by the huge oak tree, Heather and Jess sat, sketch
pads on their laps, their pencils flying across the pages. They
were always drawing, those two. Their artwork had turned
darker this summer: Gothic headstones and gargoyles, their
faces distorted and ugly. They were obviously going through a
phase, as her mum would say. They had Heather's portable tape
player between them on the lawn, and she could hear the faint,
tinny strains of "Lovesong" by The Cure. She knew that her sister was keeping guard, stopping her sneaking out to meet Dylan.
She tried to pretend otherwise, of course, but Flora wasn't stupid.
Every time she ventured outside, Heather and Jess were there,
like her own personal bodyguards, with their insincere greet-
ings and pretense of asking her to help them with the horses, or
to clean one of the caravans or any of the other mind-numbingly

boring excuses they kept coming up with. She felt like a prisoner in her own home. And it was always there, unspoken between them: Heather's veiled threat to tell their mum. So Flora found herself humoring Heather and playing along. She should never have smoked that joint—Heather was even more disapproving of Dylan now.

But it had been two days and Flora felt she was going to die of a broken heart if she didn't see him soon. He might think she was going off him. He might meet someone else. She couldn't bear it any longer; she had to see him.

She watched as Heather jumped to her feet, throwing her arms wide and spinning around, singing loudly while Jess looked on, giggling. Heather was wearing a lemon-yellow sundress and looked beautiful and innocent as she twirled on the lawn. Flora felt an unexpected pang of tenderness toward her. She knew her sister was only looking out for her. But, still, it could be stifling. She was the eldest; she didn't need her baby sister to protect her.

She pushed away the thought. This was her chance, while they were distracted. There was no point making excuses that she was going to the shops as they would just offer to go with her. No, she had to be sneaky.

Flora studied herself in the mirror, applying a little lip gloss, fluffing up her long hair, straightening her ankle-length tasseled skirt. Then she raced downstairs before anyone saw her. She inched open the front door. From where Heather and Jess sat they would see her if she walked down the driveway, so she crept around to the other side of the house, through the bottom section of the caravan park, crawling through the hole in the hedge into the field with the turnstile that led to Jess's house and the high street. From there it was just a short walk across the next field to the fair. She couldn't help but break into a run as soon as she'd left the grounds of Tilby Manor, just in case Heather or Jess appeared behind her, her heavy DM boots kicking up dust from the ground.

Even though it was only three o'clock the fair was already in full swing. The company would be moving on at the end of the summer and Dylan with it. She didn't know how she was going to be able to say goodbye.

The sun was high in the cloudless sky, and along with the crowds and the music, she felt slightly disoriented as she walked through the fair, a shimmering heat haze floating in front of her. She was disappointed to see that Dylan wasn't in his usual position on the Waltzers. Instead two other guys had taken his place, pushing shrieking girls around to the thump of "Pump Up the Jam."

Her need to see him was so great she felt sick. Where was he? Maybe it was his day off. And then, through the crowds, she spotted him and her breath caught—like it always did on first sighting. He was standing at the candyfloss van talking to someone. Dylan was wearing a linen V-necked tunic top with jeans, a beaded necklace around his throat and leather wristbands decorating his tanned arms. His floppy dark hair fell into his eyes and she thought again—*for the millionth time*—how beautiful he was.

But then she noticed who he was with and her heart sank.

Speedy. Again. Why was his mother's boyfriend always hanging around? And he dressed way too young for a man approaching forty.

They looked to be in deep conversation. Speedy was leaning toward Dylan, his narrow face creased in a frown. He was wearing an oversize T-shirt with a large strawberry on the front and Adidas trainers. Dylan nodded at something Speedy was saying, his expression serious, then reached around to a back pocket to retrieve an envelope. He handed it to Speedy, who almost snatched it, then shoved it into his tatty jeans and stalked off. Dylan stared after him, then ran his hand through his hair, looking exasperated.

Flora waited a few moments before heading over. Dylan was surprised, and pleased—she was thankful to note—to see her. "Gypsy Girl," he said, his arm snaking around her waist and pulling her toward him. "Where have you been? I've missed you."

"I had to sneak out," she said, rolling her eyes. "My sister's acting like my bodyguard."

"Can you stay out all day?"

She laughed, giddy to be in his company again. He was like her drug; she felt intoxicated just being near him. "Yep. Until nine thirty this evening." She didn't tell him her mum only let her come to the fair if she stuck with Heather. But as long as she was back by dark her mum couldn't really say anything. "What was your stepdad doing here?"

"He's not my stepdad." Then he grinned and raised an eyebrow. It was then she noticed he had something in his hand. A clear packet of what looked like white powder. Even she knew it was more than just a bit of weed. "Got us a little treat for later," he said, kissing her nose. "It'll make you feel on top of the world."

Heather had searched the house and grounds but Flora was nowhere to be seen.

"She's gone," she said to Jess, throwing her arms wide in despair. "I can't believe she's gone." So much for their plan to keep Flora away from Dylan.

Jess looked down at their sketch pads at her feet, as if the answers were among the graves they'd drawn. She sighed and bit her lip.

"What?" snapped Heather. She could see her best friend was fighting an opinion.

Jess glanced at her. "It's just . . . she *is* sixteen."

"But Dylan's no good for her."

Jess crossed her arms and stuck out her chin defiantly. "That's not your decision to make, though, is it?"

Heather stared at her, aghast. They usually agreed on everything.

"Look, what have you got against Dylan anyway? He seems okay."

"Okay? He gave her *drugs*, Jess."

"She smoked a bit of weed. It's no different from drinking alcohol."

"I've not had alcohol. Have you?"

Jess looked sheepish. "Yeah. At Christmas Mum lets me have

a Snowball. And at Gina's party a few months ago we had some cider."

Heather stared at her friend with a mixture of awe and disapproval. She knew Gina and her cronies still had time for Jess. It was just *her* they glared at when they walked past. She'd never got an invite to Gina's party and it hurt that Jess hadn't revealed before now that not only had she been invited but she had actually gone. Heather didn't want to be possessive. She knew Jess liked her best, but still. Sometimes it was hard not to feel left out.

Heather had never thought she needed anyone other than Flora. Then, when she'd made friends with Jess, she'd discovered what fun it was to have a best friend, someone in the same class who had your back. She was worried about losing them both: Flora to Dylan and Jess to Gina.

"I know you care about Flora," Jess said softly, "but she's sensible. She'll be okay. She won't let Dylan drag her into anything dangerous. And by the end of the summer he'll be gone." She shrugged. "But if it makes you feel better we could go to the fair anyway. Keep an eye out for her?"

Heather wanted to hug Jess in that moment. She'd known she would understand, despite not having siblings of her own. Jess was still on her wavelength. Nothing had changed.

She felt more lighthearted as she linked arms with her best friend and headed toward the fair.

It took hours to find Flora. It was as though she had vanished off the face of the earth. Heather and Jess looked everywhere, and asked around after Dylan, but nobody seemed to have an idea where they had gone. "His shift starts at six and it's now five thirty, so he's bound to be here soon," one of the guys on the Waltzers informed them. He was older than Dylan and had kind eyes. "I'm sure your sister will be all right with him, don't worry."

Heather tried to distract herself by using the last of her pocket money to go on the bumper cars with Jess, and although she screamed when someone slammed into the back of them, and giggled when Jess took over the driving and couldn't reverse out of the corner, in the back of her mind was the uneasy feeling that wouldn't leave her. Jess was right: Flora was sixteen—old enough to take care of herself. It was just that Heather didn't trust Dylan. She knew he didn't have her sister's best interests at heart. She was counting down the days until the fair left and Dylan with it.

And then, just before six, she saw him strutting toward where they stood by the Waltzers. It took her brain a moment or two to realize that Flora wasn't with him.

"Where's my sister?" she demanded, as soon as Dylan reached them.

"Hey, it's little Heather Powell." He draped an arm around her shoulders. "What's the matter now?"

"Where's Flora?"

He threw his head back and laughed. "Take a chill pill. Your sister's gone home. I've got to work tonight." He moved away from her to leap onto the platform. He seemed full of energy.

"See?" Jess said, tugging on her arm. "Flora's fine. Shall we go back now?"

There was nothing Heather wanted to do more. She was tired of the noise and the smells and the crowds. She'd much rather go back to the barn with Jess, sit and chat and sketch and listen to music. Her plan to watch over Flora and stop her leaving the caravan park had failed miserably. And Jess was useless, even though she'd promised to help her keep Flora away from Dylan. But she'd made her feelings perfectly clear earlier: Jess obviously felt that she was being too protective of Flora.

She would have to come up with another plan.

She let Jess lead her away. Yet the uneasy feeling wouldn't leave her.

28

Margot

MARGOT HAD SPENT ALL WEEKEND AT HER DAUGHTER'S BEDSIDE— visiting hours allowing. She wanted to cherish every waking moment with Heather. She'd nearly lost her and, even though she knows the road ahead won't be easy, at least Heather's alive and recovering a little more each day. And Margot will do her best to make sure she doesn't go to prison.

The police are still standing guard. Heather's been moved out of the ICU to a private room, mainly because of the police presence but also because the hospital doesn't want the other patients to be alarmed. The doctors—thank the Lord—aren't allowing Heather to be interviewed yet, saying she's still in no fit state emotionally to deal with the fact that all the evidence points to her shooting dead two people. Heather has said she can't remember a thing about that fateful day. Margot had tried to probe her gently, asking her if she remembered anything, but

Heather had got distressed and Adam had glared at her disapprovingly.

"Give it time," Dr. Khan said, when she passed Margot pacing the corridor. "It's common for patients to be unable to recollect any memories from the time of their brain trauma. She might never get them back."

Could Margot live with that? The not knowing? She thinks so, if it means having Heather back where she belongs.

MARGOT'S RUBBER SOLES SQUEAK AS SHE STRIDES DOWN THE CORRIDOR to Heather's room. Because it's Monday morning, Adam has agreed to stay at the caravan park to check out the young couple, whom she still thinks could be journalists. Margot's excited at the prospect of spending time with Heather alone and has with her an array of chocolate and magazines. At the weekend Adam brought Ethan in to see her and Margot had to fight back tears as he snuggled up to his mother's chest, his head resting against her collarbone, sucking his thumb, happy and contented to be with her again. Heather had kissed his soft dark curls hungrily, tears running down her cheeks as she practically inhaled him, terrified of being parted from him again. Margot understands how that feels. And in that moment she knew Heather hadn't tried to take her own life. There is no way she'd ever leave her little boy. He is her world. Maybe it had been an accident. Maybe the gun had gone off in her hand and the bullet grazed her chest. Or—she recalls the unidentified set of fingerprints on the gun—somebody else was involved.

Heather is sitting up in bed when Margot enters the room. She looks up, her eyebrows raised. It's still a shock to see the huge padded plaster on the side of her head. "Mum. Why is that policeman still outside the door?" she says. She asks the same thing every day. And every day Margot has to come up with more lies.

Today, Dr. Khan has suggested they tell her the truth. Gently, of course. The police are champing at the bit to interview her. But Margot had promised Adam not to say anything until he arrived at lunchtime.

"It's just policy, love, don't worry about it."

Heather frowns and chews her lip. It's a new thing, this frowning. Before, Heather was a smiley person. She never glowered. But today her eyebrows are so knotted together it looks as though she has a monobrow.

"And why haven't you brought Ethan with you? I need to see my baby."

"He's at nursery today. It's a Monday. Remember?"

"He's too young for nursery."

Margot takes a deep breath and perches on the chair next to Heather's bed. She deposits the glossy magazines and Maltesers on the table but Heather gives them only a cursory glance.

"You put him in nursery a few months ago. Just one and a half days a week. Don't you remember? You thought it would be good to socialize him and give you a bit of a break." Margot had been the one to suggest it. With the postnatal depression, Heather had needed some time to herself. She was such a good mother. Ethan always came first—sometimes, Margot felt privately, to the detriment of her daughter.

"I don't need a break from my son," says Heather, her voice rising.

Margot places a soothing hand on Heather's leg. The blanket under her fingers feels coarse, as though it's been washed too many times. "I can bring him in later, if you like. I can pick him up early from nursery."

This seems to mollify Heather and she sits back against the pillows, the frown disappearing. The doctors said this might happen, that Heather will find it hard at first to keep a lid on her emotions.

"I wanted to talk to you about something," begins Margot, gently.

"What's that?"

"Do you remember your old friend, Jessica Fox?"

She looks surprised. "Yes. Of course. Why?"

"She's been in touch. She's a journalist now. Working for the local paper. She's been concerned about you."

Heather examines her hands where they lie in her lap. "Right."

"I wasn't sure about her, at first, but she's been . . . well, a comfort to me in a way, I suppose."

Heather lifts her head and her eyes lock with Margot's. "A comfort?"

"I've been out of my mind with worry."

Heather averts her eyes.

"And Jess has warded off the other journalists."

Heather smiles. "She probably just wants the story, Mum."

"I thought that too. At first. But I don't know. There's more to it than that. I think she is, well, fond of you. Still."

Heather shakes her head. "It's been eighteen years."

"I know. It's a long time. But you were so close, once."

"We were children."

"I know . . . I know. But . . . would you like to see her? She's asked if she can see you. Not straightaway, of course."

Heather fiddles with a loose thread on her blanket. "I suppose. It would be interesting to see her again. But . . ."

Margot inches forward in her chair. "But what?"

"I don't know. It's all water under the bridge, now, I suppose, but she was weird with me after Flora disappeared. It really affected our friendship."

Margot's puzzled. "I thought you fell out over a boy."

"No. There was no boy. I just told you that to stop you asking so many questions about it. The truth was, she just stopped being my friend, which was weird because she used to love being with us all. She'd practically moved in that last summer. But she began to avoid me, started hanging around with that horrible Gina McKenzie again. I felt she was hiding something from me and also, I could be wrong but it was almost . . ." She hesitates and Margot has to prompt her to continue, and when she does it sends goose bumps all over Margot's body. "It was almost as if she was scared of me."

29

Jess

BRISTOL DAILY NEWS

Tuesday, March 20, 2012

TRAGIC SISTER'S EX REVEALS
SEASIDE SHOOTER'S VIOLENT PAST

by Harriet Hill

THE SUSPECT in the murder of Deirdre and Clive Wilson once attacked her sister's boyfriend.

Dylan Bird, 37, alleged that the sister of his girlfriend at the time—tragic missing teen Flora Powell—flipped out and struck him "numerous times" with a riding crop during a jealous rage.

Heather Underwood, now 32, was only fourteen when her older sister, Flora, dated Dylan in the summer of 1994.

"It was obvious Heather never liked me," said Dylan. "She was overprotective of Flora and I think jealous of our relationship. Then, a few days before she went missing, I'd gone over to the caravan park to see her one evening, but Heather wouldn't let me anywhere near her. And then she started screaming at me, spouting loads of lies about how I was a bad influence and that I was no good. And then she took her riding crop to me, hitting me with it so that I actually had lacerations to my back."

Dylan refused to report the "unprovoked attack" to the police, saying he didn't want to "antagonize things further."

Later that same week Flora vanished, leaving behind all her possessions and passport. A few days after she went missing her blouse was found covered with blood. It is a case that has shocked and baffled the local community of Tilby for nearly twenty years, and even though a body has yet to be found, police suspect "foul play."

Dylan said: "I was a suspect in Flora's disappearance at the time, of course, being her boyfriend. I was one of the last people to see her alive. But I was with my mum's boyfriend at the time. I was only with Flora for a month, but she was special to me. I still think of her."

Heather's family have been contacted and refuse to comment.

THE LANDLORD OF THE FUNKY RAVEN LOOKS UP IN SURPRISE WHEN we enter. He's standing behind the bar, buffing an empty pint glass with a cloth. The small, old-fashioned pub is quiet, just two men in their sixties standing by the jukebox, chewing the fat over a beer.

Jack strides to the bar, his camera slung over his shoulder. "Are you Stuart Patterson?" he asks confidently, causing the two men to stop talking and watch him with interest, as though he is a rare animal at a zoo.

"Who wants to know?" the landlord replies, in a thick Bristol accent.

Jack will, no doubt, mistake it for West Country or "Farmer," as he calls it. It might sound the same to nonlocals, but a pure Bristolian accent is harsher than West Country, all accentuated *r*'s and *l*'s.

I step forward, adopting my friendly, nonthreatening expression, to introduce myself and Jack. I clear my throat. "We understand Clive Wilson was barred from this pub."

Stuart has very thick, dark eyebrows that remind me of Bert's in *Sesame Street*, and are a contrast to his white hair. "That's right, he was." He glances toward the men by the jukebox; they have now resumed their conversation. "He was caught trying to sell drugs to a group of teenagers."

Clive Wilson was a drug dealer? That doesn't sound right.

"What sort of drugs?" asks Jack.

"Pills mainly. E's, I think. I told him I didn't want him dealing in my pub." He's still cleaning the pint glass and it squeaks as the cloth rubs against it.

"Did you inform the police?" I ask.

"I did. But I couldn't prove anything. The kids were too scared to come forward. So the police did nothing. Clive didn't have a criminal record of drug dealing or any history so they picked him up but had to let him go again." He sighs regretfully, and places the glass on the counter. "Do you want a drink while you're here?"

I turn to Jack, who nods. "Sure. I'll have a lager shandy," he says.

"Do you have any elderflower cordial?" I ask, expecting him to say no.

He looks triumphant as he reaches for the fridge behind him and places a bottle of sparkling elderflower on top of the bar.

I try to pay for the drinks, but Jack won't let me. He orders a couple of packets of crisps as well, and I open them, my stomach rumbling. "Do you know anything else about Clive? Or Deirdre?" I ask.

"I'm afraid not. Before that I always thought he was all right," says Stuart. "He'd come in from time to time, have a drink by himself. I didn't take him for a drug dealer, but you just never know what goes on behind closed doors, do you?" He blows air out of his mouth. It makes a whistling noise. "His mother, Deirdre, seemed like a sweet old thing. Wouldn't hurt a fly. Can't see why anybody would want her dead."

Jack sips his pint thoughtfully while I take the opportunity to shove a crisp into my mouth. "Do you think it's weird that a woman killed them?"

Stuart shrugs. "Women kill too—although it was particularly violent. A gun. I don't know."

"But it's quite unusual for a woman to break into someone's home and shoot two random people, isn't it?" he presses.

"Unless it wasn't random," says Stuart, his eyebrows wriggling up and down as though they have a life of their own. "But I've never met this Heather Underwood," he adds, wiping away nonexistent stains on the bar with the same cloth he used to clean his glass. "She never came in here, although her husband has a couple of times."

"Adam?" I ask, surprised. I would have thought his local would be the Horseshoe in the high street. It's much nearer to where they live.

He nods, his hands making large, circular movements as he sweeps the cloth back and forth along the mahogany. Can't the man stay still for two seconds? "Yep. Nice bloke. Keeps himself to himself. Actually"—he pauses midswipe—"I've seen him talking to Clive."

I'm so shocked I almost choke on my crisps. "What? When?"

His caterpillar eyebrows knit together as he remembers. "A while back now. Probably a month ago. Before I barred Clive anyway. Yes, they met up a few times and they always sat over there." He points to a table in the far corner, by a fireplace. "It looked a bit hush-hush, to be honest." He taps his nose. "A few times I wondered what they were concocting. But I recognized Adam because he used to go to the shooting range, where I'm a member."

"Do you recall anything else?" asks Jack, when it's obvious I'm unable to speak. I'm reeling. Adam hasn't once mentioned any connection to the Wilsons.

"No. Sorry. I only saw them together a few times. Adam never came in again. And then not long after that I caught Clive trying to deal drugs and, well, that was the end of that." He lifts his shoulders into a half-hearted shrug.

"And how long ago was all this?"

He frowns, remembering. "The drugs thing happened a week or so before he died, so . . . yes, before that."

I push my business card toward him, asking him to call me if he remembers anything else. Then Jack and I take our drinks and crisps and go to sit at a quiet table.

Adam knew Clive. Does that mean Heather did too? And, if so, what were they involved in?

WE'RE WALKING UP PARK STREET TOWARD THE NEWSROOM WHEN I see it. The headline jumps out at me from the stand outside the newsagent's. TRAGIC SISTER'S EX REVEALS SEASIDE SHOOTER'S VIOLENT PAST. The bloody *Daily News*. Again.

Jack, who has only just noticed I've stopped, retraces his steps to join me. He's eating a Brie baguette from a paper bag. "Shit," he says, through a mouthful of food, his eyes scanning the article over my shoulder.

"I was friends with Heather when this happened. It's not as bad as it sounds."

It had been the night we'd gone back to the fair to find Flora.

It wasn't long before she went missing. We'd bumped into Dylan on the Waltzers and he said Flora had already left. But on the way home we found her slumped in the field, absolutely off her head on God knew what. Looking back now she was experiencing a bad trip. She must have taken some kind of hallucinogenic. But in 1994 we were just kids and knew nothing about drugs. We'd managed to help her home and avoid Margot finding out, mainly because Leo had come to the rescue, helping us put Flora to bed. I'd stayed over that night and we'd taken it in turns to watch Flora, to make sure she didn't choke on vomit or do anything stupid. As far as I'm aware, Margot never had a clue, but when Dylan turned up the next evening to see Flora, Heather went absolutely ballistic, striking him with her riding crop—although I wasn't there, she told me about it later. And I didn't blame her.

It was only a few days afterward that Flora went missing for good.

And all these years later I'm still not convinced that Dylan had had nothing to do with it. He had an alibi in his mum's boyfriend, apparently, but that doesn't mean anything. His alibi could have been lying too.

I've often wondered if maybe Dylan accidentally gave her a drug overdose, then had help in covering it up; maybe he thought he could convince everyone she'd simply run away. Until it was obvious that she hadn't: no money had left her account, her passport was still at home, and none of her clothes or belongings had been taken. And we all knew that Flora wouldn't have left her family. She was close to them.

I've tried to hunt down Dylan Bird since this all happened but I couldn't turn up an address for him. "How did fucking Harriet Hill find him?" I spit, stabbing at the paper with my finger. "Shit, Ted's going to go mental. He's still pissed off that they got the Sheila story."

Jack swallows his sandwich. "Yes, but we've got this drugs thing. That's good. The *News* don't have that. And you've got the interview with Heather's uncle later."

I groan, knowing that won't be enough for Ted.

"And they printed the Margot exclusive today. Nobody else has got that either. Jess"—he places a hand on my shoulder—"don't sweat it."

"She must have bloody good contacts. Better than me."

There's nothing Jack can say to that. Harriet Hill not only works for a more successful newspaper but it's a daily and has a wider circulation. She's been there for years and probably has hundreds of contacts in all the right places. Whereas I—a recently disgraced national news reporter—am still finding my way.

Jack takes my arm and leads me along the street. "Come on," he says. "It won't be that bad."

IT IS THAT BAD. TED RANTS AT ME, JACK, EVEN ELLIE THE TRAINEE, although she hasn't done anything apart from sit at the computer typing up press releases.

"Dylan Bird," he yells. "Such an obvious one. We should have this story. Not the fucking *Daily News*."

I want to tell him we can't have everything, that we're doing our best. And what about the reporters at HQ? I don't see them helping us out with this.

"You," he says, rounding on me. "*You* know the family. You have an in, for Christ's sake. Use it to your advantage, would you?"

Before I can reply he storms back to his desk behind his partition. If he had a door I know he would have slammed it.

I don't get the chance to tell him that at least we have a story about Clive's drug-dealing past.

I SPEND THE REST OF THE AFTERNOON WITH MY HEAD DOWN, TYPING up the story about Clive being barred from the pub, although I've missed the deadline, which means it won't go in until Friday's paper. I want to tell Ted that it's not my fault the *Daily News* has one over on us—mainly the fact that they're *daily*. Their stories will always hit newsstands first, and their website is plusher and more modern than ours.

Our front-page story today was that Heather had come around from her coma (something the sodding *News* hasn't got, although did Ted focus on that? No. He's too busy worrying about the stories we don't have). I asked the subeditors at HQ to keep my byline off the story. I'm sure Margot will suspect it's me, but equally it won't be long before the other papers get hold of it. I kept it brief and to the point so as not to antagonize Margot— or, more particularly, Adam.

I haven't heard from Margot since I saw her at the hospital on

Friday. But I need to make contact—I don't want us to lose touch now that Heather is awake.

As Jack leaves the office for the day he touches my shoulder in sympathy as he passes but doesn't say anything. We're all conscious of the black cloud hanging over the office, like cigarette smoke, and I'm sure Ted's watching my every move. I was always worried that he thought I was a liability after what happened at the *Tribune*. But now I realize he hired me because of that. As long as I stay on the right side of the law he's obviously happy for me to push boundaries. But how can I when I like Margot and don't want to upset her? She's like . . . I gulp, realizing how true this is. She's like family to me. She's been more of a mother to me than my own. How will she react when I tell her about Adam being seen with Clive? And then another thought hits me: Does Margot already know? Is she pretending she has no idea why Heather killed the Wilsons? Is she protecting her?

30

Jess

The café is empty, apart from a young couple sitting in the window holding hands, and Leo. He's at a table in a corner, stirring a latte in a glass cup. He looks up as I walk through the door and I recognize him straightaway. He still has his dark brown David Essex style hair, with just a few grays threaded through the front, and his tanned skin, which has always been craggy, appears to have just a few new lines. It strikes me—probably for the first time—how handsome he is. I didn't notice it back then; he was just my best friend's uncle. I thought of him as ancient, although he wouldn't have been much older than I am now.

He stands up when he sees me and his smile lights his sparkly green eyes. I go over to him and he pulls me into a hug. "It's so lovely to see you, Jess," he says, grazing my hot cheek with his lips. He smells musky. Then he moves me gently so that I'm at arm's length from him and his eyes sweep over me. "And look how beautiful you turned out to be."

Still a charmer. No wonder he always managed to get the women. I remember the rumors about him even then, whispers of how he couldn't keep it in his pants.

I know a secret about him. Heather does too. I doubt she would have forgotten it.

We saw him once snogging a girl from Flora's form at school when she'd been in year eleven. Her name was Deborah Price and she'd only just turned fifteen. They'd been down on the beach, almost hidden behind one of the dunes, when we'd stumbled upon them. She had a bikini on and his hands were all over her. Leo would have been thirty-six. And, okay, she had a reputation for sleeping around and looked older than her years with a very curvy figure. But still. He should have known better. She was underage. We never told anyone although even then we'd known there was something unsavory about it. He'd leaped away from her when he spotted us and tried to pretend it wasn't what it looked like. But we'd seen too much.

We never mentioned it again, even to each other.

After Flora disappeared, Leo was arrested but Hayley gave him an alibi. I heard they split up not long after.

If I wrote a story about him now, would I reveal this secret? It would certainly add fuel to the fire and I know that's what Ted would want me to do. But it would hurt Margot and Heather. If it was another family I'd do it in a heartbeat.

Leo asks what I'd like to drink and calls the young waitress over. I order a caramel latte, then pull out the chair opposite him and slide into it, shrugging off my coat.

"So, Jess. I'm intrigued. Why did you want to meet after all these years?" He leans forward and gazes at me intently. A lock of hair falls into his eyes and I'm momentarily disarmed.

"Um. Actually," I say, when I've recovered, "it's a bit awkward." I can feel myself blushing. This is ridiculous.

He leans back in his chair and I notice a hint of a smirk he's trying to hide. Shit! He thinks I've called him out of the blue to hook up. Inwardly I squirm. "I'm a reporter," I blurt out.

The smile disappears from his face and he sits up straighter. "A reporter?"

"I'm covering the story of the shootings. And Heather . . ."

He fiddles with the handle of his cup, averting his eyes. "So why do you want to see me? I've tried to keep out of it."

"She's your niece."

He lifts his eyes to mine. "I'm well aware of that." His voice has lost its previous warmth.

"And Margot. She needs you. After everything she's been through . . ."

He holds up his hand. "You know nothing about it."

"Of course I do," I say hotly. "I've been in touch with Margot. She means a lot to me."

He sighs. "Not again."

"What do you mean?"

"*You*. The way you were back then. You were obsessed with

Flora, Margot, and Heather. You couldn't keep away. They might as well have adopted you."

I shift in my seat, uncomfortable. Was it that obvious? My need for them then? I'd thought I'd hidden a lot from them, like how often I was on my own, how occasionally Mum wouldn't even come home at all, preferring to stay over at her new boyfriend's house, or have a drink with a friend, leaving me alone for a few days. But then, at other times, she'd want to spend all Sunday with me, curled up on the sofa watching old black-and-white films on TV and eating chocolate. Those were some of my favorite times, just the two of us. "It's not like that. Not now." I don't need anyone now, I add silently. I rely on myself.

Leo takes a sip of his latte, regarding me over the rim of his glass cup. I stir my frothy latte and try to avoid eye contact. This isn't playing out as I'd hoped.

I take a deep breath and start again. "Do you think Heather did it? The shootings, I mean. There's another set of fingerprints on the gun. It could have been someone else."

"Like who?"

"I don't know."

Leo puts his cup down. "Listen, Jess. You seem like a nice woman. But our family, we have our demons. If I were you I'd keep out of it."

"Every family has their demons."

"Not like ours."

I decide to change the subject. "Do you ever go back to Tilby?"

He shakes his mop of shaggy hair. "I haven't been back in years. Couldn't wait to leave the place. I moved to Bristol. Somewhere more anonymous. Started over."

"What do you do now? For work, I mean?"

His body relaxes and he's clearly relieved to be talking about something else. "I work for a car dealership. It suits me. I miss the outdoors but I couldn't ever go back to Tilby." His expression darkens again and he says quietly, "My life was ruined after Flora went missing. The rumors destroyed me. Do you . . ." He gulps and glances down at the floral oilcloth on the table. "Do you know what it's like to be looked upon as a monster? A pervert? I know I'm not a saint but Flora . . . She was my *niece*, for fuck's sake." His face flushes with anger.

"I can't imagine."

"I hate the fucking place now."

"I'm sorry for bringing it all up again."

He reaches out and squeezes my hand. "It's fine. It's been nice to see you, Jess. But the story you're writing—whatever angle you're going on—well, I can't help you. I don't want to be associated with any of it. I've got a new life now. I don't want the press dredging it all up so that people can point the finger at me again. Do you understand?"

I nod. "Of course."

"I'm sorry not to be more help." He gets up from the table and grabs his jacket from the back of the chair. "Take care of yourself." And then he's gone, disappearing out of the door and onto the dark streets.

I SIT AND DRINK THE REST OF MY LATTE. I'M NOW ALONE IN THE CAFÉ apart from a woman behind the counter who's humming to herself as she cleans the coffee machine. Then I gather up my things and pull on my coat. I don't want to go home. The atmosphere in the flat has reached breaking point.

We're still only communicating out of necessity. I know things can't go on as they are; we will, at some point, have that difficult talk.

I'm disappointed in my conversation with Leo. I sensed a bitter man and, for the first time, I appreciate how difficult it must have been for him: the prime suspect in a young girl's disappearance, all those gossips and pointing fingers. No wonder he couldn't wait to flee the place.

Just as I'm about to leave the café my phone rings. It's Margot and I almost drop my mobile in my excitement. And then my stomach lurches. Does she know I've just met up with her brother? Did Leo ring her to tell her?

"Jess. I need to talk to you. Would you like to come over?"

"Tonight?"

"Only if it's no problem. But we can do another night if you'd rather."

"No! I'd love to come tonight. Thank you. I'll be with you in about forty minutes."

I put my phone away and leave the café. It's not raining but the wind has picked up. It circles my ankles, pulling at the hem of my coat, like an excitable puppy.

It's not until I walk down my cobbled street, with the row of colorful houses on the hill in front of me, that I get the same chilling feeling that I'm being followed. The river on my left looks dark and unwelcoming; the apartments opposite are empty with only the occasional light on. A line of boats is tethered to the shore and bobs in the wind. I think of the shadowy person I saw standing by my building as I was leaving for Margot's on Friday night and shudder, half-expecting to see them crouched in one of the doorways, waiting for me.

I increase my pace, trying to distract myself with thoughts of Rory and the difficult conversation that's still waiting to be had, and before I know it I've reached my building. I take the gate to the car park, texting Rory as I walk that I won't be home for dinner. He replies straightaway: *That's just as well as I've gone for a drink with some colleagues. See you later.* No kiss.

I'm reading the text as I approach my car. I don't usually feel afraid in the car park, it's well lit and there's often a resident either leaving or arriving, although it's quiet tonight. Yet I can't stop thinking of the person who was lurking outside here on Friday night. Will they come back? Who was it? I look up from my phone as I approach my Nissan. There's something on the screen, clipped underneath one of my windscreen wipers. At first I wonder if it's a flyer, but on closer inspection I see that it's a wad of small, square photographs printed on flimsy paper and cut to size. I pick them up, wondering if this is Jack's idea of a joke. I wouldn't put it past him. There are five in total, and, as I flick through them, I shiver. They look as though they've been snapped from a distance in the street, but it's plain to see that each photo is of me.

With a trembling hand I turn one over: I'm standing outside my building, turning the key in the lock. You can see only half of my face in profile. Scrawled across it are the words *BACK OFF.*

31

Margot

MARGOT POURS HERSELF A GLASS OF PINOT NOIR AND SLUMPS onto the sofa. It's been a hard few days and she closes her eyes, trying to gather her thoughts, ignoring the thumping in her temples.

She's delighted that Heather has regained consciousness and seems to be her old self, but her daughter still maintains she can't remember anything about the day of the shootings. Heather had cried when the police broke it to her about what had happened. Margot was relieved that they handled it sensitively. They didn't formally arrest her, or bombard her with questions. A middle-aged police officer, with freckles and warm hazel eyes, who asked them to call her Sarah, sat on the chair next to the bed, held Heather's hand, and gently told her what they suspected.

"But I don't even know a Clive or Deirdre Wilson," Heather wailed, her eyes round with bewilderment, darting from Margot to Adam, then landing back on Sarah. "There must be some mistake."

Sarah had replied calmly, "We have some evidence to suggest you were involved. I'm so sorry, Heather. We'll give you a few days before we come back and formally question you."

Heather had nodded, tears streaming down her face, and when Sarah had left, she'd sobbed in Adam's arms. "You don't think I'd be capable of something like this, do you?" she'd asked him beseechingly. "You know me, Adam. I'm not a killer."

Adam had met Margot's eyes over Heather's head. He'd looked panicked. "No, of course not," he'd said. "We'll get to the bottom of this. Please, my love, please don't worry."

It had taken everything out of Margot, emotionally, to stay strong. She'd had to bite her lip so she did not reveal to her daughter that Deirdre had stayed at the caravan park. She hadn't even told the police yet, managing to convince herself that it meant nothing. Heather probably hadn't even taken any notice of her, checking her in and, as was mostly the case, not seeing her again until she'd checked out a few days later.

It was just a coincidence.

Margot takes a long slug of wine, instantly feeling calmer as it slides down her throat, warming her insides.

The vultures are back again. As soon as the news had broken about Heather being out of her coma they'd returned with a vengeance, quadrupling in number. Every time she left the house there was a swarm of them, like locusts. She was still furious with Sheila for talking to the press, and had called to tell her she was no longer welcome at the caravan park. Luckily they weren't busy, and she'd find someone else to assist with mucking out the horses. Leo was coming tomorrow to stay and to help and she couldn't wait to see him, grateful that she wouldn't be rattling around in the old house by herself anymore.

She's still clinging to the small hope that Heather will be allowed home. The lawyer she'd spoken to about it admitted that Heather wouldn't get bail if she was charged with murder. Everyone has her daughter down as a gun-toting psychopath, who's a danger to society. But it's her Heather, her loving, gentle daughter.

Her thoughts are interrupted by a sharp knock on the door and her eyes ping open. It must be Jess. Margot had rung her earlier asking her over. She wanted her advice but, more than that, she enjoyed Jess's company. She was young and vibrant and she made Margot feel less alone.

But when Margot answers the door it's not Jess standing there in the dark. It's a man she's never seen before. He's wearing a bobble hat and a thick scarf, wrapped up to his chin, and his breath fogs in front of him. He looks to be around her age, maybe older, his long, pointed face etched with deep grooves. Her heart starts beating faster. She's conscious of being alone in the house. Adam is fetching Ethan from Gloria's, and although Colin is in one of the caravans, he's too far away to help if she needed it.

"Are you a journalist?" she barks, her sharp tone belying her fear.

He thrusts his hands into his pockets. "No. I'm sorry to bother you. I'm Norman Wilson. Deirdre's other son."

Her insides turn to ice. Why has Deirdre's son turned up on her doorstep out of the blue?

"What . . . what do you want?"

He steps backward, as if only just realizing his imposition. "I'm sorry. It was a stupid thing to do. I can see I've scared you." He runs his hands over his chin. "I was in the area, seeing to the house, you know . . . and I . . . I . . ." He blinks and she recognizes the grief in his expression. *My daughter did this*, she thinks. *My daughter is responsible for this poor man's suffering.*

She glances down at her slippers. She wants to tell him she knows how he feels. That she's bearing the burden of loss too. But the words won't come.

"I . . . I should probably go."

Her inbuilt politeness is grappling with her fear, each fighting it out as to what the correct response should be: She should ask him in, offer him a cup of tea and her compassion, the polite part of her says. But he's a strange man and they would be alone in the house, at night, says the other, more cautious, part of her.

"I'm . . . Heather doesn't remember," Margot blurts out, suddenly wanting this man to know her daughter isn't a monster. "I don't understand why she's done this. *If* she's done this. There was another set of fingerprints on the gun. She's not been charged with anything yet. She . . ." Margot runs out of steam.

Norman's eyes widen. She notices that they are a clear jade, like a tropical sea, flecked with brown. From the photographs of Clive in the newspaper, he doesn't resemble his brother. Clive was short and squat, with gray hair and a square jaw, while Norman is long and thin and sinewy, like one of the little wooden mannequins Heather used to have in her bedroom to help her draw people in proportion.

He holds up a hand. "I'm just trying to understand why," he says sadly. He backs away, the gravel crunching under his heavy boots. "I'm sorry. I shouldn't have come. I didn't think." He retreats down the pathway until he's swallowed into the darkness of the night.

WHEN JESS TURNS UP HALF AN HOUR LATER, SHE'S AGHAST WHEN Margot tells her of Norman's visit.

"Thank goodness you didn't let him in," she says, taking off her coat and hanging it on the peg behind the door. Margot notices her outfit: bright turquoise tights with a blue corduroy skirt and a jumper covered with small pink pom-poms. Her clothes have always been a bit . . . wacky.

It cheers Margot to see how comfortable Jess feels in her home. "I felt sorry for him," she replies. "He had an aura of sadness around him. He's just looking for answers. We all are."

"But to turn up here at this time of night? That's a bit weird." Jess follows Margot into the kitchen and refuses the glass of wine she offers but accepts some chicken casserole that's been in the slow cooker all day. She takes a seat at the table while Margot bustles about with plates and cutlery, making sure to leave enough food for when Adam gets home later.

"He said he was in the area," she says, as she hands a plate of casserole and vegetables to Jess.

Jess takes it with thanks. "This smells delicious."

Margot scoops some out for herself and sits opposite Jess at the table.

"I bumped into Norman earlier while I was doing some digging on Clive. I found out a few things about him. Like he was banned from the local pub for drug dealing."

Margot's mouth falls open. "What?"

"I know," says Jess, through a mouthful of chicken. She pauses to swallow before adding, "Deirdre only bought the house in Shackleton Road back in February and already he'd managed to get barred from the local pub." She has a self-satisfied look on her face. But then her expression changes and she seems rattled. She reaches for the bag at her feet, and retrieves something, then hands it across the table to Margot. It's a slightly unfocused photograph of Jess printed on thin paper.

"It was on my windscreen tonight. If you turn it over . . ."

Margot does as Jess says and reels when she sees *BACK OFF*. The letters are written so thickly that she's surprised they haven't scored through the paper. "Have you shown the police?"

Jess shakes her messy blond bob. "Not yet, no. But today I was trying to find out more about Clive. I wondered if this was from Norman."

Margot gives back the photograph and Jess returns it to her bag. "Really? I know I've only just met him, and briefly, but he didn't seem threatening."

They eat in silence for a few moments. And then Jess pipes up, "I get the impression Norman's hiding something, though. Or someone else could be scaring me off." She stares at Margot, as though expecting her to suggest who that person might be. When Margot doesn't reply, she adds, "And there's more."

Margot's insides turn over and she puts down her knife and fork. She doesn't know if she can take any more revelations. Her nerves are frayed enough as it is. "Go on."

"The landlord saw Adam in the pub, talking to Clive."

Margot's head swims and she has to hold on to the edge of the table to steady herself. "But that can't be right. Adam said he'd never met either of the Wilsons."

Jess looks at her and Margot detects pity in her eyes. Stupid, foolish, naïve Margot, that look says, believing your gruff and uncommunicative son-in-law.

Margot clutches the gold locket at her throat. Heather had given it to her one Christmas, a few years after Flora went missing. Inside there is a tiny photograph of her, Flora, and Heather.

The other fingerprints on the gun. The police had said one set was Adam's, the other undetected. She'd taken it for granted that Adam's fingerprints were on it because he'd used it before. But now . . . now . . . Her head spins. The neighbor spoke of seeing a woman leaving the Wilsons' house. A woman they've identified as Heather, her car leaving the scene. Not Adam. Heather. But what about afterward? In the barn. Maybe Heather hadn't shot herself. Somebody else could have done that. Was it Adam? Was it a plan between them that had gone wrong?

She pictures her son-in-law, tall and brooding with his craggy looks. Outdoorsy, curt, a little antisocial at times, but he loves his wife and son. Doesn't he? She might not have been convinced at first, but he's right for Heather: their personalities meld together, making each a better person. Heather brings Adam out of himself and Adam is a solid, calm presence for Heather, who's always been so sensible but who, underneath, can be anxious at times. He's reliable and would do anything for her. And, okay, they argue now and then, but who doesn't?

"Margot? Are you all right?" Jess has finished all the food on her plate, and is leaning back in her chair, her hands resting on her stomach. One of the pom-poms from her jumper is missing.

Margot snaps back to the present. "Sorry. I'm just in shock. I need to speak to Adam." She stands up. He'll be due home anytime soon and she wants to be alone when she confronts him.

Jess stands up too, gathering up her bag and looking a bit disappointed. "I'm sorry to have upset you," she says, her voice full of concern.

Margot waves her hand. "No. No. It's not that." She'd wanted to ask Jess if she'd come and see Heather, as a friend, not a journalist. Now, though, she wants to be alone with her thoughts. She feels as if she's being driven mad with them, jumbling in her head, making her feel dizzy.

Jess grabs her coat, shouldering it on. "I'll go. Thank you for a lovely meal. How is Heather, by the way?"

"She's getting there." Margot surprises herself by giving Jess a quick hug. "I'm grateful to you," she says, when she's released her, "for caring. You're a good girl. Thank you for telling me about Adam. I'll give you a call tomorrow. Heather wants to see you so we'll have to arrange something soon."

Jess's whole face brightens. "Really? That's brilliant. Thank you."

And then she's gone. Leaving Margot alone with her thoughts while she waits for her son-in-law to return home.

32

Jess

THE ROAD AHEAD IS DARK AS I TURN OUT OF TILBY MANOR ONTO Cowship Lane. There are no streetlights and I have to concentrate hard on the cats' eyes in front of me to show the way.

A hard ball of disappointment is lodged in my chest. I was hoping to stay longer, chat with Margot in her cozy kitchen. What is it about her, about them, that I'm constantly drawn to? Is it because they're like the family I never had? I was like this as a child and it hasn't changed. I felt so happy when Margot first agreed to see me, and now it seems we're becoming friends. That she trusts me. But when I told her about Adam knowing Clive, she shut down, and now I feel pushed out. I shake my head, dislodging the thoughts. I'm not family. Margot doesn't see me as another daughter. I'm just someone who knew them all a long time ago.

I don't know what compels me to do it, but instead of driving along the high street and out toward the M5, I take the turning that leads to the seafront. The road is small and narrow, more a lane, really, with the beach on my left and a row of houses on my right. Eventually it becomes Shackleton Road. The Wilsons' house is the fourth in a terrace of six. I pull up outside. There is no CCTV along this street. The killer's identity rests on the shoulders of Peter and Holly Bright, as far as I'm aware, unless other witnesses have come forward, although Angela Crosswell, the police press officer, informed me only yesterday that this wasn't the case. Nothing substantial anyway. A sighting of a woman fitting Heather's description boarding a bus to Bristol later that morning, another at a beach, and a café, all within the local area, but they've all been discounted because it was either during or after the time Heather lay unconscious in the barn.

The tide is in, lapping against the wall, the breeze spraying salt onto my windscreen. It's not yet 8 p.m. but it feels a lot later. The sky is moonless, the only light coming from the windows of the terraces in front of me.

I pull up, roughly where I imagine Heather parked that fateful morning, under a streetlamp, and switch off the engine as I watch the Wilsons' house. Is Norman staying there? It looks empty: no lights on, net curtains hanging limply. Someone has knocked over one of the garden gnomes and it lies on its back next to the flower beds, bright red and blue among the dull greens of the lawn. I try to imagine what must have been going through Heather's mind when she pulled up here eleven days ago with Margot's gun.

This won't do. I need to get home and sort things out with Rory. We've been avoiding each other since Friday night. All I seem to be thinking about at the moment is Heather and Margot.

I turn the key in the ignition when a rap on my window makes me jump. A long, weathered face appears at the glass. My heart races when I realize it's Norman. I could just drive away without speaking to him, but that would be mean. I wind my window down and arrange a smile on my face. "Hi, Norman."

"Oh, it's you. I wondered who was watching the house." He's wearing a woolly hat, pulled down low on his brow, and a scarf that's flapping open in the wind, revealing a colorful tattoo on his neck that looks like a bird, although I can't quite make it out. I wonder if he regrets it, that tattoo, now he's older.

"Are you staying there?" I incline my head toward the house. Although I can't imagine he'd want to after what happened.

"No. A week after the . . . *the murders*"—he swallows as though it pains him to say it—"I traveled down from Reading and I've been staying at Clive's place in Bristol, but the police have put me up somewhere else tonight. A cheap B and B."

Why would the police do that? My reporter's antenna twitches. "Oh, really? How come?" I ask, trying to sound casual.

"They had a warrant. They wouldn't tell me any more." He looks downcast. "My brother . . . Well, I think he might have been involved with drugs."

This isn't a surprise after my talk with the landlord of the Funky Raven but I remain silent.

His shoulders sag. "But we know it wasn't some drug lord who killed him, don't we? It was that woman. That Heather Underwood."

"I . . . Well, I think the police will want to look at everything. Innocent until proven guilty and all that."

He makes a *pft* sound with his tongue. I wonder why he's here at this time of night. I know he was at Margot's earlier, but what has he been doing since then? Lurking around Tilby or nipping back over to Bristol to put photographs on my car? Does he know where I live? But if he's responsible for the photographs, then why? *Back off*, someone had written. Back off from what? From finding out more about Clive?

"Anyway," he says, stepping away from my car so that he's standing on the narrow pavement. "I'd better get back to the B and B. Got to sort out funerals, for when the bodies are released."

"I'm so sorry." I don't know what else to say.

He hangs his head. "Thanks," he mutters. Then he lifts his eyes to meet mine. "You know she did it, don't you? Heather Underwood. And it wasn't because of drugs."

"What do you mean?"

He wraps his scarf tighter around his neck. "I hope they lock her up and throw away the key, that's all I'm saying."

Without another word he stalks off, hands in his pockets, toward a car further up the street. His legs are skinny and bowed, his back hunched. He's just a nearly sixty-year-old man, I think, a man who's angry and grieving. He means me no harm.

I put the car in gear and head toward home.

IT'S ONLY NINE O'CLOCK BY THE TIME I GET BACK, AND THE UNDER-ground car park is empty of people. There are spaces for seven cars—two spaces per flat and one for visitors—and only four are filled, not including mine. Still, four cars, which means that at least someone should be at home. I'm not going to be alone in my building. Although I note with a heavy heart that Rory's Fiat isn't there.

As I get out of the car, the all-too-familiar feeling of being watched makes me jumpy. Is someone taking my photograph now? I look wildly about me, my scalp prickling. But, of course, nobody's there. I hurry past the parked cars, almost running to the side door that leads to the flats, using my key fob to gain access.

And that's when it hits me. How would anybody be able to get in here? The car park is secure, with an electric gate. There is a pedestrian side access, but that's locked and only residents have a key, although there have been times when it's been left unlocked. And it's possible to climb the gate, I suppose, without being seen at night, but you'd have to be young and fit and tall. I doubt Nor-man would be able to scale it. Wayne Walker is tall and fit. Could it be him? Is he telling me to back off the story because of what I did to him with the phone hacking? But I've learned my lesson. I'd never be so stupid again.

I run up the back stairs to the second floor, my mind racing, thinking of the photographs in my bag. And for the first time in ages I yearn for Rory, for how it used to be between us in the early days, when we'd tell each other everything, me curled up in his arms before talk of babies and marriage began to divide us.

The flat is dark and empty, and I go about switching on all the lights and closing the curtains. When I get to our bedroom I pause at the window. There it is again. A beam of light from the derelict building opposite. Is it squatters? The beam is moving, as though the person holding the torch is pacing, and then it swings around so that the light almost blinds me. I step back in shock, snatching the curtains closed.

I jump when my mobile buzzes where I'd left it on the bed. It's Jack and I'm filled with relief.

"Jack!" I gasp, about to tell him everything. It's been ages since he rang me in the evening and usually only when Finn was working nights.

"I've found out something I think you'll be interested in," he says, his voice serious and very un-Jack-like. We usually have a bit of banter on the phone first.

"O-kaaay . . ."

"I did a bit of digging after you found that card with the flowers."

"Flowers?" I'm still thinking about a possible stalker in the building opposite and have to concentrate on what he's saying. "What flowers?"

"The ones that were left in Clive Wilson's garden with the threatening note attached."

I slump onto my bed. Suddenly I feel exhausted. "Right."

"I phoned the flower shop—they're in Bristol—because the name and address was on the card. I remembered it after you

let me see it. And" he coughs, sounding embarrassed—"I pretended to be Finn. Don't ever tell him—he'd kill me."

I laugh, mostly with relief that Jack sounds like his old self
again. "Bloody hell, you're getting as bad as me. What happened?"

"I scared them into telling me who purchased the flowers.
You're never going to believe this but . . . it was Adam."

"Adam." I sit upright, in shock. "Adam Underwood?"

"Yep." He sounds very pleased with himself. "Adam asked
the woman in the shop to write the note. She didn't think anything of it—he said it was a joke for a friend's birthday."

I'm going to have to tell Margot. "Good detective work, DS
Jack Renton." I laugh.

"I'm wasted in this job. No need to thank me." He's chuck-
ling when he hangs up.

I try to ring Margot but it goes straight to voicemail so I
leave a message. Even though we don't really text each other—
Margot's always preferred to talk—I tap out a quick text anyway.
If she's speaking to Adam tonight she'll want to ask him about
the note as well. Why did he send it? What's going on between
him and Clive?

I go into the kitchen, my head reeling, and make myself a
cup of tea to take to bed (Rory always thinks it's weird that the
caffeine doesn't keep me awake like it does him). I'm returning
to my bedroom when I hear the letter box rattle. I slam my mug
down, spilling tea, and dart into the hallway, thinking it's Rory,
just in time to see something fluttering to the floor. It looks like

a leaflet. I bend over to pick it up. It's a bus ticket—I recognize the local company's logo. I turn it over, expecting a note on the back but there is nothing. When I read it again I see *BRISTOL TO TILBY* printed on the front. And a date: March 9, 2012. The date of the Wilson murders. I wrench open the front door, hoping to catch the person who posted it, but the corridor is empty.

33

Margot

The back door slams and Margot's heart leaps in her chest.

He's back. Adam's back at last. Where has he been all this time? Ethan must be exhausted.

She jumps up from the sofa. She probably shouldn't have had that third glass of wine. She feels light-headed and has to hold on to the doorjamb for support. She's just read Jess's text. She'd thought she recognized the words—she'd seen them before. It's only now she remembers where: in the office when she was searching through the bookings to see if Clive or Deirdre had ever stayed here. They had been scribbled on a piece of paper and she'd moved it aside without really thinking about it.

She doesn't know her son-in-law as well as she thought.

Adam strides in and her heart sinks when she sees he doesn't have her grandson with him. "Is he at Gloria's again?" she says, trying to push away the jealousy. She's hardly spent any time alone with Ethan lately, and when she offers, Adam tells her, in a slightly patronizing way, "You've got too much on your plate at the moment." In her lowest moments she can't help but worry that he's purposely keeping him away from her.

He runs a hand across his stubble, an aura of distraction surrounding him. "Ah, yes, but Mum lives on the way to the hospital. It was getting late. I'll pick him up on the way to see Heather tomorrow."

He slumps onto the sofa, still in his waxed jacket, eyeing the almost empty wine bottle on the coffee table. "Would you mind getting me a glass, Marg, as you're up?" he asks, as he reaches for the bottle. "Although it doesn't look like there's much left." His face is pale and drawn with tiredness, the bags under his eyes making him look older than his thirty-four years.

"I'll open another," she says, going to the kitchen to fetch a bottle and a glass. To her surprise, he follows her. He leans against the worktop and watches as she pours the wine. There is something brooding about his presence tonight.

Then his eyes flicker toward the two dirty plates still on the kitchen table and he frowns. "Who's been here?"

She bites back her irritation. It's still her house. "Jess. She popped over."

"You seem to be spending a lot of time with her lately."

"Yes, well, she was once very close to Heather. She knew Flora too."

He takes the wineglass from her and clomps back into the sitting room in his walking boots. She follows, wondering how she's going to bring up the subject of Clive. He reclines on the sofa, his face even more pinched. "I understand Jess reminds you of the past. But she's a journalist, remember? You can't trust her."

Margot purses her lips. There's no point in arguing with him. He would never understand what it's been like for her all these years. Losing a child is one thing, but never to know what has happened to that child, never to know if her last moments were of fear, or pain, not to have been there to protect her. It will haunt her, torment her, forever. That's one of the reasons she's never sold Tilby Manor. Just in case Flora is out there somewhere and manages to find her way home—although, deep down, she knows that's not likely. But if there is just a sliver of possibility that her daughter might have run away, there is also a very thin thread of hope that she might return. And Margot doesn't want to cut that thread. Ever. She'll die here, she's sure of that.

For a time Jess was like another daughter. And being with her makes Margot remember the past, yes, but more than that. It makes her house feel like a home again.

She takes a deep breath. "Adam. I don't want to ask Heather. She's still fragile and struggling to remember events leading up to the shooting. But I need to know. What did you argue about the night before her"—she struggles to find the right word—"accident?"

He sits up, suddenly alert now. "Jeez, Marg . . ."

"Was it about Clive?"

His eyes are round with shock. "What? Clive Wilson? Why would we be arguing about Clive?"

"Because you knew him."

He stands up, the wine in his glass sloshing so that some of it lands on the ancient patterned rug. "What? Of course I didn't know him. What makes you say that?" He slams his glass down on the coffee table and, for one fleeting moment, Margot actually feels afraid of him. Was this what he was like when he argued with Heather? Threatening? Aggressive?

She stands up too, but she only reaches his shoulder. "Please don't lie to me, Adam," she says calmly. "You were seen with him in the pub. And I know you wrote a threatening note to him after he died. 'This was one bullet you couldn't dodge.' Ring any bells?"

He runs his hand over his chin and she notices a throbbing in his jaw. "Fucking hell. Don't you trust me?"

She flinches. Adam never normally swears in front of her. "I want to know what you're hiding. I'm Heather's mother. I'm on your side. Heather's side. Adam . . . please. What were you both involved in? You can tell me anything."

He laughs, but there is an edge of mania to it. "You really think that I . . . *that Heather* . . . would be involved in anything dodgy?" He slumps back on the sofa. Suddenly the fight has gone out of him. His chin quivers and she sees, with a jolt, that he's on the verge of tears. "I was just trying to do something good." He gulps. "The pain she was in. It was always there, since the day I met her. The guilt she felt at Flora's death. She suffered with bouts of depression long before she had Ethan. But she didn't want to worry you. You'd been through enough, don't you see?"

Margot did. Her daughter, her lovely, gentle, kind Heather, hid her suffering so as not to upset her. The thought of it broke Margot's heart. "Go on," she says, in a small voice.

"At the beginning of the year Deirdre Wilson booked two nights in one of the caravans. She said she was in the process of buying a house in the area so wanted to be near as she had a few things to sort out. She brought her dog with her. It was extremely cute. Like a bear. Heather got talking to Deirdre." He smiles at the memory. "You know what Heather's like. She's always so good at small talk. She's genuinely interested in people. Anyway, Heather was really taken with the dog, I can't remember its name, and Deirdre told Heather she used to breed them, and gave Heather her contact details as her son, Clive, still did. I remembered Heather telling me about it. We felt it would be good for Ethan—for all of us—to have a puppy."

"So you spoke to Deirdre?"

"Yes. Only on the phone to get her son's details. By this time she'd moved into her cottage in Tilby."

"So then you contacted Clive?"

He nods. "Yes. We met up in the Funky Raven, as that's near where his mum was living, and he was staying with her. The dogs were expensive. Over a grand. I gave him a deposit and he promised there would be a litter due in a few weeks. We wouldn't be able to take the puppy, of course, until it was a few months old, but we could come and see the litter and reserve one. I gave him three hundred quid up front."

Margot sits back down on the sofa again. "And what happened?"

"He was bloody lying, wasn't he? The fucking con artist. There was no pregnant bitch. I asked around and apparently he had a dog. A male dog. So I met up with him again and asked for my money back. But he continued lying about it, making excuses. Anything, rather than give me the money. I threatened to knock his block off if he didn't return it."

"Oh, Adam."

"Well," he growls, "it was out of order, Marg."

Her mind races. "Even so, a note like that after he died was a bit extreme." There is dirt under her fingernails from cleaning out the horses earlier. She picks at it distractedly. "Especially with a murder investigation going on. What were you thinking?"

He shakes his head, his eyes bloodshot. "That's the thing. I wasn't thinking straight. Heather was in the hospital . . . They were saying she'd killed him. I was just so angry, with her . . . with Clive . . . everyone. It was stupid, I know. I blamed Clive. For the money . . . and then for what happened after, with Heather killing him . . . I think he was on her radar because of that. You know she's not been well"—he points to his head—"mentally. She flipped. She was angry with the world. She had a bee in her bonnet about Flora's disappearance. She blamed herself for that . . . I think it all got too much. So, the night after Heather did"—he gulps—"what she did, I came home and scribbled the note on a piece of paper to get the wording right, then rang up a florist and told them it was a joke for a friend's birthday."

"And Deirdre? Where does she fit into all this? She must have known that Clive wasn't really breeding from his own dog. Was she in on the scam too?"

"I don't know what she thought, Marg. She was an old lady. Maybe she didn't know what he was up to."

"Why didn't you tell the police any of this after . . . after . . . ?"

"I didn't want them to think that was why Heather killed them."

"Over a dog." She laughs. "But that's ridiculous."

He frowns. "I know that, but the police would try to find any spurious link, wouldn't they?"

Margot gets up. She feels woolly-headed after all the wine. She needs a warm drink. Adam follows her into the kitchen with the empty wineglasses. "I'm sorry I got angry," he says, his shoulders relaxing. "The note, it was a stupid thing to do. I regret it."

She clicks the kettle on and Adam sits at the wooden table, his head in his hands. She can't help but think there's more to it. Yes, three hundred pounds is a lot of money to lose but that level of anger at a man who died at the hands of your wife? It makes no sense to her.

"Did you ever get the money back?"

"No. Clive wouldn't admit there was a problem. He continued to promise us a puppy."

She rests a hand on his shoulder. He still has his coat on. She desperately wants to give him the benefit of the doubt. She has to believe in him, for Heather's sake. For Ethan's. "I'm sorry, Adam."

He places his hand over hers. They stay like that for a while, then Margot moves away to make hot chocolate. After a few minutes she hands Adam a mug. "Here, drink this."

"Thanks." He takes a sip, even though it's piping hot.

She sits next to him, at the head of the table. "So is that what you argued about? The night before? Money? The puppy?"

He lifts his head, his eyes puzzled. "No. Heather was on my side about all that. She thought Clive was just stringing us along too. No, it was something else. She . . ." He stares at his mug intently, not meeting Margot's eyes.

"What then?"

"She got this idea in her head that—"

They are interrupted by the shrill sound of the landline.

Adam jumps up. "It's a bit late for phone calls. It could be Mum ringing about Ethan, or the hospital." His face is gray.

Margot is on her feet, too, almost running to the little half-moon table in the hallway where the phone is.

"Hello."

"Hello, Margot? It's Gary—Gary Ruthgow."

Her heart picks up speed. "Gary . . ."

"I'm sorry to be calling late. But we've found a body. Remains. Bones, really, dating back fifteen to twenty years. And we're not a hundred percent sure yet, but . . ." Margot's legs threaten to buckle underneath her weight. "I think you should know we're looking into the possibility that it could be Flora."

34

August 1994

Heather's hand trembled so violently that the riding crop fell from her fingers to the grass at her feet. Dylan cowered before her and she noticed blood seeping through his thin tie-dyed T-shirt. What had she done?

It had happened again, just like before. The blackout. The rage. She couldn't even remember doing it, just the familiar bubbling sensation in her head, the flickering orbs of light sweeping across her vision, like the beginnings of an ocular migraine, and then the overwhelming feeling of anger before everything went black. And when she opened her eyes she was faced with this. An injured, cowering mess in front of her.

He had his hands over his head, as though expecting another blow. When it was obvious no more was forthcoming he straightened up, staring at her with wide, disbelieving eyes. He winced as he reached around, gingerly touching his T-shirt.

There were beads of blood on his fingertips. He stared at it in horror. "You crazy, fucking bitch."

"I—I don't know what happened. I'm sorry."

"You beat me with a riding crop, that's what fucking happened." He took a step back, as though he was afraid of her. "I only asked for Flora. You just flew at me."

Heather cast her eyes around the garden. Nobody else had seen, thank goodness.

It was two o'clock in the afternoon, the sun was at its hottest, and she'd just come back from a ride. She'd been walking across the field toward the barn where the tack room was when she'd seen Dylan skulking against the hedge.

She'd seen red, literally. And now here they were.

"You've actually drawn blood." He was still staring at his fingertips in amazement.

She wanted to tell him to get over it, hadn't he seen blood before?

"I'm really sorry," she repeated, moving toward him.

But he stumbled backward, terror on his face. "Get away from me, you fucking freak. You're mental."

"And you're no good for my sister. Leave her alone. She's not interested in a loser like you," she snapped.

He smirked. "That's not what she was saying the other night when she was groaning with pleasure underneath me."

Heather felt the fury pumping through her again. "She must have been drugged up," she fired back, "because that's the only way you can get your kicks."

His expression darkened and she noticed his fists were clenched at his sides.

"You're just a scuzzy sad loser," she taunted, on a roll now that she was getting a reaction. "And at last my sister's seen through you."

"You're just jealous," he said, turning away. "Flora is in love with me."

"Don't flatter yourself. She's moved on."

He whipped around so that he was facing her again. "You'd love that, wouldn't you? You control freak. She told me about you, you know. How you were such a cling-on, always tagging along after her. Never letting her have her own life. She hates you."

It can't be true. Flora would never say those cruel things about her. Never.

"Get lost or I'll tell the police you're giving my sister drugs," she cried.

"Yes. Go ahead. Call them." He lifted up his T-shirt. Four deep whip marks were visible along his tanned back. "I'm sure they'll be interested to hear how you attacked me." He shook his head. "You're a nutter." Then the smirk was back. "Flora knows where to find me. She can't keep away. You'll see."

"If you come back here my Uncle Leo will shoot you with his gun," Heather yelled.

He flicked his middle finger at her, then turned and trudged away. She watched his retreating back, angry at his words, yet mortified that she had lost control. Again.

FLORA HAD SEEN HIM ARRIVE. SHE WAS UP IN HER BEDROOM LISTENING to her favorite All About Eve album, sprawled on her window seat and thinking of Dylan, their magical evening two nights ago. From her room she had a view of the Big Wheel's flashing lights between the trees. She wanted to go to him, but knew she had to be careful. Uncle Leo had given her a stern talking-to about drugs, and warned her that if he ever found her in that state again he'd tell her mum and call the police about Dylan. She couldn't risk it.

And then, as if her thoughts had somehow conjured him up, Dylan was there, in the garden, talking to Heather. Her heart swelled. He had come to see her. Oh, he was so beautiful, she couldn't bear it. She touched the leaded-glass window with her palm, her eyes scanning the length of the garden and the accompanying fields for Uncle Leo. Was he out riding? In the caravan park with her mum? Or somewhere with that annoying girlfriend of his?

A yelp of pain made Flora's eyes dart back to Dylan and her sister. She sat forward, in shock, unable to believe her eyes. Heather was whipping Dylan, her face filled with hatred. Thwack, thwack, thwack, over and over again while he cowered like a poor animal in pain. No. What was she doing? She was hurting him. Stop! She banged on the glass but Heather kept up her relentless, torturous rhythm, her eyes glazed and unfocused.

She was going to kill Dylan. Flora had to stop it.

Flora ran from her room and down the stairs, almost tripping over her long skirt, and raced through the living room and out of the French windows, barefoot. But she was too late. Dylan was gone and Heather was standing alone, riding crop at her feet.

"What the fuck do you think you're doing?" Flora screamed, grabbing Heather's arms and shaking her violently. "I saw you! I saw you from my bedroom window."

Heather hung her head; a patch of red had appeared on each cheek. "I don't know what came over me. I'm sorry."

"You're a little psycho," she cried, still gripping Heather. "Where has he gone?"

Heather shrugged. And Flora released her, pushing her hard in the chest so that her sister toppled backward, landing with a thump on her bottom. Then Flora sprinted across the lawn, faster than she'd ever run in her life, her bare feet snagging on stones and thistles but she didn't care. She had to catch him.

She spotted him in the distance, just as he was entering the fairground. She tried to call his name, but Flora was too out of breath, too unfit, and the word died on her lips. She panted, clutching her side. *Come back!* She had no choice but to walk through the fair barefoot. She winced as she imagined treading on gum, sweet wrappers, and God knew what else. But she was so desperate to kiss him, to soothe away the sores inflicted by her head case sister, that she would have walked over razor blades if she had to.

Dylan paused at the entrance of the fair, squinting into the sun. He reached around and touched the place on his back, near his left shoulder, where Heather had struck him.

Her poor baby. Flora took a few steps forward, her breath ragged, still clutching her side, trying to press the stitch away. "Dylan!" she called.

"Dylan!" a woman's voice echoed.

Flora's voice was drowned by another. A woman, running up to *her* boyfriend, *her love*, and jumping into his arms, wrapping her long, brown legs around his waist, her copper curls cascading down her back.

Flora bent over, in physical pain, feeling as though she might throw up as the woman leaned forward, kissing *her* Dylan deeply on the lips.

She had lost him. And it was all Heather's fault.

35

M Y BRAIN FEELS WOOZY. THE IMAGES OF THAT DAY ARE STILL ALL JUMBLED UP
so that nothing is clear. I just wish I could remember more. Everything
aches, my head, my limbs, and I never feel warm.

Underneath all the fear and the guilt, I know that Dylan is to
blame. He was the one who caused a rift between us. He's the one with
the secrets.

Unfortunately he's not the only one. Uncle Leo. My mind keeps going back to him yet I can't quite figure out why. I only know that he's an
important piece in the puzzle I'm trying to work out in my chemically
fogged brain.

36

Jess

WHEN MY ALARM GOES OFF THE NEXT MORNING I'M SURPRISED
to find myself lying on top of the duvet, still dressed in yesterday's clothes. Rory isn't next to me. I touch his side of the bed,
the covers still pristine and wrinkle-free. Did he come home
last night? I feel a stab of fear and sit up, blinking in the early-
morning light that seeps around the edges of the bedroom curtains, my mouth dry.

Despite my self-enforced rule not to drink during the week
I'd been so freaked out by discovering someone had been outside
my front door that I opened a bottle of wine and drank the lot. I
must have staggered in here and collapsed in a heap on the bed.
I'd wanted to blot everything out: the fear, the loneliness, the
fact someone's watching me.

I get up and go into the kitchen, hoping that maybe Rory fell
asleep on the sofa. But it's all just as I left it yesterday.

I check my phone, but nothing from Rory. What if something's happened to him?

I click the kettle on, then stand in the kitchen and call Rory on my mobile. Eventually I hear a raspy "Hello?"

"Rory. It's me. Where are you? Are you okay?"

There's a rustling sound, as though he's getting out of bed. "Yeah. Sorry. Ian said I could stay at his so that I could have a few drinks."

My stomach lurches. We've been together for nearly three years and he's never stayed out without letting me know. "Why didn't you ring me?" It's not like Rory to play games.

He sighs. "I thought you'd be busy. We never see each other much anyway. You're always out."

"That's not true," I say, hurt. My mobile feels hot against my ear.

"You're in Tilby a lot . . ." The words "with Margot" are left unsaid but I know he's thinking them. He clears his throat. "Look, I'm sorry. I should have called. I'm angry with you and I'm trying to punish you."

Typical Rory, telling me how it is. Despite myself I can't help a small sad smile. I nod, even though he can't see me.

"But that's not going to get us anywhere, is it?" His voice is tinged with regret.

"No," I say quietly.

"I'm teaching all week in Hanham. But I'll be home at six. Okay. Then we can talk. Properly." This is more like the Rory I know and love. The Rory who always has to find a solution, who hates going to bed on an argument, who prefers to clear the air. He's not the type to mooch about for a week in a mood, refusing to discuss our problems. Unlike me.

"Okay, that would be good," I say, closing my eyes, relief flooding through me. "I'll see you tonight." The phone goes dead, but I leave it pressed to my ear for a couple of seconds anyway, listening to nothing.

I MET RORY AT A PARTY IN HAMMERSMITH. I HAD JUST TURNED twenty-nine and was still reeling from the breakdown of my first serious long-term relationship. I hadn't planned on meeting anyone that night. I had sworn off men.

I'd been sitting on the sticky threadbare carpet, my back against the woodchip wallpaper, nursing a beer and wondering why I'd bothered to come. My friend and colleague Anita, from the *Standard*—where I was working at the time—was dancing in the middle of the room with a group of people I'd never seen before, jumping up and down to The Strokes with an abandon I'd wished I'd felt.

"You look like you need cheering up," a voice said, and a guy with floppy dark hair, striking navy-blue eyes, and an impish grin sat down next to me. He had on flares and a retro 1970s shirt with a swirly orange print. Even though it was hideous he managed to carry it off. He must have noticed me staring at it because he'd blushed a little and glanced down at his clothes. "Yeah. Sorry about the getup. I've just come from a seventies party. It was shite."

I'd laughed then. "This party's even worse."

He watched the dancers throwing themselves around the floor and cocked an eyebrow, his eyes twinkling mischievously when "Jump Around" by House of Pain came on. "It is. But they look like they're having fun. Come on." He got to his feet and pulled me up, my beer sloshing over my chipped mug. "Give me that," he said, taking it from me and shoving it on the mantelpiece next to a plant with cigarette butts covering the soil. I was mortified. I wasn't a dancer and I didn't even know this man. But he didn't give me much choice as he started throwing me around and performing outrageous moves, trying to make me laugh. And because he was sexy and handsome, I allowed myself to go along with it, before long even beginning to enjoy it. When the song had finished we flopped into a faded old armchair, breathless.

And that was when we started talking, and when we found we couldn't stop. I could have listened to him forever, the soft Irish lilt in his voice, the way he talked about his brothers and sister and parents. He told me he was a teacher and that he loved kids. And, as I sat practically on his lap, enraptured by this funny, gorgeous, off-the-wall man in the hideous 1970s shirt, I realized I needed to see him again. His optimism and love for his family were infectious. Even then, I was desperate to be part of it, and it wasn't long before I was. His family welcomed me with open arms and the same wry sense of humor as Rory. I loved them almost as much as I loved him.

As time passed, I fell deeper in love with him, this man who was so straight. So good. All my other partners had played games, had agendas, but not Rory. He was honest about his feelings right from the beginning, and he listened to how I felt. He'd never pressured me into anything. We talked about the future, of course, in the abstract way you do when you don't really believe you'll become thirty, then thirty-one in the blink of an eye, and have to make grown-up decisions, like whether to get married and have children.

But now, for the first time since we've been together, I feel the pressure.

If I don't commit to Rory he'll leave me, find someone else to marry and have his babies.

I walk to work, despondent but fearless. In the cold light of day I have more courage: I'm ready to tackle anyone who might pose a threat. *Back off.* Nobody tells me what to do, I think, as my feet pound the pavement. Someone is playing mind games with me and I'm not having it. I refuse to be intimidated. I'm a strong, independent woman. I don't need this kind of shit in my life.

It starts to rain and I put my umbrella up, the damp seeping through my sheer purple spotty tights. I'm walking by the river when my mobile buzzes in my coat pocket. I stop to answer it, expecting it to be Ted, asking me to take a detour to interview someone on my way in. I'm surprised when I find it's Margot. She must want to talk to me about what went down with Adam last night.

Her voice sounds strained, like she's been crying. "Sorry to bother you, Jess. I just . . . I needed to talk to someone. It's too early to visit Heather yet."

"Are you okay? How did it go with Adam last night? Did you tell him about the note?"

"Yes. That's all fine. He was buying a puppy from Clive. It's not that, Jess. It's . . . The police called. This is off the record until you hear from them yourself but"—she gulps—"they think they've found Flora's body."

I gasp and lean over the railings, the river rushing past me. I need a cigarette so badly that my hand trembles in anticipation. "What?" I manage. "Where?"

"They wouldn't say too much. I need to go to the police station. I need to . . ." Her voice is shaky.

"When? Would you like me to come with you?"

"They've told me to go later. This afternoon. No, it's okay, Jess. Thank you, though. I'll . . . I'll be in touch. I've got to dash now."

I open my mouth to respond but the phone goes dead.

I drop it into my coat pocket and stand there for a few seconds, gazing out across the river. A seagull swoops down next to me and starts picking apart the remains of a sausage roll near my feet.

I can't believe Flora's body's been found. After all these years.

Balancing the umbrella in the crook of my arm, I fumble in my bag for my cigarettes and light one, using my hand to shield the flame from the wind. I close my eyes as I take a few drags, instantly feeling calmer.

I always believed Flora was dead. Especially when her blood-stained blouse turned up in the undergrowth nearby. But her body having been found after all these years still comes as a shock.

I'd never told the police or Heather about the part I played in Flora's disappearance.

I'd been a teenager, young and silly and terrified. I thought, if I told the truth, I'd get into trouble. So I kept quiet. And, obviously, at the time I didn't realize that the event I'd previously perceived as so small and unimportant would become so significant, until it was clear that Flora wasn't coming home.

So I did to Heather exactly what I'm doing to Rory now. I pushed her away.

My cheeks feel wet. I'm crying. I hardly ever cry. I hate it. It makes me feel weak and vulnerable. I've always felt it serves no purpose. In my view, it's better to try to get on with things. I brush away the tears angrily. Get a grip, woman, I tell myself. This isn't about you. It's about Flora. Beautiful, exotic Flora.

Would I have been able to save her if I'd known?

"Don't tell anyone," she'd whispered to me, her long hair brushing my face as her mouth pressed against my ear. She'd smelled of White Musk from the Body Shop and fruity lip gloss. I think she knew I looked up to her, and that I'd do anything she asked. "Particularly Heather," she'd added. *Particularly Heather.*

I'd agreed, of course. She'd had a rucksack on her shoulders, one of those school ones in yellow hessian that you could write on. She'd drawn a heart with the initials DB 4 FP inside it with flouncy letters. They were going on a day trip, she'd said. Her and Dylan. She'd be back before dark, as always. "But cover for me," she'd said. "I don't want anyone to know that we won't be in Tilby. If anyone asks, I'm at the fair. Okay? Promise?"

I'd promised.

I never knew what she did that day. Because I never saw her again.

But she'd been spotted at nine o'clock that evening walking along the high street. The driver who saw her said she was alone. And then nothing. No other sightings of her. It was as if she'd walked into a black hole or an alternative universe. She simply . . . vanished.

And I kept my promise. I never did tell. At first it was because I thought she'd come back and I didn't want to get her into trouble. I wanted her to think she could confide in me. Trust me. And then, when it was obvious something had happened, I thought maybe she'd run away with Dylan. Guilt and fear kept me away from Heather and, understandably confused and annoyed that I wasn't supportive of her, Heather became aggressive and surly with me—until eventually I stopped calling for her altogether. I abandoned her when she most needed my friendship. And I've lived with the guilt of that for the last eighteen years. Not that I thought about it. That's what I do best: bury my head in the sand. If I don't think about it, I can pretend it hasn't happened.

Except—as I'm beginning to realize—these things have a way of coming back to haunt you. To make you sit up and pay attention, like a devout preacher, or a strict, determined teacher, so that you can no longer just put your hands over your ears to block out the sound.

I flick my cigarette butt onto the ground and stamp on it.

It's stopped raining so I take down my umbrella and trudge the rest of the way to the office, stopping at Woodes on Park Street to buy two coffees, handing one to Stan, who's cuddled up in his sleeping bag outside the door.

"Sounds like it's all kicking off in there today," he says, inclining his head toward the building. "Your boss has been out here asking me if I've seen you. He's tried calling you apparently." He warms his hands on the cardboard cup. He has on threadbare fingerless gloves and his nails are yellow. Sometimes he finds a bed in a shelter, but more often than not he sleeps outside, on a bench in College Green or in a doorway. I've always wanted to ask him how he ended up here. What happened? Was he a teenage runaway, hiding from an abusive family? Drugs or alcohol? He can't be that much older than me.

I check my watch. I'm not late. If anything, I'm fifteen minutes early. Has Ted heard about Flora's body being found?

"I'd better go," I say, moving away from him to open the door.

He grimaces, as though I'm about to walk into a lion enclosure at a safari park. "Rather you than me. This is why I don't have a job." He chuckles.

When I get upstairs Sue isn't in, but Ted is pacing the floor and Ellie is sitting staring up at him, all wide cow eyes, hugging her knees, and Jack is standing over his desk, fiddling with his camera. Nobody has thought to turn on the overhead light and the effect is dark and murky.

"What's going on?" I say, putting my coffee on my desk and shrugging off my coat. I hang it on the back of my chair and throw the umbrella onto the floor. The sky outside darkens and thunder growls.

"There you are!" Ted whips around to stare at me. He's got that look in his eye again: excitement and fire. I glance across at Jack who rolls his eyes. "Our boy Jack here has given us a great tip-off from his copper boyfriend." He taps the side of his nose. "Although, obviously, we can't reveal the source if anybody asks."

I pause, surprised. Finn said he never gives tip-offs—and I know Jack has asked many times.

"A body has been found."

Nothing new, I want to say, but I don't. Margot asked me not to tell anyone and I'll respect her wishes and do the right thing, for once.

I pretend to look shocked.

"The police think it's Flora Powell," he says. "You know, the sister of Heather Underwood."

"Yes. I know who Flora is."

"But that's not all," he says. He can hardly contain himself. He's like a comedian on a stage who can't wait to deliver the punch line. "The body has been found in a house in Southville, Bristol."

I frown. Southville? My stomach twists. Please no . . .

"In a Victorian house in Ridings Road, apparently owned by Clive Wilson."

I feel sick. "What?"

His eyes are shining. "That's right. At last there's a motive. It seems like Clive Wilson killed Heather's sister. She must have found out somehow, and shot him in revenge."

My head is spinning. It would make more sense than the idea that Heather had shot the Wilsons in some indiscriminate attack. Heather was always ultraprotective of her sister.

"Can you and Jack go to the address now? See what you can find out?" It's not really a question and Ted has already turned away to talk to Ellie before I can answer.

Jack pulls his camera case onto his shoulder. Without speaking, we leave the office, almost bumping into Sue as she's coming through the front door. She knocks me with her elbow and my coffee spurts over the top of the plastic rim. She's wearing new glasses that take up almost half of her face.

"Where are you off to in such a hurry?" She laughs, pushing her glasses further up her nose while I lick the coffee from the lid.

"A body's been found," says Jack. "It's all go here today, Sue." He glances at me, about to make a quip, no doubt, but I shoot him a look that says, *Don't make jokes. Not about this.* And he closes his mouth.

"What a story this is turning out to be," says Jack, as he strides down Park Street. He turns his collar up against the rain and I try to hold my umbrella over his head, but he's way too tall and one of the spokes keeps jabbing him in the ear. "Here, let me have that," he says, taking it from me. I link my arm through his while he holds it over both of us. "This must be weird for you," he says.

I sip my coffee. "It is. When I first heard, I thought there must be some mistake, that Heather couldn't possibly have shot those two people. But now . . . if Clive had killed Flora and she'd somehow found out, well, it makes more sense. It's still extreme, don't get me wrong, but more *understandable* somehow."

He's quiet for a few moments. Then, frowning, he says, "What doesn't make sense, though, is why she'd kill his mother. Why did she kill Deirdre Wilson as well?"

37

Jess

As soon as we arrive at the terraced road in Southville, with its row of almost identical Victorian houses, we spot Clive's instantly. It stands out like a flamboyant wedding cake in a line of chocolate sponges. It's been cordoned off with police tape, and a white forensics tent has been erected in the front garden, obscuring the entrance to the basement. A police officer is standing on the front steps, a notebook in his hand, assessing the small crowd of onlookers that has gathered on the rain-slick pavement, shivering in their coats. As yet I can't see any other journalists or TV stations.

The house is a far cry from the well-kept Tilby cottage. Paint flakes around the window frames, the net curtains look grubby, and the roof is missing a few tiles. I can see that the front garden is overgrown; no cute gnomes or umbrella stands here.

My recently digested latte curdles in my stomach as it hits me, again, that this is where Flora's decomposing body was discovered. I glance at the tent. Is that the actual spot where they found her? Or are they using it to block out the view into the basement?

It's stopped raining now, but there is dampness in the air and the sky is thick with gray clouds.

Jack sets down his tripod, a hand to the small of his back as he bends over. We'd parked in the next street even though it would take only fifteen minutes to walk from my place. The way Jack's acting you'd think we had to trek miles with his camera equipment on his shoulders, like a mule.

He winces as he stands up. The bruise around his eye has turned a yellowy purple, and it's in stark contrast to his pale face. "I must have pulled a muscle." He grimaces.

I roll my eyes. "Seriously? We've just walked around the corner."

He turns away from me to set up his tripod on the pavement opposite Clive's house and, for one brief, disbelieving moment, I wonder if I've offended him. Jack and I always take the piss out of each other. That's our thing. It's always done with affection. It's because we're close and have the same sense of humor. He'd normally retaliate with a killer comeback: he'd make a quip about my clothes, hair, or accent. But he's silent as he carefully places the camera on top of the tripod.

I touch his shoulder softly. "Hey. I didn't mean it. Are you okay?"

"Sure. Of course." But he doesn't look at me as he says it.

I'm about to say more when I'm distracted by someone standing at the edge of the gathered crowd. It might have been nearly twenty years since I last saw him, but I can tell it's him by the way he stands, the arc of his neck, the floppy, curly hair that looks like it should belong on a Labradoodle. He's wearing jeans and a tan leather biker jacket, with a stripy scarf thrown stylishly around his throat. Even from here I can tell he's handsome. He reminds me a little of a taller, duskier Rory. I move slowly away from Jack and cross the narrow street so that I'm standing beside the man.

I clear my throat and he turns his head in my direction. He must be nearly forty now. He has lines fanning from his eyes and bracketing his mouth, but he hasn't changed much. There is no gray amid the thatch of dark curls. His eyes are still a startling blue. He doesn't recognize me, I can tell. I bet he hardly noticed me back then. I was just a friend of Flora's sister. A kid. Practically invisible to the likes of Dylan Bird.

I decide to use my anonymity to my advantage. "What do you think's going on here, then?" I ask, flashing him my most charming smile.

He thrusts his hands into his pockets. "I heard a body's been found. They think it's been there years." He talks out of the side of his mouth. I'd forgotten he used to do that.

I wonder how he would have heard. Maybe a friend lives in this street.

"Did you know the man who lived there?"

He frowns, the lines between his eyebrows transforming into deep furrows, giving him a wolflike appearance. "I met him once or twice. A long time ago."

He met him once or twice. How? How did Dylan know Clive?

"Do you live around here, then?"

He shakes that mop of curls. "About five minutes away. I was just passing on my way to work." He looks at his watch theatrically. "Which reminds me, I'd better get going." He steps away from me but I grab his arm.

"Wait!" I cry. "Dylan. It's me. Jessica Fox. I was Heather Powell's best friend. I met you when you were going out with her sister, Flora."

His eyes narrow as he surveys me. "Oh, yeah. I remember you. And Heather. She attacked me once."

"I know. I read about it in the newspapers." Heather had played down the incident at the time. She must have been embarrassed. I would have been too. It was so out of character for her to be violent. Or was it? Now I know she shot her father, when she was only ten, I'm not so sure. The more I find out about Heather the less convinced I am of her innocence. I'm reminded of the differences that always lay between us, which I'd refused to see. Like how, out of the two of us, I always thought I was the stronger, harder, more independent one because Heather seemed quieter, softer than me. Yet the incident with the riding crop, the possessive way she acted around Flora, her justification to me of her uncle Leo when he'd killed a sheep that had wandered onto their land, all point to someone who was much steelier than I'd given her credit for.

And now this. A motive. It's a difficult thing to come to terms with, but I have to accept that Heather shot dead Clive and Deirdre.

I've been conflicted over this for so long. But now I'm almost relieved.

"What are you doing here?" asks Dylan.

I realize I'm still holding his arm, and I remove my hand, suddenly embarrassed. "I'm a journalist now. I've been covering the story about Heather."

I didn't know he was living so locally. Could he have been following me? Had he planted those photographs behind my windscreen wiper and posted that bus ticket through my door? But why? What would have been his motive for following me and telling me to back off?

I still haven't told Jack about the photographs.

Dylan swears under his breath. "I need a fag."

I open my bag and retrieve my packet of Marlboro Gold. "Here," I say, offering it. He takes one without saying thank you, and waits for me to light it for him. When I've done so, we both move away from the crowd.

"I can't get over this," he mutters, as we walk down the street. "It's like Rose and Fred West all over again."

"I hope not. They had more than one body buried in their garden."

Dylan raises his eyebrows. "Maybe now everybody will stop pointing the finger at me," he says. He takes a deep puff on his cigarette. "The police wouldn't leave me alone after Flora went missing. Even when my fairground mates vouched for me. The cops made my life a misery. They were everywhere. They questioned everyone who worked there and wouldn't let us leave. We were supposed to go up to Blackpool but we had to stay on in Tilby until the police had finished with their inquiries."

Dylan stops to lean against a wall, one leg bent backward with his foot resting on the brick. He still manages to look cool. Part of me wishes he'd become fat and ugly in the interim years. For Flora. But no. Here he is looking better than ever. Arsehole. While beautiful, vibrant Flora has been reduced to decaying bones. He might not have killed Flora but it's still his fault she's dead. He should have walked her home. She was just sixteen years old.

Jack is oblivious to me and Dylan standing further up the street—he's too busy snapping away with his camera. He's now taken it off the tripod and has it pressed up to his face as he tries to get as close to the forensics tent as possible. Any minute now I'm sure he'll be shooed away by the police officer. I had better be quick.

"When did you meet Clive?"

He exhales smoke slowly into the misty air. "Oh, years ago. My mum was dating his brother, Speedy."

"Speedy?"

"That was his nickname. Because he supplied drugs and was always on speed. But his real name was Norman."

Norman. Oh my God. "Norman Wilson was dating your mum in nineteen ninety-four?" Is he still involved with drugs? Were both Clive and Norman dealers? Were they running some kind of drugs racket here in Bristol? But Norman had said he hadn't seen much of Clive over the years.

He nods. "For a few years. They split up a year or so after Flora went missing."

"And Clive and his mum, Deirdre? You knew them too?"

"We spent Christmas with them once. There, actually." He gestures to the house down the street.

Jack is now glancing around for me. He waves when he spots me but Dylan doesn't notice. "It was before I met Flora. Must have been Christmas 'ninety-three. They seemed okay. Deirdre was nice. Chatty, fussing around us all, making sure we had enough to eat and drink. She had a couple of cute dogs. Clive was quiet, a bit odd, but nothing out of the ordinary, although it was obvious he was a total mummy's boy."

"In what way was he odd?"

He takes another puff on his cigarette. "Not very friendly. Avoided eye contact, that kind of thing. He'd stare at my mum a lot, too, when she wasn't looking. I noticed him leering at her arse as she helped Deirdre carry the roast spuds through to the dining room."

I picture Clive from the photographs that Norman's daughter Lisa had emailed across. He hadn't looked particularly sinister. But, then, it's not as though psychopaths have it tattooed on their foreheads, is it? "Did Flora and Clive ever meet?"

"That's the weird thing," he says. "I can't remember them ever meeting. He did come to the fair once, though. That summer. With Speedy. *Norman*," he corrects himself. "But I can't remember if Flora was there that day."

"And Deirdre?"

"Deirdre never came to the fair. I only met her that one time at Christmas."

I try to get it all straight in my mind. "So, the day Clive visited you and Norman, how long was it before Flora went missing?"

He pushes his hair back from his face. "I don't know." He sounds irritated. "A few days. That same week, I'm sure. But it's a long time ago. I can't remember exactly."

"But the day Flora went missing. You didn't see him?"

He shakes his head.

Something doesn't add up. "Why was Norman at the fair? Did he work there?"

Dylan drops the cigarette butt onto the pavement and grinds it into the tarmac with the heel of his boot. "No. Not exactly. He used to supply us with drugs." His head shoots up. "You're not reporting any of this, are you?" He moves away from the wall and stands up straight. "We're just old mates, having a chat."

Old mates? I want to laugh in his face.

"Yep, just chatting, don't worry," I lie. I won't have any qualms in using what he tells me if I need to. I owe him nothing.

Dylan's eyes dart toward the house and he grimaces. "I haven't seen Norman in years. I'm sure he's a reformed man. Or perhaps not. I don't know." His expression changes and he looks sad. "Me and Flora, we were kids. I know we wouldn't have lasted. But I've carried the guilt for all these years, wondering if I could have done something. I should have made sure she got home okay . . . but I left her there."

I frown, trying to keep up. "Left her where?"

He chews his lip and has the good grace to look ashamed. He hangs his head. "In London. We went there for the day. But while we were there we had a huge row and came back separately. Went to the fair. There's witnesses to put me there. I'm not lying." His blue eyes flash. "But I should have seen her home. She disappeared from the bus stop back in Tilby. Did you know that?"

"Yes. I read it at the time."

"A family drove past and saw her walking past the clock tower. It was less than ten minutes from her home."

"I know."

"She came home safely from London."

I stare at him, appalled. Does that make it better? Because she hadn't disappeared in London after he'd left her there? I should have told someone. I should have told Heather the truth, or just stopped Flora going. If she'd been in Tilby she wouldn't have been at the bus stop, and she wouldn't have been walking along the high street, alone at night. She might still be alive and Heather wouldn't have ruined her life trying to get revenge.

Dylan groans. "And now *this*."

I frown. "What?"

"Clive." He covers his face with his hands. Is he crying? "It's my fault," he says, through his fingers. "He must have killed her because of me."

38

August 1994

Flora shoved a twenty-pound note into a beaded fabric purse. It was all the money she had. She wasn't allowed to touch her savings. They were sitting in her building-society account waiting until she was old enough to buy her first car, her mum always said. And it wasn't as if she was running away. No, it was just a day trip. She'd be back by dark. Before anyone worked out that she was gone.

Her mum was so busy with the caravan park that she wouldn't notice where she was. Just as long as she returned home at the normal time, all would be well. She would have asked Heather to cover for her, but she still wasn't talking to her sister. She was furious with her for almost splitting up her and Dylan. Almost. But it hadn't worked.

When she'd seen *that girl* kissing him she'd been incensed. And then, much to her delight, he'd pushed her away. He had his back to her so she couldn't see his face, but the girl looked dejected, stepping away from him and folding her arms across her chest, her pouty lips turned down. "You know I've got a girl-friend," she'd heard him say, and then he must have sensed Flora watching because he turned, his face falling when he realized she had seen. He must have thought she was about to flounce off in a huff. But, no, she wouldn't give that hussy the satisfaction. Instead she'd marched right up to Dylan and flung her arms around his neck, kissing him deeply. When she opened her eyes the girl had gone.

They were invincible. Nobody could come between them.

And now this. London. She was so excited last night she hardly slept.

They planned to meet by the clock tower at 6:30 a.m. to get the bus into Bristol. From there they had booked a Stagecoach to London. Only ten pounds for a return trip, and Dylan had kindly paid for her. She was still unsure exactly why Dylan was so desperate to go to London, or what he planned to do when they got there, but she didn't care. She'd never been to London before. A whole day with the love of her life. She imagined them wandering around Trafalgar Square or Hyde Park, hand in hand. It was going to be so romantic and it would be such a relief to be away from Tilby, the fair, and that idiot, Speedy, who seemed to be hanging around more and more often, these days.

Despite the early hour the sun was already out, and she could hear the cockerel crowing from the farm next door. A shiver of anticipation ran through her. She dressed quickly in her favorite sleeveless ivory blouse with the lace collar and a blood red ankle-length skirt with tassels at the hem, slipping on her mood stone necklace that Dylan had bought for her. It was a deep blue. Happy. And then she crept out of her bedroom, her rucksack on her back, and padded down the landing, her black DM boots in her hand. She knew her mum would be up already, mucking out the horses with Sheila. Uncle Leo should still be in bed. He was a late riser and didn't normally emerge until gone nine.

She tiptoed past Heather's room. Her door was half-closed and she could just see the edge of the camp bed on the floor where Jess was sleeping. The girl hardly ever seemed to be at home. A floorboard creaked under her foot and she paused, waiting to see if she had woken anybody. She was just about to continue toward the staircase when she heard a movement behind her. She froze, and turned slowly. Jess was standing at the entrance to Heather's room in a Snoopy nightshirt, her hair standing on end, rubbing her eyes sleepily.

"What's going on?" she whispered.

Flora put a finger to her lips and inclined her head toward the stairs in a follow-me gesture. Jess looked confused but she shadowed Flora down the stairs until they were standing in the hallway by the front door. Goldie came bounding up to them and Flora had to shush her as well. "Please, don't make any noise," she whispered.

"Are you running away?" asked Jess, her big brown eyes wide with horror.

"No. But don't tell anyone, particularly Heather," whispered

Flora. "I'm going on a day trip. Away from Tilby. With Dylan. Will you cover for me? If anyone asks we're at the fair. I'll get the bus back before dark. Mum will never know I've gone. But, please," she urged, "don't tell Heather."

Jess shrugged. In her nightclothes with no makeup she looked younger than fourteen. "Okay."

"Promise."

"I promise."

"Okay. Great." Flora sat on the bottom step and slipped her feet into her heavy DMs, tying the laces quickly. She jumped up. "I've got to go." She kissed a surprised Jess on the cheek. "Thank you." She hoisted the bag further up her back, gave Goldie a quick hug, and snuck out of the front door, turning once more to flash Jess a grateful smile.

FROM HER BEDROOM WINDOW HEATHER WATCHED FLORA MOVE deftly over the gravel driveway, like a cat burglar. And then she eyed Jess's empty bed. She'd heard every word they'd said and it broke her heart. *Don't tell Heather.*

There was a time when Flora had told her everything. They never kept secrets from each other. And now here she was, sneaking off to spend the day with her boyfriend, asking Heather's best friend to lie for her. She remembered Dylan's cruel words from the other day. *Always tagging along after her. You're such a cling-on. She hates you.*

Was it true? She was beginning to think that maybe Dylan had been right.

If there was one thing she'd never doubted before, it was Flora's love for her. But since the other evening, when she'd whipped—it still made her cringe to think of it—Dylan, and Flora had pushed her over, her sister had been avoiding her and the chasm between them was widening. She couldn't allow that to happen. They'd been through too much together.

She'd shot their father for Flora, for Christ's sake.

39

Margot

THE AIR IS STALE INSIDE THE COMPACT INTERVIEW ROOM AND MARgot has to remind herself to breathe. Her palms are sweating and she pulls the scarf away from her throat. It feels like it's choking her. Oh, how she hates confined spaces. She's happiest when she's in the open, or when she's riding her horse across the Gallops. It's only then she feels she can really breathe. She takes a sip of warm water from the plastic cup a sympathetic policewoman had given her when she first arrived.

Adam had offered to come with her to Bridewell, but she'd refused, saying she would rather be alone. But she's regretting that now. It would have been better to have someone with her. She wishes Heather was at her side or, failing that, Jess's reassuring, no-nonsense presence.

She'd been to see Heather that morning to tell her about Flora.

Heather was making excellent progress. The police still hadn't formally interviewed her and wouldn't until the doctors determined that she was well enough. A police officer continued to stand guard outside her door. Sometimes they even came into the room and sat quietly next to the bed. Margot was sure this was in case Heather said something incriminating in her sleep. She hopes she hasn't.

Heather had been dozing when Margot arrived that morning. She was on so many drugs and painkillers, plus intravenous antibiotics because the wound to her chest had become infected, and they made her sleepy. But her brain activity was normal, there was no sign of swelling, and the doctors said once the infection had gone and her wound began to heal she could be discharged. Discharged where? That was the question that most bothered Margot.

Margot had sat on the chair next to Heather's bed and stroked her hair away from her face. "Heather," she had said, "are you awake?"

Heather's eyes had fluttered open and she'd smiled. She sat up and asked if Margot had brought Ethan with her.

"Adam's bringing him later."

Heather flopped back against the pillows. "I miss him so much. I just want to get out of here."

"I know, sweetheart."

She had turned her face away from her mother and Margot suspected she was crying. "This is all just a nightmare." She sniffed. "That solicitor you employed came to see me yesterday and was asking all sorts of questions. Do you really think I'll end up having to go to court?"

Of course you will, Margot had wanted to say. *As soon as the police are able to interview you, you'll be charged. I have no doubt.* But she can't tell Heather the truth. Not now.

"Listen, love. The police called. There's been some news."

Heather had turned her tearstained face back to Margot. "What news?" Her eyes were hopeful and Margot's heart sank. *Not good news,* she wanted to say.

"The man who—who the police think you shot, Clive Wilson, well, a body has been found in the basement of his house. A body that's been there a long time. They think . . ." She'd gulped. It never got easier to say it. "They think it's Flora."

Heather's mouth hung open and her eyes grew large and round. "What? No. No, that can't be right."

"The police will have a motive now. They'll think you found out somehow and killed him. And his mother."

Heather shook her head. "But, no, that's . . . That can't be. It's not Flora."

"There's a strong likelihood it is," said Margot, gently. *Why else did you kill Clive and Deirdre Wilson?* she had added silently. She took Heather's hand. "Listen, the solicitor I instructed— Louisa Milligan—said there's enough evidence to suggest you could be charged with manslaughter on account of diminished responsibility or . . ."

Heather squeezed Margot's hand so tightly that it hurt. "Ow," she said, snatching it back. There were three half-moon indents where Heather had dug her nails into the flesh.

"I'm sorry but, Mum, you're not listening to me. I didn't kill Clive. I've never met him. Yes, Adam spoke to him about getting us a puppy. But—and I know I can't remember that morning, what I'm supposed to have done—but why would I kill him? Surely if I found out he'd killed Flora I'd remember something as huge as that . . . wouldn't I?" She trailed off, confusion written all over her face.

"You know what the doctors said. A traumatic incident can sometimes cause temporary amnesia. The brain is protecting you from remembering something so horrific. It could have blocked out the fact that you knew Clive killed Flora."

"No. It's not Flora. It's not! It's not!" Heather began to thrash her arms about and Margot was worried she'd pull out her drip.

She stood up and restrained her daughter by placing her hands firmly on Heather's upper arms. "Honey. Stop. Please. Otherwise I'll have to call the nurses." It was like speaking to a child, not a grown woman.

Heather stopped writhing, but her face remained deathly pale. Margot continued, "I'm going to the police station this afternoon to talk to them. To—to make an identification." If you can call it that, she thought, after so many years. "And to give my DNA. I'll know more after I've been."

Now that's where she is. Stuck in a claustrophobic room in a police station having provided her DNA.

The door opens and Gary Ruthgow enters, his bulk taking up most of the doorway. Behind him a slight young woman trots in, holding a file to her chest. His face softens when he spots her sitting stiffly on the uncomfortable plastic chair with her handbag on her lap. "Hello, Margot."

She dips her head but doesn't smile. "Gary." Her heart beats faster and she has to take another sip of water because her tongue is sticking to the roof of her mouth. This is it? The moment she finds out for certain whether or not that body is her daughter's.

His eyes go to the empty chair beside her. "You didn't bring someone with you?"

She shakes her head. *Just get on with it.*

Ruthgow and the DC, who introduces herself as Clotilde Spencer, take the seats opposite. Ruthgow clears his throat and looks across the table at her, his expression serious. She notices he's wearing a soft pink tie flecked with white. "Now, obviously it won't be possible for you to identify Flora, due to the, uh, decomposition of the body." She winces at the word. She's trying not to think about her beautiful Flora being reduced to bones. "That's why we've taken the DNA sample from you. But we wanted to know if there was anything else that might help us identify the remains that we've found."

"Such as?"

"Any abnormalities, fractures, that kind of thing. Like, for example, had she ever broken her collarbone?"

"No. She broke her ankle years ago when she was about six. Her left one. I don't think it was ever set properly. It used to play up now and again. And it was weaker."

DC Spencer sits up straighter. "Broken left ankle, you say?'

"That's right."

She turns to Ruthgow and raises an eyebrow.

Ruthgow leans forward, his elbows on the table. "The body that has been found died somewhere between nineteen ninety-three and nineteen ninety-six and is believed to be a young female, aged between fifteen and seventeen. Unfortunately, due to the amount of time that has passed, we're unable to determine the cause of death at this point, although we have forensic pathologists working on it as we speak. But there is one thing we're certain about. There has only been one past breakage."

Here it comes, thinks Margot, bracing herself. She won't cry. She clenches her fists in her lap, pressing the fingertips into the soft flesh of her palms. She'll wait until she's alone in the car to shed any tears. "The left ankle?"

Ruthgow smiles. "No. Right collarbone. There is no indication that either ankle has ever been broken. We won't know for definite, of course, until we run the DNA sample you gave us, but . . ." He sits back in his chair and Margot's amazed that he looks relieved. "I don't think the body is Flora's."

MARGOT WAITS UNTIL SHE'S SAFELY ENSCONCED INSIDE HER RANGE Rover before letting the tears flow. She's not even sure what she's crying about, exactly: that the body doesn't look as if it's Flora's, or that it's somebody else's daughter and that another family, another mother, has had to live the same limbo life as she has for the past eighteen years. Part of her wanted it to be Flora so that she could finally—not move on, she'll never be able to move on—have some kind of closure and lay her to rest. Yet the other part, the bigger part, is relieved because it means there is the smallest hope that maybe Flora didn't die all those years ago, that she's alive somewhere. Happy. It's a fantasy she sometimes allows herself, but not too often. Hope is a powerful thing that, as yet, has led only to disappointment.

She reaches in her bag for a tissue and wipes away the tears. This won't do. She has to be strong. She promised Heather she'd go back to the hospital and tell her the news. And even though it won't be officially confirmed until the DNA results are through, this is what Heather will want to hear.

Because it means Heather had no motive to shoot Clive Wilson.

Her mobile rings and she answers it when she sees Leo's name flash on the screen. She'd texted him earlier to tell him about the remains.

"They don't think it's her," she says, her body sagging against the seat. She repeats what Gary Ruthgow had told her about having a DNA test just to be sure.

"That's great news if it's not her," says Leo.

"It is. And it isn't."

"But if it's not her body, it means there's no motive for Heather," he says.

"I know." She leans her head against the steering wheel and closes her eyes. "Are you still coming to visit today?"

There's an awkward silence. "I, um, listen, sis, I'd love to come back to support you. I feel dreadful I'm not there for you— and Heather, but it's just . . . It brings it all back, you know."

She does know. After it transpired Dylan had an alibi it was

Leo who was hounded most by the police. She knows that a large number of people still believe he had something to do with Flora's disappearance even though he, too, had an alibi.

"I'm sorry," he says again, into the silence, and she can hear the emotion in his voice. He hasn't been back to Tilby in fifteen years. When they meet up she and Heather always travel to Bristol to see him. Not once has she doubted him. She knows he'd never be capable of hurting his niece, yet that doesn't stop the gossip and speculation. It was his liking for younger women that did it, she knows that. She'd heard the rumors at the time that he slept around with much younger women, but she never felt he was inappropriate with her own girls. He was their uncle. She knew he didn't view them in that way, even if Sheila had once made a throwaway comment that Margot should watch him around her daughters. She insisted she'd been joking, but Margot hadn't found it remotely funny.

"That's okay. I'll keep you up-to-date with any news."

Margot ends the call, then throws her mobile onto the passenger seat, blowing her nose loudly and peering at herself in the mirror, wiping the stray mascara away from her bottom eyelids. She doesn't want Heather to see she's been crying.

Heather. Something is niggling at Margot. The way her daughter had reacted when she'd told her they thought Flora had been found. She'd been so sure the body hadn't been that of her sister. Why?

Unless—and the thought is so awful that Margot can barely bring herself to think it—unless Heather knows exactly what happened to Flora. An image of Keith's crumpled body comes to mind, the gun slipping from Heather's trembling hand to the ground.

Heather had killed her father. Could she have killed her sister too?

40

August 1994

HEATHER WATCHED AS FLORA SCUTTLED ACROSS THE FIELDS AND out of sight. She wondered if Dylan was waiting in the lane. She imagined so. The two young lovers running off for the day. She turned away from the window in disgust.

Doesn't Flora understand how much she's done for her?

That day, four years ago, had been like any other on their farm in Maidstone: another day of their father's aggressive moods, put-downs, and bullying. Their mother overcompensated for their father's lack of love and, as a result, the three of them were close. Their father was the outsider. He bullied Flora most, maybe because she was the eldest, or because she backchatted him more than Heather did. Whatever the reason, it was normal for him to shout abuse at them, particularly when their mother wasn't in earshot. Flora would sneak into Heather's room at night when they heard their parents arguing downstairs, and they would huddle together under the blankets until they heard the reassuring slam of the front door, which indicated their father had gone out. He never hit Margot. They were sure of that. But he was a hard man, devoid of humor, as though he'd just woken up one day and all the joy had seeped out of him. Their mum admitted it was like he'd had a personality transplant. He wasn't her Keith anymore.

But none of them knew what to do about it.

Thankfully, he'd never hit his daughters either, or shown any kind of physical violence.

Until that spring day in 1990.

It was their favorite season on the farm, because of the lambs. They liked to cuddle them, and occasionally feed them with a bottle. Years before, their father had joined in, showing them how to cradle a lamb's warm little body in the crook of their arm, like a baby. That was until his fun-loving humor was replaced by a prickly, grumpy, anxious state and he snapped at them all the time.

Stress, their mother called it. Obnoxious-bastard syndrome was what Flora called it.

On that particular day their father had got out his shotgun because a cow had become entangled in barbed wire and had to be put down. "I need to put it out of its misery," he'd said, carrying the gun as though he were John Wayne.

Flora had glanced at Heather and grimaced. But half an hour later, as they were leaving the barn where the lambs were kept, they saw that their father had left his gun out, leaning against the barn gate.

Their parents were so strict about gun safety. They'd taught them how to use one, of course, but in very controlled conditions, with experts. And they were not allowed to touch a gun without adult supervision.

That didn't stop Flora, who almost jumped on it with glee. "Look, it's Dad's gun."

"He'll go mental. Put it back," said Heather, her heart racing at the thought of their father's wrath. But Flora flung it to her shoulder and made pow-pow noises while pointing it toward the empty field.

"Don't!" Heather cried. "It's dangerous. I don't think the safety catch is on."

"Oh, chill out," said Flora. "It won't have any cartridges in it. Dad will have used those to kill the cow. You know he only ever loads it with one or two."

But, still, Heather felt uneasy about it. Gun safety had been drilled into her so many times.

Flora laughed. "We can be cops!"

"You know we're not allowed to play with them. And, anyway, I don't think cops use shotguns. Put it down, please, you're making me nervous."

"Oh, it's fine . . ." The words died on her lips. Their father was striding toward them. Heather began to tremble. Now they were in trouble.

When he saw that Flora was holding his gun his face turned

purple. "What the fuck are you doing? Put the goddamn gun down now!"

Flora lowered it to the ground, as though she were holding an unexploded bomb. She laid it at her and Heather's feet and held up her hands in surrender. "I'm sorry, I'm sorry," she began, her face crumpling.

It happened within a blink of an eye. Keith was suddenly looming over them, grabbing Flora by her puny little upper arms and shaking her so violently Heather thought she could hear her sister's teeth rattling. "You never play with guns, you stupid, *stupid* girl," he yelled. And then he slapped her hard around the face.

It was as though time stood still. Even the trees seemed to freeze, midsway. Silence descended all around them, as if everything had taken a collective breath, and Flora touched her stinging cheek, tears of shock in her eyes.

Before Heather could process what she was about to do, she leaned over and grabbed the gun. She stepped away from her father but with the barrel aimed at his chest. She was consumed by a sudden, blinding rage.

He looked as though he was about to burst with anger. His big, round head reminded Heather of the blueberries from the Ribena adverts. "Give that back to me, you little shit," he spluttered.

"You leave Flora alone," cried Heather, taking another step backward.

He looked confused for a second. "I'm not touching Flora. Now give me back the gun or you'll get a good hiding from me. You and your sister."

And that was when she pulled the trigger.

She'd been so consumed with anger and fear that her mind was blank as the gun fired in her hands, her arm shuddering under the weight of it.

It was surreal, like watching a movie. Heather felt as if she had floated away from her body and was looking down at them all, watching as her father flew backward, his eyes wide with surprise, the blood spreading across the front of his shirt. And then their mother's cries and Flora's screams, and Heather had dropped the gun to cover her ears because it was all too much. *Too much.*

And now Flora was scheming behind her back with Jess. Keeping secrets. Pushing her away. After everything.

The floorboard outside her room creaked and Heather jumped into bed, pretending to be asleep, before Jess realized she knew everything.

She couldn't lose Flora. Not now, not after all they'd been through. She needed to speak to her as soon as possible. She'd heard Flora telling Jess she'd be getting the bus home before dark, which meant she'd be arriving at the bus stop just outside the clock tower at no later than 9 p.m.

And Heather would be waiting.

41

I CAN'T STOP THINKING ABOUT YOUR LAST MOMENTS. THEY HAUNT MY
*dreams. And the blood. So much blood, blooming like ink across your
blouse, gathering in the ruts of concrete under your head. The shock in
your eyes that someone you love—someone who loves you—could hurt
you. I held you in my arms, after. Did you know that? I held you and I
rocked you, and I cried because I'd been unable to protect you.*

That's all I have ever tried to do.

42

Jess

BRISTOL AND SOMERSET HERALD

Friday, March 23, 2012

POLICE MYSTIFIED BY
BODY IN BASEMENT

by Jessica Fox

A BODY found in the basement of a Tilby couple who were shot dead two weeks ago is not that of missing teen Flora Powell, police have revealed.

Clive Wilson and his mother, Deirdre, were killed in Deirdre's home in Shackleton Road on Friday, March 9. While searching Clive Wilson's Victorian property in Southville, Bristol, police discovered the body of a young girl, thought to be aged between fifteen and seventeen, buried in the basement. An excavation had to be carried out after a crumbling internal wall in the basement collapsed during the routine search, revealing the bones. The body is thought to have been at the house since the mid-1990s.

Heather Underwood, who is recovering in hospital from a self-inflicted gunshot wound, is currently under police arrest for killing Deirdre and Clive Wilson, although no charge has yet been made.

Her sister, Flora Powell, went missing from Tilby in 1994 at the age of sixteen.

DCI Gary Ruthgow of Avon and Somerset CID said: "A DNA test has confirmed that the body does not belong to Flora Powell. At this stage we are ruling nothing out and investigations into the identity of the body are still underway."

TED CHEWS GUM IN MY EAR AS HE READS OVER MY SHOULDER. APART from us, and Sue on Reception, the newsroom is empty. I can see Seth in the side room going through what look like old slides. Ellie is out doing vox pops with Jack. I haven't seen much of him recently. Not properly. Not like we used to. We used to go for lunch or for a drink after work at least once a week for a proper gossip. That hasn't happened since the night he got mugged. He's been working hard and I wonder if he's looking for a promotion or another job.

After Ted's finished reading, he stands back, with a "humph," his arms folded. I can tell straightaway that he's disappointed. "This is nothing that the *Daily News* won't have," he says, half-sitting, half-leaning against the empty desk next to mine. He looks tired this morning, I observe. He's not shaved and his eyes sag more than usual. He's wearing faded jeans that are thinning at the knee and Puma trainers. "It's only Wednesday. This won't be printed until Friday. By then it will be old news. We need something more, Jess."

Inwardly I groan. Always something more. I've done as much as I can. I'm the only reporter nationally who has an exclusive with Margot. The red tops have borrowed quotes from my piece, of course, but they've had to attribute them to me and to the *Herald*. It's strange to see my name in the national press again. But how are we supposed to compete with a daily newspaper when we come out only twice a week and nobody reads our website? I've tried to point out to Ted that we need to move with the times and refurbish our online presence, but he keeps muttering that Jared, the editor at HQ, dismissed the idea, citing "budget cuts."

I flick through my notebook looking for the *more* that Ted wants. "Well, I'm working on the story I got from the landlord of the Funky Raven."

He runs his hand across his bristly chin and raises one of his shaggy eyebrows. "Remind me?"

"That Clive was dealing drugs to students in his pub. And I bumped into the guy Flora was going out with when she disappeared. Dylan Bird. He told me he thought Clive had killed Flora because Dylan owed him and his brother Norman money for drugs." I remember Dylan's pinched white face, his mumblings of "he killed her because of me."

Ted sighs heavily and my heart sinks, anticipating what he's going to say. "But Clive didn't kill Flora, did he? At least, there's no evidence of that now. The body isn't hers!"

"But if he killed this other young girl he might have killed Flora too," I say. "Dylan said he'd been at the fair around the same time as Flora. He might have met her."

Ted grunts. "'Might have' isn't good enough." He slaps the edge of one hand into the palm of the other. "We need cold, hard facts. And the fucking *Daily News* seems to be getting everything before we do." A tense silence falls between us. Ted's blue eyes are cold as he stares off into the middle distance, still chewing.

"You know, Jess," he says, still not looking at me, "HQ are looking for any excuse to shut this place down. They want us all under one roof. I'd hate that, and so would Seth. We're too old and jaded to make that move."

I'd hate it too. I love the freedom we have here.

"We're the ones who are coming up with the good stories on this," I say, my cheeks hot. "Not them."

"Only because you know the family. It keeps Jared off our backs."

Jared is ten years younger than Ted, suave with his slicked-back hair, expensive suits, and soft-top sports car. Ted is the antithesis to Jared. Ted is what I call old school. Ex–Fleet Street. There's nothing suave or slimy about Ted.

I have one ace up my sleeve, although I'm not sure how ethical it would be to use it.

But I need to prove to Ted that he wasn't wrong to employ me. He hired me because of my track record.

I take a deep breath and it all comes out in a rush. "Margot said I can go with her this afternoon to see Heather." I feel as if I've thrown a hand grenade into the room and am waiting to see if it explodes.

His eyes flick back to mine and he looks more alert than I've seen him all week.

"I'm not sure I'll be allowed to interview her," I add hastily. "But proceedings aren't active yet because they still haven't charged her due to her health."

"She's getting better, though. It's only a matter of time."

"I know. It's a long shot, but she might give me something."

He stands up, actually rubbing his hands. "Yes. Yes, she might. It's worth a shot. You'll be the first journalist to see her, to interview her. Great. Great. That'll get Jared off our backs."

"Even if they say I can interview her, I don't know if she'll agree . . ." I begin, but he's already walking away.

I'VE ARRANGED TO MEET MARGOT IN THE ENTRANCE TO SOUTHmead Hospital and she's already there when I arrive. She's wearing a wool camel coat that reaches midcalf, and a large black cashmere scarf slung around her neck. I'm struck again by how elegant she is. She's wearing lipstick and her hair is styled, the streaks of white at the front giving her a distinguished appearance. For a moment, a millisecond, really, I feel a stab of envy for Heather that's so sharp I gasp. My own mother never even called me back after our brief, awkward phone chat last Friday night.

When Margot spots me, her green eyes light up and she hurries over, pulling me in for a hug. I allow myself to be engulfed by her warmth, the smell of her familiar musky perfume, before she releases me.

"Thank you for coming. Heather will be so pleased to see you," she says, taking my arm and leading me through the atrium toward the maze of corridors while I wonder if this is true. I've no idea of the reaction I'll receive from Heather and my heart races at the thought. She'd be within her rights to tell me to get lost.

Margot's chatting the whole way, and I wonder if she's nervous. I can't help the small thrill that runs through me at the thought that I'm allowed into her inner sanctum.

But I know not to be fooled. Behind that refined politeness Margot would fight to the death for her family. I've been on the receiving end of her hostility, and I don't want that to happen again. I need to tread a very fine line here between being loyal to her but also getting Ted the story he wants.

Yet again I wonder if I'm the right person for this job. How objective can I be? I've already admitted to myself that I want to believe Heather is innocent and that there is a rational but not-yet-found explanation for all of this—although, as time goes on, it's looking less likely.

My heart starts to beat faster as we approach Heather's room and my mouth is so dry I can only nod as Margot tells me Heather's no longer in ICU and that the police will be formally questioning her tomorrow, now the doctors deem her well enough. She doesn't say it but I sense her unease about what will happen when Heather is discharged. Will she be taken straight into police custody or will she be allowed home? At least she has Margot to fight for her. I'm sure she'll get her the best lawyers, the best defense team. I imagine she has money squirreled away. She's never been one for material things, preferring to spend her cash on her animals.

I can't believe I'm about to see Heather again. How will it be between us after all these years? We've both changed so much. I swallow, wishing I had some water.

A police officer is standing outside Heather's door. A man: young and slim with closely cropped hair and a pointed chin. He doesn't smile as we approach but he nods to Margot, standing aside to let us pass.

I wasn't expecting that. She's in hospital, hardly able to go anywhere. I dart Margot a questioning look but she just shakes her head briefly.

Heather is sitting up in bed when we enter, on top of the blankets. She's wearing sheepskin slippers and lilac pajamas, and her hair—which is exactly the same as I remember it—is long and shining, as though it has recently been brushed. She's older, of course, with faint lines around her eyes, but she's still got the amazing complexion I remember, poreless, almost, with a hint of peach at her cheekbones. There is no sign that she's been so ill, apart from a bandage around her head. She blushes when she sees me but her face breaks into a wide smile—she still has that dimple in her left cheek—and in that moment she's my fourteen-year-old best friend again. My eyes fill with tears and I blink them away. I must be going soft.

"Hey, you," she says.

I rush toward her bed, then hesitate, wondering whether to give her a hug. But she saves me making that decision by leaning forward, her arms outstretched. I bend toward her and hold her, her silky hair brushing my nose. She smells of shampoo and hospitals.

When we break apart she indicates the chair next to her bed. "Please, sit down." I take a seat, and pull my skirt over my patterned tights primly, suddenly feeling self-conscious. I should have brought her some flowers, or grapes, or a magazine, or something. I bet she would have if I was the one in the hospital bed. Heather was always thoughtful like that.

Margot clears her throat. "I'll go and get us some coffee," she says, retreating from the room so that Heather and I are alone.

"It's so lovely to see you," says Heather, her eyes bright. "You've hardly changed."

"It's so lovely to see you too," I gush, surprised at myself. I never gush. I'm acting like a teenager, not my usual professional self. I have to remember who she is. Why I'm here. Not just as an old friend, but as a reporter. "You've not changed a bit. But now you're married. And a mum!" *And a murderer.*

She smiles shyly and takes the photo frame from her bedside cabinet and presses it into my hands. "That's my little boy, Ethan." She points to the man cuddling him. "And that's my husband, Adam."

For some reason, I don't tell her I've already met them in my capacity as a journalist. Instead I say how beautiful her little boy is.

"What about you?" she asks. "Married? Children?"

"I live with my boyfriend, Rory. We were in London but moved to Bristol last year."

"And how's your mum?"

I grimace. "She's still the same, but since she got married and moved to Spain I hardly see her." My voice is imbued with a bitterness I always try to hide.

Heather doesn't say anything but reaches over and squeezes my hand. I realize that this is what it's like to have an old friend, someone who knew you in childhood, someone who remembers all the hurt, the pain, and the anguish you went through as well as the good times. Someone who knew you before you had the chance to put up the barriers and become a different, more cynical person. Heather is the closest thing I ever had to a sister.

"I'm so sorry we fell out," she says now, her eyes dropping to her lap.

"Me too. It's one of my biggest regrets," I admit.

"Same. It was so silly. I was angry about Flora. It was such a horrible time. I've missed you."

And there it is, the phantom in the room, floating between us. Flora.

I avert my eyes, looking instead at a board on the wall with photos of Heather and her family pinned to it. "I pushed you away because I felt guilty," I explain. "I saw Flora the morning she disappeared. She was off to meet Dylan. They were going on a day trip to London. I never told anyone."

She squeezes my hand again. "I know. I heard you talking that morning. I pretended to be asleep."

I stare at her. "You knew?"

"I was jealous, I think, that she was telling you and not me. She was angry with me because of what I did to Dylan."

I can't help but laugh. "I'm sorry," I say. "I've only just found out the extent of what you did to Dylan."

She laughs, too, but looks shamefaced. "It was wrong of me to attack him."

"No doubt he deserved it."

"He was a dick, wasn't he? I never understood what Flora saw in him. Do you remember how she would play 'Martha's Harbor' over and over again because it reminded her of him? It used to drive us crazy. She was so in love." Her smile flickers and dies. "I can't listen to that song now."

I'd forgotten how much Flora had loved All About Eve. "I saw Dylan yesterday. For the first time since . . . well, since 'ninety-four. He was at Clive Wilson's house when they thought . . . they thought . . ." I trail off, not knowing what to say. How much has Margot told her?

"When they thought they'd found Flora's body?" she finishes for me.

I nod. "But it's not her."

She doesn't say anything in response and I wonder what she's thinking. Was part of her hoping it was Flora, so that she could finally lay the ghosts of the past to rest? Or is she relieved because it means there is still hope, even after all these years?

"Did Mum tell you that the police think I killed two people?" She looks down at her hands. She's fiddling with her rings.

Part of me wants to laugh because it sounds so absurd. Of all the conversations we've ever had, I never thought we'd be having this one at our reunion. "Yes. She did."

She still doesn't look at me. "Mum said you're a journalist. Are you here for a story?"

I place my hand over hers. "I'm here as your friend. All of this . . . it's made me realize how much you meant to me. We were such good friends. I've never found that again." I feel a stab of guilt. How can I tell her I'm here for the story too? Although the friendship thing is true.

She lifts her eyes. "Really?"

"Really. I mean, I've got Rory, of course, and Jack who works with me on the newspaper. But no really good female friends. I . . . well, I miss that."

She smiles, and it changes her whole face, brightening her instantly. "Me too. My life had become a bit insular, really. Just Adam and Ethan—and Mum, of course. I hardly see Uncle Leo anymore."

I nod, remembering our meeting the other day, reminded again of the ripple effect that Flora's disappearance has had on the whole family.

If I don't come back with an interview, Ted will be furious. But I can't ask her. Not now we're getting on so well. If it was anybody else, I would. But not her.

I'm angry with myself. I'm too close to this story. I should have handed it over to someone in HQ.

She touches the bandage on her head. "I can't remember that morning."

I'm confused. "Which morning?"

"The morning it happened. The shootings. The last thing I remember is arguing with Adam. It was a stupid row that just escalated. I was tired, overwhelmed, felt like I was doing too much and he not enough. Ethan had been teething and not sleeping. I just felt"—she shrugs—"knackered."

"So what happened?"

"We argued. He told me he'd stay at his mum's, with Ethan. Give me some peace if that was what I wanted. I opened a bottle of wine, cried a bit. Flopped onto the sofa. I think I passed out. And then"—she's fiddling with her rings again—"and the next thing I know I'm here."

I can't imagine not being able to remember something. A whole event just gone, wiped from my memory. Even when I've been at my drunkest, I've remembered everything the next morning, even if half of those memories were excruciatingly embarrassing and all jumbled up. I'm no psychiatrist but it sounds like some kind of blackout. Or maybe it's because of the head injury.

She wrinkles her nose and, in that moment, I see the teenage Heather in her. "It's so frustrating. I hate not being able to remember." She looks at me, imploring. "I just don't understand why I would kill anyone, particularly those two people. I've never met them."

"I think you met Deirdre, though. Your mum told me she rented a caravan from you earlier this year."

"Oh, yes. But I barely remember her. Only that she seemed chatty and had a really cute dog I couldn't stop cuddling. It looked like a bear. She said she bred them. That's all the conversation we had."

The outer corner of her eyelid flickers, her face impassive.

I remember her twitchy eye. It's hardly perceptible—you'd only notice it if you knew her well. If you'd maybe grown up with her or, like Adam, loved her and knew all her little idiosyncrasies.

Her eyelid always flickered very slightly when she was lying.

She's still playing with her hands, almost like she's nervous. I glance down. And that's when I notice it. The rings. There's her wedding and engagement ring on her left hand, a modest ruby among a cluster of diamonds. But also two others, one on each little finger, identical, small, and gold with an oval crest on the front that looks a bit like a lion. I remember asking her about it when we were kids, because she always wore it. Then it was on her middle finger. Now there is one on each of her little fingers. She'd told me it was a family ring, handed down through the generations. She had one, so did Flora and her mother. I'd never heard of them before and was intrigued by this grown-up piece of jewelry that she was allowed to wear to school. It sounded very posh and aristocratic to me, and they weren't like that, the Powells.

Flora never took hers off. She had been wearing it the day she disappeared.

So why was Heather wearing it now?

43

Jess

HEATHER DOESN'T NOTICE ME STARING IN HORROR AT THE RINGS. Two, when there should be one. Maybe I've got it wrong. Maybe Flora hadn't been wearing the ring when she disappeared. Except . . . I was there when Margot first reported Flora missing. Heather and I were standing at Margot's side, Heather quietly sobbing. It had been late. Gone 11 p.m. Flora was never that late. I remember Margot giving a description to the police, telling them between hot, panicked breaths what her daughter had been wearing that day, including the gold signet ring. I remember because I'd loved the way it sounded like "cygnet." My fourteen-year-old self had imagined lots of fluffy baby swans.

Why had Heather been crying? Could she have known then that Flora would never come home? As far as we were all aware at the time, she was just a few hours late. It was concerning, yes, given Flora's history of always being punctual. But to cry? Had I thought it odd? I can't remember. Because I had my own guilty secret: I knew Flora had gone off somewhere for the day with Dylan. I thought perhaps she'd decided to stay the night with him. But I wasn't worried that she'd run away; the backpack she'd been wearing that morning was too small, not large enough to hold even one set of clothing, never mind more.

Heather had left me alone at her house earlier that evening, at around 7:30 p.m. I hadn't remembered that until now. When she'd returned she had been wet and covered with mud. She said she'd slipped and fallen after getting her pony in from the field. She'd been wearing a skirt, not her usual riding gear. It had rained that night and I'd thought nothing of it. I'd waited for her in her room, happily doodling and listening to music until she came back. What time had she returned? It must have been nine-ish. Definitely before the curfew anyway, because I remember her looking at her watch and becoming agitated when it got to nine thirty and Flora wasn't yet home, muttering something about Dylan.

I haven't thought about that in years. Even after Flora went missing I didn't think it was strange.

Until now.

Heather had killed her father, whether by accident or not, and now Clive and Deirdre Wilson. She was seen exiting their house on the morning of the murders. And she was caught on CCTV near Clive's Bristol property earlier that same morning. Does she really not remember or is it just some convenient excuse? And as I watch my onetime best friend, sitting on the hospital bed, twisting the wedding ring on her finger and staring wistfully into nothing, I realize I hardly know her at all. We were friends for just over two years. Two years is such a short time in the grand scheme of things. It might have been an important moment in my life, but it's a tiny slice out of our thirty-two years. Heather is a killer. There is no disputing that, however much I've been trying to convince myself. She's killed not just once but three times. And now she's wearing Flora's ring. What does that mean?

I suppress a shiver despite the stuffy room.

She's a fucking psychopath. I'm sitting here having a cozy chat with someone who is evidently dangerous. Maybe even criminally insane. I stand up so suddenly I almost knock over Heather's water and save it just in time.

Heather looks up. "Are you okay?"

"I'm . . . just hot," I say, replacing the plastic cup.

"Not surprised. You've still got your coat on."

I can't speak. My mind is racing. Was she responsible for the photographs on my car? No, it couldn't have been her. She's been in hospital, under police guard. Then who? Adam? I thought I saw him that time, following me. Are they working together? Did he put the photographs on my car to warn me off? But what about the bus ticket? What did it all mean?

Why have you got Flora's ring?

Just then Margot bustles into the room, armed with two takeaway cups. She's all smiles. "Lovely to see you both catching up," she says, and her face falls as she notices I'm on my feet. "Are you leaving, Jess?"

"I . . . um . . ." I want to run back to the safety of my flat, jump into bed, and stuff a pillow over my head to stop these relentless thoughts. I've always been the same: I ran from Heather as a teenager because I couldn't face up to the part I'd played in Flora's disappearance; I've distanced myself from my mother because she neglected me as a kid, then remarried and started a new life without me. And now I'm doing the same to Rory. But this. I can't hide from this. I need to face it, head-on.

And the journalist in me needs this. If Heather really did hurt Flora all those years ago, I owe her nothing now. I'd happily write a story about her. The irony doesn't escape me that I would forgive Heather for murdering Clive and Deirdre Wilson because they mean nothing to me, but I'd throw her to the wolves over Flora. "I'm just taking this off," I say, folding my coat over the back of the chair. "It's hot in here."

Margot looks pointedly at it. "I'd say so in that thing." Then she seems to remember her manners, and blusters, "Not that it isn't a nice coat . . ."

I'm not offended. I know my clothes aren't to everyone's taste. That's why I like them.

Margot hands me one of the takeaway cups, which I accept with thanks. She gives the other to Heather. "I've got you herbal tea," she says to her daughter, smiling indulgently.

I place the cup under my nose. I can tell by the delicious aroma that it's coffee and I'm thankful she hasn't brought me some weak herbal crap. I need caffeine and I'm suddenly desperate for a cigarette.

I offer Margot my seat but she waves me away. "Oh, no, that's fine. I need to make a call so I'll go into the dayroom. I'll leave you two to catch up."

I watch her through the glass panel in the door as she stops to chat to the policeman on duty, although I can't hear what they're saying.

Now is my chance. I sit down and pretend to notice Heather's ring for the first time. She's holding her cup with her left hand; the right rests in her lap. "Oh, wow, I remember your family ring," I say, lifting up her right hand and pretending to admire it. "You used to always wear that when we were kids. Flora had one too, didn't she?"

I sound so fake, but I'm hoping Heather won't notice.

She stretches her fingers. "Yes. Matching ones. We never took them off."

"Was Flora wearing hers the day she disappeared?"

Heather takes her hand away and uses it to cup her tea. She gives me a long look, her green cat's eyes narrowed, and I hold my breath. Does she know what I suspect?

Eventually she says, "I thought so. But I found it afterward. In her room." She holds up her right hand and wriggles her little finger. "I wear it now."

I think back to the morning when I last saw Flora. I can't remember if she was actually wearing it or not, despite what Margot said to the police. Maybe Heather's not the psychopath I thought she was. And Margot would have noticed the extra ring, wouldn't she? If it meant something. Heather must be telling the truth.

I try another tack. "It's all so sad," I begin, "what happened to Flora and now you, in this awful situation." I reach for her hand again. "You know, if you did ever want to tell your side of the story, in your own words . . ."

She snatches her hand away. "I thought you were here as my friend."

"I am. But I can't lie to you, Heather. You're all over the news already. Everybody speculating, putting words in your mouth. People need to understand that you're human. Not some"—I pause for dramatic effect, making sure she's paying attention—"cold-blooded killer."

She blinks, studying my face, but doesn't say anything.

"I want people to know the real you. The *you* we all know and love. The wife. The mother . . ."

"The *murderer*," she adds bitterly. Is she thinking of her father? She doesn't know I know about that. She never told me. Then she adds, "Everyone obviously thinks I killed the Wilsons."

"No . . . I don't know. Look, we don't need to dwell on that bit so much. I want people to see you as I see you. Gentle, kind . . ."

"You haven't seen me for nearly twenty years," she says levelly. "How do you know I'm kind?"

"Well, you used to be. You'd do anything for anyone. And, according to your mum, you haven't changed. She said you're a brilliant mother to Ethan."

She's silent. "I don't know . . ."

And in that moment I feel it. That familiar swell of excitement in my gut, the anticipation that she's wavering, that I might be the only journalist in the UK with a story from Heather's point of view. A surge of adrenaline shoots through me. "You could read it through before anything is published. Show them all that you're just a normal wife and mother. Put doubt in their minds . . . But"—I lean forward, as if telling her a secret—"we need to be quick, because once you're charged with this, Heather, proceedings will be active and there will be restrictions on what can be printed."

"I think the police are coming to interview me tomorrow. The doctors said if I'm well enough today . . ."

"Can you put them off? Say you're still ill? Just until after Friday?"

She looks doubtful. "That's two days away."

"If we printed this, you'd get sympathy from the public. It could make a difference, Heather, especially if it ended up going to trial."

Something crosses her face. Panic, maybe. "I don't know . . ." she says again, reaching over to place her takeaway cup on the bedside unit.

Come on, Heather. Come on.

"Think about it," I say, trying to sound understanding rather than frustrated. "I could write something based on what I know already and give it to you to read. You wouldn't really need to do anything."

She looks toward the door, as though afraid the police will arrive at any second. "I suppose I could say my head hurts." She puts a hand to her bandage. "It does a bit anyway. It could be all the stress."

Guilt rushes in, like the tide. "Oh, Heather, I'm so sorry. I shouldn't be asking you this . . ."

"No. It's okay. I know you're only trying to help me." She sits up straighter in bed, looking determined. "Let's do it." She laughs and I join in, and right away we're fourteen again, giggling conspiratorially because we're planning to do something we shouldn't. "But don't tell Mum," she adds. "She'll only try to talk me out of it."

I feel uneasy at leaving Margot out of the loop, but I'm so desperate for this story that I'm sure, in this moment, I'd agree to anything.

A NURSE COMES IN AND SHOOS ME OUT, SAYING HEATHER NEEDS HER rest. Heather does look tired, the color of her face not far off that of the white pillow she's lying on. I promise to be back to see her soon.

I almost skip down the corridor and out to my car. I can hardly believe my luck. While I'm driving home I call Ted on hands-free.

"Guess what," I cry, when he answers. "I've only gone and bloody done it. Heather's agreed to an exclusive."

There's a pause and then: "Right, but we'll only be able to use it if she's not charged."

I'd hardly expected him to whoop down the phone. After all, this is the ever-cynical Ted. But I was hoping for a bit more enthusiasm. "I'm praying she can put the police off, just until it's printed on Friday. And we can put it on our website before that, of course." Not that anyone will read it, I silently add.

He doesn't say anything for a few seconds and then: "Okay. Let's hope. But good work, Jess. I knew you could do it."

I put the phone down and do a little air punch. At last, a sliver of praise from Ted.

I'm beaming as I pull into the underground car park. And then my euphoria dies, replaced by guilt.

IT'S BEEN WORTH VISITING HEATHER, BOTH ON A PERSONAL AND professional level. I just hope she manages not to speak to the police tomorrow. I long to talk to Jack and dissect my conversation with Heather in detail. But he's been acting oddly lately and I don't feel as close to him since all this has happened.

Something else has been niggling at me too. Something I haven't wanted to think too much about. Those photos on my car. When they were taken I'd been on a job with Jack in Tilby. I recognize the scenery in the distance. Had Jack taken the photos without me being aware? Then why put them on my car with the words "Back off"? Why would he want to scare me from the story? So he can take it over for himself? I feel instantly guilty for my treacherous thoughts. Jack's one of my closest friends. And he's a snapper, not a reporter. But I can tell he's hiding something from me—I know him too well.

Rory's already home. I can smell spices and curry paste as I take off my coat and shoes in the hallway. My stomach grumbles at the prospect. I've not eaten anything since lunchtime.

"Good day?" he says, as I walk into the living room, slinging my laptop bag onto the sofa. This is how we are with each other now. Polite, but distant. We could be flatmates, rather than lovers. I remember, with a jolt, that I haven't even told him about the photographs on my car and the threatening message. We haven't really conversed since I told him I'd found the engagement ring a few days ago.

"Busy," I say, walking through to the kitchen. I stand beside him, watching as he stirs the curry. Usually we'd kiss now, or I'd wrap my arms around his waist as he cooked. But we just stand there, like virtual strangers.

"I thought"—he indicates the frying pan—"we could sit down for once and talk properly."

I pull a regretful face. "I've got a bit of work to do. I went to see Heather today."

"Heather?"

"The woman I used to be friends with," I say, surprised that he doesn't remember. How can he not know about Heather, when she and her family are all I've thought about for the past couple of weeks?

"The woman who murdered two people in Tilby?" He turns to me, a horrified expression on his face. "You went to see her?"

"Yes. She's still in hospital. She agreed to an interview." He turns away and his shoulders tense. Disapproval emanates from every pore. "What?"

He sighs. "It's nothing."

"It's obviously not *nothing*," I spit, tiredness making me tetchy. "It's my job, Rory."

He spins around to face me, wooden spoon still in his hand. "I understand that. But . . . I don't know. You're so secretive. I thought we told each other everything, yet you lied to me about your last job. The phone hacking. The threats. The reason we left London. I gave up everything to follow you here and I feel like you're doing it all over again."

"Doing what?"

"Pushing me out. Not being honest."

I fold my arms across my chest. "I knew you'd be like this about it."

"Like what?"

"Sanctimonious. Disapproving. Judgmental."

He takes a step back from me as though I've punched him. Hurt flickers in his eyes. "Is that what you really think of me?"

"I . . ." Is it? Is that why I didn't tell him the truth about the phone hacking? Because I knew he'd disapprove and judge me? That he wouldn't love me anymore if he knew what I was really like, what I'd do to get a story? "You don't like what I do for a living, do you? It doesn't sit well with your social conscience. You want to make the world a better place. You're a teacher! It's one of the most important, worthwhile jobs there is. And you see mine as—"

"Don't put words into my mouth! You're always doing that, telling me what I think or feel, and it's bullshit, Jess. Journalism can be worthwhile. You don't have to lower yourself or be morally corrupt to be a good journalist. Have you ever thought that it's not me who's being judgmental but that you're judging yourself?" A pulse throbs in his jaw and his eyes darken. "I just wish you'd trust me a bit more."

"Just then, though, when I told you about Heather, you sounded . . . disapproving."

He takes a step forward, his expression softening. "I wasn't disapproving. I was worried. Because I love you. I care about you. I want you to be safe. That's all. I think you're a wonderful person. You're funny, kind, confident, clever. It's you who's got a downer on yourself, for whatever reason."

He's right. Whatever he says, I can never shake the feeling that he's too good for me, that I don't deserve him.

We stand and stare at each other for a few seconds. Then he reaches his hand out and takes mine. "I'll always love you," he says. "No matter what."

And I realize I love him too. Really love him, in a way I've never felt about anyone else. He's never been the problem, it was me, pushing him away because I felt I didn't deserve him, scared that eventually he'd find out what a fake I really am and leave me anyway.

I've never really trusted anyone in my life. But I need him. I need to stop running away from forming deep relationships, not just with Rory but with friends too.

I lead him to the sofa. We've a lot to talk about. I need to tell him everything.

WE SIT UP FOR HOURS, JUST TALKING, LIKE WE USED TO. I ADMIT HOW lonely and isolating it's felt, always having my barriers up in case I get hurt. I tell him why I've always been a bit obsessed with the Powell family, never having much family of my own. Margot was the mother I wish I'd had, Heather and Flora the sisters. I tell him about my guilt for never revealing to Margot or Heather (until now) that I saw Flora the morning she disappeared and that she was off somewhere with Dylan.

"And now I feel someone is watching me," I say, explaining about the photographs and the figure standing outside our building. "Maybe even more than one person. At first I thought it was Wayne Walker—the man I was telling you about from London. But I don't think it is. It's something to do with the story I'm working on. Why else would they write 'Back off'? And then someone pushed a bus ticket through the letter box." I get up and go to my bag to show him.

Rory's face grows more concerned. I sit down again and hand him the bus ticket. "And sometimes I think it's Adam who's following me—Heather's husband," I clarify, when he looks confused. "Other times I'm convinced it's Wayne Walker. I've even begun to suspect Jack."

"Jack?"

"Because the photos were taken when we were together. He's so ambitious. I have a feeling he wants to move into reporting instead of taking photos. He's good. He worked out that Heather's husband had written this threatening note . . ." I fill him in on that too. It's a relief to tell him everything.

When I've finished he takes my hand. "Come on," he says, leading me into the bedroom. It's dark outside, and the light is off. Rory doesn't reach for the switch. Instead he leads me to the window. The curtains are open and the full moon makes it easy to see across to the derelict building. He squints to get a better look.

I stand beside him. We're still holding hands. "Usually there's a person with a torch. And they shine it right into the bedroom. And it always seems to be when I'm alone," I whisper.

"They could just be squatters," he replies, in the same low voice.

"I think whoever it is posted this bus ticket to me. They're trying to tell me something, I think. Or scare me. I'm still not sure. I've never seen anyone coming in or out, just a shadow moving behind the windows, and the torchlight." And then I laugh. "Why are we whispering?"

He laughs too. It's such a lovely sound and I feel so happy and safe beside him that, for the moment, I no longer care who's watching me.

We wait for a few minutes, but there's no sign of torchlight, or shadows moving. I'm disappointed, worried he'll think I'm making the whole thing up for a bit of attention.

He moves away from the window. "I'm going over there," he says, the determined look I recognize on his face.

"Wait! *What?*"

He holds up a hand and I see the teacher in him. "You stay here and watch. I'll take a torch. If I need your help I'll flash it three times."

"No! You could get hurt." This isn't what I expected from Rory. "Don't try to play the hero."

His jaw sets hard. "I'm not. But you're afraid and you have been for weeks. If it's a squatter, they won't hurt me."

Before I can say anything else he's off down the hallway,

poking his head into the shoe cupboard for our torch. I race into the kitchen and take a knife from the knife block. "Here," I say, catching up with him by the door. He opens his mouth to tell me no but I insist. "Take it. Just put it into your pocket. Please. If anything happened to you because of me and this story . . ."

"I'll be fine," he says. "But keep watch, okay? And if I flash the torch three times, call the police because it means I'm in danger."

My mouth is dry. I can't believe he's going to do this. "Should we just call the police anyway?"

He shakes his mop of dark hair. "No. Not yet. We don't want to waste their time. It could be a homeless person or they might have moved on. Nothing to worry about. I'll go over and see."

I hug him to me, not wanting to let him go. He's tall, over six foot, but he's slim built. He cycles a lot but he's never been to the gym. Would he be able to protect himself in a fight?

He pulls away. "Hey. I grew up with two older brothers. I'll be fine," he says, as if reading my mind. "Now, keep watch."

He slips out of the door and I run back to the bedroom. I watch as he crosses the street. He's wearing his big padded coat and I can see he's got his hand in his pocket where the knife is. When he gets to the door he stops and fiddles with something for what seems an age. Then, eventually, the door swings open. He turns to me and gives me the thumbs-up. And then he disappears into the building.

44

Margot

Margot sits in the corner of the room watching Heather with her family. Adam is sitting beside his wife's bed and little Ethan is on her lap, trying to nuzzle into her neck while she reads him his favorite story, *Guess How Much I Love You*. She resembles the picture of contentment as she rests her cheek against his soft curly hair while he sucks his thumb. Adam watches them with a little smile on his lips. He's brought in some of the daffodils that he grows in a part of the field they use as their allotment, and they fill the room with a scent that Margot has always found slightly cloying. It looks like a normal family scene, except Margot knows it's not. The police officer's presence reminds her that her daughter is under arrest for murder. Tomorrow they will come in to interview her and Margot knows she will be charged. Their lawyer has said she'll fight for diminished responsibility, but even if that's the case and Heather gets the lesser charge of voluntary manslaughter instead of murder, she'll still have to go to prison or a secure hospital under the Mental Health Act. She'll have to leave her husband and her son and go away for goodness knows how long.

Will Adam wait for her? How much does he love her? Margot has always found him so hard to read. He's a good father, she can't dispute that, and she's always thought him a good husband to Heather. But they'd argued a lot since Ethan was born, and the night before the *incident*—Margot can't bring herself to call it anything else—he'd walked out on her, taking his son with him. Why? He was going to tell her the night she got that phone call from DCI Ruthgow, but they were distracted by the possibility that Flora's body had been found. And she's not had the chance to ask him again.

Eventually Ethan starts to get wriggly and tired and Adam picks him up, but Ethan holds out his arms to Heather. His little chin wobbles. He doesn't want to leave his mummy and it breaks Margot's heart.

"It's okay, little man. Mummy will see you tomorrow," says Heather, smiling encouragingly, although Margot can see it's killing her having to say goodbye. Adam bends over to kiss Heather and she leans forward to hug Ethan once again, smelling his head with her eyes closed.

It's not until they leave that Heather allows the tears to run down her cheeks.

Margot's by her bedside in an instant. "I know, sweetheart," she says, pressing a tissue into her daughter's hand. "It's hard. I know."

"I can't bear being apart from him." She sobs.

"Hopefully not for much longer."

Heather turns to face her, fire suddenly blazing behind her wet eyes. "Soon it will be even worse. Soon I'll only be allowed to see him once a week. He'll grow up not knowing me. Not really. A prison is no place for a child." She's crying so much now that her shoulders are heaving.

Margot pulls Heather into her arms. "Please don't cry. I've got a brilliant lawyer for you. We'll do what we can to fight it, okay?"

Heather rests her head on Margot's shoulder and cries as if she's still a child. Margot rubs her back, feeling powerless. It's in-built in her, the desire to make everything okay for her daughter, but how can she prevent this? Eventually Heather pulls away, her eyes red and puffy, and Margot sits on the chair. She glances at the clock on the wall. It's nearly seven thirty. Soon visiting time will be over and she'll have to go. She doesn't want to leave her in this state.

"Mum," says Heather. She pulls her knees up to her chest. She looks impossibly young and vulnerable, thinks Margot, assessing her daughter in her oversize pajamas. She's lost weight since the . . . *incident*. She swings her legs out of bed and Margot jumps up from her chair. Heather is still a little unsteady on her feet. The head injury has caused a lack of balance, although they've been assured this is only temporary.

"What is it, sweetheart? Do you need the loo?"

She shakes her head, then winces, touching her bandage gingerly. "No. I need . . . I need to tell you something." She pats the bed next to her, and Margot sits. The bed is high off the floor and Margot's legs dangle like a child's.

"What is it?" They're sitting so close that their thighs are touching. Margot realizes, with a jolt, that Heather has suggested she sit so close so that the police at the door can't hear what she's about to say. Straightaway Margot's heart begins to beat faster.

"Jess is going to write a piece about me. With my blessing. I'm hoping it will make the public understand a bit more, that they know I'd never be capable of killing the Wilsons. Not when I have Ethan to think about. It might help if . . . when . . . this all goes to trial."

Margot's holding her breath. "Right?"

"My brain's been all over the place since the accident. I can't remember taking a gun to the Wilsons. I can't remember driving back to the caravan park and trying to shoot myself in the barn. I can't remember falling and banging my head. Since . . ." She swallows, and Margot's insides feel as though they've turned to ice as she wonders what her daughter is about to say next. "Since it all happened I've been dreaming a lot. All these different thoughts have been racing through my head, fragments of memory. I've been trying to piece it all together . . ." A tear falls from Heather's eyes and drops onto her hand resting in her lap. Margot stares in horror at the teardrop, unable to move, to comfort.

Heather swipes at the tears. "I loved Flora. You have to believe me when I tell you that. I wanted to protect her. She was different from me. Flaky . . . dreamy. I never meant to hurt her . . ."

Margot puts her hand to her throat and fingers her gold locket, bracing herself for Heather's next words.

Heather turns to stare at her mother and grasps her hand with such intensity that Margot almost pulls off the necklace. "Now I've got Ethan, I understand," she says. "I can imagine how you must feel. The pain of never knowing what happened. The torment. It's not fair to you, Mum. I'm so sorry. I knew the body at Clive Wilson's house couldn't belong to Flora. I'm going to tell you what really happened to her, okay?" She squeezes Margot's hand. "And then you can decide what to do."

45

August 1994

THE SPELL HAD BEEN BROKEN. JUST LIKE THAT.

They were walking in St. James's Park, admiring the pelicans. It had been romantic. The sun had been shining and she'd linked her arm through Dylan's, like they were a proper couple. How grown-up she'd felt, how she'd enjoyed the admiring glances they'd received. Until Dylan went and ruined it.

Now he stood before her, in his tie-dyed T-shirt and baggy jeans, his dark hair flopping into his bright blue eyes, and smiled the slow, lazy smile that used to turn her insides to mush. But not now. Now, instead of rushing up and throwing her arms around him, like she would have done earlier, or yesterday, the only desire she felt was the urge to punch him hard in his stupid, idiotic face.

"What?" he said, throwing his arms out. "What have I said?"

She placed her hands on her hips, like her mother did when

she got cross with them. "Oh, I don't know. Perhaps the little thing about wanting me to help you peddle your pathetic drugs. I thought you wanted to come to London to spend time with me. Away from Tilby. But no . . . no, of course not. You just want me to join your . . . *empire*," she spat.

He lowered his voice so that the couple next to them couldn't hear. "Speedy has a good contact here. Said he'll give them to me on the cheap." He walked toward her with the arrogant swagger she used to find so attractive, but now repellent. "Come on, babe. You're sixteen. You could come with me when the fair moves on . . . There's good money to be had from this, if we play our cards right."

"What a great future you're offering me." She couldn't help the sarcasm that dripped from her tongue. "A Bonnie and Clyde future."

He laughed, but his eyes darted about nervously. She was getting loud and he was worried who could hear. "I'm not suggesting we kill anyone."

"Aren't you?"

He stepped forward and tried to encircle her with his arms. "Babe. You like it. I know you do. I saw how you were when you snorted that coke the other night . . . but you don't have to take drugs. Just help me sell them." His eyes clouded. "I owe Speedy and his brother, Clive, money, babe. I need to do this. I can't mess with them."

She pulled away from him. "It's wrong. I don't want any part of it." She'd felt out of control at the party the other night and she hadn't liked it. She'd looked around at the crowd she was with, most of whom were off their heads on some substance or other, and she'd been disgusted by them all.

Dylan's expression became more alarmed and he moved away from her. "I thought you were cool."

"Maybe I'm not. I want a career. I don't want to be a drugs pusher or an addict."

He laughed nastily. "You're a baby. Just like your sister. A fucking prissy small-town girl with no ambition."

"No ambition!" she shrieked, causing the couple in front of them to turn to look at her. "I've got more ambition than you. Heather was right about you."

She stalked off before he could answer, heart thudding against her rib cage. When she'd calmed down a bit she stopped by a tree to catch her breath, expecting Dylan to have followed her. But he was nowhere to be seen. She felt a flurry of fear. She was alone, in London, with no idea how to get back to the coach. Calm down, she told herself. She could work it out. Marble Arch. That was where the coach had dropped them off. It would be okay. She took deep, gulping breaths, trying not to panic. As long as she was back before the coach left at five it would be okay.

FLORA'S FEET HURT AS SHE TOOK HER SEAT ON THE COACH. SHE'D spent all afternoon wandering around by herself. A kindly old man had pointed her in the right direction and she'd spent the last two hours hanging around the coach area, terrified she'd miss it if she strayed too far.

She didn't see Dylan get on the coach, and was beyond caring if he came back or stayed in London. She sat near the front, by the window, next to a middle-aged woman who had her head in a book the whole way back. Flora clamped her headphones to her ears, so she could listen to her favorite song, "Martha's Harbor," on her Walkman. She wouldn't allow herself to think about him ever again. What a lucky escape she'd had. There were plenty more fish in the sea, as her uncle Leo always said when one of his relationships failed, which was often.

Suddenly she longed to be at home, with her uncle and her mum, Heather and Jess. Safe and warm, away from Dylan and his druggie mates and the fair. She didn't want to go back to the fair ever again. Behind the bright lights and the loud music there was a rotten, seedy underbelly.

It began to rain as the coach pulled into Eastville and she had to walk for fifteen minutes across town to the bus station. The rain continued to lash down and she only had her little velvet jacket to protect her from the onslaught. By the time she arrived she was drenched and shivering in her summer blouse and floaty skirt. The only sensible thing she had on was her trusted DMs. She sat on the bench trying to keep warm as she waited for the Tilby bus. Despite herself, she looked around for Dylan. Then she spotted him. He had bought himself a hot drink and was standing at the other end of the concourse, watching her. She caught his eye and he smiled, looking relieved to see her, but she didn't return his smile. He'd left her in London. She'd never forgive him. She turned away, hardening her heart against him. It didn't matter how sexy he was, or how he made her feel, she knew, deep in her gut, that he was bad news, and if she stayed with him he'd drag her further into his murky circle. She was sixteen, with the whole world at her feet. She'd meet someone else. Someone better. She didn't need him.

HEATHER HID IN THE BUSHES, SHELTERING FROM THE RAIN, WAIT-ing for the bus to come in. She'd been there for more than an hour and she was cold to the bone, despite her waxed jacket. Because of the sudden change in the weather, the sky had darkened even though it wasn't yet nine. Did that mean they would miss their curfew of "before dark"? This used to be nine thirty but the nights were already drawing in very slightly, and the bad weather made the sky darker than usual. Either way, Heather was past caring. She needed to see Flora, to make things right between them. She was still smarting that her sister had chosen to confide in Jess over her.

The clock tower was empty. The rain was too heavy for the usual youths to hang out there tonight. The streets were wet, with only the occasional car driving past, the whoosh of water under tires making her think of her best friend. They loved to huddle in the barn, listening to the rain and sketching.

Then she saw the bus rattling toward her, screeching to a halt next to the bus stop. She was surprised to see Dylan get off first, alone. He had no jacket on, just his thin T-shirt, and his shoulders were hunched against the rain as he walked along the street, then turned off toward the fields that led to the fair. Heather's heart fell. Where was her sister? Why was she not with Dylan? Another couple got off the bus, holding hands and occasionally smooching, not caring about the weather as they wandered in the opposite direction toward the beach.

And then Heather saw Flora stepping daintily from the bus, her heavy DMs landing in a puddle and splashing the hem of her skirt. Her hair hung in dark tendrils and she had her earphones in, the yellow leads snaking around her velvet jacket and toward the bag on her back. Heather's heart swelled. Her sister looked utterly miserable. A car drove past, obscuring Flora for a second, before moving out of sight.

Heather stumbled out of the bushes and into Flora's path, making her sister jump in fright. She put a hand to her heart. "Shit, what are you doing?" she hissed, pulling off the earphones so that they dangled in one hand. Her family signet ring glinted under the streetlight.

Family. They were linked, her and Flora. They shared the same blood. And that stupid little dickhead Dylan wouldn't come between them.

"Where have you been?" she said, although she knew. "You've been with him again, haven't you? Sneaking off to God knows where. What's wrong with you, Flora? Why can't you see what a loser he is?"

"Not now, Heather." Flora looked weary, like she'd rather be anywhere else than there, talking with her. "Go home."

Heather felt the familiar white-hot rage flare up inside her. *Go home.* Was that how little Flora thought of her, or respected her? She'd confide in Jess but not her. Her own sister.

"Why are you freezing me out?" Heather demanded, her hands making fists by her sides.

Flora sighed. "I'm not."

"You told Jess where you were going this morning but not me. Don't you trust me?"

"It's not that . . . Listen, I'm tired. It's been a long day."

The rain had stopped now and the air smelled fresh, like washed clothes. Flora went to walk away but Heather ran after her, tugging at her jacket. "I was only trying to protect you. That's why I hurt Dylan. Listen to me . . ."

Flora stopped walking and spun around. "I just want to go home," she said.

"You pushed me the other day. You've not been speaking to me."

"Oh, grow up. I've got bigger things to think about," Flora replied.

"No. We need to talk about this now."

"We'll be late."

"I don't care!" Heather screamed. That got her sister's attention. Heather always cared about being late.

Flora stared at her sister dispassionately. Flora's hair had begun to curl in the damp, and her face was ashen with mascara streaks under her eyes.

Before Heather even thought about what she was doing she

grabbed hold of her sister's arm and began pulling her toward the lane that led to the fields. "Ow! Get off! What are you doing?" cried Flora, trying to shake her arm free.

"We can walk and talk," said Heather.

"Leave me alone, you little psycho," shrieked Flora, losing her temper now. She pushed Heather away so that she stumbled backward, landing in the mud. Heather gawped at Flora in shock, then stood up, mud caked on the back of her skirt and down her legs.

"Why are you so mean to me?" she cried. "I'm only trying to help you!"

"Are you going to get your riding crop out and whip me too?" Flora said, her eyes flashing.

Heather flew at her, pushing her so hard that this time Flora went reeling backward. Her head snapped back against the wet pavement, and she must have bitten down on her lip when she fell because it burst open, pouring with blood, her eyes round with shock as she landed, before closing.

And then there was silence, apart from the rustle of the leaves in the tree above them.

Heather leaned over her sister, shaking her. "Flora. Oh, God, Flora. I'm so sorry. I'm so sorry. Please wake up. Please . . ."

To Heather's relief, Flora's eyelids fluttered open and she sat up, groaning. "You pushed me!" she cried.

"You pushed me first. And I fell into a muddy ditch!"

Flora touched her lip and blood came away on her fingers, dripping down her chin and onto her blouse. "I'm bleeding."

Heather knelt down, her bare knees snagging on the concrete pavement. "Here, let me help you."

But Flora pushed her away. "Leave me alone." Her voice sounded weird with the fat lip, which had already swelled to twice its normal size. She stood up shakily, brushing down her wet skirt.

"Flora, I'm sorry. I—" She reached out, but Flora slapped her hand away.

"Go home. Now! Before I fucking kill you!" spat Flora, blood bubbling on her lip. She picked up her Walkman from the pavement and Heather could see that it had smashed in the fall. Flora crouched over it, tears spilling down her face.

Heather wanted to cry too. "I'm so sorry." She touched her sister's shoulder. "I'll buy you another. I shouldn't have come to find you. I was worried."

Flora covered Heather's hand with her own and squeezed it gently. "I know. But please just leave me alone now. I'll follow you. Just go. There's no point in us both being late."

Heather knew when she was beaten. If she stayed it would only make matters worse. Flora was too cold, tired, and angry to listen to her now. She'd follow on. She just needed some space. It was still only a little past nine and not yet properly dark. And Jess would be wondering where she was. She'd left her in her bedroom nearly an hour and a half ago, telling her she was sorting out the pony. Because it was raining Jess had been happy to stay behind. Jess didn't love horses like she did.

Heather turned back just once as she walked off down the

road, before taking a left along the lane that led to the fields. Flora was kneeling on the ground and stuffing what remained of her Walkman into her rucksack, her hair obscuring her face. Heather wanted to rush back to her sister and throw her arms around her. But she knew it wouldn't be welcome.

And then, her heart full of guilt and sorrow, Heather trudged down the lane that led toward home.

46

Jess

TIME SEEMS TO STAND STILL AS I WATCH FROM THE WINDOW. I PRESS
my face to the glass, trying to spot Rory in the building opposite.
I've got my boots and coat on in preparation, my phone in my
hand, ready to call the police if he flashes his torch three times.
Nothing. The silence seems worse somehow. I'm imagining all
sorts: he's been stabbed before he can alert me that he's in danger; he's been beaten up—murdered.

"Come on, Rory," I mutter to myself, stamping my feet impatiently as though trying to dispel some of my nervous energy.
"Give me some sign you're okay."

And then I see it, an arc of torchlight. Is it him? I don't know
what to do. I'm paralyzed by indecision. Rory's put himself in
danger for me and now I'm letting him down by being a flake.
Perhaps he's just searching the area and has found nothing.

I can't bear the not knowing.

Before I change my mind I race out of the flat and down the stairs to the entrance. The street is empty, the door of the building opposite slightly ajar where Rory broke in. I falter. I don't think of myself as brave. I'm not one of those journalists who constantly puts themselves in danger on the front line, or who goes undercover to investigate some criminal gang. No. I might be headstrong, reckless at times. I make wrong decisions, like the part I played in the phone-hacking scandal. But I'm not brave. Yet, as I stand here dithering, I can't stop thinking about Rory, playing the hero for me. Without allowing myself to think any more about it, I dart across the road, slam my shoulder against the heavy door, and step inside the building.

It's dark and dusty and I instantly sneeze. It was once a warehouse and it still has those large, square windows that are murky with dirt. I blink, trying to adjust my eyes to the dark. The room is immense; open plan with stairs in the far corner. A large dust sheet is draped over something near the stairs. I turn slowly. Where is Rory? And then I see him in the opposite corner, underneath the window, the moonlight bleaching his dark curls. He's leaning over what looks like a body.

"Rory?" I hiss, stepping toward him.

His head swivels toward me, his eyes wide. "I've just called an ambulance. There's a woman here, unconscious." He gets to his feet, and that's when I see her. The woman. She's sprawled on top of a dirty old sleeping bag and there are used needles littering the concrete floor, as well as empty crisp packets and a cereal box. A drug addict.

Rory kneels beside her and takes her hand. He looks visibly upset and I'm suddenly struck by the horror of it. "She's so thin," he says sadly. "What makes somebody end up like this?"

I go to him and put my hand on his shoulder, wanting to comfort him. I know this will affect Rory greatly. He's the first person to put his hand into his pocket, or donate by mobile, when an advert for UNICEF or the Royal Society for the Prevention of Cruelty to Children comes on the TV. He can't walk past a homeless person without stopping to give money, or a *Big Issue* seller even if he already has that particular copy. I kneel down beside him. The woman looks older than me, her skin sallow and sunken, her long dark hair matted and greasy. She's wearing a colorful maxi dress and only a cardigan for warmth. Her fingernails are bitten down and dirty. But there's something familiar about the shape of her face and the dimple next to her full, chapped lips.

Rory still has hold of her hand. "It's okay," he says to her, in a soothing voice. "The ambulance is on its way. We'll stay with you. My name is Rory and this is my girlfriend, Jess."

At the mention of my name her eyelids twitch and her mouth moves.

"Rory," I whisper, "she's not unconscious. She's trying to say something."

Her eyes open slowly. Cat's eyes. For a second I stop breathing. "Jess . . ." Her voice is raspy, as though she's not used to speaking out loud.

Rory turns to me in shock. "Do you know this woman?"

Her eyes close again and her hand goes limp in Rory's.

I sit back on my heels in horror, thinking I might be sick as the sirens sound in the distance. It can't be. It can't be her. But even in her current state the resemblance to Heather is striking. "I think . . . I think it's Flora."

47

Margot

I NEED TO TELL YOU THE TRUTH," HEATHER SAYS, STARING AT MARgot intently. "Flora's still alive."

Margot stares at her daughter, speechless. The damage to her brain must have been greater than any of them had understood. She's spouting rubbish. She's confused, bless her.

She takes her hand. "Sweetheart, we have to accept that Flora is dead."

Heather snatches her hand away and adjusts her position on the bed so that she's facing her mother. "No. Listen. Please listen. It's important, Mum. I know I sound deluded. Mad, even. But . . . I don't know if it was seeing Jess again or just my brain healing but I've remembered. Ask Adam if you don't believe me. Ask him what we'd been fighting about that last night."

Margot puts a hand to her head. "I don't understand what you're trying to tell me."

"I found out about Flora when Deirdre came to stay at the

caravan park. She had a dog with her. Big and fluffy. You know, one of those chow chows. And I remembered Flora telling me about them when she was going out with Dylan. She said the mother of the guy his mum was seeing bred them. And the guy's brother, Clive, had come to the fair and brought it with him. And then there was the ring . . ."

Margot gets up from the bed and begins pacing the room, her mind racing. *Flora's alive?* "Where is she?" she snaps, suddenly not caring about the logistics, only that she wants to see her daughter again, her baby. She burns with it, the desire to hold her elder daughter in her arms again. "Where is she, Heather?"

Heather starts crying. "That's just it. I don't know. I found her, Mum. In Clive Wilson's house in Southville. I found her and then I lost her again. Call the detective guy that you like. Get him to find her."

Margot wants to believe all this is true. She's dreamed of it so many times over the years. But Heather's been in a coma—she nearly died. "Are you sure you didn't . . . dream this?"

"I'm telling the truth. It's a long story, Mum." Heather's face is a picture of desperation. "I'll tell you another time but, for now, please, *just find her.*"

RUTHGOW SOUNDS JUST AS SKEPTICAL AS MARGOT FEELS.

"And Heather is telling you this only now?"

Margot is patrolling the length of the atrium, her mobile clamped against her ear. There are a few people at tables, nursing vending-machine drinks. The cafés are now closed. "I don't think she could remember before. The . . . accident. Her head . . .

her thoughts were all over the place." Her voice sounds echoey in the vast space.

"Please try not to get your hopes up," he says softly. She wonders if he's at home. Perhaps with a significant other. Are they clearing up after dinner or about to go out for the evening? She's sure she can hear someone humming in the background. "I understand how badly you want it to be true. But this could be a figment of Heather's imagination after spending a week in a coma."

"I—I know."

He clears his throat. "Leave it with me. I'll do all I can, Margot, I promise."

After he's hung up, Margot slumps into a chair, feeling as though all her energy has been sucked from her. She doesn't even know where to start with her thought process. She needs to go back and talk to Heather.

She hurries along the winding corridors to the area where Heather's room is. Visiting time is nearly over. The nurses and doctors—they all know who she is now—are usually happy to be a bit lenient, but Margot doesn't want to break any rules.

The same policeman is still outside Margot's door and he raises an eyebrow when he sees her. "Back again?" He smiles. He's young, this policeman, with twinkly hazel eyes and a round freckled face. He's young enough to be Margot's son. She likes him. Out of all the police officers who have stood guard in the nearly two weeks since Heather was admitted, he's the only one who bothers to talk to her or treat her as though she's an actual human being, rather than the mother of a criminal.

"Forgot to ask Heather something," she says, throwing him a benign smile. He steps aside to allow her to pass.

Heather is lying on top of the bed in her dressing gown, her head resting against the puffed-up pillows; a nurse is taking her blood pressure and temperature.

Heather lifts her eyebrows in surprise but doesn't say anything until the nurse has left.

"Well?" she whispers.

"I've called Ruthgow. He's going to look into it. You need to tell me everything, Heather."

"Some of it is still patchy. I can't remember what happened before . . ." She touches the bandage around her head. "And I don't remember shooting the Wilsons but"—she flushes—"I do remember getting obsessed with her in the weeks leading up to . . . it."

Margot perches on the edge of Heather's bed. "With who? Deirdre?"

"I just couldn't get it out of my head, the thing with the dogs and the ring." She holds her right hand up. "This ring, Mum. Flora's."

Margot takes her hand and examines the little gold ring. It's identical to Heather's, passed down through the family. Margot's grandfather had been a bit of a snob and decided that their family's crest needed to be immortalized in the shape of rings, even though he had no ancestral lineage or blood. Margot had worn his since she had handed hers to Heather, and Leo had given his own to Flora when she was a baby, saying he knew he'd never have kids and it was all a load of pretentious crap anyway that he didn't want to be a part of. Margot had had to have it made smaller so that it would fit on Flora's little finger when she had allowed her daughter to wear it as a teenager. Heather hands it to Margot now and she studies it, looking for the very faint join. She reaches down to the floor to retrieve her reading glasses from her bag, slips them on, and peers at the rings. Heather takes hers off, and Margot holds them in her palm. They are identical.

"It's exactly the same as mine, see? Too much of a coincidence we'd have the same family crest, isn't it? I know it's not some ancient coat of arms and that my great-granddad just wanted to say he had a family ring. But still. That's Flora's ring, isn't it?"

Margot nods. Why hadn't she noticed before that Heather was wearing Flora's ring? If she had, she'd have questioned her about it. It might have prompted Heather to remember earlier. There are so many questions buzzing around her head that she can't think straight for all the noise. Then she asks urgently, "What happened to my little girl? Tell me. I need to know."

Heather opens her mouth to speak but is interrupted by one of the nurses bustling into the room. It's the one Margot has never taken to. Brenda. Skinny and upright with thin lips that refuse to smile. "Right," she says, clapping her hands and shooing Margot off the bed. "Time's up, I'm afraid. It's really late. You should have left at eight."

In that moment Margot could quite cheerfully have throttled Brenda. "Can you just give us a minute, please?" she says. "I need to talk to Heather."

"You can talk to her in the morning."

"But—"

"Come on. Out."

Margot catches her daughter's eye. She's waited eighteen years but she doesn't think she has it in her to wait any longer.

Brenda touches Margot lightly on the shoulder. "Off you go, then," she says, in the kind of voice you'd use on a wayward child.

"I'm sorry," mouths Heather, her expression one of panic.

Margot shakes her head. "It's okay. I'll be back first thing."

But she doesn't have the chance to finish her sentence because the door is closed firmly behind her.

The nice policeman chuckles. "Gosh, she's not to be messed with, is she?"

Margot doesn't have the energy to summon a smile. She staggers along the corridor, feeling as though she's drunk. There's a funny vibrating sound coming from her handbag: her phone. She drops her bag in haste and rifles through it. It could be Ruthgow with news of Flora. Why hadn't she kept it in her hand? Stupid. Stupid. She's on her hands and knees now. By the time she finds the phone right at the bottom of her handbag the person has rung off. She grabs it and sees Jessica Fox's number under missed calls. Before she has the chance to ring back her phone springs into life again with Jess's name flashing up.

"Margot?" she says, before Margot even has the chance to say hello. "It's Jess. This is going to come as a shock. But I've found a woman who I think is Flora. Margot? Margot? Are you there?"

48

Margot

THE PLEASANT-FACED POLICE OFFICER, WHO SAYS HE'S CALLED DALE, helps her to her feet and guides her to a chair in the dayroom.

"Are you okay, Mrs. Powell?" He leans over her and pats her shoulder, like she's an old-age pensioner. He holds a white plastic cup of water under her nose. She notices a hairline crack in the rim.

The magnolia walls are closing in on her. She still has her mobile phone in her hand. With the other hand, she takes the cup and sips the water slowly from the side with no crack.

"You had a funny turn. Shall I go and fetch Nurse Brenda?"

"No!" she says, too quickly.

He laughs. "I don't blame you. Maybe just sit here for a bit, then. I'll be just across the way outside your daughter's room."

The dayroom is only small, maybe ten foot by eight, with just a few chairs and a bucket of plastic toys piled high in the corner. There's a noticeboard with leaflets pinned to it and a poster encouraging people to talk to their doctor if they find blood in their wee. Margot takes a few deep breaths, like she was taught in her yoga class, until her heart rate slows. Then she stands up gingerly and dumps the plastic cup on the table.

She walks down the corridor carefully, feeling much steadier on her feet now. She can do this, she thinks, giving herself a little motivational pep talk. She's strong.

At last she's a cat's whisker away from finding out the truth about Flora. Heather says she's still alive. Jess says she's found her. *Jess*. She needs to ring Jess.

Her fingers tremble as she scrolls down to Jess's number in her phone. "Hello." Jess sounds worried and slightly out of breath. "Margot. Are you okay?"

"Where are you? Where's Flora? I need to see her."

"I'm at Southmead Hospital. Flora was brought in less than ten minutes ago."

Southmead Hospital? Flora's here. She's actually here. "I'm at the hospital too. I'll meet you in the atrium, near Costa," she says, her pace picking up so that she's almost running down the corridor.

Jess is already standing outside Costa with a striking man when Margot gets there. He must be the boyfriend. He has his arm slung protectively around Jess's shoulders. She looks like she's been rubbing her eyes: her mascara is smudged. Her face is pale and drawn, her hair a mass of blond fluff, and she's wrapped up in her llama coat. Margot notices a ladder in her patterned tights.

Her face lights up when she spots Margot. "Come on. I'll show you where she is," she says, linking her arm through Margot's and almost pulling her along.

"I don't understand," Margot says, allowing herself to be led, her mind still playing catch-up. Jess is acting like she's just had an adrenaline shot and she doesn't bother to introduce Margot to her boyfriend, not that Margot cares. All Margot wants is to see her daughter again. Jess is still gabbling as they hurry toward Accident and Emergency, something about derelict buildings and a person sleeping rough who turned out to be Flora. She can't quite comprehend it all. It's as though her brain has stopped functioning properly so that thinking is like wading through glue.

In A and E Jess explains to the receptionist who Margot is and a doctor appears straightaway: a tired-looking man with a crumpled face who introduces himself, although Margot instantly forgets his name, and asks her to follow him. She turns back once to see Jess and her boyfriend standing at the desk, looking helpless.

"Can you ring Gary?" Margot calls to Jess. "Ruthgow, CID," she adds, when Jess stares at her blankly.

Jess nods and is already reaching for her phone as the doctor leads Margot away.

"I'm afraid your daughter is very poorly," he says, his face grave. "She overdosed on heroin and, if she hadn't been found just then, she would certainly have died. We've given her naloxone, which will help to reverse the effects, but she's finding it hard to breathe and I think one of her lungs has been affected.

She'll start to get withdrawal symptoms. It looks like she's been an addict for a long time. Suffice to say her health isn't good."

An addict? Flora is a heroin addict? Margot can't get her head around it. *Please, God, let her survive this.*

He stops when they reach a line of cubicles: groaning and shouting are coming from behind a curtain. Thankfully he goes to a cubicle further down the line and Margot takes a deep breath, trying to steady herself.

The first thing that strikes Margot about the woman—*woman, not girl; she had pictured Flora as a sixteen-year-old*—is how tall and thin she is. Margot glances at the doctor for reassurance but he gives her a look that says, "Go on."

This woman, this creature in the bed, looks nothing like her beautiful little girl and Margot has to suppress a sob. She has an oxygen mask over her face and, although she has blankets and sheets up to her waist, Margot can see she's wearing an ugly hospital gown.

Oh, Flora, what have you done to yourself? How could her clever, naïve daughter end up like this?

"Flora?" she whispers, moving closer to the bed. She looks so old, this girl—*woman.* Her once glossy dark hair is now dull and matted, hanging in strands over her shoulders, her skin no longer young and fresh but sunken and lined. Margot's eyes fill with tears as she runs her fingertip over the chicken-pox scar just in front of her daughter's left ear. It's her baby. She can hardly believe it, but it's true. She gently brushes the hair away from Flora's forehead. It's been a lifetime, yet the curve of her forehead is so familiar that Margot's heart feels like it might burst with love, fear, and sadness for all the lost years. She takes her elder daughter's pale hand in hers and holds it to her face. She wants never to let it go.

The doctor touches her upper arm gently and says he'll be back in five minutes. Margot hardly notices him leave.

And then, much to her delight, Flora opens her eyes, those beautiful green eyes, so like Heather's, and she squeezes Margot's hand. "Mum?" she croaks.

"Oh, my baby. It's me. It's Mum. You're okay. You're safe. You're safe."

A tear slides from the corner of Flora's eye and seeps onto the pillow. She turns her head slowly toward Margot and pulls away her oxygen mask. "I'm so sorry." Her voice is raspy, as though she's been smoking twenty cigarettes a day.

"You don't have to be sorry, my darling," Margot says, a weight crushing her chest. "I've missed you so much."

"I've missed you too . . . Please . . . Heather . . . Is she alive?"

"She's alive and well. Don't worry about Heather." How did Flora know? She must have read about it in the newspapers. Is that why she's come back? Because of Heather?

Margot replaces the oxygen mask over Flora's face. "We can talk later. You need to get well. It's okay. It's all going to be okay." Flora's chest rattles as she breathes and the sound worries Margot. Her eyes slowly close again and Margot sits on the cold, plastic chair next to the bed, still clutching her daughter's hand and watching as her chest rises and falls. She only lets go when the doctor comes in and checks the monitor by Flora's bedside. There is a flurry of activity and noise as another doctor rushes in. Then an overweight nurse with a kind face ushers a startled Margot out of the cubicle.

"What's going on? Is there something wrong?"

"They're just taking her to the right department, pet," the nurse says. "She needs more specialized care, that's all. Come with me, and when she's settled, you can see her."

Margot wants to scream and kick the woman, this nurse, who's keeping her apart from her child. She wants never to be parted from Flora again. But she resists the urge, instead allowing herself to be led away.

Jess and the boyfriend are sitting at a table holding hands and murmuring to each other when Margot stumbles into the waiting area, blinking from the harsh overhead lighting. Everything has changed. Since Flora went missing Margot has been going through the motions, like an actress playing a part, but it hadn't felt real. She'd been numb, even when something good happened, like being with Heather or Ethan, and any elation would swiftly be followed by a surge of guilt. And now. Now everything feels hyperreal, too bright, surreal almost. She still feels like she's in a play, but one in which the ending has suddenly changed without anyone telling her.

When Jess sees her she drops her boyfriend's hand, pushes her chair back, and darts over to her. "Is it her? Is it Flora?"

Margot can only nod and Jess has to help her to the table.

"No," says Margot, stopping in her tracks. "I need to go. I

need to see Heather. She knew Flora was still alive. I need to tell her that her sister is here."

Jessica's eyes widen in surprise. "Wait. What?"

"Heather knew. I don't . . ." She gulps. "I don't understand any of it. Not yet."

"I did wonder if Heather knew more than she was letting on," Jess says, a blush coloring her cheeks. "She was wearing Flora's ring."

"What happened? How did you find Flora?"

The boyfriend steps forward. "I found her, Mrs. Powell." He holds out a hand. "I'm Rory." And then he proceeds to tell her everything.

THE WAITING ROOM IS REMARKABLY BUSY FOR A WEDNESDAY EVEning, but Margot feels as if she's been sitting there forever, even though it can't be longer than half an hour.

She has sent Rory and Jess home. There was nothing more they could do. She doubted they would be allowed to see Flora, and Jess in particular had looked shattered, unable to stifle her yawns. As Margot hugged Jess goodbye and thanked Rory, she promised to call in the morning with any news.

Flora. Her baby is home. She feels a surge of relief and elation, quickly followed by fear that she'll lose her again. She can't let that happen.

She gets up and begins to pace. She's desperate to see Heather, although visiting hours are long over and she knows she won't be allowed.

"Margot?"

She turns to see DCI Ruthgow charging toward her, a determined look on his face, which relaxes as he approaches. He's wearing a long wool coat with the collar turned up over the top of a suit.

"Gary." Her mouth goes dry. "Is everything okay?"

"Jessica Fox rang me. Told me about finding Flora. That's wonderful news." He smiles, although the deep furrows in his brow don't disappear.

"But?"

"But nothing. The main thing is that she's been found. There'll have to be an investigation into where she's been, of course, to determine if there's been foul play."

Margot dips her head. "I know. Heather . . . she already knew Flora was alive. She'd found out before the incident with the Wilsons. I was shooed out by a nurse before I could get any more information from her but I need to know . . . She said she'd found her at Clive's Bristol house." She bites back tears.

The grooves in his brow deepen. "I thought Jessica found her?"

"No. I don't understand it all."

He's silent for a few seconds as he assesses her with those heavy-lidded eyes of his. "Come with me," he says suddenly, and strides off down the corridor.

"Where are we going?" She has to trot to keep up with him.

"To speak to Heather."

"But we won't be allowed."

His mouth is set in a grim line as he says firmly, "Well, we'll see about that."

49

August 1994

FLORA STUFFED HER BELONGINGS BACK INTO HER BAG. HER WALKman was broken, and the tape spooled out of her All About Eve cassette, like two shiny brown ribbons. She didn't understand what had happened to her sister. She was just so angry all the time.

The rain was coming down heavier now, and her hair hung in wet strands around her shoulders. She shivered in her thin white blouse. It was covered with the blood from her lip. She'd never get those stains out and her mum would go mental. She had on a white body stocking underneath, so she stood up, peeled off the wet blouse, and threw it into the bushes, covering herself with her black crushed-velvet jacket.

Despite her good intentions of dumping Dylan, her heart still ached when she thought of him. It had all been going so well until today. And now he'd just stalked off, not even caring how she got home.

She hoisted the bag onto her back and set off down the road toward the lane that led home. It would be muddy now—the rain was already pooling in potholes and gushing down drains.

She thought she heard something in the bushes. A rustling, a moan . . . but she couldn't be sure and she hurried on, her head down.

She didn't hear the car approach until it was right next to her. "Flora?" said a voice she vaguely knew.

She looked up to see a large red face peering at her. He had the window down and rain was spotting his forehead, landing on his pale eyelashes, although he didn't seem to notice. Or care. She recognized him as Speedy's brother. Clive. That was his name. She'd only met him briefly a few days ago. She thought he seemed a bit leery. Beside him sat an older woman with a fluffy dog on her lap that looked like a bear. She'd seen Speedy with that dog and had raved about it to Heather.

"This is my mum, Deirdre. Do you want a lift?"

It was so tempting. It was still a good ten-minute walk home, and she was cold and shivery. She didn't like the way Clive's eyes traveled to her chest but his mum was in the car. He was hardly going to do anything inappropriate with her there, was he?

"Okay. Thanks," she said, getting into the back. The car smelled strongly of wet dog and there were cream dog hairs all over the fabric, but she didn't care. She was warm and off her feet. That was all that mattered.

"You poor thing, you look exhausted," said Deirdre.

"That's a shame. I was going to invite you to a party at mine," added Clive. She could see his eyes in his rearview mirror.

The pupils were huge so it was hard to see any iris. A party? She glanced at her watch. It was gone nine. It would be getting dark soon. She'd be in trouble with her mum if she was late. And Heather . . . She bristled when she thought about her sister and their fight. She'd never forgive her for breaking her Walkman.

"Dylan will be there," Clive added, turning to grin at her. Then he put the car in first gear and moved away from the pavement. She stared through the rain-splattered window. The high street was deserted.

Dylan would be at the party. The thought was enticing. His cruel words of earlier filled her head. *You're a baby. Just like your sister. A fucking prissy small-town girl with no ambition.*

She'd show him. Heather and her mother too. She'd been good her whole life. Always toed the line and done everything that was ever asked. But where had that got her? Wasn't she allowed a bit of fun? To have a wild night out?

"Where is the party?"

"In Bristol."

Bristol? Bristol was a bit far. How would she get home?

"Oh, I don't know. That's a bit far. My mum would kill me."

Deirdre's laugh was tinkly, like a fork against glass. "You're a young girl. You should be going to parties and having fun." She shifted her weight so that she could see Flora in the back. "I grew up in the sixties and I expect your mum did too. I bet she had her fun back in the day."

Flora doubted that. Her mother was born sensible. Like Heather. And Deirdre looked twenty years older than Margot, who was probably closer to Clive's age. She did a quick calculation. Deirdre must have been at least in her late twenties in 1964. Clive was born before that.

"I live down there," said Flora, pointing to a road that led toward the caravan park.

But Clive ignored her and kept driving. "Oops, sorry, missed the turning," he said, laughing. "Looks like you're going to have to come to the party now."

"Don't worry," said Deirdre. "I'll make sure you get home safely. I'll call you a taxi later. And you can ring your mum from our house."

Our house? Clive still lived with his mum?

"I don't think I can afford a taxi home," Flora admitted, "but maybe Mum or Uncle Leo could come and collect me."

"That's it. You call them when we get there," said Deirdre, flashing Flora a reassuring smile. The dog fidgeted on her lap, then jumped between the two front seats to join Flora in the back. "Oh, he likes you and he's a good judge of character."

Flora smiled, trying to quash the unease that rippled through her. She sat in the back seat and cuddled the dog as the rain lashed down and Clive's windscreen wipers whooshed back and forth. She shivered, her wet skirt clinging to her legs. She just wanted to go home but she also didn't want to offend. And part of her couldn't resist the thought of letting Dylan see her at the party. She'd show him she wasn't some provincial mummy's girl.

"I've got some hot chocolate in a flask if you want some," offered Deirdre. She handed it to Flora. "Just pour it into the little cup. That's it."

The hot chocolate was delicious and slid down her throat, warming her instantly, although her lip throbbed. She hadn't realized how thirsty she was, and before she knew it, she had finished the whole cup.

"Have some more if you want it," said Deirdre. "It will warm you up."

Flora poured herself another cup gratefully and swigged it back. It wasn't piping hot but it was more than lukewarm. When she'd had enough she returned the flask to Deirdre with thanks.

Clive didn't say much and Deirdre faced the front again, fiddling with the radio. "Let's have some music to get you in the mood for a party," she said, settling on Ace of Base's "The Sign."

Flora appraised Deirdre, although from where she was sitting she could see only her profile. But she was attractive, Flora suspected late fifties, with blond Marilyn Monroe hair and a full figure. She was wearing a blue spotted 1950s-style dress, which suited her figure, and a white raincoat.

"Will you be at the party too, Deirdre?" she asked politely.

Deirdre laughed again. "Oh, no, dear. I'm too old for that kind of thing now. No, I'll leave you young people to have your fun." She touched Clive's hand where it rested on the steering wheel. Flora wanted to laugh to herself. Clive had to be nearly forty. He was far from young. Why did he and his brother hang out with people half their age anyway?

"I like to provide the entertainment." Clive grinned, his eyes flashing at her from the rearview mirror. Of course. He provided the drugs. That was why he was having the party. It was a job for him. Still, it didn't mean she'd have to touch them. She'd go for a few hours, then ring her mum and Uncle Leo would come and pick her up. And, okay, they were bound to be angry with her. But she was sixteen. She was entitled to a bit of fun. And it would piss off Heather. She smiled at the thought of her irate sister. Her eyelids were heavy now. It must be the lull of the car and the sound of the rain. It was sleep inducing. Soporific. She liked that word. Yes, it was soporific.

Ace of Base sounded very far away now, as did Clive's voice. She thought she heard, "I like her. She's a keeper." But she couldn't be sure. Then she felt the car stop and she tried to prize her eyes open, but they kept falling closed. She felt strong arms lift her from the back seat and something being thrown over her, covering her face. Maybe a blanket. It smelled damp and fusty. Then the click of a door opening and closing, a dog barking.

"Where's the party?" she muttered, although her tongue felt too thick for her mouth.

She was sure she heard Deirdre reply, "There is no party, darling. It's just us." And in that moment she knew she had made a huge mistake in trusting them. She wanted to scream, to put up a struggle. She longed to be at home with her mum and Uncle Leo and Heather, huddled on the sofa with Goldie on their laps. But her body felt too heavy, her mind fuzzy.

And this time she was unable to prevent her eyelids from closing.

50

Margot

Tears stain Heather's face and Margot thinks her daughter looks young and vulnerable in the huge hospital bed, her legs drawn up so that she's hugging her knees under the covers. "I never gave up hope that she was alive somewhere," Heather says.

Gary Ruthgow is perched on a chair on the other side of the bed to Margot. She was surprised when the hospital staff allowed him to talk to Heather at this time of night. But Heather had readily agreed, hungry for any news of Flora. Margot has a pager in her hand, given to her by Flora's doctor, who promised to let her know if there is any news on her elder daughter.

Margot stays silent as she holds Heather's hand for reassurance. After all these years she's finally going to learn the truth.

It was the ring that did it.

"I'd been cleaning Deirdre's caravan when I saw it," explains

Heather. "It was nestled among Deirdre's cheap costume jewelry. I picked it up and compared it to my own—it was exactly the same. And I knew, then, that it was Flora's. So I took it. It wasn't until she checked out the next day that I had the courage to ring her up at home—she'd left her number when she made the booking so I knew where to reach her. It was a Bristol number. I know now it was the Southville address.

"She'd been affronted on the phone when I asked her about the ring, accusing me of stealing. Her defensiveness caused alarm bells to ring. She eventually admitted she'd bought it from a charity shop but I didn't believe her. The ring—coupled with the dog—made me suspicious. I don't even know exactly what I thought her involvement was then, just that she must have known something about Flora's disappearance. And it was the way she acted around me too. There was something odd about her. While she was staying she'd been too interested in the caravan park. And in me. She stared at me a lot. I don't know, in retrospect I wondered if, on some level, she wanted me to find out."

"Deirdre had cancer," says Ruthgow, matter-of-factly. "It was terminal. So maybe she was trying to find some kind of redemption."

Heather shrugs. "I couldn't get it out of my head. The dog. The ring. So I did a bit of my own detective work."

"Why didn't you come to the police?"

"I didn't have any evidence. I didn't even know what I thought had happened at that point."

"Did you tell anyone about the ring?"

Heather sighs and blinks. "I told Adam. But I'll get back to that.

"After I found the ring but before Deirdre checked out, I asked her if she had any children. She said she had two, Clive and Norman. Her eyes shone when she spoke about them. I asked her if one of them dated a woman in the early 1990s with a son called Dylan. I didn't say anything about Flora going missing. She pretended to think about it before answering that, yes, one of her sons had dated a woman with a son called Dylan. And then I just knew. I *knew* that one of her sons knew more about what had happened to Flora.

"So I found out where Deirdre was living—this was a few weeks before she moved to Tilby so she was living with Clive in Southville still. In one of the windows hung a West Ham flag and the house was a bit grotty. And I stalked them. I watched when they left, saw who they spoke to. Clive went out mostly in the evenings. I asked around but a lot of people were scared of him. He had some dodgy connections. One thing became evident, though. He was a drug dealer with a perversion for underage girls."

Margot stares at her daughter, horrified. "Do you mean that Clive and Flora were . . . together? That she knowingly ran off with him?"

Heather looks appalled. "No. God, no. Mum, I'm sorry, I wish it had been that. But it's a lot worse."

Margot's head is pounding and bile rises up in her throat. All her worst hideous visions, the ones she tried not to think about but that came late at night when she was alone in bed, burrowing through to her brain like a determined rat, flooded her thoughts. Visions of Flora being raped, murdered, tortured. Suffering. In pain. Screaming for her to rescue her. She puts her hands over her ears and shuts her eyes to get rid of the images. A moan escapes her lips.

"Mum . . ." Heather squeezes her hand. "I'm so sorry . . ."

"Please . . . go on." Margot senses Ruthgow's gaze on her but she avoids looking at him.

"So, for the next few weeks I hung around their street in Southville when I could. I saw Clive help Deirdre move to her cottage in Tilby and took that opportunity to knock on their Southville neighbors' doors and ask questions. They said they'd seen Clive out and about very occasionally with a dark-haired girl younger than him. And, no, they didn't know her name. I became convinced it was Flora. I thought maybe she'd run off with him, but it didn't make sense to me. I couldn't understand why she wouldn't have contacted us to let us know she was okay.

"Then—a few days before the shootings—I found out that Clive was staying with his mum in Tilby. Getting away from all the people he owed money to, was the rumor going around. I think moving to Tilby was a way for them to have a stab at pretending to be respectable. So I took that opportunity to knock at the house in Southville, hoping Flora would answer. But, of course, there was nothing. Then I sneaked around the back. They have a basement with a grubby-looking window that looks out onto the garden. I was sure I saw a shadow move beyond the glass. But when I knocked nobody answered."

"You should have called the police then," says Ruthgow.

"With what evidence? You wouldn't have believed me. Adam didn't." Heather hangs her head. "I told him, the night before the shootings. He was already stressed and angry with Clive because of the puppy and losing money to him—money we could ill afford."

Until now Margot wasn't aware of any money issues. But she keeps quiet, willing Heather to continue.

"He thought I was being delusional, that my postnatal depression had returned. He said I was obsessive. He didn't even listen to me. We rowed and he walked out, taking Ethan with him."

Margot shuffles in her chair. Why hadn't Adam told her the truth about the row?

"So . . . after the row with Adam, and on the morning of the shootings, I couldn't sleep and woke up early. I thought I'd go to Clive's Bristol house again, hoping he was still in Tilby with his mum." She sighs. "I left here early and drove there while it was still dark, but of course nobody answered when I got there. So I went around the back again. I was sure I could see movement behind the window, like before. A shadow. I knew somebody was there."

"You could have been hurt," says Ruthgow.

"It was stupid. And reckless. I was desperate. But I called Flora's name. I banged on the glass and called her name until someone came to the window."

Margot sits up straighter in her chair. There are so many questions she wants to ask but she'd promised Ruthgow she'd be quiet if he allowed her to stay for this informal interview.

"The face. It was older, haggard, but I knew straightaway it was Flora."

Margot holds her breath.

"Flora recognized me too. She looked dreadful, and fearful. The fear . . ." Heather shakes her head, as if trying to dispel the memory. "Anyway. She opened the window. I helped her climb out. She . . ." She glances at Margot almost regretfully before turning back to Ruthgow. "She became agitated when I told her to come with me. She—she refused. At first."

Margot opens her mouth to speak but Ruthgow throws her a warning look. "What do you mean, refused?" he asks, calmly.

"She seemed reliant on Clive. There were track marks on her arms. He'd obviously got her hooked on drugs."

"He's a monster," hissed Margot, before she could stop herself.

Heather squeezes her mother's hand. "I know, Mum. But he's all Flora knew, for eighteen years God knows"—she gulps—"God knows what he did to her."

"Held her prisoner."

"She lived in the basement, that much was obvious. But, Mum, the weird thing is, it wasn't locked. She could have left . . . before."

Margot can hardly believe what she's hearing. "You mean she stayed there voluntarily?"

Heather looks uncomfortable. "Maybe not at first. But, yes, by the time I found her, yes."

Margot stands up, suddenly furious with Ruthgow. "Why didn't you find her? She was under our noses this whole time! We could have saved her from all those years of horror!"

Ruthgow's expression darkens. "Margot, please keep calm or you'll have to wait outside. This is important."

Margot sinks back onto her chair, but she darts him a look of anger.

He turns his attention back to Heather. "Go on," he says gently.

Heather reaches over and takes Margot's hand again. "I had to coax her out of there. She was . . . she was like a wounded animal. All wide-eyed and cowering. It was awful. The basement she'd been living in was squalid. She was like a zombie, disheveled, dirty, high on drugs. If I hadn't been looking for her I would have mistaken her for another drug addict—there's a surprising number of them in this city, as you know. She was so skinny, Mum . . ." Heather wipes tears from her eyes but continues, her voice wobbly. "When I tried to convince her to leave with me she became panicky and violent, trying to hit me. I wanted to call the police but she wouldn't let me—she was trying to protect Clive and Deirdre. She sobbed that they had abandoned her. That Deirdre was sick and now she was getting all Clive's attention. It was sordid. It disgusted me. It was like they'd brainwashed her."

Margot closes her eyes, not wanting to picture it.

"But I knew it was the drugs talking," continues Heather, "so I told her I was taking her to see them in Tilby and she willingly came with me. She told me then about the day they had kidnapped her, given her spiked hot chocolate so she blacked out. When she finished talking she was exhausted and fell asleep on the back seat of the car. It was still early morning when I half carried her into the house and laid her on her old bed in her room."

Margot had left everything as it was the day Flora disappeared. Even her old posters of the Psychedelic Furs and Joy Division were still Blu-Tacked to the walls. "I thought being back in her old bedroom might help Flora to remember who she really was when she woke up," adds Heather. "Clive had used her as his pawn, his plaything, for years, keeping her dosed up on heroin and threatening her that he'd come for me if she"—Heather's crying now—"if she left or told anyone."

Margot's head is reeling. Deirdre had known. All this time. She'd helped her son, her sick, perverted son, keep Flora a prisoner for years. She's a *mother*. How *could* she?

"'And then," sobbed Heather—Ruthgow hands her a tissue, which she uses to blow her nose, "she was so hooked on drugs I don't think she cared where she was, as long as she was getting a fix."

"Oh, God." Margot groans, feeling sick. It was like the horrifying stories she'd read in the newspapers, young girls being kidnapped and kept locked up as prisoners for years.

"And then?" probes Ruthgow, gently. "What happened after that?"

She lowers her eyes. "I . . . don't remember."

Ruthgow looks at Margot, his lips set in a grimace.

"Can I see Flora?" pleads Heather.

"I'll see what I can arrange," he says, getting up from his chair and adjusting his trouser legs. They've gone slightly saggy at the knee, observes Margot. "Thank you, Heather. You'll have to come into the station next week and give a formal statement. If you're up to it, that is." He pauses at the door. "You have a motive now, Heather. I have to warn you, you might be charged with this."

Heather sits up. "But I can't remember what happened."

"Well, I suggest you try."

Margot stands up, fists clenched at her sides. "You can't charge her with this. If she did kill those—those *bastards*," she spits, "I don't blame her. I don't—"

"Margot," Ruthgow says, his voice firm. "We'll take a formal statement next week. Please try not to worry about all of that for now." He shoots Heather a knowing look before leaving the room.

THEY ARE ALLOWED TEN MINUTES WITH FLORA, HEATHER RIDING IN a wheelchair, even though she insists she's strong enough to walk. But Brenda's having none of it. "You're lucky you're being allowed to do this," she says, tucking a blanket around Heather's legs.

"Her sister has just been found after nearly twenty years," snaps Margot. "She should bloody well be allowed to do this."

Brenda shrinks away in surprise. "I'm just saying. I don't want my patient getting pneumonia." She insists on accompanying them to see Flora, even though, reluctantly, she allows Margot to push the wheelchair.

Flora is in the corner of the small four-bed ward with the curtain pulled closed around her bed. The others are empty.

Margot wheels Heather into the cubicle, leaving Brenda sitting in a chair next to the ward's entrance.

Flora has a bit more color in her cheeks and a sheen of sweat above her upper lip but her chest still rattles when she breathes.

"The naloxone is working. But it means she'll have withdrawal symptoms. We're trying to manage it as best we can," explains one of the doctors. A different one this time. A young woman.

Margot bends over and kisses Flora's forehead, which causes her eyes to open. And then she notices Heather and tears seep out of the corners of her eyes and run down the sides of her face.

"Hey," says Heather, taking her sister's hand. "It's going to be okay. We're here for you. You'll get through this."

"I thought . . ." She coughs. "I thought I'd killed you back at the barn. I'm sorry. I'm so sorry. The gun, it just went off . . . There was so much blood on your blouse and on the floor when you hit your head."

Margot frowns. "What do you mean, sweetheart? What gun?"

Flora tries to sit up but Margot stops her. "Don't try to move."

Heather lowers her voice. "We struggled over a gun. I remember that much. In the barn."

Margot turns to Heather. "But why didn't you say that to DCI Ruthgow?"

Heather glances at her sister and Margot notices a look pass between them.

"Mum," says Heather, "do you mind if I have some time alone with Flora?"

"Of course." She kisses Flora's clammy forehead and steps out of the cubicle. "I'll be back in five minutes."

She goes and sits next to Brenda, who pats her arm sympathetically. From where she's sitting she has a view of the cubicle and the mint-green curtain surrounding Flora's bed. She can just see the wheels of Heather's chair underneath it. She can't quite make out what they're saying, but she can hear one of her daughters faintly crying and the word "sorry" floats across the room toward her.

And in that moment warmth engulfs Margot, like she's just downed a glass of brandy. She'd hoped and prayed for this moment so many times over the years that she's lost count. But here they are at last: she and her two precious daughters. All under one roof for the first time in eighteen years. Safe.

Then Heather pokes her head around the curtain and calls Margot over. She stands up, an uneasy feeling in the pit of her stomach instantly dispelling her happiness of a moment before.

When she reaches the cubicle Heather pulls her in and indicates for her to sit on Flora's bed.

"What is it? What's wrong?" she whispers, dread swirling in her stomach. Although she thinks she knows what they're going to say.

51

MUM LOOKS AT ME WITH SUCH FEAR IN HER EYES THAT IT BREAKS MY HEART. *After everything I've put her through all these years and the not knowing what really happened to me. It's aged her. I can tell her the truth now. I can finally see a bit more clearly now the drugs are leaving my body, and I can put things right. At last.*

I try to prop myself up on my elbows, but they tremble with the effort. I feel so weak. "I'm so sorry, Mum," *I say, my head falling against the pillow, cradled by her warm, comforting hand.* "But you need to hear the truth. It wasn't Heather." *I glance across at you sitting with your head bowed. You have tears on your cheeks. I was terrified I'd killed you in the barn that terrible morning. I'm so grateful that you're alive and here with me now. I turn my attention back to Mum and squeeze her hand gently.* "She didn't shoot the Wilsons. It was my fault. I was the one who killed them."

52

Jess

BRISTOL DAILY NEWS

Thursday, March 22, 2012

SEASIDE SHOOTER'S SISTER FOUND ALIVE IN VICTIMS' HOUSE

by Harriet Hill

THE MISSING sister of the alleged Seaside Shooter who killed a Tilby couple has been found in the victims' basement.

Flora Powell, now 34, who went missing when she was just sixteen, has been found alive at Clive Wilson's Bristol property. It is thought she was kidnapped and kept a prisoner, hooked on drugs, for nearly eighteen years.

She was found living rough along the Welsh Back by

two residents and is said to be in a critical but stable condition in hospital after a suspected overdose.

Police have delayed charging Ms. Powell's sister, Heather Underwood, 32, due to her recovery from a head wound. But now police believe that Heather may not have killed Deirdre and Clive Wilson after all.

A source said: "The police are now looking into the fact that it may have been Flora who actually committed the murders. An eyewitness at the time of the killings recalled seeing a 'dark-haired woman,' which would also fit Flora's profile. After what they put her through, she definitely has a motive."

A spokesperson for Avon and Somerset Police confirmed that Flora Powell had been found but refused to comment further on the case.

"Fucking Harriet fucking Hill," I spit, to a startled Rory. "How did she get this story when it all happened just last night? Has she got spies at the hospital or something? Shit." I fling the newspaper onto the coffee table.

"I'm sorry. I thought you should see it." Rory had gone out to get milk this morning and had bought the newspaper when he saw the headline.

"Now they're saying it's Flora who killed the Wilsons? " I throw my hands into the air.

"It makes more sense, though, doesn't it? You said Margot

told you there was an unidentified fingerprint on the gun. And it means Heather's off the hook."

I groan. "That might be the case—but poor Flora. And poor Margot."

The sofa sags as he sits down next to me and pulls me into him, kissing my hair.

"My story about the body in the basement not being Flora is going to be old news now, isn't it? It's published tomorrow." I sigh. "I don't know. Maybe I should work for a daily again."

"If that's what you want?"

I turn to face him. "You'd follow me a second time? Leave Bristol?"

"Of course. I haven't got a permanent job here yet. I'm just supply teaching."

"I couldn't ask you to do that for me again. It wouldn't be fair. And, anyway, we've got a good thing going here, haven't we? Especially if we're saving to buy our own place."

He stands up, half smile on his face. "That's true. But only if that's what you want."

"It is," I say resolutely. I mean it. Rory's not my father and I'm not my mother. We'll make our own way, Rory and me. If what Heather, Flora, and Margot have been through has taught me anything, it's that you have to grab happiness when you can as you never know what the future holds. Hold on to the ones you love.

He checks his watch. "I need to get off. What time are you going in?"

"I don't fancy seeing Ted this morning." I have Heather's interview still to finish writing up, so at least that should pacify him for a bit but I know he won't be happy about this. And my last article will have to be scrapped as it will no longer be relevant. "I'll walk down in the next ten minutes. I've got a lunchtime deadline and at least my story about Heather will be an exclusive."

Rory bends over to kiss me goodbye. When he's gone I read through Harriet Hill's article again. I wonder if she knows the "two residents" who found Flora were Rory and me.

I gather my things together and make my way to work. It's not raining but a mist has settled over Bristol, giving everything an ethereal quality. As I walk the cobbled streets of the Welsh Back and turn left at the Llandoger Trow, I can almost imagine I've gone back in time. What had Flora been doing in the derelict building across from mine? It still doesn't make sense. Was she the person who's been following me? Did she post the bus ticket through my door in a bid to reach out to me? To tell me? How did she get into the building? And what about the photos and *Back off*? I can't imagine they were from her.

It's nearly nine as I trudge up Park Street and bump into Jack coming out of the newsagent's with a can of full-fat Coke in his hand. "Need some energy," he says, holding up the can with a guilty look on his face, as though I've caught him with an illegal substance.

"I could do with some of that this morning," I admit, and quickly fill him in on what happened last night.

"Bloody hell!" he exclaims, when I've finished. "So what does this mean for your friend, Heather?"

I push open the door to the building. Stan isn't huddled on the ground this morning, which gives me hope that he might have found a bed last night.

"I don't know," I say. "But it throws doubt on the investigation. I suppose the police will question Flora."

"If she admits it, make sure you get the story before smug Harriet Hill has the chance." He smirks. "I've got some news also. Shall we go somewhere for lunch? Can't really talk about it here." He lowers his voice to make his point.

"Sure," I say, feeling lighter despite everything. I've missed Jack and feel guilty that I'd been silently accusing him of leaving the photos on my car.

"Great." His eyes are shining as he slopes off toward Seth and the picture desk—if you can call it that.

I plonk my bag down and am taking off my coat when Ted strides over, holding a copy of the *Daily News*. "I know," I say, before he can start. "But I was the one who found Flora last night. I was the one who was at the hospital with her mother. I don't know how Harriet got hold of that story before I've even had the chance to type it up." I jut out my chin, daring him to have a go at me.

To my surprise, he doesn't. "It's bad luck, I know," he says, running a hand across his stubbled jaw. "But we can print your Heather Underwood interview tomorrow. Maybe you can include a quote from Flora, if she's well enough."

I pull a doubtful face, although I'd love to see Flora again. I still can't believe she's alive.

"But even so," he says, thrusting his hands into the pockets of his jeans, "what you've done so far is great."

I can only stare at him in shock as he walks back into his office. I smile to myself as I sit at my desk to type up the rest of Heather's story, wondering how Harriet Hill found out that Flora had shot the Wilsons before I'd had the chance to.

I WAIT FOR JACK OUTSIDE AS HE'S FINISHING UP. I'VE HAD A PRODUC-tive morning, completing the Heather article, which will be front-page news tomorrow. I even had a call from Jared congrat-ulating me on my "scoop." Even Harriet bloody Hill won't have that story, I think, as I light a cigarette and huddle in the door-way. It's gone cold and we've been predicted snow, even though it's late March. I see Stan walking down Park Street wrapped in a dirty blanket, a cap pulled down over his frizzy hair. I no-tice how people flash him sidelong glances of disapproval or pity. Others press their chins to their chests and hurry past, pretend-ing not to notice him.

"Hey, Jessie," he says, when he approaches me. He's the only person, apart from Rory, who calls me Jessie. But it's stuck and I don't like to correct him now.

"Sorry, Stan. Am I standing in your spot?"

"You're in my home." He grins, and I move out of the way so he can make himself comfortable in the corner. I hand him a couple of my cigarettes and he presses one to his lips so I light it for him. "Did you catch up with that bloke in the end?" he asks, after he's taken a few drags.

"What bloke?"

"The bloke who came looking for you last week."

"A bloke was looking for me last week?" This is the first I've heard of it.

"Yeah, tallish fella."

I think of Flora and my suspicions that it had been she who was following me. "Could it have been a woman?"

He shakes his head and picks what I hope is a bit of ash out of his beard. "Nah. Definitely a bloke."

I think of Wayne Walker. "What did he look like?"

"Stocky. Quite handsome."

That doesn't sound like Wayne. Unless it was Adam. "Did he have dark hair and a beard?"

"Nah. He was blond."

I frown, trying to think. Was it Norman? "Was he quite old?"

"He was young. Well, about your age, I reckon."

"What did he want?"

He pulls the blanket firmly around his shoulders. "Wanted to know your movements. What time you left, that kind of thing. He looked official, actually. I thought he was a policeman."

A policeman? Why were the police looking for me? "Did he . . . did he say anything else?"

"Nah. He stalked off when I wouldn't tell him anything."

I smile at him, overwhelmed by fondness for this man whom

I've talked to every day for the last nine months but don't really know. "Thank you."

He grins. "Anytime."

"So, what's the big secret?" I ask Jack, as we sit at a table in the café near the top of Park Street.

He fiddles with his paper napkin. "I'm leaving."

I stare at him, speechless, the glass of elderflower cordial nearly slipping out of my hand. "But—but why?"

"I'm going back to Brighton. Got a job on the *Argus*. I miss my hometown, Jess. I'm sorry. And, also, it's as a reporter."

A reporter? I knew it. Has he been tipping off Harriet Hill? Would he do that? Undermine me? No. I can't believe he would.

"I've been earning extra cash selling contact details to the nationals," he adds, his cheeks flushed. "I'm sorry I didn't tell you, Jess."

I shrug. "There's no law against it."

"I thought it could be a way in, that's all."

"But what about Finn? Will he move to Brighton with you?"

"We're over."

Again, I'm reeling. "What? When?"

"I'm sorry I haven't been myself for the last few weeks. Finn, well, he turned out to be a knob." He smiles sadly.

I've always thought so but I've never admitted that to Jack. "In what way?"

He leans back in his chair and stretches his long legs out underneath the table. "Urgh. You name it. Controlling. Bullying.

Possessive." He ticks them off on his fingers. "And then . . ." He glances at me, almost shyly.

"What?"

"He started to get violent. It began with a slap across the face, then a punch to the thigh. But lately he'd just fly into these jealous rages. That night when we met up, I didn't get mugged. It was Finn. He punched me because he was jealous. He said he noticed a"—he adopts a silly French accent—"*frisson* between us. He was convinced something was going on."

I can't help but laugh, the idea is so ludicrous. "Uh . . . Hello, you're gay!"

"I know." He sighs. "But I've"—he lowers his voice and glances around the café—"slept with women before."

"So he thought we were sleeping together? Oh my God, Jack!"

"I know." He stares down at his gourmet cheese and chutney sandwich. I've ordered the same yet neither of us has taken a bite yet. "The awful thing was, he hated me having any friends, male or female, because he was convinced I'd end up sleeping with them."

I'm suddenly full of rage at the thought of Finn beating up my lovely friend. "What a bastard! You should report him, Jack. Seriously."

He hangs his head. "I can't."

"It's wrong. He deserves to be prosecuted." I remember how subdued Jack had become, how he'd flinch if I touched him. I wonder how long it had been going on.

He looks shamefaced. "But it sounds ridiculous. I'm six foot five, taller than him. I'm—"

"No!" I slam my fist on the table, causing our plates to jump. "For fuck's sake. It's assault. And a police officer too!" *A police officer.* "Wait. Was it him?"

Jack opens his sandwich and begins picking the lettuce out of it. "Was what him?"

"Stan said some bloke had been asking after me. He said he thought it might have been a police officer."

Jack's head shoots up. "What?"

"And the photos on my car."

"What photos on your car?"

With everything that's been going on, I haven't even had the chance to tell Jack all about it. But as I explain I notice his face pales. "What is it, Jack?"

"I found a photograph of you. In our bedroom." His gaze goes to my coat hanging over the back of my chair. "You're wearing that coat in it. I asked Finn about it. He said it was mine. Accused me of taking it because I fancied you." He shakes his head in disbelief. "Shit. What a bastard."

He must have scaled the gate to get to my car. He's certainly strong enough.

I reach over and squeeze his hand. "I'm so sorry." *Back off* makes sense now. Not someone warning me off the story, but a jealous lover warning me off their boyfriend. "Have you moved out?"

"Finn left yesterday. He's staying with"—he rolls his eyes—

"Harriet Hill of all people. Oh, yes, it seems the two of them have struck up a friendship."

"Harriet Hill? I—I just can't—" We burst out laughing at the absurdity of it. "Hey," I say, a thought striking me. "You don't think he's 'the source,' do you? We wondered how she was getting all her stories."

His eyes widen. "Of course! What a wanker! He'd have knowledge of the case through his job. And then he fed the information back to her."

"So much for his *I don't give tip-offs because it's unprofessional crap.*" I mimic Finn's voice. "He wanted to make me look bad, no doubt, by giving her all the good stuff."

He pats my hand, which still rests on top of his. "I'm sorry. And I love you, you know. Just"—he winks—"not like that."

A lump forms in my throat. "I can't believe you're leaving. You're my only friend in Bristol."

"You have Heather now."

That's true. All this time I'd wanted to believe my old friend was innocent and now I know she is, we can move on, resume our friendship as women.

"And Rory. He's a good bloke."

"I know," I say, taking my hand from his and picking up my sandwich. "I'm lucky to have him."

"You're lucky to have each other." He pauses as he takes a bite of his sandwich. "You know what really pisses me off?" he says, his mouth still full. "I could have had that fucker Finn but I didn't hit him back, even when he punched me in the face and in the ribs."

"That's because you're a million times the person he is," I say. "I wish you'd told me."

His eyes are downcast, as he says softly, "I was ashamed."

"Oh, Jack. He should be the one who's ashamed." Then: "Can I come with you?" I say, the idea popping into my head. "To Brighton? Do you think they have a job going for another reporter?"

Jack stares at me. "I can find out, if that's what you really want."

I fidget in my seat. Is that what I want? A new place to live? A new start? But I'd be running away. Again. I've moved around so much there's never been enough time to put down roots. But now I have Heather and Margot and Flora, as well as Rory. I don't need to be afraid that I'll lose the people I love, or that I don't deserve to be happy. Margot's strength all these years has inspired me. She didn't run away when Flora disappeared or when everyone thought Heather had killed the Wilsons.

"Don't get me wrong," Jack says, wiping some chutney off his chin with the paper napkin, "I'd love to work with you in Brighton. But your job. Ted. Rory. You're living virtually rent-free here, and Brighton is expensive."

"Actually," I say, taking his hand in mine, "I'll miss you tons but I want to stay in Bristol. Make things work with Rory."

He places his hand on top of mine. "You're a big softie at heart, aren't you?"

"Don't underestimate me. You always said I was as hard as nails, remember?"

He takes his hand away and resumes eating. "I never for a moment thought that was true. I could see right through you, Jessica Fox," he says, his mouth full of bread.

"Well," I sit back in my chair. "I'll tell you this for nothing, Jack Renton. You might not want to report your nasty ex for beating you up, but I'll be watching him. And if he takes one step out of line I'll be onto him. I can promise you that."

53

Jess

BRISTOL AND SOMERSET HERALD
Tuesday, March 27, 2012

TILBY MURDER VICTIMS
RESPONSIBLE FOR MORE DEATHS
by Jessica Fox

**POLICE ARE looking into the possibility that Clive
and Deirdre Wilson, who were murdered in their own
home earlier this month, are responsible for the deaths
of two young women.**

The body found in the basement of their Bristol property has been identified as missing teen Stacey King,
who disappeared from her home in 1991 when she was
seventeen.

Stacey, from Clevedon, lived with foster parents at the time of her disappearance and was described as "troubled and vulnerable."

A forensic pathologist who conducted an autopsy on Stacey stated that the cause of death was a heroin overdose and he believes she died around 1993. She was found buried beneath a false wall in the basement.

Police are now reopening the case of teenager Marianne Walker-Smith, who was found dead on Clapham Common in London last year of a suspected heroin overdose, as they look into claims made by witnesses who saw her with Clive Wilson before she disappeared.

Clive, along with his mother, Deirdre, was shot dead in Deirdre's Tilby home earlier this month. As yet, the police haven't charged anybody with their murders.

Clive's brother, Norman Wilson, has been questioned by police as to his involvement in the kidnapping of Flora Powell and the murders of both Stacey King and Marianne Walker-Smith.

The police have only "scraped the surface" of what they believe is a drug and kidnapping ring in Bristol, with connections in Reading and London.

Norman's daughter, Lisa, said: "There is no way my dad is involved. We didn't see much of my uncle or my grandmother over the last ten years and we never visited their Bristol home. I'm not saying my dad was always a saint, and he spoke openly of his battle with drugs when he was younger. But he has been clean for years. I believe him when he says he knew nothing about it."

Dylan Bird, who was Flora Powell's boyfriend at the time of her disappearance, has also been released without charge.

He told the *Herald*, "Norman Wilson supplied me and my mates with drugs in the early 1990s but we lost touch after that. I cleaned up my act and I'd heard that Norman moved away and settled down with a wife and kids. I don't believe Norman had any involvement in the abduction of young girls. Unfortunately his brother and his mum used Norman and myself as bait to lure my beautiful girlfriend into their trap. I'll never understand how Deirdre Wilson could have stood by and allowed it to happen."

A police spokeswoman confirmed that a man has been arrested and released without charge.

I DON'T HEAR FROM MARGOT UNTIL THE NEXT DAY.

I'm halfway home when she calls.

She's crying and her voice is thick through her tears. My stomach tightens. "Margot? Are you okay? Is it Flora?"

She's died. That's what I'm expecting. But instead Margot says, "Flora's had a stroke."

I stop in my tracks, gazing out across the river, even though it's dark and I can't see much, except the occasional light in a window at the apartments. The river looks black in this light, undulating, stagnant.

A stroke? "But isn't she too young for a stroke?" It's a silly thing to say, I know that. But all the people I've ever known to have a stroke have been old, like my granddad and Rory's great-uncle Cian.

"It's a result of the many years of drug abuse." Margot's voice sounds so sad that my eyes fill with tears. "It's severe, I'm afraid. She may never recover, fully."

"Oh, Margot . . ." The unfairness strikes me. This cruel, shit world, I think, and I kick the wooden bench that overlooks the river hard, hurting my foot. Then I slump onto the bench, no longer afraid that I'm being watched. That particular fear is over now that I know it was Finn who'd been following me.

"Before the stroke, she admitted it all," continues Margot, in that same resigned voice. "She hadn't meant to shoot Heather. Heather had been trying to stop her. Clive and Deirdre had kept her prisoner for years, a prisoner to heroin, and she was pushed to the edge."

"Did Flora ever tell you what happened that day?" I ask, as I light a cigarette.

I listen in silence, taking the occasional drag as Margot tells me the sequence of events of that fateful morning.

Heather had taken Flora back to Margot's house at the caravan park with the idea that she would work on convincing her sister that they needed to go to the police. She left Flora sleeping in her room to make a cup of tea but when she returned Flora had gone. The drawer to the half-moon chest in the hallway was open and, straightaway, Heather knew what her sister was about to do because it was where the key to the gun cabinet was kept.

Heather raced into the barn just in time to see Flora taking the shotgun from the cabinet. "It's the only way I can stop them doing this to someone else," Flora had said.

Heather tried to wrestle the gun from Flora's grasp. But it went off and the bullet struck Heather's chest, the force of it throwing her backward. She stumbled and hit her head. Flora thought she had killed her. She was so devastated that she no longer cared what happened to her. She took Heather's car ("God knows how she drove it when she's never had a lesson even if it is an automatic," said Margot) and headed for Deirdre's house in Tilby. She knew the road name as she'd heard them talking about it. The West Ham sticker in the window made her sure she was entering the right house.

After she'd shot them she took a bus back to Bristol. She was too scared to hand herself in, instead managing to score heroin and sleeping rough. One day she saw me coming home from work and followed me, dossing down in the derelict building opposite. Apparently she was trying to reach out to me. She worked out which apartment was mine and then she managed to sneak into my building behind a neighbor and pushed the bus ticket through my letter box in an attempt to tell me she was in Bristol. But I hadn't made the connection because I'd thought Flora was dead.

"She thought she'd killed Heather," Margot finishes. "And she was scared to come forward. She told the police everything before her stroke. Gary"—she coughs—"um, DCI Ruthgow, has been amazing. Heather will face no charge. And poor Flora . . ."

"What will happen to Flora now?" Surely she won't be prosecuted for murder, not after everything they did to her and what she's been through.

Angela at the police press office told me earlier that this was just the tip of the iceberg. Clive had been prolific and Flora was getting too old for him. If Heather hadn't found her when she had, I've no doubt Clive would have killed her. Maybe he would have given her just that little bit too much heroin and buried her in the basement too.

It was just by chance that Clive and Deirdre had bumped into Flora that August night, although they were obviously hoping to pick up someone. The spiked hot chocolate that Deirdre had been carrying meant it was premeditated. They'd been coming back from the fair where Clive and Norman had been doing some dodgy drugs deal. Apparently, according to Margot, Clive had recognized Flora from the fair and had taken the opportunity to lure her into the car, knowing she wouldn't be afraid if his mother was there.

It's Deirdre's role in all this I can't get over. How could she have helped her son to abduct these women, turned a blind eye as he drugged and raped them? I'll never understand it.

"Flora's too ill to face charges," says Margot. "Temporary insanity would be her plea, though I'm sure if it ever . . . if it ever came to her being fit enough to stand trial, although that's not likely . . ."

"Oh, God, Margot. I'm so sorry."

I close my eyes, tears seeping out from underneath my lashes as I think of Flora as I like to remember her: a sixteen-year-old girl in love, floating about her sunny bedroom in her long skirts and DM boots, singing along to "Martha's Harbor" and no doubt thinking of Dylan.

"Despite the stroke, and how ill she is, at least she's safe. She's away from those monsters," says Margot.

"I know. I understand."

"Don't forget about us, will you?" she says suddenly. "Heather would love to see you again. She's allowed to come home at the weekend."

I open my eyes, blinking away the tears. "You're both stuck with me now," I say, as I gaze across the river. "I'm not going anywhere." And I realize that this is what I want. To grow some roots. To enjoy my life with Rory here in Bristol. Maybe to have children one day. To be a mum. I'll learn from my parents' mistakes, not become like them. Because I have Margot as a role model.

"I'm glad." Her voice sounds lighter. "Thank you for being there for me. For being a friend to me and Heather, above being a journalist."

I'm surprised. I never consciously understood that that's what I've done. But it's true. I've held back much more than I would if another family had been in the same situation. I kept Margot's confidence, when asked, not writing about finding Flora having overdosed on heroin, or going after Leo and revealing what I knew about his dalliance with the underage Deborah Price. I'd needed Margot and she'd needed me. We were there for each other.

I'm smiling as I end the call, promising Margot that I'll visit Heather at the weekend. And then I stand up, pocketing my phone as I make my way home, to Rory and our future.

EPILOGUE

Heather

THREE MONTHS LATER

My sister is propped up in bed, her head resting on a layer of pillows when I visit, her dark hair sleek and shiny and cut to her shoulders. She's no longer in a hospital but a rehabilitation center for stroke victims. It has a view of Tilby Bay from her window and sometimes, when it's quiet, you can hear the waves crashing against the rocks below. It's therapeutic, and Flora has always loved the sound of the sea.

I take out the book I've been reading to her every day for the last week. *Rebecca.* She never got the chance to finish it before she went missing, and even though she occasionally reads to herself, her eyes get tired. I take her hand, her good hand, and she squeezes mine, a sign for me to continue. The signet ring on her little finger glints in the late-morning sun. She'd been delighted when I returned it to her. Before the stroke, Flora told me Deirdre had stolen it when she'd snatched her.

It's been a long road to recovery for Flora. She's only now starting to regain a little speech; before she'd communicate with me by blinking, once for no and twice for yes. I take her out when it's a nice day, wheeling her chair along the seafront, and she closes her eyes and takes deep breaths, cleansing her lungs. She's no longer dependent on the heroin that ravaged her body over the last two decades. She has put on some weight and looks healthy, younger now that her face has filled out. She has defied all the odds, but I knew she would. She's strong, my sister.

I visit her every day without fail. Making up for lost time, I suppose. I often bring Ethan with me, although today he's at nursery. When he first met Auntie Flora he'd been scared, running to me and hiding behind my back. But eventually he'd warmed to her, no longer noticing that one side of her face droops and that she finds speech difficult. I think the fact we're so alike helps. He knows this is Mummy's sister. Sometimes Jess comes too, and the three of us sit together and listen to 1990s music in companionable silence, born out of our shared history and a bond that growing up together can sometimes bring.

Flora has never been charged. She was too ill to be formally interviewed under caution, and then she had the stroke. The drugs have done so much damage to her nervous system. But I haven't given up hope. I have no doubt she'll make a full recovery. It might take a while, but she's determined. Even though the stroke isn't what any of us would have wished upon Flora, I still thank my lucky stars every day that she's here. And I know Mum does too.

Mum, as always, has been amazing. The caravan park has been sold and she's put in an offer on a large bungalow with sea views where she'll live with Flora. They are due to complete any day now. Adam and I have bought a smallholding not far away, just big enough for a few horses. Adam has taken a job at the shooting range, and starts there next month. We've had to work on our marriage. He feels guilty that he never believed me about the Wilsons having something to do with Flora's disappearance, and it's taken me a while to forgive him for that. But life is too short: the last few months have taught me that much. And I love Adam. I want it to work between us.

Mum and the police officer, Gary Ruthgow, have grown closer, going on dates and enjoying each other's company. I always suspected she had a thing for him. But it's wonderful to see her truly happy at last.

Watching how Mum tends Flora so patiently and with such love has made me want to be a better mum. A better person. Everything I did—have done—was for love.

I wish I could say the same for the other members of my family.

Two weeks ago I had a phone call from Deborah Price. She'd been in Flora's year at school and, once, Jess and I caught her getting off with Uncle Leo in the sand dunes when she was barely fifteen. I was surprised to hear from her after all these years. She wasn't friends with Flora and had never really spoken to me, even when we caught Uncle Leo's hand in her bikini top.

"I know it's a bit weird to be calling you," she'd said, her voice husky, while I wondered who had given her my number, "when we don't really know each other." A baby cried in the background. I'd heard through the grapevine that she had five children and I occasionally spotted her around Tilby, looking stressed, her hair scraped back into a greasy bun, as she pushed a double buggy and pulled on a dog's lead, a fag hanging from her mouth. "How is Flora?"

"She's getting better," I'd replied curtly, wondering if she was only calling to get the gossip on my sister.

"I read about what happened in the newspapers." The press had had a field day with the story and it had run for weeks. Everybody from the past got dredged up: Norman pleading his innocence that he wasn't involved in any kidnapping; Marianne Walker-Smith's brutish-looking stepfather, who cried on TV over her death; an old girlfriend of Clive Wilson's, who said he liked her to dress up as a schoolgirl in the bedroom.

I was on the verge of putting the phone down until she added, "I've always felt guilty about that night. It's haunted me for years."

I'd cleared my throat. "What night?"

"The night Flora disappeared."

I'd frozen, mobile clamped against my ear. What did she know about that night?

Her voice was heavy with unshed tears. "I was with Leo that night. We were having it off in the bushes near the lane that led to your house. He had a girlfriend but he couldn't keep away from me. We heard you and Flora having an argument and you stomping off home. We saw a car pull up and Flora get into it."

"You saw Flora getting into Clive's car?"

"Yes. But we hadn't known it was Clive. Not then. Not until all this came out."

"And did you tell the police any of this, that you saw her getting into a car?" I shot back, already knowing the answer. If they'd told the police they could have run a trace on the car. They could have saved Flora years of torment and abuse.

"I'm so sorry. I wanted to when it became obvious that something awful had happened to Flora. But Leo, he said we'd get into trouble and he'd end up in prison. I wasn't yet sixteen you see. I wasn't sixteen until the thirty-first of August. Leo was in his late thirties. It would have looked wrong, ruined his reputation."

"It was bloody wrong," I hissed, feeling sick. I terminated the call, not wanting to hear any more of her excuses, and instantly called Leo.

He acted all cheerful to hear from me until I asked him if Deborah's story was true.

His silence said it all.

No wonder he'd left Tilby. He always maintained it was because everyone secretly thought he'd hurt Flora. But I think it was because the guilt of what he'd done was too much. He'd kept quiet all these years to save his own skin.

I'll never forgive him. And neither will Mum. As soon as I told her what he'd done she went straight to Gary Ruthgow about it. I'm hoping Leo will get his comeuppance.

I do feel bad for lying: to the hospital, to my mum, to Jess, to the police. But of course I remember that fateful day. I've always been able to remember.

I remember hearing a cough and turning to see Colin, our long-term tenant, standing at the entrance, assessing me with concern in his baggy eyes. Colin, who I knew was very fond of me, took my word for it when I assured him all was fine and he returned to his caravan. It was only later, when he looked back on that morning, when he noticed I'd already been out, that he must have realized what had really happened. Jess told me she always felt Colin knew more than he was letting on. And it's true, but he kept quiet. For me.

He'd gone by the time Flora came into the barn. He didn't see her confront me when she saw the gun was still in my hand, or the struggle that ensued between us.

He wouldn't have known the gun had gone off as we'd wrestled with it, or witness Flora run from the farm and board a bus back to Bristol. He didn't know that I lay on the floor of the barn, unconscious.

Later, in the hospital, Flora begged me to tell our mother, and the police, that it was her. "You could have died because of me. I want to do this. Think of your son. They'll go easy on me after everything I've been through," she'd said. "You saved me. Now it's my turn to save you."

And save me she did. I'm here, free, able to walk around, to push Ethan on the swings in the park, ride my horse, be with my husband. Live a normal, full life. An even better life than the one I had before because Flora, my brave, beautiful sister, is in it.

It doesn't always sit well with me, letting Flora take the blame. But I continue the pretense for Ethan's sake.

After all, I'm good at keeping secrets: my father's death was no accident.

When Flora and I argued in the barn over the gun, the Wilsons were already dead.

I'd driven to Tilby and shot them while Flora slept in her room. She caught me trying to put the gun back in the cabinet: she'd been withdrawing and said she needed them for her next fix. That moment only cemented it for me. I'd done the right thing—I didn't even think of the consequences of my actions. I just knew I couldn't let them live and risk them luring Flora back into their sordid world.

No, it wasn't my sister who killed Clive and Deirdre Wilson. It was me. And I'd do it all over again.

As for Uncle Leo, let's just say I'll be watching him.

ACKNOWLEDGMENTS

I STILL HAVE TO PINCH MYSELF TO BELIEVE THAT I'M A FULL-TIME writer and on my fifth book. I couldn't have done any of it without the most fabulous, hardworking (and best-dressed) agent in the world, Juliet Mushens, who always goes above and beyond. I'm so lucky to have her not only as my agent but as a friend.

The same goes for my two wonderful editors, Maxine Hitchcock and Matilda McDonald, who, along with all the amazing Michael Joseph team—from the sales to the art department— have made my books into *Sunday Times* bestsellers. I couldn't ask to work with a nicer, more dedicated team of people and I feel very lucky to be an MJ author.

A huge thank-you to Hazel Orme for her meticulous copyediting and her encouraging and supportive emails.

When I was writing this book I was fortunate to be introduced to a retired CID detective, Keith Morgan, who gave me invaluable help with this story, answering my endless questions about police guards in hospitals, what would happen to a suspect if they were too ill to be questioned or arrested, etc. Before I finished the book, Keith sadly passed away. He was such a lovely, kindhearted man, who went out of his way to help me, and I am so thankful to him.

Writing can be a lonely business so I really appreciate my writing buddies, Gilly Macmillan, Nikki Owen, Tim Weaver, Liz Tipping, Joanna Barnard, Fiona Mitchell, and Gillian McAllister for the chats, support, meetups, WhatsApp messages, and laughs.

Thank you to all the bloggers and readers who have bought, shared, borrowed, and recommended my books, and to those who have contacted me on Twitter, Facebook, or Instagram—your messages really do mean so much to me.

To all my friends, who have been so kind and supportive, reading and recommending my books, particularly the wonderful netball team for all our pub chatter.

To my mum and sister for being my first readers, and to my lovely stepparents, stepsister, nieces, and in-laws.

My family, as always, has been incredibly patient while I wrote this book. To my husband, who spends hours listening to me droning on about plots and characters, who's always honest if he thinks something won't work, and helps me brainstorm tricky plot points. To my children, who are still too young to read my books—although I suspect my daughter will be reading them soon!

And last, but definitely not least, to my dad, Ken, to whom this book is dedicated. From a very young age he taught me and my siblings that we could do anything if we put our minds to it and worked hard. Thank you, Dad, for always believing in me, for your continued support, for forcing my books on all your friends (whether or not they want to read them!), for your humor, your generosity, and your strength.

ABOUT THE AUTHOR

CLAIRE DOUGLAS has worked as a journalist for fifteen years, writing features for women's magazines and national newspapers, but she has dreamed of being a novelist since the age of seven. She finally got her wish after winning Marie Claire's Debut Novel Award for her first novel, *The Sisters*, which was one of the bestselling debut novels of 2015. She lives in Bath, England, with her husband and two children.

DON'T MISS THESE OTHER NAIL-BITING THRILLERS!

DO NOT DISTURB
A NOVEL

"Douglas is a true must-read thriller author. . . *Do Not Disturb* is yet another reminder of just how good she is at putting the reader on the edge of their seat and keeping them there until the final page."

—*PopSugar*

LAST SEEN ALIVE
A NOVEL

"Thrillingly tense and twisty, a great read."

—B. A. Paris, bestselling author of *Behind Closed Doors*

LOCAL GIRL MISSING
A NOVEL

"*Local Girl Missing* has a supple, twisty shape and a sense of menace that never flags."

—*New York Times Book Review*